IndieReader RATING: 4.8 stars (out of 5)

TO HOVER OVER WATERS is a speculative YA novel that follows five children as they navigate a world where no one can see, hear, or remember them.

Author Jesse Banner effectively shifts perspectives throughout the novel, with each chapter focusing on two or three characters; this approach keeps the story moving and brings insight into the core experiences that shape each child. Beyond simply learning how to survive while unseen, Banner revels in exploring the deep emotional impacts.

IR Verdict: *TO HOVER OVER WATERS* is a reflective, unique and lyrical literary novel for young adults with nuanced characters, global adventures, and dreamlike storytelling that uses its intriguing premise as a backdrop to explore the far-reaching trauma of abandonment. Jesse Banner's intentional and eloquent storytelling creates a captivating, character-driven novel that is hard to put down.

—*IndieReader* Review

Banner, who has worked with trauma-centered youth organizations, offers nuanced insight into the tumultuous lives of lost children. He conveys it beautifully . . . both YA and literary fiction fans will savor Banner's colorful characters and elegant, dreamy writing style.

Festive settings in international locales cleverly provide foils for the children's isolation. Magical powers, hallucinogenic visions, and a dash of romance pepper the deeply philosophical narrative. The mysterious ending suggests preparation for a sequel, a welcome notion because the Rahirrem's adventures have only just begun. As these "chosen" children grow, grapple with their pasts, and nurture one another, their experiences are sure to uplift the reader.

Takeaway: This lyrical fantasy delves into childhood trauma, resilience, and solidarity for fans of both YA and literary fiction.

Great for fans of: Neal Shusterman's *Skinjacker Trilogy*, Andrew Clements's *Things Not Seen*.

–**BookLife** Review, *Publishers Weekly*

TO HOVER OVER WATERS

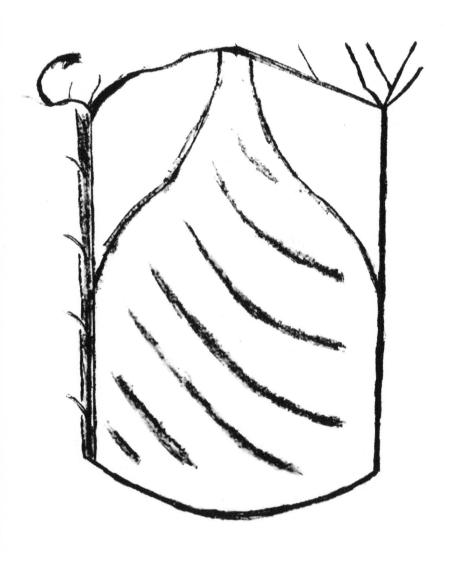

TO HOVER OVER WATERS

JESSE BANNER

Idun

NASHVILLE, TENNESEE

Idun is an imprint of W. Brand Publishing
j.brand@wbrandpub.com
www.wbrandpub.com
Printed and bound in the United States of America.

Cover design by designchik.net

To Hover Over Waters / Jesse Banner—first edition

Available in Hardcover, Paperback, Kindle, and eBook formats.
Hardcover ISBN: 978-1-950385-74-4
Paperback ISBN: 978-1-950385-68-3
eBook ISBN: 978-1-950385-69-0
Library of Congress Control Number: 2021912204

CONTENTS

T he vast, desert terrain surrounding the RV park was flat and uninterrupted. At dusk, the occupants watched the day's warmth gradually fade by the spectrum in the sky; a florid maroon settled on the horizon and was fleshed out in layers that ascended heavenward, culminating in dull blue high above.

Dusk fell; the bustle of the people eased, as did time itself. There was an icy bite in the air, in stark contrast to the heat that had weighed upon the campers less than an hour prior. Against this change, the tenants swiftly retreated to their tents and RVs.

The campsites—each consisting of a cement slab, a grill, and a wooden table—radiated out from an asphalt U-turn connected to the highway. At the center of this hub, inside the half oval, stood the park manager's office: a tawny box of a lodge with minuscule excuses for restrooms on either side. Atop towered a fluorescent cactus. Its neon tubes flickered green for the outline of the desert plant and then swapped to red, circling back down to form the letters.

This glowing cactus became elongated across the windshield of a late-evening arrival. The RV sped along the empty highway and made a reckless turn into the park. Sand exploded into the air as the bulky beast missed the entrance, broke through the dirt, and barely dodged the office. The churning cloud followed the RV's course correction back onto the asphalt and the search for a vacant spot in the second row.

With one hand still clenched on the wheel, the father tenderly massaged the fresh sunburn on his forearm. He jiggled the keys from the jammed ignition before hoisting himself from his seat. Hawaiian flowers stretched over his midsection when he pulled his shirt down to cover his navel. The sagging trousers had to be adjusted as well. And his legs wobbled slightly, becoming reacquainted with his pompous weight.

Seconds later, a chewing gum bubble popped, and some foul namecalling flowed from the passenger seat. Reddening at the cheeks, his wife worked to clear her lap of the dashboard trash that had slid her way. A petite creature wrapped in an extra-large sweatshirt, she tossed an empty food wrapper at her husband. This projectile was followed by a second wad, tossed by the daughter, squeezed into the seat with her mother.

Ignoring the mother's curses and the daughter's echoes, the father clapped his hands and announced to the back of the RV that they had arrived. His words stirred a tremor; the two nine-year-old boys raced to be the first out. The tornado of flailing limbs brought everything in the kitchen toppling to the floor. The mother popped a particularly furious bubble. But before she could get a single threat out, the twins were gone, scurrying to explore the park. Too tired to give chase, she rolled her eyes at the distant sounds of their hoots and hollers.

Even as they descended the retractable steps, the little girl refused to leave her mother's hip; it was an ordeal for the two to wiggle through the narrow door together. The father watched them leave, took the time to recover some of the displaced belongings, and then turned toward a small makeshift bed crammed behind his seat—a mound of tossed blankets bordered by pillows. Quiet in his approach, he went to one knee and began pulling the blankets away until one of his youngest sons was un-covered. The drowsy boy fought against the intrusion, pressing his nose deeper into his pillow. The man tickled at the small cheeks. He gently tugged on the small fin-gers and squeezed the tiny toes. Finally, the boy gave in to the coaxing and sat up with a crooked grin, his eyes still closed; but, it was enough for his dad. The father sang in a whisper as he picked the boy up, and together they made their exit.

Inside the building, the park manager had felt the vibrations through the thin walls of his office. After emerging from beneath his desk and re-straightening the picture frames on his wall, he came outside with a flashlight. The building was unscathed, but the chaotic entrance had an ill effect on the atmosphere. In a wave, guests were unzipping their tents and poking their heads out of their mobile homes. They sent heavy looks to the manager and then to the father walking, with his son in tow, to their picnic table.

And so it was that no one would see what the man had forgotten; not only forgotten—the man didn't see him, and neither did the woman, nor the four other children.

The fifth child sat upright. The blanket that had been tossed over his head moments earlier fell off and folded into a circle around him. He liked how soft it felt, yet he hesitated to pull it back to his shoulders; he didn't believe that it was his to use; it was his younger brother's—not meant for him.

He wanted to join his family outside but was unsure if he was supposed to, wondering why his father had taken his brother and had left him. The boy pondered this for some time. And the more he thought about it, the more he began to worry that he had done something wrong.

Eager for his father to return and forgive him, the five-year-old boy wanted to get his attention and knew the best way to do so. Climbing into the driver's seat, he stood with one foot on the steering wheel and pulled down the sun visor. Tucked inside was one of his father's fish hooks. It was metal, rather thick around the curve, and had quite a sharp point. This was his way to start a game he often played with his father.

The homemade hooks were becoming increasingly difficult to snag around the house, but no matter how high his father placed them or where he hid them, the boy would always find a way to climb or snoop. The real fun, however, was watching his dad look for them when it was his turn to hide. The man would scratch his head and make a funny, frantic face, eventually spotting his son, waiting eagerly to be found. The boy would be given a stern word and at times a whooping; it all depended on his mom, who hated the game and would often ruin the fun by scolding his dad for allowing him to nab them. They would say the hooks were not toys, but the boy got the reward of their attention, so he still enjoyed the game.

He bunched the blanket in his fist, tucked the fish hook inside, and hurried out of the RV. The soft green blanket dragged behind his quick steps, collecting dust as he trekked toward his mother and sister at the table.

The boy wanted to show his dad that he had found the hook—not so well hidden in the visor—but it did not seem like a good time. The park manager had arrived to collect payment, and the boy's father was already bouncing with rage about the price. A ripoff is what he kept calling it. He stood high on his toes; his sole source of balance was a finger pressed into the manager's chest. The fingers on his other hand formed a gun, pointed at the numbers on the cactus sign.

Those at the table barely noticed the argument, too engaged in a game of hide-and-seek. His brother raised his cupped fingers to cover his face, and as he did so, the two girls acted as though he disappeared. They pretended to panic, calling his name and turning in their seats, and checking under the table. The longer they pretended to look, the more distressed they became and the more the boy giggled. Only when the mother held his brother's arms and pulled them away was she able to find him.

The game looked like fun and the boy wanted in.

Positioning himself on the opposite end of the table, the boy watched his brother take one last turn. The mother let his brother hide behind his hands and then found him with a laugh and a tickle.

Then the boy tried to play along. He let the blanket drop from his head as he covered his eyes. The neon glow was lost in the dark, his fingers were so tight. He pressed his hands against his eyes; no one would be able to say that he was cheating. The world disappeared.

The boy's arms soon grew tired, but he remained stoic in his hiding place. He knew they would find him but feared they would be disappointed if he broke the rules of the game and revealed himself too soon; they may not want to play again.

The final bark from his father made his arm jerk, but the boy kept his eyes closed. There was some murmuring between his mom and dad and he thought that they were growing concerned—he was hidden and playing so well.

Then a greater commotion broke out around him, a busyness. Without revealing himself, the boy listened to the activity. He didn't give in but allowed himself a smile at the thought of them combing the entire park, searching and rustling through the bags as they had for his younger brother. He wanted so badly to be found; their faces, all of their faces full with relief, would be his reward.

When the silence came, he thought they must have given up. He imagined that he had played so well that they had to quit. Not wanting to make them worry any longer, he threw his arms open wide. His eyes squinted; the light of the neon glow was bright and blinding. And it took him a moment to see clearly that the cement slab was empty. The RV was nowhere to be seen. His father had disappeared. His mother and siblings had gone with him. The park manager could be seen drawing the shades in the window of the office. The other tents and vehicles were closed to him.

The boy was alone.

He did not cry that night; he did not feel sad. He only felt weightlessness, as though he might float up and out of his seat, but chose to stay on the table where they had left him. In a way, he was still safe, sitting there in his motionless state, nestled in the circle of the soft blanket, not quite ready to venture into the world beyond it. He was numb—but safe.

The loose desert sand was carried by a gentle breeze and stuck to his clothes and face, layering on his blanket and sprinkling his hair until he resembled an earthy creature that could have sprouted from the ground.

When the first spark of true acceptance came, the boy felt it deep inside. He did not simply lie down—it wasn't that gentle a motion. He crumbled inward. A puff of dust sprouted up when he sunk, curling into a fetal ball and becoming completely enveloped in the green blanket. It cushioned his body from the hard, wooden table. It was then he realized no one would come to wake him. And no one did.

. . .

The bough broke in the night. The merciless momentum of the eastern wind collided with the barn, a bent and straining structure that had already been weakened by time and neglect. The wind thrashed through the tattered wood, causing a chilling howl.

The four horses inside were spooked by the sound. Their legs kicked. Their heads flung back with wild eyes. The small band whinnied and cried for all to run, making their escape. In the surrounding tall grass, they circled in a startled frenzy, their hooves adding to the thunder.

The girl, buried in a bed of hay, did not follow immediately. Her tired eyes shot in every direction as the light strobed through the splits in the barn. The support beams bent so far they looked to be made of rubber. The shower from the patchwork roof was quite heavy; she feared that the top of the barn had already been stripped away completely. The horses called and kicked in the pasture; her view of them was broken by the barn door swinging freely on loose hinges. Her thoughts were foggy and unable to judge which would be safer: the buckling barn or the thrashing storm outside. But the choice was lost with a deafening crack. The barn wavered briefly in quiet suspension and then began to buckle in a series of escalating crashes. As the earsplitting blasts sounded, the girl rolled toward her family's tractor. Calamity rained down. She had just reached the rear tire when the nearest wall smashed over the high seat of the rusting machine. Her body trembled under the tremendous reverberations and jerked about in pain as splinters were fired like buckshot through the wet hay.

The conquering of the barn was the storm's magnum opus, and it subsided soon after. It was then that the girl was able to compose herself and twist out from her dubious shelter.

Anelie, her favorite horse, was grazing nearby, calm once again. The girl walked away from the wreckage. The horse followed, with a slight gimp in its step; the girl realized that there was a stain of blood on the horse's white sock.

"Anelie!" cried the girl. *"Bitte . . . bitte vergib mir."*

Less than an hour later, the girl and her horse stood in the first breath of daylight and watched her father pace in circles, surveying the site in a stunned daze, his eyes wide and mouth agape. Caution steered his steps. The carpenter moved amidst the wreckage with his arms slightly held away, as though he were walking on brittle ice; each step he took with his toes before trusting it with his full weight. Rarely did he feel confident enough to disturb what had fallen, but when he did, it was to recover small, accessible tools and supplies strewn amongst the debris.

The girl's grandmother forgot to close the gate behind her when she entered the pasture. Her son stepped from the pile of wood and metal, trying to hide his hurry to meet her, keeping her from getting too close to the ruins. She offered a thermos of hot coffee and a couple of warm muffins, wrapped in a dishtowel. The man devoured the muffins in a few bites, washed them down with the coffee, then spoke in hushed tones about what they were to do with the remains of the barn. He would cut the salvageable pieces to use in his shop and collect the rest for winter firewood. The old woman kept her eyes locked on her son, unable to look at the shambled remains of the barn built by her late husband. The emotional toll was displayed in her son's passionate stomping and swinging of his arms; his mother remained composed in her outward response, her hands gently patting the air between them and her neck slowly bowing her silver head, impassive opposite her son's frustration. The lethargic bow of her head hurt the girl, who watched from afar—she wanted to comfort them both.

With a brave breath in and out, she hurried down the hill, leaving the horses to graze. The girl lifted her knees as she ran, leaping through the tall grass as quickly as she could and letting the great grade of the hill assist her acceleration. The man turned away with his hands on his hips; his mother lingered with her eyes fixated on the cloth that had been returned to her. Just as her granddaughter kicked her heels at the dirt to slow down, the woman looked toward the house and started back.

"Oma!"

The elderly woman didn't turn to the call; she did not spread her frail arms to meet the rush of love the girl offered; she kept her gaze locked ahead and shuffled away. The dissonance and disregard stopped the girl in her tracks. Her feet planted, but her pleas carried forward. Gradually, the tone hardened, from affectionate to desperate. But no matter how loud the girl called, the woman didn't hear.

"Oma!"

The gruff in the carpenter's wheeze accented the end of every pull of the saw. He crouched low and worked with his arms moving near his knees. Each cut was stacked in a pile at his feet and, once it reached his knees, he carried it out from the ruins. The re-usable pieces were gathered in neat, straight rows based on length;

the wood for burning was tossed in a bundle a few paces away. The girl watched her father, and even followed him into the mess at times, waiting for her chance, waiting for him to notice her.

It had been a while since she had first noticed that her father and grandmother no longer spoke to her, looked at her, or heard her. Eventually, she had stopped expecting them to call her name. She had been named after the grandmother who now looked through her. So the girl had even considered giving that name back and taking another—San.

This would be another penance for what she had done, even though she didn't know what that had been exactly.

"Vati." Although it was as soft as a coo, it was difficult for her to believe that her father didn't hear it, and so she decided to continue. "*Es tut mir leid. Vati.*" Her entire being quaked as it gave her apology. But nothing seemed to penetrate the withdrawn look in his eyes. For a moment, the girl allowed herself to become angry at this; she bit her lip and balled her fists. And it was at that moment she remembered the anger she had felt the night prior. The rage—she wondered then if that rage was in any way to blame for the wreckage before her.

The night before had not been the first she had slept in the barn; she had maintained a bed and a routine with the horses for quite some time. But on that evening, she had walked along the fence with the horses, passed the main gate, and saw her family in the window—joyful and content—sharing a meal. There was no sign of celebration or special occasion, but the girl knew that the meal should have been for her sixth birthday.

She had spent the proceeding hours screaming, crying, and breaking everything she could get her hands on. In her anger, she wished that her father and grandmother would feel as she did, broken and devastated. It was this wish, she now believed, that brought the storm and its destructive end.

"*V-v-verzeihung. F-für den Sturm.*" The girl's voice shook as she apologized for the storm she had brought upon them. "*B-bitte, bitte. S-seht—*" A lump stopped her sound completely. Closing her eyes, she gathered a great breath and powered through, forcing her voice out in a shout. "*SEHT MIR!*"

When she opened her eyes in hope that her plea was heard, she saw her father standing with his spine arched backward and right knuckles pressing into his sore thigh; he didn't give any response to his daughter's crying. But he was standing still, and she took this as her long-awaited opportunity. The man's left hand hung by his side; she studied it like it was prey, wiping her eyes and tiptoeing forward, and lifted her hand.

The girl's father had always possessed a special ability to communicate a multitude of things through the way he held her hand. She could feel strength in his grip, the same strength that had allowed her to first feel safe around her grandmother's horses. He had held her hand until she could offer the carrot without dropping it, no longer fearing that the horse would take her fingers with the chomp. His grasp could also be serious and firm, as in the times she did wrong. But there could also be tender comfort given; his calloused carpenter's hands could feel soft as they enveloped hers when she was sad.

The girl felt none of these, she felt nothing when she touched his hand. When her petite fingers slid into his palm, his hand didn't close around them, unflinching to her touch. The girl felt a chill run from her arm and shiver through the rest of her body. She yanked back her hand and put it to her chest.

"Vati."

The contrite numbness seeped through San as she ran through the open gate, past her grandmother's garden, and away from the small square home.

. . .

Every morning at dawn, the boy would wander the park in search of his family van. He did not see anyone he knew, and no one acknowledged him. No matter what he did or said, no one in the park paid any attention to him. Moreso, they could be looking right at him and yet not see him. It was the strangest sensation; there was a dullness, a haze in their eyes when they looked through him, and it made him feel as though he were not there at all.

The boy could search the entire park in a single trip but his daily laps became increasingly smaller as he lost willpower, returning to his original table earlier each day. Meals were comprised of whatever scraps the other campers tossed into the garbage or neglected to put in their coolers before bed—never enough to feel full.

"Please?" the boy finally spoke one evening, amidst the symphony of forks hitting plates, smacking lips, and gulps of tea. But no one at the picnic table answered— no one even heard the question. Defeated, he sunk back to the ground and pulled the blanket over himself like a green cocoon. This worked to muffle the torment of the appetizing meal, but it also trapped him in with the loud rumble of his stomach.

When the meal had ended, the table was cleared. To stay out of the way, the boy somersaulted underneath the table, still in his blanket bundle. He poked his head out and watched them throw the scraps of the meal in the trash can and then break into groups on their way to the restrooms. Seizing the opportunity, he kicked his way free of his blanket and tumbled back out from under the table. Mid-sprint, his head was turned askew to monitor the restroom doors when he collided with the can, which toppled over and started to roll. The bottom was grounded by a short chain; the can was only able to go in a small circle. What emptied was more than the boy had expected, and he had to retrieve his blanket and fasten it into a sling to carry the jumbled mess of meat. The load weighed heavily on his back as he made the return journey to his base.

Watering at the mouth, he looked at his scavenged meal. He spread it across the table and marveled at his loot. The growl in his stomach sounded more like a joyful cheer, and yet the meal was unfulfilling—the greater need remained unmet.

After the first few chomps and swallows, the boy stopped and looked around, staring far down the stretch of highway. The road was vacant; his family's bus was not racing back to get him. This was the best meal he had enjoyed since they left, and it only made him miss them more.

The hook was knitted through the frayed blanket. He ran his finger along the inside of the curve. "Come back," said the boy to emptiness.

Although he searched every day, a part of him already knew that his family would not be found in the park, that leaving was his only hope of finding them. They had gone on.

. . .

Mom'll be mad. She gets mad that I take things. "Not yours!" she yells. No! She is. She is mad at me. Everyone is. That's why they pretended and then . . . and then left. In a poof! But they won't poof back. Then they're gone away. They wooshed and drove home. And they forgot me behind.

II

A t the gas station, the truck shuddered to a stop, the exhaust ceased to spill from the tail, but the boy continued to shake in the bed.

It had been an awful ordeal, crawling into the random truck, followed by the even more terrifying ride down the highway.

The boy scrambled out of the bed, plopped onto the pavement, and rolled beneath the frame. The underbelly sizzled and the rubber warmed the boy through his shirt as he pressed himself against the inside of the rear tire.

Peeking out from under the truck, he spied the driver popping open the door, sliding from his seat, and scratching himself at the pump. He rocked back and forth on his heels in rhythm with the click of the numbers and the chug of the gasoline, checking his watch frequently. And when the numbers stopped and the handle released, it was like a starter pistol; he returned the hose in a flash, dripping gasoline on the pavement, and hobbled toward the station's double doors in a hurry. His right leg may have fallen asleep while driving because he dragged it in a delayed limp. The boy watched him go and only came out when the store's glass doors closed.

The blanket had collected enough twigs, mud, and dried stains that it was no longer soft to touch, yet it remained comforting; he brought it over his shoulders, wrapping it around his neck like a scarf. The blazing sun hit the boy as he made his way to the storefront windows, his panting breath fogging a spot on the clear glass. He pressed his face against the pane and peered in. The sight made his jaw drop—bags, boxes, and shelves of pure treasure. He moved toward the door; his face slid along the glass. A trail of smudges followed after his fingers and nose. His gaze broke from the food for a split second and caught something that made the track of smudges stop—the counter and the woman standing behind it.

But it was not just her. There was a crowd inside; the woman was taking money from a jumbled line that snaked down one of the aisles. There were too many. He feared that he would not be able to sneak in and out without getting caught.

The boy spotted his driver's face over the top of a shelf of candy bars. A forlorn grimace was etched on his face as he shot looks down at his watch and back at the immobile line, ahead. He didn't see the boy pressed against the glass. Neither did the woman at the counter. No one did. Still, the boy had always been wary of strangers, and he was sure they would grab him if he tried to take something. They would punish him.

The boy pulled his nose from the window in despair, shoulders slumped and arms loosely swinging, and started his return to the truck without lifting his head. His mother's voice in his ear advised caution for the cars that may pull through, but the boy kept his head hung, only stopping a few feet from the truck when he found himself looking down at a pair of shoes—blue shoes. He raised his gaze slowly. Next came blue pants with a blue shirt tucked into them, draped with a matching tie that was tightly gnarled at the neck. The face, which was only a little higher than his own, was not blue, but fiery red at the cheeks.

Another boy—someone who could see him. The thrill of this was quickly lost to fear when the newcomer shoved him backward a couple of steps. A stern finger then flicked over the blanketed shoulder, toward the glass doors. Startled at being seen again and confused as to why the stranger was pressuring him to go back, the boy moved to the side only to have the blue-shoed boy outstride him and repeat his demand with a deeper burn in complexion. The boy in the blanket knew that he couldn't outmaneuver this kid, and so he simply shook his head, harder and harder.

With an assured walk to match the smile, the boy high-stepped through the doors. They shut behind the mysterious blue shirt like the mouth of a beast, swallowing him whole. Bewildered, the other small creature ran for cover. The blanket was trampled and abandoned without a second thought as he hid behind some crates stacked nearby.

The stranger must have been caught stealing. The crowd had jumped on him the second he reached for the food, the boy was sure of it.

After what felt like hours, the boy in blue emerged with the same confident strut. Nothing chased after him. There was no sign of alarm. At the edge of the sidewalk, in what could have been a dance, he skipped in a circle and wagged a sub sandwich in the air. The plastic wrapper rustled and fluttered like a flag. A bottle was pinched in his armpit, and his pockets were overflowing with candies. In a sweeping gesture, he waved back through the glass to the woman at the counter. The boy behind the crates clenched his fingers tighter at this taunt but was surprised at the woman's complete disregard for the show. She didn't even look. This puzzled the boy so much so that he came out from hiding.

The boy in blue saw the wheels turning behind the younger boy's curious expression. He held the sandwich out with a grin. The boy recoiled from it and shook his head once again. His scared eyes whipped toward the door, and he expected them to slide open. The thief followed the gaze to the glass, rolled his eyes, and tried to comfort his new friend.

"Psh, they dunno. Get it? They don't see us."

. . .

The six-year-old went by Mar—he had picked the name himself and took great pride in that fact. To the point that when the boy asked, Mar would refuse to tell what his real name was.

Mutually relieved to finally have someone to talk to, there was rarely a quiet moment. The boy immediately cried to Mar about being left alone and overlooked. He talked about his family and how badly he wanted them back. He told story after story about home, but Mar said little on that subject; he talked more about the places he had been since becoming invisible and where they should go next.

"Show 'em. We can go anyplace we wanna."

Mar's story was rather difficult to follow; his retelling was frequently interrupted by his scattered focus and the diversions he called adventures—mostly climbing, throwing, or breaking anything that caught his eye. But over days and several false starts, the boy managed to build a reasonably coherent sequence of events.

Mar didn't have any brothers or sisters; it had been just him and his parents in a "big BIG house."

"All for me. All to myself. Kids on my team and others and . . . and school, they always, always, *always* wanted to come over."

One afternoon, Mar had fallen asleep while playing in one of the rooms on the top floor—his favorite place to play because of the view it provided of the valley.

"I played treehouse. There were trees below. I had another treehouse. In the yard. Backyard. But there . . . my room, that room felt like a bigger one. Like our house, our *whole* house, all was a bigger one. Living in a treehouse. With a window over the other trees."

He had woken, hours later than expected; his parents had not come to get him. A meal had passed, and they had let him sleep. The daylight had gone, but they had not carried him to bed. He had scurried downstairs, expecting to find them either searching for him or asleep themselves. But instead, they were sitting contently in the den, reading something on his father's computer. They didn't notice when he entered nor when he asked them to tuck him into bed.

"I yelled from the hall. I yelled from the door." Mar put his face to the boy's until their noses touched. "Then I yelled from here. *This* close." His parents continued to look past him, not seeing or hearing anything he did. They didn't hear when he called their names—not even when he cried.

"I was loud. Louder than everybody," Mar boasted to the boy. "But they ignored me. I was not quitting. I followed them. I did chores. I made a mess. I sat in my seat at lunch. Every lunch. But no plate for me."

"You left them?" the boy asked the question to which he already knew the answer if only to keep Mar on track. They both spotted a swing set on top of an approaching hill, but the boy wanted Mar to continue with his story.

"I left. Yeah. They played like I wasn't there, so I said—" Mar paused, allowing time for him to slurp his spit and hock it at the nearest tree. *"Peww.* To get 'em for their nasty, mean game."

Mar seemed to lose interest in his own story at this point, switching topics to the collection of action figures he had had at home. The other boy didn't listen to this; his mind was on something Mar had mentioned earlier in his jumbled tale—the cloud in people's eyes. Mar had used that phrase to describe the way everyone looked through him. The boy thought that it was the best way to describe what he had experienced as well.

"I was not me. Not here. No, no, no more. It was like I was never ever there. At all. Nothing. But who cares! I went by myself. Went everywhere. And . . . and saw that everyone was in on it. Everyone was treating me that way. They're all against me. I'm *in-disible* to them. And I gotta win. Then I see you. And they ignored you. Like me. I saw you and I knew. I knew you were on my side."

. . .

The boy had cried almost every night since the separation, but not like this. The sorrow that turned his stomach was like a foreign disease his body was not prepared for; it sprung suddenly and crippled him, resilient to the normal remedies—holding his dad's fish hook, singing his mother's lullabies, and breathing in the scent of home that he believed still lingered in the blanket.

The ground around the jungle gym was hard, and the sparse trees of the park provided a minimal break from the punishing wind. The best shelter the boy could find was under the spiraling slide. The large plastic overhang blocked much of the chilly breeze and the sand was more manageable. There was a decent indention, almost as though an animal had recently dug there; it was enough for the boy to curl into if he pulled his knees to his chest.

Mar had been rather upset when he left some time before and had pressured the boy to come along. "Stop crying. Come and you'll see and you'll feel better. They don't say no. You sneak . . . sneak in . . . shhh." He had added a whistle. "Find some stuff. Take a little. *Bop.*"

"Uh-uh." The boy had furiously shaken his head. He regretted mentioning that he had been hungry.

The boy's body began to tire from the crying fit, but he wanted to stay awake, to be sure that Mar returned safely. To combat the lull, he forced his eyes to stay open wide and pounded on the slide, hoping the hollow thumping would be enough to keep him awake.

The action spurred his father's voice out from his memory. A stern shout told him to stop pouting and go to bed. It sounded in his ear again, and so he didn't stop hitting the slide. He kept up his drumming to keep his dad's attention. Along with his voice, the boy sensed his father in other ways. He breathed his dad's scent—a combination of a favorite coffee, hot cinnamon gum, and sawdust. The feeling of his coarse flannel sleeves wrapped around the boy, and he tumbled in, allowing himself to be taken.

. . .

Mar thinks it's a game. A game we gotta win. Mar calls . . . not fair. They started it and that's no fair, but . . . ha ha ha . . . they'll lose. And then we'll win. Na na na. 'Cause . . . 'cause we're a real team. That's what Mar said.

But no. No way. Not me. I don't think Mom is playing. I think she's just mad and then left. But then she'll say sorry. And they want me to stop playing too.

Mar wants me to make up a name for the game. I don't want to, but he barks at me, and won't stop when I say my really real name. Like a dog. Bark. Bark. Rarr. Woof. I want him to stop it, so here I go. I choose one I like. The best. I'm gonna be Des. My name is gonna be Des . . . D-E-S. Des.

III

Des straddled the high branch; his feet dangled beneath it, one hooking on the opposite ankle. Seeking more stability in his lofty perch, he draped one arm over a smaller branch that jutted against his ribs and leaned back against the tree. There was an unfortunately placed knot in the bark behind him. Squirming his shoulders, Des rolled his back against it like it was a lump in fresh dough he could smooth out.

His tree was on a ridge overlooking the town and its swarm of headlights. Shutting one eye, Des reached out and began following random sets of headlights with his finger, using the perspective to make it look like he could pinch them and control their path. His lips sputtered and his throat rolled with the sound of an engine.

He pretended the car belonged to his family. His guttural rumble went lower to match the right pitch; the van always sounded like it was struggling, running low to the ground as it was weighed down with his brothers, parents, and sister. Des could feel the lazy bounce of the large vehicle, hear the music his mother would find on the radio, and see them each in their place.

And the longer he followed, the more he wished that the lights would miraculously turn around and come to fetch him. He would much rather follow any of the lights below—family or not—than be pulled along for another day by Mar.

Des had settled into his chosen name in the months since being separated, but that was the only thing he was at peace with.

Mar—his sole source of company—was also his greatest annoyance.

For the majority of their time together, he had been trying to keep up with Mar's whimsical mind. The cycle began with Mar; he would see the smallest of signs—a city on a TV in a passing window, mountains on a billboard, a theme park featured on a passerby's shirt, or some other random lure—and read it as a profound epiphany for their next adventure.

"That's where we gotta go! That's it. Come on. We have to."

And Des would then spend the following weeks hurrying to keep up with Mar's driven pace, all the while listening to him preach that something special was awaiting them, but there was never fulfillment.

Mar's cheerful fever would eventually die out and, after a day or two of reticent murmuring, he would change his mind. He would stop dead in his tracks, spin on his heels, or push Des toward a new destination—usually in a completely different direction.

Des had fallen into the role of a complaisant yet silent follower, almost like Mar's second shadow. He had yet to muster the courage to oppose Mar's confident tone—as empty and pale as it was. Tired of the perpetual cycle of dead ends, he had yet to say or do anything to stop it. Silence was his only given defense, neither contradicting nor supporting Mar's sense of direction.

Des spotted a row of streetlights dotting an outer road. There were no cars or homes to add and blur their lights. The vacant road presented a clear row of six lights, and Des counted more than once to be sure. These, he imagined as flickering candles for him to wish upon—six lights for his sixth birthday. Solitary and brief, this would be his only celebration; Mar hated the very mention of birthdays or any sort of track of time. One wish—Des closed his eyes and blew, willing himself to imagine that the lights would go out and it would come true.

The whistle started high in pitch then shot low as Mar popped his lip from his gapped teeth. Des spun around and looked down. This quick motion messed with his depth perception, and in turn, made his head feel light. Bearhugging the branch provided stability and relief.

Mar threw his whistle again, this time acting out the casting of an invisible fishing line and drawing in a catch. Des played along by untangling his feet and kicking one down toward the fisherman like a hook was tugging on his pant leg.

Descending the jagged arrangement of branches was arduous. Trusting his arms more than his legs, hesitant to jump between the thick wooden wings, he draped himself over each branch and sluggishly slipped his legs off. His shirt bunched beneath his chin and his belly became raw from chaffing.

When his feet finally wobbled down onto solid ground, Des patted his right pocket to make sure his father's fish hook was there.

Mar saw none of this; his eyes were squinted beneath the brim of a cowboy hat. The cap was glaringly large for his head; it tilted with one side perched on his right ear and the other falling against a cheek that was smeared with a black marker. The sloppy imitation of a beard seemed to give Mar more confidence in the persona, and he bared his teeth in a snarl and spat at Des's feet when he grinned.

"Where's mine?" asked Des, pointing to the hat hanging down to Mar's nose.

Mar raised his chin high enough to allow the hat to slide up and back against his forehead. With one eye still covered, he glowered and said in the deepest voice he could muster, "No, no. You're too scared to come . . . come with me. You don't get one."

This was true; Des had been too afraid to go with Mar on his scavenging trips. He still feared that people would see himand punish him if he walked into their homes and searched through their belongings.

The closest he came was hiding across the street or around the corner. Des could only watch in anxious anticipation as Mar tramped through the doors or clamored up to the windows. He would then wait and count the idling seconds in agony, listening for sounds of discovery and anger. Mar would occasionally take advantage of this, screaming at the top of his lungs and bursting out of the house in a frantic run, only to stop short and smile at Des's desperate gasps for air.

"It's a trophy prize, 'cause I'm brave."

. . .

The floors had been liberally coated; the green linoleum tile sparkled in the rising sun and gave the room a majestic atmosphere like visitors were stepping in a bath of emerald waters. The rickety frame of the beds, which were packed in rows with narrow spaces between them, were faintly reflected in the shine. Over each of these cots were draped ephemeral mosquito nets. These patchwork veils were pulled taut along the sides and over the four posts. With fine lines at these ends, they looked to the boy named Pab like silver pyramid boxes in which the patients rested and magically healed.

"*Shikamoo.*" Pab greeted the wrinkled woman in a whisper and a bow like he had seen the doctors do; he unbuttoned the crease in the mosquito netting and spread the wings apart and stepped in, letting the net fall back together behind him. He had traveled a very long way from his home, so he was unsure the woman understood him, but she didn't seem to hear him in any case. "*Jina langu ni* Pab." He pointed to the three letters he had marked onto the breast pocket of his doctor's coat—a spare he had swiped from the linen closet. Its tail was far too long, and Pab had to fold it up and tuck it in the back of his rope-tied waistline.

Pab had settled on his name only days before he had found the curbside sickbay. Before that, he had still been clinging to the name his parents had given him—the same parents he had left in that humble home he had once thought was the entire world.

Their unwillingness to look him in the eye, to speak to him, or to hear him had been received as a sign that he had done something wrong; he had upset them. He had waited for them to tell him what he had done, all the while wishing they would punish him in some other fashion. A verbal rebuke or extra chores—his usual punishments—would be preferable to the silence. Unsure what his sin had been, Pab was equally confused as to what he needed to do to atone for it.

The old woman in the bed had fulvous cheeks, murky eyes, and a worrisome tremor in her hands. Pab started the day by washing these hands as she slipped in and out of sleep. This appeared to ameliorate her discomfort. He dried them with a towel that matched the color of the floor. Her fingers seemed to steady as they interlocked over an embroidered heart stitched into her gown; they trembled less than before—at least he thought and hoped they did.

Pab kept a keen eye on the woman with the knitted heart as the day progressed.

Amidst the rounds of the nurses and doctors, he picked up where he saw slack—refilling cups of water, applying a cool cloth to a feverish sweat, and closing the window when the insects swarmed in the hottest part of the day.

But no matter what he did to help, the woman's health continued to fail—her coughing fits were worse, her body shook with painful tremors, and Pab could do nothing.

Evening approached, and the doctors came in and gathered around the woman. Pab stopped his sweeping and sat on the empty bed opposite hers. Leaning forward, he tried to gather what was being said. The doctor spoke with a rapid-fire tongue in an unfamiliar dialect, but while Pab was slow on following the language, he had learned the doctor's body movements—particularly, his hands. If the man interlocked his hands and kept them pressed to his stomach and far from the patient as he spoke, then he was typically giving grave news; if his hands were free and he ended their talk with a handshake or a touch on their shoulder, the outlook was more positive. This time, the doctor's hands were steady. Pab waited and watched closer, clinging to the hope that she would heal; he liked this woman.

But there was another motive that fueled his hope; he wanted to know that he had made a difference, that he had played some part in her recovery so that he could add her to his list.

Pab reached behind his back and removed a shabby notebook from his rear pocket. A few unbound pages tried to escape when he flipped through the booklet. On each leaf of paper, there were several lines, and each line would be a space for him to fill with a name or other indication, charting his progress toward his goal—*wema*.

Wema was his answer to everything that had happened.

After much reflection on what it would take to be seen again, his answer had come in the form of a single word, taken from his sister's name. He had observed that his sister remained seen by their parents. She had not been removed. Furthermore, it had long been his devastating suspicion that his mother preferred his sister; she had never been shy with her rebukes and constant comparisons. And so Pab had reasoned that he needed to become like her in order to be seen again. Wema—like his sister, kind and generous and acting on the behalf of others—was what he needed to become.

He would do more good deeds, to be like his sister. The separation, he hoped would then be over. And on that joyous day, he would return home, and he would take back his name.

However, not every deed or day was added to his list; some only increased the lonesome dread. Such despair was felt when the man in the coat began fidgeting at the hands and walked away with a pitiful bow but no comforting touch. Pab didn't know what ailed the woman, but his reading of the doctor's signs came true; the woman passed by noon the next day. He had only known her for a short time, she had not even known he was there, and yet he wept for her as though she were another mother from whom he was lost.

. . .

A spooky wail of a sound woke Des and immediately gave the impression of an animal, growling with hunger and crouching to strike. His eyes shot open, but the rest of his body remained motionless. The darkness was so thick that he could barely see the brick wall he had slept against. Imagination took hold of that canvas, an emptiness that was quickly filled with sharp claws, razor fangs, and piercing red eyes. The monster formed and grew to match the sound of the moan; Des could almost feel its steaming rank breath on his face.

The strange sounds did not seem to be getting closer; Des thought it was safe to turn on his back but did so at a delicate pace. He cringed and gritted his teeth; the sound of his sleeping bag, rustling and deflating, would surely startle the beast. It was a painstaking process that ended with a sudden jolt—on the opposite side of the alleyway, Mar's spot was vacant, and his blankets were strewn about. Where was Mar? Images of his friend being attacked and dragged to his death made his heart stop.

"Mar!" Des called loud enough for his friend to be able to hear him from inside the monster's stomach.

Des sat up, to better determine where the wails were coming from. His eyes were slowly adjusting and, down at the end of the alley, where the lane met the backside of another building, there was something curled on the ground—the true source of the cursed noise.

Des stayed in his sleeping bag as he started his approach, scooting forward. If there was danger, he could slip back inside and zip the monster out. But as he crept closer, the echoes lost some of their effects. The messy noise became less jumbled; the more distinct sounds—a low, rough moan, a peppering of heavy sniffles, and a few gasps for air—were less frightening when they were not overlapping and reverberating off the walls.

"You're alive!" exclaimed Des, when he realized that it was Mar who was causing the symphony of sounds, momentarily forgetting that the monster was entirely his creation.

"Shut up," barked Mar. Des doubled back from the heat of the rancorous retort.

Mar sat with back hunched, legs crossed, and hands rubbing the opposite elbow.

With his arms stretched and hands open, Des guarded himself upon his second approach. He leaned forward with his feet set and ready to spring, putting a hand on his friend's head. Instantly, Mar's body leaned into the slight touch. Des felt how tired his friend was, as though he had been awake for days and the crying fit had taken its toll.

"What's the matter?"

Mar's sobs shook in a thick, low tone. His head slumped down with each cry, and his shoulders rose in arduous tremors, heaving buckets of tears from a deep well within him.

Following an ephemeral moment of strength, Mar spoke. "I don't know."

"Don't know?" Des stood up and looked about, searching and hoping he could find the tangible thing that had taken control of Mar like a puppet on strings. "Huh?"

"S-stop. Leave me alone!" Mar ordered Des away.

Des retreated, this time on foot and dragging his sleeping bag, and pretended to fall back asleep. He could tell that Mar worked harder to keep his whimpers lower, but Des could still hear them. While the image of the creature had left the canvas of his mind, the boy struggled to fall asleep, toiling over what could have cracked Mar, who had always seemed impervious and invisible.

. . .

He doesn't want to talk about it, Mar. He plugs his ears and shakes his head—no—when I say it was his turn to cry, when I ask why . . . why was you crying? Then he said, I'm a liar. He said, I'm the crybaby. And then he makes fun of me for not going with him. To get mine and his things.

Mom will make him stop it! She'd tell him, stop being a big bully! And she'd make everything better. Singing. And then rubbing my head. Gah, I want her here. Now! For everything, I want her here. For everything.

But I'm on my own. I've gotta do it by myself. No mom. Me. I'm six. Like Mar. Same age. I'm just like him. So I can stand up to the bully. I can.

IV

*T*he entire town seemed to be involved in the same party. Everywhere Mar went, people were dancing, singing, playing, and eating. Small vendors had sprung up along the street selling treats, flowers, dolls, and so much more. Random concert stages were scattered with bands and dancers. Floral designs decorated the homes, matching the vibrant colors worn on the dresses, woven in hair, and painted on faces. There was a parade on almost every street; everyone was in equal spirits and the onlookers were encouraged to join. There was no break in the sea of people nor the flow of jubilation. Mar had yet to catch up with the change in dialect, so he was not sure what they were celebrating, but he could not help getting swept by the fever.

It was hard to navigate the crowd since no one made room for him and the process was made all the more difficult by how much Mar was carrying. He was squeezed between two bags, one on his front and one on his back. The loot had settled heavily and rounded the bottoms of the packs. They flopped up and back on him, hanging low on his short figure and forcing him to jut his knees out as he jogged. Undeterred by the sweat dribbling to his chin, Mar stayed focused and maintained his tenacious pace, pushing through but more often bouncing off people.

Mar was tempted to stay in the parade a little longer but knew that Des would already be worried.

Des, after well over a year, was still too frightened to scavenge for food or join in on many of Mar's adventures.

Upon his return, Des asked Mar what happened. The worst-case scenarios had already been forming and flustering: he had somehow been injured, captured, lost his way, or simply left.

Most of these were ridiculous but the concerns of trouble were somewhat understandable given Mar's wild eyes, matted hair, and drenched face. He was also walking with a disconcerting limp due to the positioning of straps. And the exasperated grin he panted through looked more confusing than comforting.

"Ready?" Mar's question was distorted by a large gasp for air, and so Des did not understand him. "They got so much. So much!"

Mar didn't bother to pull the backpacks off; he gave in to their weight and came down with them. "There's food—all yummy. Stuff I never ever, ever got before. Good stuff. And funny hats. And they're having fun. You gotta try." Mar continued to boast as he writhed his sore but nimble limbs from the tangle of straps.

The bags became lighter as Des raised them higher; the load emptied in a radiant shower. The individually wrapped candies and treats were intact, but the baked goods had been smashed. He had tried to keep them separate, rolling them in different rags and napkins, but his work had been undone in the journey. Des didn't seem to mind; he grabbed handfuls of the mess and shoved it into a beaming smile. Mar was rejuvenated by the sight of his friend's excitement, thinking he could capitalize on it.

Mar could hear the parade's music. Mimicking the dances that he had seen in the streets, he spun around the pile of treasure on the ground, clapped his hands, and took short, quick steps. He imagined that he could move as effortlessly as the people did; but, from the confused look on Des's face, Mar knew that he was not getting it quite right.

"What's the matter? What's wrong? Gotta go?"

"No! It's fun. They dance like this. Like that. And whoo." Mar spun a couple of times. "Out there. Let's go. Let's go. Let's go." Mar started backing away toward the exit, but Des sunk lower to the ground and shook his head. It was a valiant effort, but nothing seemed to get through to him, so with a disappointed groan, Mar gave up on the festivities outside and stayed with him.

. . .

An eight-year-old girl named Ren sat atop a newspaper vending machine, crossing her legs and centering her weight on the wobbly base. She didn't want to fall and humiliate herself in front of the handsome man playing his guitar on the street corner.

Ren's cheeks blushed when the attractive musician smiled over a wool scarf and gave a nod to a stranger who dropped a bill in the open guitar case—his first take of the day. If she had any money, Ren would have done the same.

The lid of the case kept getting blown shut by the morning breeze, but when it did, he never quit strumming; he simply balanced on one foot, gripped the top with the heel of his boot, and flipped the case open again, never missing a beat.

Ren was reluctantly drawn away from the dimpled smile by the tasty aromas wafting from a nearby bakery. She hopped from the machine, tossed a flower she had picked from a grove in the case, and braved a smile up at the man—a smile he didn't see.

A soft jingle from the chimes above the door welcomed her. The mixing temperatures in the air tickled her skin; the warm, sweet breath from the large ovens behind the counter contrasted with the chilly morning air flowing in from the windows, which were thrown open by the owner, allowing the smell to attract more customers and it worked; the place was packed with people, and Ren watched many more stop, do a double-take, and be lured away from their morning rush.

She snagged a *sfogliatella* from a fresh pyramid of goodies on a sampler tray. "*Grazie*," giggled Ren to the employees in the back, who were lost in a swirl of buzzing oven timers, barking orders, and flour-covered aprons behind the counter.

The cool fresh air was a relief, even after such a brief time in the rising heat of the crowded bakery. Ren let her feet start into a skip with little mind for where they would take her. One hand swung her last, frail flower through the air while the other pressed the *sfogliatella*, into her full cheeks. The bread was delicious and disappeared before she had covered more than two blocks but it left her tongue parched.

She stood at an intersection, smacking her dry lips and licking her fingers, and was teased by the sound of swishing water and heavy gulps coming from a cabbie sitting in his parked car waiting for a fare. The engine rumbled and he stretched himself into an insouciant slump, tugging the brim of his derby over his brow, hanging his hairy arm on the rolled-down window, and poking his head out so that he could tilt the bottle fully. Before the bottle could be sucked dry, Ren tramped closer and lowered herself in front of the man's squinted eyes. Supporting her elbow on the side mirror, she offered a flower in exchange for the drink. She spun the flower, pinched between her small thumb and middle finger, hoping this would hide the fact that the stem was bent and most of the petals were lost. The driver didn't free his gaze from under the patchwork derby. He did not see her at all. He finished the bottle, crunched the plastic in his fist, and let it fall into the seat next to his. A satisfied burp was his only response. She was not insulted by the fact that he didn't see her—she had already grown accustomed to that—it was the grungy smell of the man's breath, a rank concoction of tobacco and stale coffee, that made her recoil. To get back at him, Ren chomped down on the flower she had offered him, letting the earthy taste settle as she moistened the petals with her tongue, which she then stuck out at the cab driver. She crossed her eyes for good measure. The driver stared through this with a placid distance in his eyes and a benign snarl on his face as he picked his teeth in the mirror.

Mouth still dry and throat gagging with regret at the festering bitter taste of the flower, Ren continued her way down the busy market street.

A rickety stand was set up on the next corner, tilting off the curb and into the street. Ren had seen many of these in the city market streets with people selling food, jewelry, and cheap oddments, never paying much attention to them—just more obstacles in congested walkways. Yet, as she came near a stand that was blanketed with artwork and price tags, her prance came to a quick stop when the sharp color of the painted eyes snatched her gaze.

There were portraits of solemn faces, strange collages of puddling colors, and a great variety more; but what stuck out to Ren most were the green eyes that appeared again and again, in some form or another, in each of the paintings.

She was transfixed.

If it had not been for the wind pattering and flipping the pages of the book in the vendor's lap, Ren may not have seen the woman sitting next to the stand, her posture was so stoic and fixed, with her legs crossed and her eyes downcast. Ren had to kneel low to the ground to get a proper look at the woman's face. Her features struck Ren as pleasant and softly alluring, and she found it difficult to turn away, caught in particular by the subtlety of the aged eyes crisping underneath the young, freckled skin.

A man in a suit walked by, holding a hat to his head. He slowed and shuffled under the small awning to see the collection. The woman didn't greet the man, nor did she start into a sales pitch, as Ren often saw these street vendors do. Neither did she stop the pages from turning or hold her place when the next gust of morning breeze rippled through the cramped street; she let the pages flutter, almost as though she were not intent on reading, but simply needed a reason to keep her eyes down.

"Chiara." A man at the front door across from the stand juggled three grocery bags in his arms as he searched his pockets for his keys. He didn't stop searching to allow time to look at the woman, saying her name as a blunt greeting, out of forced courtesy and he did not expect a reply. Ren did not hear her give one. The man disappeared into the apartment building, and the woman named Chiara remained like a statue.

Though Chiara did nothing overt to solicit her attention, Ren was captivated by an incredible stirring. The fascination grew the longer Ren stayed and observed—the long hair spun in a tight bun atop the woman's head, the stains of paint that had become ingrained in her delicate hands, and the resemblance between her aged eyes and the blue of a quickening stream. She studied the woman, seeking an answer to the question that was tightening her chest—was this the woman she had been looking for?

Ren's father had told her very little about her mother, despite the ceaseless pestering and pleading of his child. She had learned earlier on that she must catch her father in the best of moods to get anything back and even then, he remained vigilant and subdued in his replies, giving only bits and pieces, just enough to temper her badgering. He would respond in a monotone and distant voice as if he were guessing her mother's favorite song or hometown or hobby or any such small anecdote. And yet, the smallest morsel would whet Ren's appetite for more.

In all parts of her life, Ren placed at least a modicum of significance and relation to her mother, real or imaginary. She would be filled with delight at the mere sight of her mother's favorite color or the chance to eat her favorite meal. When her father brushed and cut her hair, she hoped that it was in a style similar to hers. Ren would inspect her appearance in the mirror, focusing on the parts of herself that were unlike her father—her blue eyes, stringy smile, and thin neck; her father had mentioned these were given from her mother and so they became Ren's most cherished features. Since her father kept no photographs, Ren relied on these as clues to piece together, to guess what her mother looked like and who she was.

In this vein of desiring connection, Ren had easily reasoned that her mother was the purpose of her removal; while everyone else didn't see her, Ren believed that her mother would—all Ren had to do was find her. As a form of dedication to the quest, she had taken a new name, the nickname her father had once given her mom—Ren.

Now, facing this silent woman in the town far from her own, the girl instantly felt the maternal intimacy she had sought and it told her that this woman must be who she had been looking for. She felt like there was a string, invisible but strong, holding her to the woman. Ren stayed by her side all morning and then followed the woman when she packed away her paintings and carried them up the stairs to the tiny apartment on the top level of the nearby complex.

The narrow door opened into a room that was divided into a sitting space and a kitchen by a domed archway and a change from carpet to tile. Directly across from the apartment's entrance was another door that led into a bedroom with a small bathroom and walk-in closet joined off it.

There were shelving units of various sizes. Some of these were filled with books and photo albums. Other shelves were deeper and built more sturdily, with sliding drawers and panels. These held supplies such as paints, chalks, and blank canvasses. In the rare open spaces between the shelves and other pieces of furniture, Ren could see that the walls were painted in Chiara's style. A small television sat on the floor opposite a two-cushion sofa and a wicker rocking chair. Outside the apartment, between the window of the living room and the window of the adjacent bedroom, Chiara had fed a clothesline with hand-dyed dresses and shirts. Everything Ren saw, she loved; it instantly felt like home to her, like she was returning and not simply arriving.

"Mamma!" Ren finally called in a howling laugh. Her excitement was so great that her imagination layered over reality; she could almost will herself to believe it, that the woman had stopped with a stunned expression on her face and come to kneel in front of the girl for a loving embrace—and a sweet embrace it would be. But the daydream could not last; the woman walked right past her without the slightest flicker of acknowledgment.

Chiara instead focused on her records. The soft scrape of a needle was followed by the opening notes of a symphony coming from speakers wired in every room.

Ren's arms flopped against her sides, her head dropped, and she turned, following the woman into the kitchen.

Chiara prepared herself a plate, sat down at a table pressed into a corner of the kitchen, and began conducting the symphony with her fork between bites.

Ren braced herself for a swell of tears; she even squinted her eyes and frowned against it. But to her surprise, she did not cry. The devastation did not come because the feeling of belonging did not go away. The imaginary string slung between her and the woman, Ren could still see it. Feeling the tug of that invisible tether, she breathed a deep sigh of resolve, whispering to herself that she would remain with Chiara—even if she remained, unseen.

. . .

"Take that one." Des steadied himself with his foot on one rail, gesturing to the parallel line of iron. "We'll race. But! But you have to stay on your track. Stay on. Balance. Can't step off. That's cheating." He hopped in the air a couple of times, switching his pivot foot and teetering his arms.

The boys stepped onto their respective rails.

"Back, back, back to this marker," Mar called as he reached across and tapped Des's toes with a stick, prodding him to shuffle backward so their line was even. "And chase the train."

With one foot flat under their weight and the other bent at the toes behind them, the boys set themselves in starting poses.

"Ready?" asked Des.

Mar responded by imitating the sound of a gun and tossing heaps of gravel as he pushed himself into a sprint.

Des launched himself to match the pace but quickly slowed, straightening his arms out, biting his tongue, and dropping his gaze from the tracks ahead to maintain his center. Mar soon pulled ahead of Des's deliberate and balanced steps, but he did so by barely staying on the rail at all.

"Cheater. That's not—"

The burning anger at the sight of Mar's taunting grin took Des's concentration away from his balance and his footing was tripped. He was sent forward in a sprawling and unintentional leap, his leading leg still raised in mid-step. His threatening whistle-blow was cut short as his hands shot forward to break his fall; they clapped on the rail a second after his knee collided against it.

Watery eyes blinked through the sweltering pain, and he rolled down the gradual slope of the embankment. The wool of his sweater gathered a good number of small rocks and clumps of dirt before he came to an unpleasant stop at the bottom of the small hill.

"Des. Are you okay? Let me see it."

Des let his arm lose its grip on his knee long enough to slap Mar away. "You cheat!" This was all Des could get out; his breath was held down in his clenched gut. And when it did come out, it was a hacking cough with a heavy gurgle of spit. "Get away! I hate you!"

Mar was then treated with spurts of foul names and threats, backing him away until he found his boundary and gave Des his space.

As the pain slowly alleviated, dulled to a tenderness, Des remained in his curl for something close to an hour. After such time, the tears continued to dribble over the small, bump on the bridge of his nose.

"I wanna go home." Des knew that he needed to hold his ground. "I'm going home."

The words seemed to repulse Mar as he shook his head and threw himself backward, away from Des's sickening suggestion. "Just 'cause you got a little hurt."

"No. It's not . . . stop. Stop. Stop! I want to go home."

Mar brushed his pant legs and stood up. Then he waved his arms to bat away the words Des left in the air between them. "No! You can't just quit!"

Mar let out more of his aggression in an angry fit, roaming around in a fidgety fury, hurling rocks into the air and breaking a stick over the tracks.

"Baby. *Wah.* You're being a baby. You don't! You don't know where . . . You don't know how to get back." He stomped back to Des, huffing gulps of cold misty air and holding his arms out with claws extended to make himself look more beast-like.

"I can find it." Des straightened his back to sell his resolve.

This only provoked Mar more. He stepped forward and loomed over Des. "They won't see—"

Des cut him off, screaming, "SHUT IT," and standing up so quickly that he almost headbutted Mar on the chin.

The rush to his feet also rekindled the flare in his knee, forcing Des to scream against the pain. "SHUT IT!"

Des pushed past Mar and limped back up to the tracks, his choice of left or right was arbitrary. As he walked, he listened desperately for any sounds following behind him. Mar stayed down, in the ditch a good distance away, but moved parallel to him, as though there was some force keeping him at bay. He was not happy, but he was moving in the same direction; Des decided that he couldn't ask more of Mar than this and limped ahead.

. . .

I'm going home. Mar can come if he wants, but I'm finding it. I'm done. They won't see me. That's what Mar thinks. I am being a quitter. He doesn't want to lose and tries to boss me around. Stay away. Stay away. And stay out and go where we want. That's what he wants. But I don't think what he thinks. He's wrong; this isn't a game. There's no winning. Something just went bad. Something's wrong. Very, very wrong.

V

The evening rain stung the top of San's head, mocking her for choosing the open field over the dry cover in the town, though it was not much of a conscious choice. It was instinct that diverted San, as soon as she spotted the spires of the church and the speckle of homes. In her exodus, San had, to the best of her ability, stayed away from the larger towns and homesteads, traveling primarily in the farmlands and woods. She did so to avoid people as much as possible, after discovering that it was not just her father and grandmother who looked through her. The dull haze in their eyes lit a fire in her chest and she wanted to evade it.

Only when absolutely necessary would she venture into a town or, preferably, a lone house on the outskirts to restock her satchel. Taking what she could carry and what would last, San was surprised by how much they had to spare. She took from their abundance, never enough to make a significant dent and they never seemed to notice.

On these supply runs, San was also surprised at how different and rather odd the people sounded; she found it amusing to listen and mimic the strange names they called each other and the particular words they had for things. She would then recite them on her walks to keep her mind busy.

The downpour worsened by nightfall and a dense fog settled, causing her to walk into the barbed wire that was looped and tangled between the rusting poles. She freed the front of her coat that had been snagged and let her bags sink into the ground at her feet while she assessed her options. The wire seemed to go on forever in both directions, but she knew that her limited visibility added to this illusion. A faint glow of a lone homestead appeared on the other side of the fence. It teased and taunted her pride, and San relented.

"*Eine Stunde,*" San growled to herself as a compromise with her instincts to stay away; she would seek shelter in the home for only an hour, or until the storm rolled on.

With the promise of a dry warm space, San hurried to get through the fence without taking the time to search for a gate or even bring her bags with her.

The limited light and thicket of wire made maneuvering through the fence difficult. It was too slick to balance or step over. The stakes gave a little when she tried to work them from the sloppy topsoil, but this only caused the coils of thorns to slide along the pole and cut at her hands. So she went to her belly and started to dig. Her cuts and their trickles of blood were coated with globs of mud as she tunneled herself beneath the fence and slid into the gunk. She felt a hundred pounds heavier when she rose to her knees on the other side; mud padded her shoulders, chest, and thighs. San started toward the house, marching through the neglected growth of weeds and shaking the loose mud off each limb. Yet her complexion had collected more green than it lost brown by the time she came to the brick wall that ran between the house's rear courtyard and the pasture.

The grass of this quartered lawn was well-maintained compared to the brush she had pushed through, but it was cluttered with tools, toys, and animal feed. As she navigated through the obstacles, most of which were farming and gardening tools, she wondered if there was anything left in the storage shed stuck in the corner where the wire fence met the wall.

The doorknob on the back entrance to the house didn't budge and neither did the surrounding windows. Feeling slighted, San moved to the other side, trying everything. There was a pyramid of firewood stacked under a high window on the eastern side of the house. Steadying herself on the logs, she pressed against the window, but it was locked as well. San was given a curious stare by a mangy cat lounging on the inside windowsill. She hissed at the pet and scared it away.

San got to the front of the house only to find it, too, was locked. She pressed her shoulder against the door as though she was going to ram it, but only had enough energy to slow her descent, sliding into a ragged pile on the soaking wet welcome mat.

She tried to capture any warmth radiated from within but only received the sweet smell of cooked meat and fresh bread—just out of reach.

The rickety door to the toolshed had to be worked back and forth to open far enough to squeeze in, scooping and slopping the loose earth.

The shelves and hooks along the walls were mostly bare, except for a cardboard box full of bent nails, a hatchet, a gardening trowel still on its hanger, a larger shovel, and a flashlight with engine oil stained on the bezel and lens. She clicked it on and used the blurred light while propping the shovel against the door to keep the wind from blowing it open.

The shack was longer than it was wide. San rested her head on an overturned saucer at the door. There was a stretch of darkness beyond her feet, she didn't know how far it went, but she could easier touch the walls on either side. The odd dimensions were evocative of a coffin and made her claustrophobic.

The flashlight bulb was dim, but it gave enough light for San to spot a bag of feed on a bottom shelf. Her stomach made a desperate growl of relief, louder than any thunder roll yet. She cut open the burlap sack with the blade of the hatchet and her heart raced as a stream of chicken feed flowed out onto her lap.

Her fingers cupped and dipped into the feed and held some to her nose. The tiny pellets did not have much of an aroma and San didn't expect that they would have much taste, but they would suffice for the night. She spat out most mouthfuls without swallowing, but the munching seemed to trick her stomach into thinking she'd eaten.

A strange sound popped from the darkness beyond her feet. Sitting up and letting the feed fall back to her lap, she tuned out the dribble of rain and listened for the sound again. The lightning and thunder lapsed, giving her time to focus. When it came, she could tell it was closer. But it took a third time for her to recognize it as the quiet cluck of a chicken, moments before the boney animal, with its feathers matted, hobbled out of the shadows.

"Hallo."

The gawky, sopping-wet creature ignored her and peeked at the small bits of feed that had stuck in the mud on her leg. She tried to remember the other greetings she had learned as she watched the chicken follow the line of seeds, but her mind was too sodden and hungry. Before it reached the pile in her lap, San reached out and offered the bits in her hand. The chicken's head bobbed up and down, slowly diminishing what was on her palm, following it like a leashed dog when San pulled her hand closer to her waist.

The sudden frenzy of bawling *bawks* and beating feathers woke San to the fact that she had unconsciously grabbed the chicken with her other hand. When her mind became more lucid, she didn't let go of the chicken, even though she was met with a rush of fear and pain from the claws. She gripped it tighter, and out of some instinct, brought it up and wrung it down hard against the wall. San slid to her knees, pressing her weight down on the animal's neck. Bracing it into the corner lessened the chaotic fury of claws and flapping wings, but the sting of the shrill cries continued. Patting the ground behind her, the wooden handle of the hatchet was found. The blade came down with a swift slash. She was startled by how close she came to her fingers; she hit more of the wood than anything and had to pry it out, drag the bird away from the wall, and breathe again before trying another chop. This time, she was more precise, and the shrieking cries died to an echo.

When the storm lifted, San opted for the longer route, following the fence all the way to the corner and then turning toward her original entry point. Skimming over the loose earth and kicking slush high in the air, she slid with each stride.

If her feet hadn't stumbled over her satchels buried in gloppy mud, she may have skated past them.

A crescent moon was peering through wisps of grey. San nestled against the moist moss on a large tree and then peeked around the trunk on both sides to check the forested terrain. The coast was clear. No one had been pursuing her, but her heart continued to race, and her ears were alert for the smallest sound of trouble.

San's lighter was out of fluid—she lit fires almost every night. The matchbox striker strip was soaked. She had yet to master her father's method of just those special rocks and steel to spark a fire. So the chicken would be tried raw.

Her first hesitant cuts with the pocketknife removed nothing but feathers. The next shaky slices gave thin slivers of the outer skin, barely enough to chew, giving a bitter and metallic taste; this may have been her sweat and the bird's blood that coated her fingers. After a few breaths to settle her nerves, San was able to carve deeper.

With blood-stained arms and hands, the seven-year-old finished plucking the feathers and gnawed at the meat. The bits and threads she pulled made her throat gag and stomach lurch, and she couldn't even finish what was in her hand, but it was enough to fill her with pride. To celebrate, she chopped up what was left of the bird, intrigued to see the bones and innards.

The carnage was terrible, like something a pack of dogs may leave. Within the hour, she threw up her minuscule meal. And yet, through the gummy bites and bitter results, San was filled with sensational satisfaction that was strong enough to negate her hunger and lull her to sleep.

In her dream, there was a fire roaring beside her. She was in the same forest, only the trees appeared taller and fuller. And it was darker; the blaze was towering, yet San couldn't see far into the night. Footsteps were approaching but she was not frightened. She felt relieved—without knowing why. Then her father stepped into the light. He was thinner than he had been when she left him; the shadows on his cheeks and eyes had grown as his face was scrawnier, and his presence was not as intimidating as she remembered. He appeared as brittle as glass, and yet his frame managed to carry a massive carcass that he laid next to the fire. The limp body was quite large and didn't have the shape of any animal San could recognize.

"*Ich vermisse Dich,*" San told her father—as she had said many times while falling asleep. Her father didn't say anything; he didn't joke or tell her that he missed her as well. His only response was to rotate a piece of meat on a spike over the fire. As he worked, he gave the occasional glance toward San, not as a summons, but to insinuate that she should be watching closely; she could tell that he was teaching. When it had cooked to his liking, he took it off the heat and placed it on the ground in front of San. Then, without a word, he stood and disappeared into the shadows. He left her to smell the sweet fragrance of properly cut and cooked meat. Permeating, it stayed with her even after she woke in the morning, as did a resounding truth she believed her father was trying to tell her—if she could learn to hunt and cook like that, then she could stay out where she wished and never rely on the people again.

. . .

The festive market occurred once every month. Taking place on the first Saturday—weather permitting—it was a time that Ren eagerly anticipated; she loved how the town square transformed into a happy maze of tents and stalls, in which Chiara and other artists sold their work. There were fellow painters, as well as photographers, carvings, and metalwork. Homemade crafts and jewelry were available to trade or purchase. Farmers hauled and sold their harvests. And the town residents swarmed for the magnificent congregation of merchants.

The rented tent provided more space than the rickety stand that Chiara would post on her apartment sidewalk;

therefore, she was able to bring a greater portion of her collection for display; Ren loved seeing the full breadth of her artistic flair.

Yet Chiara always struggled with sales. It wasn't for a dearth of talent—as far as Ren was concerned—but a debilitating lack of confidence. The other artists, craftsmen, and farmers would force themselves into the crowd, striking conversations and herding customers to their spots. Meanwhile, Chiara was far less charismatic, choosing to sit quietly by her table, concealed by her work, and wait for the rare patron.

The regular vendors would send customers her way. This was done subtly—for example, a quiet recommendation at the end of their sale—never meant to embarrass; they genuinely recognized her skill.

This group of artists—most of whom were also in her weekend art class—was one of the few social circles Chiara felt comfortable in.

Otherwise, the world didn't seem to welcome her—no one came to see her or urge her out. But she didn't project herself, either. Chiara was aloof; she lived, ate, and slept alone, doing very little to change it. Her discomfort with people was not just in presentation or sales but in the regular and mundane exchanges. The common ease of speech eluded her, and that set her apart from the normal flow.

She seemed a pariah—an alien—and Ren could relate; the young woman was removed, just not to the same extent, the main difference being that Chiara's separation was self-inflicted.

It was this strange common ground that had convinced Ren, almost immediately after meeting Chiara, that she was meant to stay, taking it as her mission to learn through the woman.

Chiara was not the biological mother Ren had expected, but there was a lasting comfort with her. Ren had made her home with Chiara. She had chosen to live vicariously through the artist—their lives becoming interwoven—and in doing so had rekindled a sense of belonging in the people's world. The separation had diminished, the chasm had narrowed, and Chiara was her line across it. Ren had taken to her as a surrogate mother, and the tether she imagined between them had only grown stronger.

. . .

"I went somewhere very different from anywhere we could go. And I saw people and creatures and things that nobody has ever seen—weird and magical things." Des stood up and raised his arms like they were long enough to reach mountaintops, and then dropped to crouch low to the ground. He always tried to animate himself when he told his stories, hoping to garner some sense of approval, or perhaps envy, from Mar.

The cold had become too formidable; the boys were forced to cut their day's trip short and retreat indoors.

Movie theaters had proven to be suitable retreats in such instances, as they offered ongoing entertainment and an endless supply of sugar-fueled treats. Almost every town had one, so it gave them a consistent and decided destination when the weather got bad—one of the few things the boys could agree upon recently.

But Des preferred their time after the final show when they got to tell their own stories instead of trying to understand the people's drama.

"I was flying. Over mountains. Big mountains that poked the clouds. Not a lot of people were brave enough to cross them, but I did." Des closed his eyes and imagined the sensation of flight he had felt in his dream—the cotton-soft touch of the clouds and the rush of the wind.

In his dream, the movement had felt so real. The tremendous velocity of the wind filled his chest with pressure, his ears with howls, and his eyes with tears. When he turned his head, he saw mirages of feathers overlapping his fingers. In the next blink against the wind, Des gracefully landed in a lush garden, supremely dominated by a single, ancient tree with grey aged bark. Everything else in the garden was lively with color; the tree was swarthy, and it drew the eye with a foreboding gravitas.

The garden was the center of a village, tiny huts made of thatch and stone scattered around, which was collectively enclosed by a wall with a golden shimmer. Des walked along this border and saw that it was not built with brick or stone, but rather random objects both large and small. It was curious how they were able to stay up and support the impressive height.

"There was a spell on the wall that gave the objects a glow. The wall was made from the people's things. Everyone who lived there gave something. You gave anything you wanted. When you were old enough. And then a spell was used to add it to the wall. Build it up and up and up."

"What did you give?"

"All I had were my shoes." Des looked down, momentarily surprised to see that his shoes were still on his feet, but also a little disappointed—their disappearance would have impressed Mar, who could only manage to scoff and ask what he, himself, gave to the wall. Des had to answer, "You weren't there, Mar."

Averting his attention from the look of insult on Mar's face, Des explained the significance of the tree. "The wall was built to guard the tree and everyone—"

"Is that all?" Mar guffawed with a demeaning smile that curled his lips back.

Des stared back, silent.

Mar shook his head, lowering it to blow bubbles in his drink through a straw.

Des sank to the ground, let the feathers fall from memory, and blinked at his friend. The story was not finished, but Mar did not seem at all interested in hearing the end, which happened to be Des's favorite part. He bit his lip and considered persisting through the rest of the dream—how he had seen the girl.

The girl had not been in the village or anywhere close to the wall. He found the girl with scarlet hair that swathed over her eyes, kneeling in a bleak field of parched and pedal-less flowers. Although she was placed at a great distance, Des could hear when she started to cry. A gentle rain from a cloudless sky accompanied her tears but she remained dry. The curiousness did not stop there; time seemed to speed ahead, and the flowers suddenly rose to bloom. The most glowing beauty came from the ground, and he stood in the radiance of tranquility for a moment. Des took great care to not disturb a single petal when he stepped closer to the girl but awoke before he saw her face.

Des decided that none of this was worth sharing with Mar and chose to accept his failed attempt to impress by simply muttering, "Mhmm—your turn."

With a forceful burp and a shake of his head, Mar snorted, "No. I'm not gonna. It don't matter, Des. Nope.

I thought we're on the same side. But you don't want it. You quit my game—I quit yours."

Des felt like Mar punched him in the gut. He wasn't sure how he regained enough breath or managed to steady his lips enough to speak. "I just want to go home. Mar. You know that you can stay with us. You—"

"This could be great, you dud!" Mar's bark was deafening. He turned on his heels and marched away, fists thrusting. "A gift! We can go where we want. And do what we want. And you want to go back!"

. . .

I try—I do—to read the signs and such, and I try to know which way to go. Directions. But nothing! Nope. Nothing looks right. It all looks the same to me—different. Nothing hits. I wish one of the signs would say, Hey, hey, hey dummy, go this way! And I would get it. But they don't. I got nothing. I got shlop. And he doesn't even want to get there, but I feel bad for Mar. I feel like I'm letting'em down.

VI

A much larger vessel cruised alongside the ferry and its sizeable wake caused the smaller to sway. The captain sounded the horn in vain objection, and Pab bellowed a deep *yawp*, trying to match the pitch. The tilt of the deck could have sent him tumbling, but it wasn't the first time he had traveled on water, and his legs steadied themselves well.

The fog was thickening, which could have been the reason the greater ship had not seen the ferry and passed so close. It also kept Pab from seeing either shore. He even had trouble seeing the other occupants of the deck; he had to find them in the mist, and when he came upon someone he found especially fascinating, he made a game mimicking their mannerisms—it was the closest thing he had to conversation.

One such character was a slender man hunched over the starboard rail with his elbows propped on the polished wood. A burning cigarette was held tenderly between the fingers of his right hand; bleached-blonde hair nearly concealed the phone he held to his ear with his left. The strands of hair were as straight as bristles, shading an already glum mien. The stranger spoke with his lips pursed, smoke puffing out with each word.

Pab was not tall enough to lean over the rail; he settled with wrapping his arms through the square bars and resting his forehead against them. He balled his fist and parted his index finger with an arch at the knuckle, mirroring the man's sullen frown and draw from the cigarette, filling his lungs with the spray of the water when he circled his lips. He couldn't fully understand what the man was saying on the phone, so he improvised with mumbles jumbled together, casting in the few words he had picked up and trying to match the tone.

Pab's next find was a couple dressed in very elegant attire. The woman's shoulders were bare; her dress started under her arms, curving down and flowing out in a long train that she held up and away from the grimy deck. The man wore a black suit with a white scarf and a top hat.

Finding the couple fascinating—they seemed rather out of place in the drab scene—Pab followed on their stroll. His back was straight, but his lumbering feet felt awkward as he tried to mimic the sophisticated sashay of the woman's steps.

Calamity struck when the man leaned in for a kiss and a gust of wind knocked his black hat off. The brim bounced on the rail, teetered for a moment, and then started to tumble toward the water. Pab was quick though, dropping to a knee and thrusting his arm between the bars in time to catch it. He smiled in relief but more amazement at his luck. Not wanting to bend the hat by squeezing it through the narrow bars, Pab alternated his hands and worked the hat up and over. Dusting it off, he offered it up with a humble nod that the man didn't accept. They were already moving off, with no mind of the hat. They didn't see it in Pab's hand, only a few feet away—the same way they didn't see him. Feeling defeated and glum, Pab let the couple wander away, placing the hat on his head and meandering in the opposite direction.

It was too large for his head and plunked the rim of his nose. Adjusting for the difference, Pab tore pages from his journal, crumpled them, and stuffed them along the inside of the hat. It was noticeably heavier, slid slightly, but was a much better fit. He was glad the pages were finally of some use.

It had been nearly a week since the last space on the last page had been filled, since he realized that it had made no difference.

His mother had never promised to look at him again. No one had told Pab that if he accrued that list of kindness, long enough to fill this random booklet, then the separation would be broken. That motivation had been entirely of his design, originating in his own desperate hope. Pure, unfounded hope had driven him through years of small favors and acts. He had written each of them down until every line and space in the book were filled. But it was not right or not enough, not enough to be welcomed back.

Why had it not worked? Was there more that needed to be done? Or would wema always be out of his grasp?

With his sight obstructed by the hat, he didn't see what was ahead, and his knee bumped into a bench that was set against the rail. He moved to sit but stopped when he saw that the seat was already occupied.

Everything the woman wore appeared to be made of the same continuous piece of cloth, a stitched pattern tracing from her legs to her head. The fabric was loose at her arms—where she had it wrapped to cradle an infant against her chest. Pab couldn't make out her face, but he did hear her voice—her singing. It was a tenderly sweet melody that kindled warm embers in his chest. The child didn't make a sound, and he assumed he or she was asleep, but the woman continued to sing. Soon, Pab could hear nothing of the waves, horn, or churning engines.

Suddenly the mist sparkled, illuminated, but not yet fully dissipated by some unknown light source.

There was a soothing feeling that loosened Pab's body, making him more vulnerable to the sway of the boat, so he locked his fingers around the frame of the bench. This was his anchor and he trusted it enough to close his eyes and surrendered to the weightlessness.

Pab heard the creak of warped boards bouncing. He looked down and saw his feet crossing the makeshift bridge, the one he and his siblings had constructed to traverse the backyard stream. He had used it every day on his way home.

Before him, walked his mother. He held the train of her gomesi, and they stepped across the trickling stream that wove through his family's garden. She didn't reach for him but he also didn't risk ruining the moment by trying to get her attention.

They approached the back entrance of their home. He could hear giggling coming from inside and knew the names that belonged with each laugh. His mother stayed outside in the garden. She did not work or tend to the plants but simply sat in the dirt. It was then that Pab noticed that she was singing—the same tune the mother on the boat had been—the song that had carried him into this daydream. Beyond that, he could understand it more, now that it was in his mother's words.

Pab was standing in the water now. Legs steady in the soft current, he could have remained upright and yet felt the urge to dive, as if there was something to retrieve in the water, something he was meant to find. Pab pursued this guess and fell to the side, spreading his arms as he tipped. Another's hands were quick, catching him before he hit the water and hoisting him up for a tight embrace.

Pab assumed it was his mother and savored the reunion, his heart soaring. Tears formed a stream down his cheek and added to the one they were standing in. He had envisioned his family, almost every day and night, but never before had they given back. They had never talked or even looked at him, let alone held him like this before. Something was different, and when Pab opened his eyes, he saw what had changed.

It was not his mother nor his sister; another woman held him. Pab didn't recognize her but did not pull away. He was startled by the stranger, but not afraid. He allowed himself to remain in her embrace. There was something in the way she looked at him; Pab's memory could not match her face, yet she looked at him like she knew him. She snuggled him closer, then peppered his cheeks with kisses. Each press of her lips was warm and lingered. Then she began to rock him back and forth as though he were a babe. The woman was quite strong; he was almost ten years old, his body had grown so much, but her arms were sturdy.

She spoke only briefly. The few words were stirring; so much so that he was rattled awake, finding himself back on the boat. The rocking sensation remained but that could have been the waves returning below. What was unmistakable were the words that continued to ring in Pab's ear and the assurance they gifted, to not lose heart, that wema was within his grasp.

· · ·

Des stunned Mar with how easily he agreed to the plan; Mar had expected convincing Des to take a plane to be more of an ordeal.

The real conundrum turned out to be finding the airport.

This process involved a few exhausting days, several mistaken turns, some irritating maps, and many misleading rides. They could see planes flying overhead, but had trouble tracking where they were landing and departing. Finally, Des thought to wait outside a hotel and join a party that hailed a taxi for the airport. They had to wait for a cab with enough space, but after hitching a ride with a woman who traveled light, Des and Mar spent the night sleeping in a terminal surrounded by frustrated travelers griping about their delayed flights.

The next question was which plane to get on. Ultimately, they decided that finding the shortest boarding line was their best option, as it would likely mean there were open seats.

The hull was much tighter than they had expected, and the passengers jostled forward bumping each other and smashing their luggage overhead. The boys managed to squeeze through and find an empty row near the back. They each carried only one pack; Mar tossed his into the bin without a worry, but Des took the time to retrieve his father's fish hook from the special pocket; he didn't know how it could possibly get lost or damaged but didn't want to take the chance.

Des buckled himself in; Mar was brash and remained in the aisle even after all the other passengers had taken their seats. He mimed the hand gestures and directions given by the attendant, pride soaring that he was the last man standing. Des did his best to ignore Mar's boasting. When the plane sped up, the runway streaking by outside the window provided a fair distraction. Then he heard Mar yelp with fear and hurriedly click his seatbelt closed at the first turbulent rattle. Des laughed through the pop in his ears and the pressure in his chest, as Mar gritted his teeth and clawed his fingers into the armrest. The plane tilted and shook in its climb; the shrinking world disappeared beneath the clouds.

Mar hollered that it was not a cloud, but smoke billowing outside the window. His rapid breaths and wild eyes were fueled by the persistent shaking of the capsule. The sign for seatbelts was illuminated above them, and there were several worrisome rings of a bell. Mar swore that the plane was going back down, that they had made a terrible mistake. Des tried not to listen to his trembling tirade and took the opportunity to be the braver one for once, faking an imperturbable yawn and a shrug of his shoulders, as if the incessant shaking was somehow soothing him.

Moments later, to their astonishment, the blinding grey broke, as did the dread in Mar's voice. The boys were stunned to behold the rolling, peach-colored hills above the world. The plane leveled out, the shaking stopped, and Mar's grip released. It did not seem as though they were moving but rather coming to rest on the pillow. They had entered a new place—a dreamland that left the boys utterly speechless.

· · ·

The cheerful anthem from the crowd outside roared through the open window, drawing the girls from the television. Chiara brought her cover around her shoulders and leaned over her small balcony, immersing herself in the fever of the growing party on the street below. The other tenants went farther, leaving their apartments and gathering on both sides of the street, answering the beckoning call of the parade. The sidewalks were packed; the people were barely able to keep out of the street. The night air was set aglow by the lights on the floats and flashes from cameras in the crowd.

Beside Chiara, Ren straddled the rail, ducking under the blown windchimes, mouth agape at the marvel below. From the top of her head to her hips, she swayed to the rhythm of the music.

A progression of elaborate floats, boisterous bands, and costumed dancers slowly made its way down the street. The closest was in the shape of an elephant made entirely of flowers and strobing lights. A line of red traced around its large ears, down the trunk, and ending in a bloom of flowing ribbons at its snout. Ren and Chiara laughed and cheered as trumpets sounded somewhere nearby, simulating the elephant's call.

The next was an electric rainbow that spiraled up in the shape of a cone with occasional fireworks shooting from the top and exploding high in the night sky. The crowd applauded with every colorful shower. A woman danced on the float, wearing a robe that matched the loud colors of the tower. Beefy men in face paint wearing skin-tight vests rode around her float on child-sized tricycles, barely avoiding each other and the crowd. They beeped on hand-held horns and wheeled toward the audience with looks of shock painted on their faces, and the crowd reveled in the levity.

The irresistible energy flooded into Chiara's apartment and took hold of the girls. The young woman clapped her hands over her head and danced backward into the open space of her apartment. There, she spun around the room with her cover sailing behind her. Ren joined from the balcony, hopping on the armrest of the sofa and cartwheeling across the back. She undid her hair tie and shook her head to emulate Chiara's shimmering cascade. Ren envied her angelic beauty, thinking her own hair was too frizzy.

Chiara disappeared into the bedroom. Ren hurried in her shadow. In glee, she pushed against the sides of the doorframe with her hands and bare feet, scooting herself higher. Chiara picked a dress from within her wooden wardrobe and held the hanger by the shoulder, her other hand floating in the delicate embrace of an imaginary partner; the two swayed and twirled around the bed, kicking the loose laundry on the floor. Ren left Chiara to dance with her gown; she needed to get ready herself.

A veil scarf was wrapped around Ren's waist—long enough to trail at her heels—and a diamond-printed bandana went around her neck. She dipped her smaller fingers in dishes of paint that Chiara had left on the easel, dotted her face with yellow, brushed lines of blue on her cheeks and over her eyebrows, and then swirled the two colors in a mix to draw an upside-down triangle around her mouth.

Bounding for the window again, Ren found the street was overflowing; the crowd had grown, and a live band was calling for more to come. The huge floats had been replaced by a crisp white convertible with its top down. Swaying back and forth, with his feet tapping on the leather seats, a young man in sunglasses, white pants, and an unbuttoned shirt sang into a microphone. His voice seemed to ring from the sky and resound in the wave of the crowd. They sang along with his ebullient antics, lauding every wink and smile he sent them.

To Ren, bubbling on the short balcony above, it felt like the crowd was calling to her. She imagined the man in the car turning to wave in her direction, the band pausing midbeat to beckon her, and even the crowd raising a plea for her to join. Ren bowed to the music's seduction and went back inside to see if Chiara was ready.

"Chiara," Ren laughed, already out of breath, and rounded into the bedroom. *"Andiamo!"*

Ren's excitement ceased; it was extinguished by something in the air she entered. The scene had changed—drastically. The room was bleak, much darker than before. The wardrobe was closed, looming like a formidable beast in the dark. The dress was no longer in Chiara's hand; it was lying flat over the windowsill, appearing as though she had tried to toss it out entirely. The shutters were hasped together, pressing the dress onto the wood and blocking out the lively music. This gave the singing and the drums outside a haunting tenor. The pulsating lights flickered in the window's outline, casting eerie shadows that floated around the room . It was difficult for Ren to find Chiara in such a place.

Ren was at the end of the bed, only an arm's reach away when she finally saw Chiara, wilting against the wall next to the wardrobe, now naked—her blanket and bathrobe were on the floor. Her head sank to the side. The beautiful, loose hair had tarnished into a drab shroud over her face.

"Chiara?"

She didn't answer. Nor did she seem to feel the lively call from the ever-growing party in the street. Chiara stayed in her slump. All signs of the cheerful spirit that had taken hold were gone. The energy that had sent her twirling on the balcony was spent, leaving a shell to wither in the dark. The echoes from outside sounded more like an elegy than a celebration.

Despite how drastic and sudden this change was, Ren was not surprised, merely disappointed, disappointed to see the devastating phenomenon rear up again.

The onset of sorrow was always sudden, or at least it was to Ren; she had yet to note consistent signs and forewarnings. Chiara could be painting, eating, walking, or as in this instance dancing when the sadness would strike. In what felt like an instant, the woman would be depleted, unable to paint or dance or do anything else. Ren called it an attack, although she didn't know from what.

Ren crossed her legs at the end of the bed and listened to Chiara's breathing as the young woman drifted into sleep. Her mind puzzled to no end, left in the silence, left to watch and wish more than ever that Chiara could see her. If they could see each other, it may help. It would be good, Ren thought, for her to know that she wasn't alone, that Ren saw her. If only her chosen mother could see her.

. . .

We crossed off three years. Counted again. And we guess three. Three years since they left me. It doesn't feel like it. But woosh. Three years and still no luck. But that's it. We won't reach four like this. We'll find them.

I hope we are still together when we do. Mar should stay when I get back. Stay. I would miss Mar if he doesn't. He's my best friend. No. We're brothers. He's my brother.

VII

The brick building had ivy green spreading over sun-bleached red. The plant bled up in the crevasses to the third level of the four-story apartment complex. Des and Mar scaled the fire escape and topped the structure—one of the tallest in the town—for the best look at the stars.

It was an especially brilliant sight—a revelry of diamonds in a dark dome. And the longer Des and Mar gazed skyward, unblinking and transfixed, the more stars they were able to see. Des hoped the spectacular view would be a favorable omen for the morning start; but, although the sky remained clear at daybreak, with the sun sharing the sky with a veiled moon, Mar soon cast a grim shadow of his own.

"I'm not budging. I've decided to stay here." Mar hunkered down and locked his arms over his chest. "On the roof, you were gonna ask? Yes. How long? Umm, forever."

Mar had been more and more irritable the longer they searched for Des's home, displaying his displeasure through an assortment of mischievous acts: flouting Des with complete silence for days, taking longer than necessary to come back from scavenging runs, and purposefully neglecting to bring back food that Des had requested. That was his more established repertoire. Refusing to leave in a timely manner and thus limiting their daily journeys to a few hours had been the most recent addition.

With no true progress to show in their search, Des didn't have a lot with which to combat his friend's protests.

They had not come across anything—home, town, or land-mark—that sparked any memory. And he had nothing but a gut instinct to tell him which way to go each morning.

Des stayed on the rooftop for the next hour or so, pre-tending to be distracted and conversing more with the birds than with the immobile friend, who sat stoically against the ventilation unit. He didn't complain, nor did he beg Mar to get up. He strolled the length of the flat roof as if he were in a lovely park, keeping his distance from his opponent's pout. But this disregard only made Mar angrier. "Get lost!"

The fire escape was fixed with a small terrace at every level, which could be accessed through an apartment win-dow that was low enough and large enough to be used in the case of emergency. The same floorplan was on display on each floor—a spacious living room, the apartment's front entrance to the far left, and the kitchen shrinking down a hall to the right. But the scene was drastically different between floors. Each apartment had a décor and mood that were as unique as the families living there.

The apartment nestled on the fourth floor felt cozy and quaint. The walls were painted a calming sea green with white trim. There were no pictures on the walls, but plenty of plants in pots and jars scattered on the floor. Flowers sprouted up around a couch with a shamrock slip and a dining table with a tree bark finish. It was as if they had left the window open, and the green vegetation had made its way inside.

Des stepped down to the next level, but it was closed to him. The window was covered by striped curtains, thick and dark. Des felt slighted, as if the people meant to shut him out from their lives.

The next floor down was easily his favorite. A couple lived there, just the two of them, which seemed more fitting for such a small space. These two reminded Des of birds, a pair of robins with room to flap their wings. They fluttered around, making the small room feel like an open cathedral. They talked, laughed, and listened to music.

There was no furniture and only a speck of decoration in the bottom apartment. It appeared unfished: the walls were plain white and most of the floor was bare. There was a mountain of boxes blocking the hallway. Des watched the woman wipe sweat from her eyes. She was worn down but worked eagerly. Boxes were emptied, possessions were sorted, and space was utilized. Her task was made all the more difficult by the watchful eye she had to maintain on the toddler waddling around the apartment.

Looking through the square windows made Des feel like he was watching a television set, perusing the different channels by clamoring up and down the iron steps of the fire escape for a good portion of the day.

Des settled on this second-floor platform, joining the lovebirds for lunch. The webbing of iron was uncomfortable. The hotdog he pulled from his bag was cold, and most of the ketchup came off when he peeled away the napkin. But he enjoyed their company.

When he decided that he had given Mar enough space and time, he gradually made his way up one more time.

Des mounted the final stretch of the ladder, came over the edge, and was immediately toasted by the immense heat. He had not realized how cool it had been in the shade along the building's side and how rampantly the layers of heat had gathered on the roof. It felt like stepping into a frying pan.

Mar was still by the metal box with the large fan. His limbs were sprawled out, body tucked against the unit. Des shielded his eyes with his hands pressed to his forehead and started toward his friend.

"Mar," Des called at his friend, who was slow to respond; when he did, it came as a quiet mumble. Des looked over Mar's dazed eyes. He turned over at a sloth-like pace.

"Oh, Mar. You need water! And food!" Des tried to remain calm as he flipped out their packs. But there was no water in the bottles and only scraps in the bags of chips and pretzels. Desperate, he tried to feed these crumbs to Mar, but he could only keep them down for a short time before vomiting them up, which sent Des into a panic.

"We need to get water. Can you get up?" asked Des, but he already knew the answer from Mar's grave features. Vines of red stung the edges of his eyes. His cheeks were flat with his face sagging to hold a jaw that seemed to have come unhinged. No expression showed on his arid, barren face. Every breath was labored in a prolonged wheeze.

Des knew that Mar needed something, quickly. He pictured the kitchens he had seen in the apartments below. But to get to them, he would have to cross through the windows and into their homes.

"I can't." Des whimpered. Long-established fear forestalled him. "Help!"

. . .

Ren was rattled awake by the reverberations of a scream in her ears. The living room was dark, as was the world outside the window. Everything was asleep, and the only sound her keen ears picked up was the quiet ticking from the kitchen clock.

Heavy sweat soaked her forehead as well as the thin pillow upon which she had slept. Her favorite oversized t-shirt was stuck to her back; it had to be peeled away so that she could fan some air against her warm skin. Her throat was raw. It took all this for Ren's tired mind to finally conclude that it must have been her scream that had sounded the alarm in her head.

But what caused it?

She felt that something was near. There was a presence lingering in the room. The feeling reminded Ren of how she could smell Chiara's perfume after the woman left for work.

In Chiara's room, the night air was untouched and everything was quiet. The woman was sound asleep underneath her blankets, completely undisturbed by the ruckus. Ren was relieved, but also envious. She desperately wanted to sleep. She wanted the tension to leave her body.

Hoping to absorb Chiara's radiant peace, she climbed into the bed, gingerly crawling with soft paws like a cat. "Chiara." Ren tucked herself under the comforter that had been tossed over the side of the bed and curled up close to Chiara. "*Qualcosa è sbagliato.*" While Ren could not see it, she felt it—something was wrong.

. . .

Despite having just spent the entire day climbing up and down the fire escape, Des suddenly lost all confidence in its structural integrity. He was wary of putting too much weight on the iron that now appeared as frail as a dried leaf.

Des's legs jittered down the first stretch and as soon as he hit the highest platform, he flattened himself against the wall. His fingertips dug on the clefts among the bricks with nail-splitting strength.

Confident in his grip on the wall, but not in his footing, Des wedged his toes onto the sill of the window before reaching down with a trembling hand to pull up on the lower sash. He fumed through every curse word he had ever heard—the window refused to give. He kicked at the bricks underneath the window and spat on the glass.

Taking the next ladder two steps at a time, Des was steadier. The thought of Mar, lying on the roof, fading from consciousness and wilting with thirst, was his antidote. Without looking to the window that had been blocked to him before, he started down to the second level, hoping fervently that his favorite couple would allow him entry, but was stopped by a quiet pattering sound. The third-floor window was open like it had been waiting for such a moment of desperation to reveal itself. The dark curtains looked like two cloaked arms reaching out and gesturing for him to come in.

These ghostly arms came to rest on his shoulders as he knelt and stuck his head under the frame. He thought of Mar and held that image in his head with the same grit that he used to trap a breath in his pounding chest, the last breath before the plunge.

His heart fluttered and his wary eyes adjusted to take in the scene.

The family sat in the corner of the room to his left, eating their dinner: a grandfather, two parents, and three children. There was a television displayed in an extravagant cabinet but it was off. The focus was on the grandfather, seated in a leather recliner. Even in the dim lighting from the two tall lamps positioned on either side of the entertainment center, Des could see the shadows in the deep wrinkles on his face and hands.

All eyes were on this man, and it was difficult to ignore him. While his skin showed age, his voice maintained the vigor of youth as he told a story—something about a past trip to the mountains in his younger years. It was captivating enough to pull Des in as well.

Des joined the family's circle and lowered himself to the floor between the mother and grandfather. The fear of being caught and punished was fading like vapor. Admittedly, the urgency for Mar's aid dissipated as well. He didn't mean for it to. He just lost track of his bearings, and the worries were left outside. It had been so long since he had been in the comfort of a family home, and without being fully aware, Des wanted to stay.

Des loved watching the smiles, winks, and raised eyebrows the family exchanged with each other as one story turned into two and then a third. He soaked in the feeling of ease, their familiarity with each other. There was a nuance of care and tradition being communicated, so subtly that Des may have been the only one to truly grasp it. And he was able to do so because he was looking for it; he had been yearning for it since the day he had become unseen.

The mother's slippers brushed Des's back as she shuffled behind him and into the hallway. Straining an ear to hear, there came the sound of a door being pushed open. Through the wall behind him, Des heard the woman's footsteps slow as she crossed what he guessed was a bedroom. The soft beats of her steps returned after a short delay. And this time, they were accompanied by a duet of giggles.

The woman came from the hall, swaying from one foot to the other. Her slippers glided across the wood floor, and she danced in slow motion. Taking his eyes from the smooth sashay, Des saw that there was a drowsy child pressed to her chest. The wisps of his hair were tucked into her neck, his head resting on her shoulder as she reentered the group. But the group had changed—so had the woman.

The mother who had returned with the child was not the same as before. Des noticed the transformation in stages: first, the change in her height, then the length of her hair, and finally there was the sound of her voice. The latter was the most curious for Des, because he was able to recognize the voice—it was his mother's.

"Mom!"

Des's mother was dancing toward him, cradling his little brother in her arms. He stood to meet her, but she twirled around him. His seeking eyes followed her. She joined the rest of his family, who had appeared while his back was turned. There was his father, two older brothers, and sister.

The room had transformed as well. The ceiling had become vaulted with a fan hanging down from its crest. A cobblestone fireplace with picture frames on the mantle replaced the television. The loveseat was facing the fireplace with a crochet blanket stretched over the back. Next to this was a handcrafted rocking chair. Des remembered it only vaguely, but it had appeared in sharp clarity.

"I-I did it. Oh, I'm h-home." Des stumbled forward in a daze. "I made it. I made it, home."

The family was squished together on the sofa. His mother held his little brother in her lap, bouncing him on her knee. Des watched him take turns smiling up at her and then at one of the twins, who was perched on the arm of the sofa. They both had their mother's eyes. The last brother sat on the floor in front of their father. These two were lost in the crackle of the fire before them, which was reflected in their chestnut brown eyes.

Sandwiched between the parents was his sister, sinking between the two cushions.

"No more. That's enough. Please, let it stop. I'm . . . I'm home." Des took a circuitous route around the room, brushing against the walls, and taking in all the familiar sights, sounds, and smells. He was greeted by the smiling faces in the photographs, the scent of pine needles, and the furry feeling of the rug between his toes. He touched, sniffed, and marveled at everything.

As he tiptoed around the room, the smallest chip of his senses was strong enough to break the levees he had built to keep the memories at bay; every part of him was flooded with a sweet sense of nostalgia. His father's ashtray was on the mantle—Des could hear the crisp sound his cigars made when he stamped them out. The feel of the stone chimney—he remembered how his brothers once climbed it. There was the antique clock on the mantle; its gears and heavy pendulum had continued to tick under his mother's meticulous care, and Des could hear the stern reprimands she gave whenever the children played too close to the heirloom.

All that he had held so dear was there, and it all welcomed him home—everything except what mattered most.

Their eyes eluded his.

His family did not take notice of him, even when Des stood with his back smoldered by the fire and his shadow cast directly over them.

How could this be so? How could he have made it home and still be removed?

"Sweet boy." His mother laughed and pressed her lips into his brother's chubby cheeks.

Watching his brother squeal and kick in her lap, Des was hit by a realization—none of what he was seeing could be real. There was an eerie sensation. He fought against it, pleading for ignorance. But the likeness was too pristine—it couldn't be real.

Des pled to stay in the dream. "Please. I'm back." Tears flowed. Des began to cry, fighting the reasoning that was making too much sense in his head. "Say my name too."

His name—he wanted his old name back. He didn't want to be Des anymore. He wanted to leave it all behind, along with Mar, the games, the dull look in the people's eyes, and everything he had felt in the intervening years. "Say it! My name! My name! Please . . . please let me back." Longing dripped from his quivering lips.

The picture frame was broken in his fist before he sent it hurtling at the wall. "Let me come back!" Des screamed, again and again, flinging and kicking everything within his reach. He knocked the ashtray from the mantle and stomped on it, spreading ceramic shards and cigar ashes over the floor. He overturned the ottoman and poured out the magazines and newspapers, which he shredded with his claws. Paintings were hit off their nails and shattered on the floor. "Let me back! Why won't you look at me?"

The longer the family kept him in isolation, the more ambitious his anger became. The rocking chair was flipped on its side. One of its joints was splintered under his heel. He toppled the heavy old clock from the mantle, broke the hands from its face, and used them as spears to stab into the side of the loveseat.

Exhausted, and with little left in the room to destroy, Des had nothing to do but scream. He clenched every muscle and thrust his arms down at his sides. His knees buckled and his gut rumbled. The painful howl was ready—it had been building strength for over three years—and boomed against the walls. It fell on the deaf ears of his family but rattled the windows. Torn pages of the magazines swirled in its fury. And then the whole house began to shake. The fragments of glass, wood, and stuffing left in Des's wake vibrated. Not only that, they were lifted—the debris was levitated by his voice and then sent flying into the fire. The pieces whizzed by him and into the burn, feeding it to grow and consume. The blaze was fomented, and it bloomed higher and higher. The once-dying sizzle grew into a burning roar with tongues lapping out and around the stone. They tasted and then devoured all that was around the fireplace until the house was engulfed. Billows of smoke clouded the room, and the fulvous waves spread.

Des stood amidst the smoke. When he had nothing left, the howl stopped, as did the fire behind him. The blaze died down as quickly as it had sprung up. The smoke took longer to clear.

When it finally did, and Des was able to see past the end of his nose, he found himself back in the third-story apartment. His home had disappeared along with his family. The grandfather had returned and was continuing his story as if Des had never left. There was no sign of his journey beyond the tears in his eyes and the lingering scent of pine.

Mar finished two bottles of water in three gulps each, sucking the air and letting the plastic crinkle. Des sat at his side, trapped in a phlegmatic daze and staring over the tops of the buildings around them. He took the smashed plastic bottles and gave his friend a cut of a sandwich. Mar munched on it for a moment or two but then asked for another water, slipping back into a more peaceful sleep before it was empty.

Des knew that Mar was snoozing, but still asked, "Do you remember what you said when you found me at that station?" He paused for a beat but did not wait for Mar to answer. "You said that you saw me. And you knew. You knew that we were on the same side." Mar smacked his lips with bits of tomato and lettuce stuck to the corner of his mouth. "The same side. And I didn't listen."

The ephemeral image of his home flashed in his head. In an instant, he saw his family sitting in front of the fire, which was once again under control. The room around them was unharmed; everything intact and in its place.

Des looked down at his friend and spoke in a stolid tone. "We're going be okay." Des was certain that Mar was too deep in his sleep to hear him, but he, himself, needed to hear it again. "We're going be okay."

. . .

It was my brother. My little, little, brother. He can't be that little. Not anymore. Because I'm not. I'm older and taller and changed. They should have too. And they have.

It doesn't matter if I find them. They left me behind. And they went and changed without me. They have grown up without me. And I am growing up without them.

VIII

A t first light, San departed from her nest and began her route through the forest, checking the traps she had set the previous evening. There was a brisk chill to the morning and, considering her last three days yielded little success, her body was not eager to leave her warm burrow of blankets.

Ribbons had been tied around tree branches to mark the traps' locations and assist her mental map. Her eye caught the first fluttering in the breeze as she walked by a curt bend in the stream where water pooled. Even from afar, she knew the trap remained un-sprung; the slender tree was bent, tethered to the tripwire strung over the bait. This trap had easily been the most complicated, requiring the greatest time and number of failed attempts to properly set.

Morose, she leaned against the marker tree and allowed the ribbon to bat under her nose before it was blown down by an aggravated snort. Her legs were reluctant to move on from the empty trap.

The second site on her route was at the bottom of a sharp slope. The weight of her backpack threw off her balance, even when she tightened the straps to her shoulders; this made it difficult to control her pace and remain upright. Rubble rolled underfoot. The supplies in her pack bounced and clattered with each awkward spurt and gallop. The wooden baseball bat sticking out from between the top zippers constantly bonked her on the back of the head. Ultimately, San resolved to sit on her bottom and scoot down the last length of the hill.

Her labored trip down was not rewarded. She growled with displeasure at the sight of the empty snare and the fresh tracks in the damp earth, picturing the potential catch strolling by without a care.

Her spirits rose at the sound of rustling leaves on her approach to the third ribbon—something had been caught. Readying herself, San marched with more determination, hair pulled back and tied with a purple yarn she kept on her wrist, and knife drawn from its sheath.

The rabbit sensed her arrival, curled, and trembled, sending vibrations down the cord tied to its right hind leg. The ball of matted fuzz shrunk as San crouched and shuffled forward on her toes. Her hand slid down the taut rope from the stake to the rabbit's leg. Her final breath before the attack came as a high-pitched whistle. The sound sent the rabbit back into a frenzy, moments before San pinched both hind legs in a fist. With her other hand, she drew the bat from over her shoulder and whacked the animal hard, until it was stilled.

It was not until she walked with the paltry weight strapped to her hip that San realized how slender the animal was; she could barely tell that the limp body was there and would have thought that it had fallen off if it wasn't for the gentle brushes of the ears against her knee. There would be very little meat to glean from the gaunt figure, but at least the previous day's work had not been entirely wasted.

Wishing to postpone any disappointment she may find at the next stop, a longer route was chosen by way of a weaving brook. She waded in, taking turns lifting one foot behind the opposite leg to remove her shoes and let the chill of the water nip at her bare feet. A chipper tune was hummed as she splashed against the easy current.

A smooth stone could occasionally be felt deep in the squishy mud, and San entertained herself by wiggling her toes through the gunk, making the water murkier, and digging out these pebbles.

In her bliss, she didn't realize how deep the stream's ditch sunk. Consequently, when she recognized a bush speckled with white flowers and purple ribbon fluttering in the wind, San had to search for sturdy footing to climb out. A tall old tree on the embankment was sufficient. Its roots had been exposed by erosion, and San used them like steps in a ladder.

Another commotion was coming from the other side of her fourth ribbon. Bits of dirt and twigs were flying from both sides of the large trunk, along with the bleats of an animal echoing in the air. Her heart jumped when she realized that it had to be something larger than usual, and she broke into a dash through the brush. She did not stop completely to retrieve and replace her shoes, hobbling forward and working the laces as she went, which took her guard away and opened the pale skin of her face to the abuse of passing branches. But once the shoes were secure, she pulled out the bat, and swung it hard with both hands, trying to clear a path ahead.

A roe deer was caught in the snare. Desperation filled its eyes and fueled every leap for escape. It was large enough to have yanked the stake from the ground and, by the looks of it, had been briefly free, only for the stake to get jammed between two protruding roots. Its left hind leg was cuffed to the trunk.

San widened her sidestep strides until she was face to face with the deer. The animal was stricken with fear, its entire body rigid as it stared back at her. The two were locked in unblinking tension. Without taking her eyes away, San retrieved a second roll of rope with a carabiner attached at one end and flicked the clip with her thumb. The soft sound was enough to trigger the animal into another flurry, crying, and tripping over itself. Too eager to take the time to tie another knot, San fed the rope through the closed clip to make a quick lasso and tossed the line toward the deer's frantic hooves. She yanked back on the rope when she saw the pointed hoof stab into the circle, but the leg was able to step out before the loop closed. Rubbing her watery eyes and shrugging the tension from her shoulders, San reopened the lasso and tried again. She flung the loop further, and it came to rest under the animal's belly. Almost immediately, the leg returned to the trap's ring, and this time it stalled long enough for San to snag it. She jerked the rope, stood, and backpedaled, using her weight to force the animal off balance. The deer floated for a moment, with its legs pulled out from under its body, and then crumbled to the ground with a thump, stretched out in opposite directions.

San tied the open end of the rope to another trunk a few paces away and hurried back to the animal sprawled out on the ground. She noticed that the loop with the carabiner clip was already slipping and knew she had to act fast. Squaring her feet and bending her knees, San brought the baseball bat down like an ax. It took three swift strikes before San felt that the deer's leg was damaged enough. The deer's agony was released in wailing cries that rose and fell in waves. Not wasting any time, San let the straps loosen on her shoulders and the backpack fell to the ground behind her. From within it, San brought out a ratty towel she often used to clean her hands after skinning animals. She brandished her knife, tossing it between her hands to see which was less sweaty for a better grip. The cloth was whipped around the snout and pulled back to better expose the neck. Another whistle, just as she had done with the rabbit, sounded before the kill strike. The throat was slit.

The surrounding area provided ample twigs and dried leaves for kindling, but she had to break a few branches down for the bigger pieces. Logs of greater size were too heavy to carry and had to be dragged or rolled to her site.

San's mind was mayhem, but her hands were smooth, and her movements were certain, driven not by experience, but sheer victory and pride. While parched, San panted with a smile on her face. The fire was lit.

. . .

There was a young man a few rows ahead on the bus, flopped across two seats. While the bend in his spine over the armrest appeared quite uncomfortable, it did not show on his face. Instead, there was pure bliss in his closed eyes and short grin as he strummed the guitar resting on his chest. The musician played like he was alone; he didn't seem to mind making mistakes and beating through a bridge time and time again until he got it right. The beard-covered mouth moved, but he did not seem ready to let the lyrics out of his head.

The guitar case, which had been given a separate seat, was covered with stickers and decals from around the world, and Des studied the collage of places, sigils, and languages. He was unimpressed with his music but presumed that the travel experience advertised on the case qualified the young man as an erudite guide to the city—

guidance that could prove useful since it was by far the largest one they had ever visited.

Mar was reluctant, preferring and eventually persuading Des to explore on their terms—a decision they momentarily regretted when they stepped off the bus and were plunged into the overwhelming noise and monstrous size.

The boys lingered at the station, acclimating to the massive buildings that seemed to block out the sun and the never-ending swarm of people knocking into each other. It was difficult to tell who was the first to step— who was leading and who was following—but the boys ventured into the fray of the city without any real destination in mind. Both were tempted to turn back, find, and follow the musician; but, they had one another, and although it was never spoken, they drew courage from the shared trepidation. When one would hesitate, he would watch his friend move ahead, daring him to follow; each did their best to hide their concern and thus enabled one another to explore more freely.

Their anxieties were cleansed by a sense of wonder. The massive structures and hordes of people felt less foreboding and more inspiring. Curiosity won over dubiety, and in due time, the boys were not frightened, but astounded by the size of it all. There was so much activity, so much to see and do. Food, music, and things they had never heard of were suddenly at their fingertips. New adventures and attractions were around every corner, and each led to the next.

Des and Mar found their way onto a bridge with suspension cables webbed between stone towers. Three lanes of traffic wove in each direction, cruising through remarkable arches in the stone turrets. The other pedestrians, some of whom were in professional attire, but most in casual wear, strolled down a wide walkway that ran down the middle of the bridge elevated above the cars. The boys trekked over the river numerous times that day, racing each other back and forth. They marveled at the cityscape around them but wanted something more exciting, to push beyond what the people were able to do. This led them to hop over the short fence that lined the walkway. They could already feel the rush of the automobiles, but they could still go further. The boys balanced on the large steel beams and sat with their feet dangling over the traffic.

This defiance of the people's boundaries happened frequently. The boys would initially follow a crowd of sightseers, falling in with the current of people, trusting that the groups with cameras and maps would know where the best attractions were. Once they were there and had seen what the people could, the boys were not satisfied until they audaciously pushed the boundaries, climbing higher or walking farther than the people, to capture a moment or a view that was theirs and theirs alone. This was Mar clambering onto the stalks of organ pipes in the cathedral, or Des jumping onto the diamond field and watching the final inning of baseball from the outfield, or both sneaking through the ropes to touch the various exhibits in the history museum.

"Rahirrem!" Mar would often call in triumph, and beckon Des to follow—this being his most recent favorite phrase, parroted from a movie the boys had seen. He would even hike up his leg and raise an arm to impersonate the warrior on his horse, leading the charge into battle. Des assumed Mar meant it as a nickname for their duo.

· · ·

Ren adored the way Chiara bit her lip when she was seized with inspiration. It was the early indication that a new piece was taking shape in her mind, to be followed by a lapse in Chiara's concentration. She would be so lost in her idea that her mind would miss its bearings on everything else; and it would then become Ren's job to shadow her around the apartment, turning off the faucet that was left running, removing the tea kettle from the stovetop when it whined, and stepping up for any other task Chiara left half-done in her lightheaded trance. The third sign would be the transformation of the living room into a studio. The furniture would be covered with large sheets and scooted to corners to clear the space. Chiara would then bring out the drafting table, painting easel, or pottery wheel and set it at the room's center. Finally, she'd select a record to match the mood brewing behind her eyes.

On that day, Chiara selected a somber piano melody to soften the air and slow time. This torpid atmosphere made it difficult for Ren to measure how long Chiara sat on her stool, suspended in contemplation, fixated on the blank canvas propped on her easel, before a single stroke.

The portrait on the album cover, which Chiara had dropped to the floor, was of a man with a short curly beard that drew from a thicker mustache with a distinct tuft just below his lip. The scruffy hair on top of his head was combed to slope down his forehead and away from a distinguished partition—Ren thought he was adorable.

The thinnest brush painted in tempo with the music. Her hand moved as though she were conducting, wrist flicking the notes onto the canvas. The shapes became more defined as the tempo rose.

Each motion was precise, and the paint seemed to obey perfectly. Her brush jumped from one side of the canvas to the other. Ren was impressed with how she was able to keep her place on the large blank space. It was as though the image was already there, latent to the world, waiting for Chiara to reveal it.

There came two vertical lines, running parallel with a bumpy curve to connect their bottoms. Their tops were connected or were nearly linked by two diagonal lines that rose, almost to a peak but not quite. A thicker horizontal line was then drawn, supported by the diagonal lines and balancing over the rest.

Finally opting out of the basic black, Chiara added an earthy brown under the rim of the curve and up along the two horizontal lines, which she topped with lush green.

The pace quickened and Ren had to focus more to keep up; just as she lingered to appreciate one thing, some other detail was added.

Ren slowly came to see the image of a canyon—the vertical lines and rounded bottom—depth and layers were formed within the ground, adding grandeur to the ravine. Across the chasm was a bridge with diagonal supports.

Chiara bent over her small clay bowl and meticulously mixed her paints, trickling single drops at a time. Ren perked up in her seat when she recognized the shade of green conjured in the bowl.

Starting at the trough and using varying brush widths and breadths of stroke, she filled the canyon with what looked like water—green water—and as it rose Chiara began to linger mid-stroke, allowing her paint to collect and thicken there. These darker lines in the middle of the waving lines were stacked until a circle began to take shape amid the waves. Ren gasped when her vision adjusted to see the canyon was the eye. The scratchy curve of the crater outlined the iris and the pupil appeared low amidst the depths like a trick of the light in the darker shades of green.

Chiara let her hand float back down, touching up and patting the paint, making the green appear more fluid and blurring the impression of the iris at the bottom. Ren had to strain her eye and trick her focus to see it again.

Like faint shadows on the horizon, the shapes of several figures dusted into view, perched on the bridge as well as the cliff to its left. Some were standing, others were kneeling, but all were in a line for their turn to use one of two buckets being lowered from the middle of the bridge. As one went down empty, the other was being reeled up with drips of green spilling over the brim. And to the right of the pulley system, Chiara drew more people. Fewer and farther between, these departing figures were more defined, with heavier strokes.

The fringes of the canvas were still blank when Chiara let go of her brush and flexed her fingers. She stretched her arms above and then behind her torso as she inspected her work—appearing satisfied. But Ren knew that she was not finished; Chiara's process couldn't be completed in a single sitting. She would continue to work on it in intervals over the next few days, with the smallest detail or addition catching her attention as she went about her day in the apartment.

Chiara gave it a nod of triumph and began to wipe her hands with a cloth. When she stood, Ren noticed how drained Chiara was and how feeble her movements appeared. There was a great heaviness in her eyes and frailty in her steps, as though she had returned from an arduous journey.

Chiara closed the bathroom door behind her, and Ren was left alone with the painting. The daylight outside had vanished into the night. The needle on the record player was curbed off and the speakers were running static. The tea in Chiara's mug was cold. Ren had completely lost track of the time. Yet, even as the hours caught up with her and she regained herself, she didn't feel tired. There was something powerful about the painting. Ren moved closer to the canvas and decided that it was without a doubt her favorite—even though she wasn't sure what it meant.

· · ·

Mar says we are the Rahirrem. That's his word. And we are. Rahirrem. The wild pups. Free and running with fire. A fire to fill the sky up. We go. And we do. Whatever we want. I'm ten and he's eleven and we are kings of it all. Awoo!

I'm sorry it took all that for me to get it. To see what he was seeing. Yup, he knew. And now, I get it, too. We are on our own! Left to our way. I was a dumb little kid. Scared and stupid. I wanted to go back and get told what to do. Because I was scared to say, so what! Now, I'm big. And I know that I would've lost this. Missed this. Missed out. I would be them. And they're scared.

Hell to them! We get to say what we do. We make the rules! Don't need them to tell us nothing. Don't need 'em! Being away is free. Being separate—it's a gift. And we can do whatever we want with it. We're special for it. Chosen for it. You have to be chosen to be the Rahirrem.

IX

Quartered near the village center, the church and school were encircled by a hefty stone wall on three sides and an iron gate at the front. The building for classes was between the chapel and an office. Between the administration building and the classrooms was a playground. On the other side of the school was a court-yard. And finally, there was a small cemetery on the far side of the church.

Mar and Des followed the teachers down the main corridor as they deposited the students into their rooms according to grade. No matter the age, the children wore uniforms and sat at assigned seats. The boys found the students that were closest to their height, sat in the back, and tried to imagine what it would be like to spend their years in the school and have their seats.

The kids spoke in a language that was new to the boys, and the life Des fantasized with them looked very different from his own. Not long before, it would have bothered him to be in such a place. The blatant differences would have signified that they were far from home, far from his destination. But since he had embraced the removal, he now cherished the experience, knowing that he would have never been in that school or town or with these kids if he had not been separated. He wanted to see the lives in that place and so many more. He wanted to go and see everything that was different from the family that had left him behind.

One subject transitioned into another. The day's regimen was a tiresome mental exercise, cramming facts and questions on top of each other. The students fidgeted in their seats, legs kicking under their desks. Auditing the class was enough work; near the end of the day, Des struggled to stay attentive to the teacher's arithmetic lesson, finding the tone to be extremely dry and wondering how the poor prisoners were able to tolerate it every day. The students were given breaks: one for lunch and one for recreation. This was too few in Des's opinion.

The uniformed students broke from the doors at the end of the day and found their cars in the bumper-to-bumper line parked in front of the gate. Those who were not picked up in the family vehicles walked to their neighborhoods in packs or took a bus.

The street cleared of parents and the faculty departed, and the buildings became eerily quiescent. Even staying in their rooms, the children had been active every moment of the day and Des had not noticed how lively the place had been until everyone had gone. The lights were turned out and the air seemed to go still. It was in this twilight, vacant and silent, that Mar and Des found the boy, sitting in the grass at the juncture of the iron fence and stone wall.

His uniform was the same as the other children, only far more unkempt—the front was wrinkled, the lapel was stained, the sleeves were rolled, and two buttons were missing.

His eyes were clear, but there was deep coloration under them, wilting in his sunken cheeks. The boy sat with his back against the wall, legs flung before him, and a hand gripping one of the iron bars at his side.

"Hey, you!" Mar called, crouching in front of the boy. They were within arms-reach, but Mar spoke as if they were a great distance apart. The boy's head rolled over in response; he looked at Mar, but his lips remained tightly closed. The acknowledgment was enough to send Mar into a carnival of ecstatic laughs and whoops, rolling about and pounding the ground with his fists.

The boy turned toward Des, who was startled by the sensation of being seen but better kept his composure. What stunned Des more was that boy didn't share the ebullient mood of the experience. He looked at Des with dull eyes, as if he didn't care whether they could see each other or not. Without speaking, he seemed to ask if Des could make Mar stop. There was also hostility from the kid—a hint that he wanted them both to leave.

Des presumed that he was around the same age he had been when first separated. "How long you been here?" asked Des, forgetting that it was unlikely that the boy could understand his language. The boy seemed to grasp enough of his intention and dropped his head away, frustrated at Des for not obliging his wish to be left alone.

Mar, completely oblivious to the cues and tension, made matters worse by crawling closer to the boy. He did his best to ask the boy his name, in his language. Des appreciated the attempt, but the boy only seemed more annoyed. Speaking rapidly and crossing the languages again, "What do you want your name to be?"

The boy yanked his shoulder away from Mar's grip, allowing his arm to slip out of the jacket. The boy eased away, and Mar dropped the uniform, putting his hands up like he had been caught stealing it. "Whoa. It's okay. We've been there." He started in on their full history, a rapid account of their time in the separation. Des quickly became overwhelmed by Mar's bombastic chatter, but the boy no longer seemed to mind. He didn't appear to hear it anymore.

If he had not run out of air, Mar would have kept on his tirade, but thankfully his lungs gave out and he had to pause. He sat next to the boy, panting to catch his breath. And the boy kept his head turned away, focusing on the empty street. Des recognized this yearning, the waiting that had lasted beyond the point of tears.

For the first time, Mar seemed to notice the boy's agitated posture. He dropped his expression, pushed himself to his feet using the wall for support, and backed away as though the child had suddenly changed into a vicious animal—one that was ready to strike.

"It's all right," Des bent down. He took a breath in and let it out, pausing between each sentence. "I know you're scared. It's okay. To be scared. And I know you think you can wait it out. But you can't."

Des's nuanced approach seemed to peeve Mar. He stomped his feet in place and crossed his arms like they were postponing something of the utmost importance.

Undeterred, Des continued to talk softly to the boy. "I'm glad. That we found you. Now. You have us."

Mar was growing more impatient with each steady and slow word. By the twiddle in his fingers, there was clear agitation, like they should already be off on some grand adventure.

"It's going to be okay now. Because we are on the same side. Us. We're on the same side."

Fed up with Des's subtly, Mar rushed forward and lifted the boy by his elbow. "Come on then. They aren't coming back."

Des shot his friend a scolding scowl. Mar shrugged, but the next moment snarled in pain when the kid bit his hand. His teeth dug in and held Mar's two fingers even after he had released. Mar shoved the palm of his free hand into the boy's chest, bouncing his back against the wall. When his jaw widened, and Mar was able to pry his hand away, the boy dropped back to his corner. He returned to his watchman post with his back to Des, paying no mind to Mar's fit of rage.

An arm and a leg were stuck between them to protect the boy from any retaliation. Des had to hide the way his arms tensed, and his balance went on edge. The soft tone he used with the boy wouldn't work on Mar—it would only add fuel to the fire. The only option was to stall and to see if Mar could rein in his anger. After beating the wall for a couple of rounds, Mar stormed toward the doors of the church, flashing his eyes at the boy and leaving Des to console.

"We'll wait. In there. When you're ready."

. . .

The pyre was unlit. Its pyramid of gangly sticks and kindling was neglected long into the night—a hollow and unstable structure. No fire meant there was nothing to keep the bite of the crisp night air at bay and the darkness would have swallowed her completely, if it were not for the immense glow of the pearl moon in the otherwise vacant sky. But San despised this light, in her malaise, she would have preferred total blackness. She wanted everything to disappear.

The crag had provided a spectacular view, but it was a considerably poor choice for a campsite in retrospect. The bare rock rolled from the tree line and protruded like a beak over a deep crescent valley. It was naked terrain, lofted up to the punishing whip of the wind that careened through the dell and constantly beat against San's back as she tried to sleep. It also made quick work of her tower of firewood, toppling the twigs and spreading the kindling. Her campsite's lack of cover would be a relatively easy fix; the forest was not far, but her discomfort and consequent sorrow were crippling, the thought of exerting herself was unbearable, and she was left marooned and vulnerable.

The thread-thin towel made for a minimal cushion for her sore side. Every bump and knot in the rock was felt underneath. There was a sharp crick in her neck due to her unlevel head. She tossed back and forth, trying to find some elusive position in which every part of her body didn't hurt. This despairing effort was made all the more infuriating due to the memory of the soft, luxurious quilt she had the night prior.

The quilt had been her favorite because it had reminded her of what her grandmother made. If the evenings were warm enough, she would fold the layers beneath and make a mattress out of it. But the night prior had been frigid, and San had needed layers. Large enough to roll around her twice, the quilt had turned into a plush cocoon.

She had awoken in the morning with a strange sensation on her thigh. Wrestling free and peeling away the top layer, San had found that her beloved blanket, as well as her sweatpants, had been soiled in the night. The miasma of blood lingered still, stinging her nostrils.

"*Teufel!*" San had bellowed as she hurtled the quilt off the ledge—followed by the pants. She had done so in a heated rage and had regretted it immediately.

Sleeping on her best blanket had been against her better judgment. She had foreseen that she may ruin it. The signs had been there: the elk meat she had devoured for lunch had tasted bland, the joints at her knees and ankles were sore, and her fur wrap had suddenly squeezed her stomach and made her sweat. The truth was that she had simply wanted to salvage a solitary comfort at the end of a terrible day.

This had happened before. The first time—San had screamed. The bleeding had been so sudden that San thought she had been attacked; this fear consequently led her to refer to the regular phenomenon as the work of a devil. She had since come to expect it with the onset of aches, a change in appetite, and other reoccurring tells.

San had been quick to realize that she wouldn't die from it—although she cried in angst that she would prefer that. Stubborn, San had been reluctant to accept that it was unavoidable and had tried everything to beat it. Experimenting with what she ate, changing how far she traveled and how much she rested and even alternating which side she slept on—nothing she tried helped. The Teufel became a consistently loathsome and macabre experience.

"*Oma*," San called out to the wind howling in her ears, caught and astonished at the change in her voice.

To summon the comfort of her grandmother's spirit from her memory and keep it close, San began to sing a nursery rhyme Oma had taught her. It was a short and sweet melody, about a bird carrying a letter of love in its beak. As brief as it was, San stuttered and paused once or twice. The precise words had been forgotten. Yet, there was enough to stir the feeling of love and safety for which she longed.

A shred of paper kindling fluttered in the breeze and landed in her hair, which fell about her face. Her fingers combed through the tangles and unwound the paper. It was a quarter of a page she had ripped from a hardback book—one she had used to practice reading but had grown tired of carrying. San considered making a pillow by piling the pieces together. She knew this was a silly notion but was desperate for the slightest relief.

The discomfort refused to desist, and San soon felt childish whistling a lullaby at the stars. She had grown too old for such juvenile remedies and didn't think that this was how a woman would handle the situation.

San abandoned the tune and chose a more confrontational way of dealing with the nuisance. She rolled onto her back and reached for her bag, which was tucked into a crevasse in the rock. The knife was kept in the side pocket; she withdrew it and held it in her teeth. Slithering on her belly, San moved using her elbows and dragged her lower body limp toward her pelts.

The animal skins were stretched between two wooden poles, using thread sewn into the corners. They were set to dry in the sun and by the night fire—if San had lit one. This was a process being learned through a few books, occasional observation, but mostly trial and error. She had spent a great amount of time and had lost several good kills as she slowly taught herself how to make something useful from the skins.

San didn't think of the tremendous amount of time she had spent on them as she pushed herself up and balanced her torso on one palm. She simply wanted to stab something.

The skins were desiccated, and the blade made a crisp crunch as she slashed at the pelts. She imagined that she was stabbing the devil that tormented her. When her eyes closed, she could hear the yelps of agony. Ruby eyes flared in front of her and then disappeared along with the sounds. She surprised herself by laughing, then flopped onto her back and opened her eyes.

. . .

The church smelled of bread, a deliciously intoxicating scent that grew more pungent as one walked down the nave. It also gave Des an insatiable appetite, one that he couldn't seem to satisfy, munching through half of their supply.

Des had expected the child to join them at some point in the night, but the boy had slept in the yard, foregoing the shelter and warmth of the church. He remained there through the rush of the school day, only venturing away to visit his classmates in their room and then later to the cafeteria.

The time waiting was not wasted. Des rather enjoyed the chapel. It felt like an old and majestic castle with its lavish decoration and aged stone. There was an expansive sense of history and purpose to explore.

Des walked atop the long pews, leaping across the aisle and taking high strides over the backs, his muddy shoes soiling the cushions of the seats, which were a deep burgundy to match the carpet. A song was stuck in his head, and he sang it out to the high vaulted ceilings. The echo made it feel as though there was a full choir filling the seats. The best place to shout was in the middle of the stage, behind a tall wooden pulpit; he was tickled by the way his voice bounced back to him from the mural-covered apse. If only he had an audience.

The figures and symbols in the stained glass were studied. Des tried to connect them and understand the message. But it was like deciphering a new language. Although they had been to many of these spiritual gatherings before, having listened to the harangues from the leaders and the worship sung by the audience, he couldn't remember enough to recognize the characters and stories in the windows—so he simply imagined his version.

Statues of all sizes were scattered throughout the chapel. Some were porcelain, most were stone. Names and stories were given to these as well. His favorite sat atop a central shelf—a woman with candles resting in cups at her feet. She was in a place of high honor, but what drew Des the most were her eyes; the tearful woman with the elongated face and hands held in contrition had mysterious eyes that seemed to track him everywhere he went.

Thrice throughout the day, Des visited the boy. Once, he found him sitting in the back of his classroom, snuggled against the coats and backpacks hanging on hooks. Twice, the child was back on the playground, crouched in the corner and staring at the still vacant street. They never spoke to each other; everything that could persuade the boy had already been said. He left it to the child to work through his situation and decide. Des would simply smile at the boy and offer his hand, but he was silently rejected. This was discouraging, but truth be told, Des did not entirely mind the boy's stubbornness. He was more concerned about Mar, who was behaving oddly.

Returning from the third trip to the boy, Mar was found standing, back hunched and knees bent with fatigue, and talking in a low slow but deliberate tone, as though they were already in the middle of a conversation.

"He looks sick."

There was no one in the graveyard Mar was facing through the window.

"The kid?" Des asked.

"It looks like he's sick or something," explained Mar.

Des was surprised by the remorse in Mar's voice. "He could be. Sitting outside all night. In the cold. I don't think he's eating. I remember how bad I felt . . . at first. Didn't eat a lot. I looked like a skeleton." Des sucked in his cheeks and closed his eyes to make his face look bonier.

Des laughed through his nose, hoping to coax one out of Mar. It didn't work.

"Did we die?"

Des's mouth fell agape with a long droning sound, his mind working itself into knots trying to get a word out.

"Did we? Are we dead? Like ghosts or something?" asked Mar.

A chill quivered through Des. The smell of bread was replaced with a repulsive stench of something rotten.

"That's why they can't see us," Mar averred.

Des shivered as though a blizzard had stirred inside the steeple. He rubbed his hands together, trying to warm them again. Mar didn't seem to be affected, his body not flinching. And Des wondered if he had acclimated, having been stuck in the cold all day.

"Come on. We can go." Des started toward the door but had to tug Mar along by the back of his shirt. "We've waited long enough. That rat isn't coming with us."

. . .

It's taken days. But I think I've gotten him off the ghost idea. And that's good. He was starting to scare me with all that blabbing about being dead. Dead? No. Hell no. We're not dead. I know it's not that. No!

But he is stuck on something else. On and on. He says there are more of us. There are others like us, out there.

More of us. More to come. Get together. Join. I like that part.

X

The man was conspicuous, even from afar, even in the bustling mob of people. He sported a bushy wool suit, which struck Ren as strange considering the day's humid heat. The heavy shoes clopped against the pavement. Their thick soles added at least two inches to the man's height. He had the smooth skin of a young man but distinguished silver in his hair. There was a sparkle in his cheeks as the light bounced off the sweat trickling down his face, which did not seem to embarrass him.

When she had finally adjusted to his peculiar fashion, Ren was dumbfounded further when Chiara finally spoke at the sight of him.

"*Benvenuto!*" The sound of Chiara's voice scared Ren as she came skipping forward to greet him.

The man in the wool suit raised his eyebrow and barely separated his lips far enough to let the words out. "**Bon**-*giorno*." He put strange stress on the beginning of his greeting and Ren could tell that Italian was not his native language and that he was still learning to mask his accent. Nonetheless, he seemed exuberantly pleased with himself—like he had just recited poetry.

"Oh, I have been expecting you," said Chiara with a quick nod, which puzzled Ren. Why was Chiara acting so strange? "My name . . . is Chiara." She gave her name slowly and offered him her hand with a quick curtsy. "Welcome."

The man didn't shake her hand, but rather stared at the way her knees shook with nerves. This even seemed to delight him. "Afternoon, Kara." Ren did not like the way he bluntly mispronounced her name; Chiara didn't seem to mind. She simply spread her arms, gesturing him forward to see her collection on the tables and shelves.

Ren had never seen Chiara be so attentive to a customer. Usually, she was awkward and impersonal. The man made his round, starting at the entrance and moving around the tent from piece to piece. His inspections seemed to be perfunctory. Ren didn't hear him ask about price, nor did he say much at all. The only sound he made was a tumid sniffle. And Ren quickly realized that it was a sign of reproach, meaning that he had grown tired and wished to move on to the next painting, cutting off Chiara's explanations.

The longer she spoke and the longer the man ignored her, the less confident Chiara became in her work. And by the time he strutted to the next portrait, she would be speaking harshly about her work, criticizing her paintings, saying that a piece was not her best work and that she could do better. Nothing she said seemed to appease the sententious critic. Chiara's poise lasted just long enough for them to take in Ren's favorite—the canyon eye—the one she was sure that he would like.

"*Dono* d—" Chiara paused, having forgotten that she may need to find a translation without insulting the man. "Gift of *Varmundi*. Uh, *scusi*, gift of . . . varmundi. It is mine—my word—gift of energy . . . gift life." Chiara was smiling when she said this but shut back down when the man turned to inspect her instead of the painting.

Chiara continued, "Peculiar but beautiful, yes?"

Ren stomped her foot and bit her lip when she saw how the man abashed Chiara with a crooked smile that steamed with arrogance, but she was relieved to see that Chiara was too lost, too entranced in her thoughts to see the judgment in the man's posh swagger. What she couldn't ignore was the snort. It was not the same sniffle; it was a belligerent snort, a haughty laugh through his nose.

The man dabbed his nose as though the noise had been an accident, but Ren could see the smirk he was trying to mask. Chiara saw it as well. Her face went blank, arms stiffening at her sides and hands clenching her apron. Ren was not sure what Chiara was going to do; it was just as likely for her to cry as it was for her to attack the man—she hoped for the latter. But to her disappointment, the moment was interrupted by a ringing from the man's breast pocket.

"**Bon**-*giorno*. How are you?" The man took his call and moved like he was making his exit, but stopped short, just outside the flow of people, still within earshot. Ren wished that he would go and never come back. "Yes. Stayed an extra morning. Owed a favor." Ren was able to approach, but even when she stood closer only caught snippets. Her best guess was that the critic had been asked to evaluate Chiara as a favor to a mutual contact. "He said she had shown—*promise*." The critic or collector or whatever he was said this loud enough that it startled Ren and Chiara, who had been leaning forward.

Ren spun toward Chiara. Her hands still gripped the sides of her apron. Tattered holes were made larger from her fingernails poking through the fabric. In the next moment, however, her fingers relaxed. Chiara's eyes perked up as the words were absorbed through her stone casing.

When the man spoke again, it was difficult to understand him. He was already laughing. "He and I will have to disagree on the meaning of the word."

Ren was slow to pick up on the vituperative retort, but she saw its effects immediately. A dark cloud rose behind Chiara's eyes and her body seemed to lose its form, trembling like water.

"Must be going. *Ciao.*" It was unclear if the man was talking to Chiara or if he was still on the phone. Either way, he did not turn to offer an apology or bid her a proper farewell, and before Ren could get her hands on him, he stepped his thick-soled shoes back into the congested street.

Everything Chiara had brought was shoved into the trunk or back seat of her car—a rushed job with no concern—canvases and gear were piled on top of each other. Ren barely had space to squeeze into her seat, and she was sure she heard a few frames crack when Chiara slammed the doors shut. Nothing was unloaded once they arrived at the apartment. The complete collection was left unattended and unwanted in the car, which Ren was fairly certain Chiara had left unlocked.

. . .

The doctor pressed her fingers to the child's throat, caressed his neck, and finished with a contemplative sigh. Notes were jotted on the pad resting in her lap. Pab read over her shoulder, trying desperately to decipher the scribbles. The ratty top hat he was wearing started to slide when he tilted his head and Pab had to catch it before bonking the doctor. After properly situating his hat and removing his gloves, he put his fingers where the doctor's had been. The patient didn't see Pab investigate his sore throat, repeating the doctor's motions, gently pressing his fingers around. He didn't know what he was supposed to be looking for, but he persisted and hoped some instinct would come. When the doctor spoke, Pab listened as intently as the patient and the worried parents on either side.

There was so much to do in the hospital. Trailing behind different physicians, observing as much as possible, and finding it all fascinating, Pab was having the time of his life.

He would study the patient, mimicking the doctor's techniques to the best of his ability, and then try to guess what was wrong. The diagnoses were more complicated, there were times when it was hard to know if his guess was in the same vicinity, and yet Pab enjoyed it.

Ever since the vision of the mother, Pab had a renewed hope in wema—the purity, the good that perhaps only he could achieve. He no longer kept a tab of his deeds and experiences, nor did he believe they would break the separation; the desire for wema was reworked. He was not striving to do good in order to be seen again, but simply because he could. The separation gave him the freedom to choose to do so. It was a gift, not a punishment, and he hoped to use it well.

One evening, Pab found himself alone in an elevator. The ding on arrival was pleasant but the low metallic grind and slide of the doors were concerning—it pleaded for maintenance. But what was more startling was the silence that greeted him; it was a stark contrast to the hurried noise he was accustomed to in the hospital. The highest number was illuminated on the panel, but he didn't remember pressing it or why he would have chosen this level; still, feeling adventurous to explore this unknown wing, he shuffled off before the doors closed.

The layout was similar to those below: open floorplan, rooms along all sides, and a staff station at the center. The difference was, again, the quiet and stillness.

Walking past a few doors, he discovered that they were more spread out. The patients' rooms were larger than the ones he had seen in other parts of the hospital. The extra space could be used to hold more beds, but there was only one in each, positioned in the center. Beyond their greater space, the rooms were grander in their accommodations.

Most of the patients were asleep, watching television, or talking softly with visitors. Nothing seemed rushed and there were no signs of alarm or distress. He knew they must be ill, but the bedridden people looked to be content and comfortable like they were on a holiday instead of in a hospital.

The longer he walked, the more aware he became of the strength in his steps. There was no clear direction in mind, but his feet said otherwise—he walked with a certain purpose. Turns were made and swinging doors were chosen as though they were familiar, finding himself in another ward in the same silent state.

The floor seemed to slope downward. His steps shot forward to catch himself even though he was not falling. Something was pulling him forward. A destination lay ahead that he didn't know. There was a growing certainty, matched only by the anticipation to know what it was for. Pab had once seen a tugboat tow a larger ship out from the harbor to sail. He felt like that ship, feeling the pull and trusting the tow to guide him safely.

On the outside, room 541 lacked distinction in appearance and location. It was just another room in a series of hallways. The same basic lettering numbered the door.

There was no clear indicator that he had arrived anywhere special, and yet Pab felt as though he had done just that.

There were two occupants: an elderly man in the bed, watching a news program, and a boy, watching the man. The tow line was stronger entering the room, which gave him the idea that he had found what he was meant to. More questions came to mind, the most prevalent being, was either the boy or the man like him?

With strong resemblance and vast age difference, Pab presumed they were grandson and grandfather. A glance around, at the assortment of photographs resting on the bedside table helped fill in the gaps and generations.

The grandson was young, younger than Pab—about eight—and yet he wore the clothing one would expect of a much older, professional gentleman. Hands clasped behind his straight back, the boy exuded a maturity, not just in dress, but presence, again very unlike a typical child. The boy did not turn to greet Pab, which was the first indication that his hopes were failing, and neither did the grandfather.

The silence created an uncomfortable atmosphere. Families were usually hugging, kissing, and crying over their loved ones in the beds, but there were no signs of love or even anything of the sort between the two.

Silences, such as the one freezing the room, were usually reserved for after death, and Pab wondered if that was well on its way.

No response was given; Pab remained unseen, a fact that was made clearer when he was bumped from behind.

"Hugo. Come away, Hugo." The nurse's determined step struck Pab as strange. The boy wasn't doing any harm. He gave a quick nod and started to shuffle away, but not far enough apparently because the nurse pulled him by the arm and positioned himself between the boy and the old man's bed.

"W-wanted to help," Hugo muttered.

"Don't cry. You're a good lil' bloke." The nurse patted Hugo's arm for comfort. "But let us handle'm." As the nurse turned, his expression changed from kind to cross, shooting a look over the shoulder to the patient in the bed. Pab then realized that the boy was ushered away for his sake, not the patient's.

"I'm the one dying 'ere. Now, do you mind moving yer bum and getting me 'nother shot?"

Pab was astonished by the ferocious bite the weak voice could carry.

"I have—" the nurse started but was interrupted by a bark. The man in the bed barked—there was no other way to perceive the sound.

The nurse kept hold of Hugo, huffed a composing sigh, and said, "Are you sure you don't want to come along? If you're looking to help, we could use you out at the hull."

The nurse was not subtle in tone. It was less of a hint and more of a plea to allow him to take Hugo from the room, but the grandson chose to stay and so did Pab.

Later in the evening, as the last light was peering through the wide window on the far wall, the grandfather was reclined in bed, body eerily still and seemingly asleep.

A brittle moan came from the throat. Hugo and Pab simultaneously looked to the doorway to see if it had been loud enough to beckon one of the nursing staff.

"Sir?" the small voice called back cautiously, Hugo assessing whether he needed to disobey the nurse's warning and investigate the noise.

Eyes closed, Wallace's head began to churn in large circles. The rotation of his head on such a reedy, veiny neck was a strange sight.

"Sir." When his shadow was cast over Wallace, the unnerving spinning stopped, and the eyes opened. What came next was a deep and hollow cough. Suddenly, the grandfather's shoulders lurched forward, carrying his head off the pillow before it fell back down with a shudder. This happened again and again, as though some force was pushing against his back, causing his spine to arch and his shoulders to hunch. Pab guessed he may be choking, as did Hugo.

"Aye!" Hugo hollered, even though he was only inches from his grandfather. His voice was loud but steady and controlled.

Wallace's eyes began to blink with each tremor until his mouth opened, then releasing a sickening hack followed by a hiss. Pab expected Hugo to take his grandfather's hand—family members tended to do so in similar crises—but he didn't; his hands went to the emergency call button on the bed.

As soon as the soft beep sounded and the button was illuminated, the hacking stopped. Hugo and Pab looked back at the bed to find a bizarre contortion on the grandfather's face. Bony cheeks were raised and darting eyes squinted like a smile, but the smirk was unnatural, the top lip was pouting, almost to his nose. It held there as the head cranked backward. Hugo didn't have time to react. His grandfather's head jolted forward, and a wad of mucus hurtled at the boy's chest. Hugo twisted his nose up and away from the mess dripping on his tailored vest.

"Ay, when those bastards get 'ere, tell them, their response time's a goddamn disgrace."

Moments later, the nurses were at the door, pushing a crash cart into the room; their urgency switched at the sight of Hugo, holding his tie and wiping his shirt with a towel.

Hugo was gradually ushered away in a flood of empathy and compassion from the staff. He seemed to comply only for the staff's benefit. The composure Hugo kept made Pab deduce that he was well-versed in his grandfather's spiteful ways, no matter how the doctors explained that it was a result of the sickness. More worrisome was the weariness in Hugo; the kid looked like he wanted a way out. Not just out of the room or away from his grandfather—the boy wanted out. Pab could recognize it better than the others. It was strange for Pab to see a boy who wanted to be like him—removed. This disturbed Pab, but it also gave him an idea, a possible answer to why he had been brought to this family.

Wallace could not see Pab, so therefore he couldn't mistreat him as he did the nursing staff, Hugo, or any other—the removal made him immune to the cruelty. Within this separation, if he attended to Wallace, then the boy would be spared the old man's depravity. Pab could give Hugo the distance he desired.

"Kaka," Pab whispered to the empty doorway. He was filled with resolve and devotion toward the boy, whom he considered to be like a little brother he was there to protect. "*Niko hapa.*"

. . .

The summertime social took place on the town's largest farmstead, located on the eastern outskirts. The massive garage was emptied of its farming machinery. Long tables were set end-to-end and covered with checkered tablecloths for the feast of barbecued meat, home-cooked casseroles, and endless side dishes. The remainder of the cement floor was left open for the dancing, spare a few tall lamps, some speakers, and a chorale of folding chairs in the far corner for the band.

The warehouse was disguised using decorations: rainbow streamers were threaded with tape across the walls, colorful balloons were tied to the table centerpieces, pots holding flower bouquets were arranged around the perimeter of the dance floor, and strings of white lights were lofted in the rafters. When one looked up at the high ceiling, these bulbs twinkled like stars in a second sky.

The dancing was the heart of the festivity. The band was a clump of stocky men, all sporting different sizes and shapes of beards. Their instruments sat across their laps and their fingers strummed along, acting without much attention. One man wasn't playing an instrument and instead gave directions to the dancers.

There were three distinct groups of dancers trying to follow his instructions but doing so with varying success, progressing in age and capability.

The section closest to the tables was made up of children, all of whom were younger than Des and Mar. Their dance was unbridled chaos, with little semblance of form. They didn't stay with their dancing partners, nor follow in line, nor listen to the singing orders coming from the speaker. Des noticed that there was a rope nearby, strung between traffic cones, creating a barrier between the children and the rest of the dancers. Its purpose was soon apparent; random boys and girls shot from the circle and if it hadn't been for the rope—which the kids had been taught to mind—they would have hurtled into the next group over.

There were more dancers in the adjacent set, and its members were older—closer to Mar and Des in age. The adolescents did a better job of keeping with the music, but it was clear that they, too, were still learning. There were a lot of toes getting stepped on and quick turnabouts for corrections. The boys were nervously steered around by the girls, tripping over their own feet and looking down most of the time. Hesitation stifled each step, and they were frustrated with each slip-up.

The final group was designated for the experts. These veterans danced with great ardor, lost to the music and oblivious to the envy of the youngsters. Their lines moved in flawless synchrony. Deciding that he would learn the quickest by working with the best, Des settled on this final group, standing at a distance, almost against the wall, and trying to move his feet as they did. It was tougher than it looked, and he felt like a blemish on the otherwise perfectly smooth choreography.

To Des's displeasure, the caller stepped down after only two more songs. And in the flannel shirt's place came a young lady with sparkly boots. The dancers and the people at the food tables applauded as the woman took the microphone. With a nod to the band behind her, she started to sing. The rhythm of her song was slower, but the band was no less lively. The adults split from their squares as they started to dance. Pairs formed for a more private dance. Some couples were waltzing leisurely in small circles; others were more improvisational in their twirls around the floor. Nothing was the same, and Des was disappointed, having only just begun to anticipate the next steps.

But as he was working his way off the floor, dodging the twirling couples, Des caught a glimpse of scarlet hair—he recognized the color immediately.

Crouching then leaping like a frog, high as he could, Des found her again, sitting in a chair next to one of the floral arrangements, gaze down, hands folded in her lap, and legs crossed. The girl may have been the only person still wearing her coat.

She looked at him with the most beautiful green eyes. Stunned and transfixed, Des was paralyzed by them.

With a peculiar tilt of her head, the girl seemed to grow impatient for Des to regain command of his feet. She then stood and stepped onto the dance floor. As she entered, all music and movement stopped—everything became as frozen as Des. Only the girl seemed to be able to move, and she did so toward Des. She stepped delicately amid the couples, who were stuck like statues in the middle of their spins and dips. The girl came face-to-face with him.

This close, he could see that she was wearing a thick fleece jacket. Three strange emblems were hand-stitched onto the sleeve. The one closest to her wrist was the most appealing to Des—an arrow and a string from a broken bow. She removed her jacket, to reveal an elegant purple dress.

Then the scene began to change.

The walls dissolved. The tables, chairs, and lamps evanesced as well. Only the strings of stars above remained in the scene. Des looked up and marveled. The lines of lights grew, stretching down with more bulbs blinking to life until the extending lights formed a sparkling dome.

Life returned when her hand came to rest in his. Des and the girl began to dance, and the others soon followed. They danced at the center of two massive rings, with dancers forming the inner circles and their partners creating the second. The music changed as well and there seemed to be more variety in the instruments and voices. Although Des couldn't see them, it sounded as if they were dancing to a massive orchestra and an equally skilled choir. The lights were singing as well, shining brighter in tempo to emphasize the notes and lyrics.

Des was bewildered at his newfound proficiency; every count and turn was sound. He somehow knew the dance by heart. Not once did he look down at his feet, nor worry about keeping time in his head. He was far more taken with the girl and the way her hand returned so eagerly to his. Fingers with painted nails lingered at his shoulder. It was as though he was her sole source of much-needed warmth. And through it all, he dived deeper into the breathtaking green pools.

The sound of Mar whistling broke the couple apart. The rattle of bits of ice hitting the ground brought Des to his senses. Being thrust back, he once again stood at the wall at the edge of the floor. The glittering dome was gone, as was the music, as was the girl.

Des cussed in a voice that rang louder than the nearby speaker. Mar didn't hear it. He was too consumed with his own game, stacking cups of ice water in a line and using a borrowed raincoat to whip them down, one at a time. After sending the cups toppling to the floor for another round, he flicked the coat over his shoulder to offer Des a turn, but his friend had already left the dance hall. Mar tossed the raincoat back over a chair. Confused, he hurried to catch up, racing along the garage walls and through the giant doors. Des wanted to be left alone, yet Mar didn't want to lose sight of him, so he had to stay close. He could barely see Des in the fringes of the dying fire's light, slipping away into the night.

. . .

Everywhere we go, she's there. Before, it was just in one or two dreams. Once or twice in a while. I would see her with her. Her . . . with her red hair. No big deal. But now, it happens when I am awake. Here and there. Here and now. In the crowd. And, I don't know. I don't know how to explain it. I just feel weird and warm and stuff. I get all weird, and my head gets fuzzy. And I can't do anything but stare like a dummy. It's been worse since I'm about to turn thirteen.

Worst part. I feel like I did before. Like I am missing something again. Not my old people. No. Don't worry. Not that. I'm missing her. Not them. I was enjoying this way but now she comes along and I'm without . . . missing something again.

XI

It was troubling how sorrowful and confined Chiara's home could feel. A place that was once vibrant with energy and color now felt cold and bleak. The doors and windows were clasped shut—no noise of life or the world outside could get in. The curtains remained drawn and only minuscule slivers of light peeked through, making it quite difficult to trust that there was a world outside at all. It was like something out of Ren's nightmares, but the most unsettling sensation was waking and finding herself in an equally dismal place.

The fits of misery would normally linger through an evening—a day or two at the most—but this bout was stubborn, for nearly a month, and Ren was beginning to doubt what she could do against it. What could she do to help Chiara? What good had she ever done? Ren was slipping into despair, herself.

A stench knocked Ren's head for a spin, waking her from a restless slumber. Alcohol had become a staple presence to the apartment, its aroma common at all hours, but these fumes were especially pungent. She crept to the bedroom door. Her mouth pursed and her eyes squinted as the stench gained strength. The apartment was rank as if Chiara had doused the furniture and walls, dangerously ready to set them ablaze.

The painting was on the stand, on full display for Ren upon her entrance. Her heartbeat quickened; Ren had not seen it since the fateful day at the market—*The Gift of*

Varmundi. But before she could begin to hope that Chiara had come out of the despair, that she had returned to her art, Ren could see her true intention, and it made her stomach lurch again. Four canvases were already piled on the floor, soaked and ruined.

When Chiara held the bottle over the easel, she put her thumb over most of the mouth, hampering the pour into a trickle—she wanted it to be a slow death. Although she had some difficulty with her aim, the bourbon fell like raindrops, slowly collecting in larger coats and blotches, until most of the painting was soiled.

. . .

San breathed freely in the solitude of the forest. Her mind was unfettered. As she walked into the sunrise, she spread her arms wide. Taking smaller and smaller steps, she savored her morning stroll in the oasis she had found.

Even in the forests, it was difficult for her to be at peace, to be as removed as she wished. Whether it was a remote cabin, electrical wires or towers, a rural highway, or even a plane flying overhead, there always seemed to be some sign of the world waiting around the corner to ruin it and remind her she was not alone.

That morning her silent seclusion was shattered by an eruption of barking.

The mangy mutts' odor wafted in the breeze. Petrifying growls rumbled as they wrestled in such a frenzy that it was difficult to tell how many there were. San started toward them, stomping louder than she realized, and the fighting ceased when the dogs took notice of her. There were three nasty hounds, three boney backs arched, and three sets of teeth bared at San. Two of them had black fur and the other was grey. One of the black dogs—the largest and most likely the alpha of the horde—had patches of missing fur. The other dark one had a gimp leg from a wound that had festered. And the grey beast had a coating of mud around its eyes and snout.

The three appeared strikingly large. San was unsure if this was due to proximity or the paralyzing fear that closed her throat, holding the putrid air in her chest. Dropping her head in a submissive bow, she diverted her eyes, only to find a sight more gruesome and terrifying than the blood in their teeth—their carnage. San saw that what had been causing the scrap was a pile of animal carcasses, shredded beyond recognition. She nearly tripped over her own feet as she backed away.

The dogs didn't track with her as she eased up the nearest hill. They stayed in the clearing, and having successfully scared off the competition, returned to their meal.

San made it out of earshot of the carnivorous thrashing, but her body stayed tense with fear. She limped away in small steps, straight-legged and head tilted back, sniffing the air. Her hands were stretched out and back, fingers flexing, feeling for the change in the air that would warn her of a dog's potential attack—but it did not come.

On the other side of the hill, there was a narrow trail that wound away in both directions, and she tried to cross, but something was holding her back. Something inside, a weight in her feet, was too heavy for her to move forward. And when she obeyed it and stopped trying to force herself to the other side of the trail, the true source became clear—it was her pride. San felt ashamed, disgusted with herself for obeying the fear that had muddled her thoughts and forced her off her course. She felt like a coward, running away from a fight, and the weight in her feet wouldn't let her take another step—until she set things right.

The meal had finally been split accordingly, and each was devouring its share, the largest of which was held by the alpha. San was much quieter on her return, trekking furtively as she descended the hill behind the dogs, squatting at the last tree before the clearing, and going to work.

A quick slip knot was looped on one end of the rope. The other end was wound around a nearby tree, twice, overlapping the lines. Then San tightened the straps of the backpack and took one final breath. This practice of composure was out of instinct, but in fact, she found that her mind was already clear, and her heartbeat was steady—she was ready.

San came out from behind the tree and planted her feet in a runner's pose. Her high whistle caught the ear of the black dog with the gimp leg and its head shot up. After a few galloping steps forward, the lasso was tossed. The two others stopped eating in time to see the first get roped; the loop got hung up on the dog's snout but fell to its neck when it turned its head to search for her. San wrenched on the end of the rope that was in her hand. The tree was smooth, and the rope slid freely around its trunk, yanking the dog onto its back. San sprinted back into the thick of the forest, dragging the yelping dog towards the base tree, its legs sprawling wildly, reeled in like a fish to the tree's base.

When the dog finally regained its footing and started straining against the rope, San stopped and tied her end to the nearest trunk. Her catch was still in the clearing but contained by the leash, close to the first tree.

The grey one spotted her and began barking at her furiously, coming straight across the clearing.

San drew the baseball bat from her pack and ran to confront it head-on. The momentum of her run aided the swing of the bat, connecting with a dog's head. It dropped to the ground, legs kicking wildly.

There was no time to draw a breath before the last dog pounced. Pure instinct sent her to her belly, and the alpha dove overhead, the jaws snapping shut, its hind legs landing inches from her side, and the tail swiping across her forearm. San reached back and drew her hatchet. Swinging without rising from her stomach hindered the amount of force; the hatchet didn't stick, merely gouged the dog's underbelly, enough to make the dog leap and give a short cry before rounding on her. She rolled to her back, lifted her bat, and thrust it into the dog's open jaws as it jumped towards her. Saliva and blood dripped on her face.

The dog's fury on the bat, fighting to take it from her, gave San some control. She pushed it back a few steps, steering through the lever of the bat. When she opened her hands and released her grip, the beast thrashed its head back and forth brandishing the bat in its teeth as though it a torn limb. San snatched up the bloody hatchet and brought its blade down hard, splitting the dog's crown down the middle.

Powerful pain shot through her right shoulder and an immense weight crashed onto her back, knocking her forward over the bleeding corpse of the dog she had just slain. The grey dog ripped the backpack off and tossed it aside, then clamped down on her shoulder again.

Out of desperation, she reached out for the hatchet that was still stuck in the other dog's head, but the one on top of her clawed at her arms, forcing her to yank it back and tuck both arms under her chest.

Mind racing and tears streaming, San waited for what seemed like an eternity, but the dog did not release her. It held the bite on her shoulder with a constant trembling growl that grew louder every time San moved a muscle.

Moving as slowly, and hesitating whenever the dog's growl grew, San slid her hand to her hip, feeling for the pocket. The folded pocketknife was then brought back up to her chin.

San didn't try to breathe or brace herself. There was no way she could properly prepare for the sheer pain she knew was coming. All she could do was scream, loud and hard, as she punched her fists out. The scream rang through the surge of agony and over the snarl from the dog. Then she flipped the blade open, thrust it over her shoulder, and stabbed at the dog's head. It was an awkward angle, but it stuck the dog right beneath its eye. It yelped, unclamped its jaws, and writhed back.

San crawled forward on her hands and knees toward the dead heap of fur as quickly as she could, working the hatchet free from the wedge in the mutt's head. The dog was squealing, pawing at its eye. It dodged her first swing and tried to dash to its left, but San hurled her weapon and caught it in the side. It stumbled but kept in its escape. San forced her shaking legs into a run so she could catch up with the animal, and she finished her vendetta.

As she knelt next to the dead dog and tried to catch her breath, San was surprised to hear the sound of barking again, having forgotten about the dog still tethered to the tree.

Without looking to that end of the clearing, San tossed the hatchet toward the leashed dog, hoping it would scare it into silence—this did not work. The dog was only incited into more of a rage.

She wobbled on weary legs to her backpack—a strap was broken, but nothing beyond repair—and retrieved the larger knife and the gunny sack she used when collecting berries.

The dog gnashed its teeth as San slowly crept closer with the sack held open and knife in its sheath. Vision disturbed by the coursing pain in her shoulder, she managed to compose herself long enough to send out another high-pitched whistle. The dog responded to the sound with one last, desperate lunge, but this was reined in by the rope. San took advantage of the restraint and forced the bag over the dog's head. San locked her arm around this muzzle, dropped to her knee, and pinned the animal to the ground. A smile came to her face as she pulled the knife, wound back, and stabbed through the bag, again and again, at all angles. The dog jerked about and squealed; San had to apply more of her weight to keep the animal down, continuing to stab at different spots until the bag was riddled with holes and soaked in blood. She didn't stop until the muffled cries faded and the rising of its chest stopped completely.

It did not take her long to find the trail again, and this time she crossed it without a moment's hesitation—the weight in her feet was gone.

. . .

Pab's chair was tucked in the corner. His legs stretched out and his feet rested higher than his chest on the windowsill, elbows on the armrests and shoulders scrunched up to his ears. The thick coat enveloped his neck and tickled his nose, stifling the sound of his breathing. The cumbersome top hat had fallen from his head and was caught between the wall and the back of the chair.

His eyes were closed, but Pab was not yet asleep, listening to the strange symphony of sounds around him in the room: the rhythm of Wallace's monitor, the old man's labored snore, the blinds being rustled by the fan, and the occasional squeak of the wheel on the cart pushed by the nurse on her rounds.

Pab could have taken the vacant bed down the hall or the comfortable chairs in the waiting room, but he chose to sleep in the rigid seat in Wallace's room—a compromise between his exhaustion and his desire to stay attentive to his patient—even though he had only grown more resentful of the cantankerous man.

It had been almost a month since Pab had arrived, and nothing seemed to be better for anyone involved. Wallace seemed to be growing increasingly cruel as his health declined.

Despite his surly manner, the old man had plenty of willing visitors. Many of these well-wishers were finely dressed on their visits as if they were attending an important dinner or business meeting. They would smile and offer cards, flowers, and other gifts of appeasement to the stubborn animal. Some even tried to combat his discourtesy with laughter, treating it like a joke—this only riled him more.

Most of the visitors seemed to be business associates or other acquaintances. Pab struggled to label anyone as friends. Of family, Hugo was the most present; others visited in rotation, but they seemed to be distant in relation and visiting merely out of obligation. They never stayed long and never showed great concern for Hugo who, due to the absence of a connecting generation, Pab presumed was being raised by his grandfather.

Pab didn't know if he had provided any relief to Hugo—or his splenetic grandfather, whose health had deteriorated at an alarming rate. The doctors could do nothing more to prolong the fight. Their initial barrage of medications and treatments had been reduced to an agonizing wait-and-see.

Pab was sharing in this wait.

On that night, sleep-deprivation was gaining the upper hand and Pab was slipping.

Then there suddenly came a startling noise from near the bed; the pictures on the nightstand clacked together.

Pab jumped to his feet and toppled the chair behind him.

Wallace's left arm appeared to be working independently, swiping at the collection of frames while the rest of his body remained motionless. His head was turned away, sunk in the blossom of the soft pillow. It was spooky, the way the arm flung itself about, almost like it was trying to detach itself from the rest of the body.

Wallace had taken every opportunity to push the pictures off, cracking a few frames and Pab presumed that he was attempting to do the same.

One of the frames tipped over, balancing precariously on the table's edge.

Feeling that there was no real emergency, the only assistance Pab could think to give would be to close the door, so that the commotion wouldn't bother Hugo, who had chosen the comfort of the waiting-room chairs down the hall.

Pab knelt to lift his wooden seat and retrieve his top hat, which had been crunched under the toppled seat. Balling a fist, Pab punched the hat to make it straight again.

Suddenly the noise stopped. Wallace was sitting up—or at least he was trying to. His head was craned forward, straining his veiny neck and hoisting his shoulders from the sheets. The blankets were shaking with his frail body under the effort. Wallace held something in his hand, between fingers that were wrenched into a claw.

The necklace and locket had been hanging on the largest photograph. The portrait was of Wallace's wife, Hugo's grandmother, who seemed to have already passed. Wallace held the necklace as though it was as fragile as glass. By the gleam in his eye, he was looking at a precious jewel. Pab had not known that the locket could be opened, nor that there was a miniature picture kept inside.

The locket started to slip. The hand shook, but the fingers were not agile enough to clench the chain and keep it from rattling on the floor. Devastation crippled Wallace's face, his mouth and brow contorted, and he began to cry. It was one of the first authentic cries he had seen from Wallace, spurring the first sympathies in Pab.

Taking a step back, Pab went to recover the necklace, slowly lifting it by the chain, with a hand cupped beneath the heart-shaped locket in case any pieces were broken and would fall. He moved to place it back in the hand, only to find that the wrinkled arm had been pulled back. The fingers were clenched in a fist, pressed tightly to Wallace's chest.

Pab thought Wallace was experiencing heart problems and began to race through every procedure he had ever seen one of the doctors perform, but nothing useful came to mind. Pab started to panic. He didn't know what to do. An alarm began to blare from Wallace's machine, and Pab looked at his hauntingly pale face and his bulging eyes—eyes that were fixed on Pab.

Wallace's eyes pierced into him with tremendous force, that knocked around his chest and caused him to stumble backward. And as he moved, the eyes followed. The distance was gone. The two stared at each other, unblinkingly until the fringes of Pab's vision blurred, until all he could see was Wallace's face, the anger pouring from his eyes.

"Bloody hell!" Wallace thrust his arms forward, toward Pab, who backpedaled into the wall.

Then there came a movement to Pab's left, but he had to blink and shake his head to restore his vision. The nurse hurried in, with Hugo in his wake. The attendant came to the opposite side of Wallace's bed and began checking Wallace's vitals and the readings from his machine. Hugo, his back to Pab, tried to corral the swinging arms. But Wallace jerked his hand away, again and again, jabbing a finger at Pab.

"Sir!" Hugo bellowed as if they were a great distance apart.

Wallace's lips were crooked, and his tongue threaded between his teeth as he stammered. Hugo called again, even louder. His voice shook; Hugo was more frazzled than Pab had ever seen him—he finally looked like a child.

Pab dropped the necklace, but the old man's episode continued.

"W-where? Get him!" Wallace finally gasped, the words exploding from his flapping lips. "B-bugger! Bugger'm. Get him!"

Hugo turned, following the direction of the frantic stabs. Pab braced for the second flip of his gut, but it didn't come. Hugo didn't see him standing there, pressed flat against the wall. The boy scanned the room around and over Pab, with a curious and concerned arch in his brow, before returning to his grandfather. The nurse glanced over Pab as well, for only a moment, and then resumed his work with the needle and the tubes at Wallace's side.

It only took one more desperate lunge from Wallace—who would have thrown himself out of bed if the nurse had not caught him—for Pab to make a run for it. He grabbed onto the doorframe to his left and propelled himself into motion. The hallway was nearly empty, but every roaming nurse caused Pab instinctively to put his head down and cover his face with the top hat. He expected someone to stop him, but no one even saw him—he was invisible again.

. . .

What's wrong with me? I can't get past it. I don't know where to go.

I know we can go . . . anywhere. But it all just feels hollow and so-so. Because . . . wherever we go, we don't really belong there. We can't stay. Not like them. No. We can't have lives like them or make friends like them or just stay like them. We are just drifting through. And that's all we've been doing. Drifting. And I want that. 'Cause we got nowhere we can go.

The only time I feel like I should stay is when I see Ada. The girl with red hair. That's what I've been calling her. She's there but not, all at once.

an was disoriented, blinded by searing pain and
erratic body-temperature changes. There was an
undeniable chill in the air and yet San had shed all
but her undershirt and shorts. Her throat felt dry with
a ravaging thirst that would not submit, no matter how
much she drank.

The wounds on her shoulder from the dog's attack had
become infected. The skin had swollen. It had become
too painful to turn her head far enough to look, so San
could only imagine how disgusting it must appear.

San hit the ground about every ten steps, unsure if
she had tripped or if her legs had simply given out. There
would be no conscious attempt to rise back up; San would
be content to stay in the soft grass and dirt with her
mind awash. But then, in the next brief lucid moment,
she would find herself back on her feet, walking again—it
must have been something deep inside that pulled her
strings up and pushed her forward.

In one of these frequent falls, San did not make it to
the ground; returning to her senses, she found herself
propped against a wooden fence. She had not seen it on
approach and didn't know how long ago she had hit it.

The top rail was underneath her chin and armpits. The
wood was warped, gave a little at the nails, but was able
to support her, taking the weight off her legs. She hung
her arms and her head, which suddenly felt a hundred
pounds heavier, and watched spit dribble from her gap-
ing mouth.

Something nudged the top of her head. It was a gentle push and San was reminded of how her papa would place his massive hand on her head and ruffle her hair.

"P-a-ra?" Her mouth barely moved, not even enough to distinguish syllables.

A gust of air rushed by her left ear. It was a jarring sensation and San finally lifted her head from the fence rail. It was not the wind but the snorting of a horse, which had its long face lowered to her.

"Ah-a-anelie?" San mumbled, amidst a cacophonous, hacking cough.

San inspected the horse—the vision of the horse or whatever it was—to see if it could be her childhood pet. The horse on the opposite side of the fence was the right shade of brown, but there was a problem with its legs; this horse had four white socks, and San could remember how many Anelie had.

"*Ich habe dich gefunden.*" San hugged the horse's neck. It felt real enough. Her sweaty face was pressed firmly to the finely groomed hair. She could feel the horse's steady breath and it was alarming for her to compare it to her own—weak and delayed.

Bearing an unfathomable shot of pain, San lifted a leg and stepped on the bottom rail of the fence, using it as a ladder to mount the horse. The animal remained surprisingly tolerant and stoic as San struggled to steady herself on the fence, relying greatly on the animal for support. She then spent her last ounce of strength to leap and flop her stomach onto the horse's back. Feeling completely drained, she stayed in that unpleasant position, draped over the back like the blanket her father would put under the saddle. It was only when she felt her weight give slightly and she began to slide that San grabbed the mane and rotated herself until one leg was dangling on each side and her weight was better distributed.

"Anelie," San gave the command in her mind, loud and clear, but when it reached her lips, it was incoherent and barely audible. "*Hamm.* Anelie. *Wir . . . e-einf . . .* Anelie— *heim. Heim.*"

San straddled the horse's back and rested her head in its mane, locking her hands together beneath the neck. She knew that she would tumble off if she tried to sit up. Through her murky vision, San spied a nearby opening in the fence where the boards had fallen and repeated her command to take her home.

. . .

The stage was empty, spare the milling of a few men and women with matching black shirts and headphones who were setting thick bundles of wires and situating the equipment. One technician was frantically typing on a computer, which caused a slideshow of images to project onto massive screens hanging on both sides of the stage—most of the pictures contained the same smiling face of the event's main attraction.

The colossal auditorium flourished out from the stage with rows of seats filling three levels. Every section was packed. Anticipation was almost tangible. The rumble of the audience was deafening.

Mar and Des were in the thick of this crowd, pushing through to get a better view of the enormous set of speakers and screens. They didn't know why the man was famous but the large crowd clogging the sidewalk had astonished them, and the energy had been too enticing to resist.

The house lights dimmed, a hush spread over the crowd, and the isles were soon clear as people found their way to their seats. A few moments later, the lights were turned out completely and the crowd simmered in suspense.

A burst of music boomed from the stage and echoed through the speakers positioned throughout the levels and in the scaffolding. It was a wave of percussion and horns that rose to a crescendo and then disappeared. The audience followed it with a bellowing cheer, begging for another round. When the music returned, it was accompanied by a greater assortment of sounds and a spellbinding display of lights. Multiple colors shot through the air, strobing from fixtures spinning on a rigging that encircled the stage. A dominant spotlight dropped on center stage and, at the same moment, the image of the empty microphone flicked onto the screens. The man stepped into the light, and the crowd raved with thunderous applause that filled the gigantic space, overwhelming the music.

The only person seemingly immune to the frenzy was Des, who stayed in his seat, arms crossed as he stared up at the image on the screen. The man's face, magnified on the screen, appeared much older than the pictures on the posters outside or in the slideshow. His hair was slick and shiny, with distinguished streaks of grey. His face stretched in an unnaturally wide smile that pushed on his high cheekbones, but it was the wrinkles that drew Des's attention, and to such a degree that he could barely concentrate on what was being said.

The pulse of the crowd did not lessen. The man sang and spoke and frequently paused for applause. The crowd would go along, mouthing his words and dancing in their small spaces.

Des sunk in his chair and tried to block out the noise, which became increasingly difficult when the man was joined on stage by a band. The drowning event felt unbearably long with no end in sight, so he turned to his right, to beg his friend to leave, but Mar was not there.

Des didn't know how long he had been gone, how long it had taken for him to get on stage but there he was, suddenly dancing around the band and imitating the guitarist.

Rushing to the edge of the stage, already sweating in the burn of the lights, Mar motioned for Des to come forward, then turned and danced another lap around the stage before returning to the ledge and gesturing more fervently.

"Why are you trying?" Des whispered to himself. Mar almost seemed to hear this inaudible blow and jumped off the stage. He was smiling as he made his way back to his seat. "You look ridiculous," Des growled, mouthing the words slowly for Mar to read as he came closer.

"What? Were you scared, huh? Intimidated by the crowd?" Mar yelled over the buzz of the audience around them.

"Why would I be? They can't see me. Doesn't matter how many there are. I'm tired of faking it and being dumb!" It was hard to be heard over the crowd and not sound furious.

"I bet Ada would come if she were here!"

Des bared this slight, refocused on the stage, and was struck by the realization that—up close—the man was not as tall as his pictures made him appear.

. . .

Pab stepped on the bumper, over the hitch, and into the bed of the truck that was idling at the red light. Crawling over the toolbox, shovel, folded tarp, and bags of cement the man was transporting, he plopped down under the rear window of the cab. The crown of his top hat was folded and it was stuffed inside his bag, to keep from flying off. He hunkered himself down, wishing for the vehicle to move.

There was a part of him that was itching to stay, to go back to Wallace's room, and to see if the nightmare had been real.

The anger he had felt from Wallace told him that he had done something wrong, even if it had somehow made him seen—it was wrong. He had scavenged before without breaking the separation, taking things from the people, but this had been different. There was something special about the necklace—at least to Wallace—and Pab believed that somehow he was not meant to have it.

The fresh scars on his side and back—self-inflicted punishments for what he had done—made the hard truck's bed even more uncomfortable. Coupled with the persistent temptation to stay, Pab couldn't stop fidgeting in the bed of the truck, even after the light had changed and the truck had cruised through the square and toward the outskirts of town.

He was thankful to leave. The farther the truck took him away, the easier it would be to keep himself from returning—perhaps he would be able to convince himself it never happened—but the truck did not make it far out of town before there was an unexpected stop.

The toolbox slid and collided hard against his bent knee when the truck suddenly skidded to the side of the lone, gravel road. Pab was alarmed further as the door popped open.

For a moment, he feared that he had been seen again.

But the driver left the engine running and quickly crossed the street. This confused Pab, as did the calls and whistles. Sitting higher in the bed, Pab saw what he was calling: a horse trotting in a pasture, along a sizeable ditch that ran with the road.

The horse was merely a silhouette in the moonlight, but Pab noticed there was a strange bulk at its withers like the saddle was lopsided—the rider had possibly fallen off. But then the mass began to move, bend, and rise. The change in the shadow was spooky, but Pab was eventually able to figure that it was the rider, barely holding on to the steed—a girl with her head slumped to the side and hair draping down to her elbows.

"Oye come'ere," the man called as he took a long stride over the ditch and extended his hand to show he meant no harm. "Lost, girl?"

But the girl did not speak. Only the horse responded with a buck of its head and soft whine.

As the man approached, the rider began to waver back and forth. Her shoulders swayed and bounced, as they would if the horse was galloping, full speed. The girl oscillated farther back until she was sprawled on the horse's croup. An arm waved a bit, almost as if she had momentarily regained her senses and was trying to recover her seat, before toppling to the ground.

The thud of the fall was audible from the truck. It pushed Pab into action. He sprung onto the pavement and took a running jump over the ditch. The horse sidestepped away from the girl—who was motionless on the ground—and had to be corralled by the man. Pab was a little put off that the driver didn't even try to catch the injured girl or break her fall, keeping his attention on the horse.

"Shhh," the man whispered to the horse. "Whoah, now."

Pab hurried up the embankment toward the body on the ground. The horse took notice of Pab on his approach; the man did not, nor did he tend to the girl, even after the horse was calm.

These clues didn't connect in Pab's mind until he was leaning over the girl, staring at the ghostly pale skin and damp strings of hair. He did not touch her, nor try to wake her, only spoke in a way he hoped she would understand, "He doesn't see you."

. . .

I'm gonna find her—the girl I keep seeing. Ada. Mar thought we should at least try to find her. This surprised me. I thought he'd think it was dumb. But he says go, 'cause he says he is tired of dealing with my dreaming and sulking. But I just want to know who she is. Another question, is she seen? Or is she like us—separated?

Mar did have one good idea. Writing it down. Everything or anything that I can remember. Where do I see her? What kind of places? Listen for her voice. How does she talk? Anything to help narrow it down. He asks me about it every day, everywhere we go. Is she here? What about now? And I feel bad when I've got nothing to say. Sometimes, I think he is more determined than I am. I'm just glad he believes me. I'm glad he thinks she is real, too.

XIII

There were no wrinkles in the river's water. Had San not been in the water herself, she would have assumed it was completely still; but the current was swift enough to carry her with ease. She floated on her back with unbelievable buoyancy, without needing to kick or stroke.

It felt more like flying, and she even spread her arms like wings, with the rippling wake of her arms and fingers combing the water forming her feathers. There was also a mist along the river that blurred the banks, helping San feel more like she was in the clouds.

A clear blue sky treated her from above. Steady over her ears, every sound was silenced by the water. She opened her mouth and stretched it to the side. The water's sweet taste trickled onto her tongue and added to the blissful serenity.

Turning to float on her stomach, San peered through the crystal-clear river to the stones scattered in the bed. The river was shallow. San could have reached for a stone and plucked it from the dirt. She waited for a fish to swim in the space beneath her, but nothing came. She seemed to be the river's sole inhabitant.

San was just growing curious about how long she had been holding her breath when her river came to a bend and converged with another stream. The temper of the current quickened as the two rivers became one and started down a sharper slope.

While it continued to carry her well, San now worked to hold her head out of the water and paddled with her hands, having lost some of her perfect buoyancy. The river was gradually deepening, but the most notable change was the concoction of color. There was a sweeping, dominant tint from the tributary that darkened the water.

She tried to relax and trust the current again. She leaned back and kicked her feet up, but any possibility of peace was soon lost; an exploding roar boomed through her head. The river suddenly leveled and then curved to the left, bringing her to the bottom of a tremendous waterfall. The deafening collision of water was startling, and San tried to turn back, but only managed to slow the pull. Luckily, the plunge pool was wide enough, and San avoided getting swallowed under the falls.

When she spun in the swelling waves, she looked back at the waterfall and the lofty ridge from which it plummeted. She had not realized it, but as the river trailed downward, the banks had risen, and she was now at the bottom of a gorge. The river snaked through a canyon with sheer rock walls on both sides.

The river was turning into rapids, the surface chopped by waves. The depth had increased exponentially. San could no longer paddle gently; she had to kick her feet furiously just to stay afloat. The water had also darkened, and she couldn't even see down to her waist.

Then the strangest thing yet occurred; the river started flowing uphill. The cliffs on either side lowered in unison as the river rose like a ramp out of the canyon. There were no more bends or bumps: the water streamlined up and out.

When the river became level with the cliffs, it plateaued abruptly, and San was tossed into the air from the forward motion of the uphill current. She flailed, suspended in midair for a moment, and then plunged into the water. The rays of sunlight faded out. There was fear that she was sinking too deep to recover.

When her feet finally brushed through the muddy riverbed, San was able to stop herself from turning by digging her toes into the gunk like an anchor. Her head kept whirling, but she was able to compose herself, kick off the mud, and paddled her feet as hard as she could. Keeping her body rigid, San shot up through the water like a torpedo. Fortunately, the river was not as deep as feared—she had simply been spun so many times that it felt like she had dropped much farther.

San neared the top, but gasped for air too soon, swallowing another gallon of water. Above the surface, when she had finished hacking and coughing, she realized that the river was flowing uphill again, but at a lesser grade, and it narrowed ahead, at a crest. San could not see what came on the other side, but her attention didn't stay on that for long.

Two massive trees stood on opposite banks of the river. They rose into the heavens, taller than anything San had ever seen—natural or man-made. The one on her left was alive—lush and thick with plenty of bushy branches—while the opposite was equally as tall but thinner and bare, appearing dead. Between them and above the river, their branches met. Looking like huge umbrellas, most of the branches jutted out at the top, forming a massive canopy that was interwoven. It was difficult to tell which branches and vines started on what tree. San had the impression of a natural and ancient archway.

San was so taken by the spectacle that she forfeited her swimming technique. Her body bobbed on its own for a moment before sinking back below the surface. The natural archway was blurred and distorted by the wake, but the overwhelming sensation lasted.

San then felt a pull come from her waist like something had grabbed her by the back of the belt. And the vision flew from her, but San did not want to leave the trees. So, as she woke, San kicked her feet—a final desperate effort to surface and get one more look at the trees.

. . .

San had not spoken. Her eyes were still closed, she had barely stirred, but Pab had seen her toes twitch—the first sign of life in an alarming amount of time—and that was enough for him to yelp with joy, tumbling back into the pile of opened boxes and spilled bottles of medicine.

After her fall from the horse, a few nights prior, Pab had brought San from the pasture to the truck. Her feet could barely manage the weight or coordination of a single step without his assistance. Once in the truck, they could do nothing but wait in agony while the driver made a few calls about the horse, before finally returning and driving them to the next town.

Pab had pulled San out when the truck was stopped at the light. The town was much smaller than the one with Wallace's hospital, but a shopping center was spotted with a fully stocked pharmacy.

The storage room seemed to the best place to stash San, where he thought no one would walk over her while he gathered medicine. Notes from his shadowing and observations had been his source for a supply list. Pab had scoured through the aisles for anything that could help.

The wound had been cleaned using the sterilizer and ointment from the store. Supplies he had taken from the hospitals included a kit that came in handy for the stitches. He had previously practiced this procedure on a leather jacket—but the application with real skin and blood had been far more frightening than he could have imagined. Torn padding from a stuffed animal had been placed with gauze under the bandage, which he wrapped in several layers. Fluids, pain relievers, and antibiotics had been forced down her throat.

At that point, Pab could do nothing but wait for days, which was the most challenging task of all.

Although it had not happened quickly, San's recovery was miraculous to Pab. Although the medicine may have helped calm the fever and swelling, the real healing seemed to come from beyond his trivial efforts. Pab could not claim it. She fought her way back from the brink, and the first real indication came in the form of a word uttered so faintly that he worried he had imagined it. "*Fluss*."

. . .

San made her turn and started to come back to Pab. It took until the afternoon following her vision of the river for her to keep her eyes open for any significant amount of time and when she did, her confused mind was fueled by instinct.

Where was she? How did she get there?

The last thing her mind could bring back, other than the rushing river and the swirl of which her body still felt, was the soft warmth of Anelie's mane.

San didn't notice the dull ringing in her ears until it was interrupted by a squeaking, coming from the figure, its shoes scooting forward on the cement. She didn't know how long the stranger had been there. Why hadn't she seen him first?

Before her vision cleared enough to distinguish the features of his face, San could tell that there was something odd happening—she sensed that the stranger could see her. It had been so long since she had been seen, her instinct overcompensated. Her body suddenly felt a chill colder than the floor. She ignored the revelation, casting it to the side in her need to protect herself. The fight in her told her that, to be seen was to be targeted, so she labeled him as a threat.

She regained enough focus to better grasp her bearings and look for a possible weapon. Among the assorted shreds of bandages, spilled bottles, and torn wrappers, there was a pair of scissors—the only sharp object within reach. They were next to Pab's left foot and she doubted she would be quick enough to get to them first.

There were plenty of boxes, which meant there could be something else sharp or hard inside them but choosing a random one seemed too risky and time-consuming. A container was turned on its side near her left hand. Powder spilled from its top. San wasn't sure how much was left in the bottle, so she decided that her best option would be to grab what was poured on the floor and toss it at the boy's eyes. This would disorient him long enough for her to get up, shove him backward, and clear her way to the scissors. These would then be taken to his throat.

San's mind fixed and altered her plan a hundred different ways, but when she saw him reach for her shoulder, it was time to act. She went for the powder but kept her eyes fixed on the scissors. The burst of motion was supposed to be startling and throw him off guard. But

San's body was not alive enough to implement her attack and so all that came of it was a strange jerk of her head and a momentary writhing of her left side—the right arm and shoulder were completely limp. San took notice of this and started to scream.

"*Shhh*." Pab tried to keep her from ripping off her bandage. He picked up her right hand and held it with both of his.

San used her mobile arm to smack him on the side of the head. Her teeth gnashed at his arm. Prepared, he dodged the clamp of her jaws. She bit a second and third attempt, but to no avail.

He smirked at her frantic snaps and showed her the towel he had taped to his forearms, giving San the impression that it was not her first attempt at biting him.

How long had she been with him?

She tried to reconstruct the past few days. The longer she struggled, the more confused and angrier she became.

"Pab." He patted his chest as he introduced himself. San looked at him but didn't give a name back. She leered at the spot where his hand rested on his chest with a sinister glare, imagining ways to break his hand or crack into his chest.

Pab wished to explain that she was safe, how they were alike, but she wasn't listening.

"*Geh' zum Teufel!*" A splatter of spit came out with the cursing. She smacked her lips and slurped another wad to hack at Pab.

"Uh . . . *Nein*," answered Pab with a stunned look on his face, but a confident shake of his head. "*Ich . . . ich bleibe . . . hapa . . . no. Hier! Ich bleibe hier.*"

San was a little stunned but mostly annoyed by his ability to follow her language. The surprise on her face seemed to amuse Pab, who continued to switch dialects, again and again, repeating the same sentiment.

" . . . I'm staying. I'm staying."

. . .

Ada. She is calling me to something greater. Something that is ours. Not theirs. She rarely speaks or answers my questions. But seeing her is less painful now that we are looking because I know it will be real.

There are so many people in our way. And so many places to go. It's like the people are trying to hide her, making it difficult. They want us to remain separate. Removed. Alone.

XIV

Ren spent her afternoon in the town's most-populated shopping center. It was a daily trip that had became a necessary escape. She needed the sustenance, to see other people, to feel the movement of the world outside, and to have the silence broken.

The sadness consuming Chiara remained, only strengthening with time.

The sparks within the small apartment were gone completely. The things that had once breathed life into their world had been taken away.

First, there was the sweet aroma of Chiara's cooking that no longer wafted from the kitchen. Chiara didn't cook such pleasures anymore; in fact, she barely ate, and when she did, it was something from the microwave or delivered in bags—Ren hated the stale smell of this food.

The music had followed. Chiara had fallen out of the habit of playing her records or singing her tunes, and Ren missed the way the music could transform the small room into an enormous concert hall. Without it, Ren became more aware of the silence between them. She felt more removed from Chiara. There had never been a word spoken or exchanged, and yet Ren had felt they were able to communicate something through what they both heard in the music.

But what she missed most of all were the paintings— through which the most had been shared. Chiara had either ruined or disposed of her works. There was no indication that they ever existed. And the supplies had been cleared from the shelves, leaving little hope that she would ever create something new.

When Ren returned home, she found Chiara passed out in her bedroom closet. This small cubby was already crammed with racks, hangers, and clothes so she did not entirely fit; her legs and hips stuck out the door, what was in the closet was mostly buried in a pile of dresses, sweaters, and pants that had fallen from their hangers. The nightgown she was wearing had slipped above her waist, revealing her bare bottom. Ren adjusted this slight immodesty even though no one else was there or would come. She knew that she would have the evening to herself, again.

Brittle petals drooping, the wilting flowers were barely recognizable. The pots that lined the balcony appeared empty, the plants were so thin and hard to detect in the dark. Ren scratched at the rough drought of the soil, reminiscing the way Chiara would play her records and sing to her garden as she watered—the first task in her daily regimen, as though she cared for them above all else.

Returning with a cup of water from the sink, Ren closed her eyes and tried to bring about the memory. She poured water over the plants and their parched soil. Her fingers dug into the softened bedding, searching for the feeling of strength and life, but recovering something else: a paintbrush.

After Chiara had ruined and disposed of her finished works of art, she had transitioned into clearing the materials. Ren had been away when this process had begun; most of the cabinets were already cleared by the time she returned. In a moment of desperation, she had nabbed a few supplies between Chiara's trips down to the garbage bins, to save what she could.

Reminiscing on that dreadful evening, Ren re-collected them from their hiding places around the apartment. There were two brushes that she had buried in the soil, three vials of paint in the spice cabinet, and a rectangular canvas hidden inside the loose fabric of the sofa's back. A roll of clay and some graphite pencils bound in the string had also been saved, but only temporarily; Ren had stored them in a shoebox that was later lost when Chiara's purge moved on to the bedroom.

The collection was placed on the kitchen table, arranged like a shrine. Her touch was overly gentle like they were fragile artifacts. And she marveled, awestruck, at the last remnants of Chiara's once-vibrant passion.

What would she do with the supplies?

There had been no long-term plan when she had taken them; she simply had not wanted to see everything thrown out.

It seemed hopeless to wait for Chiara to regain interest, and so her best option was to use the supplies herself. She briefly considered making something from her imagination, but there was only one thing that she wanted to see—the canyon eye.

The brush dabbed into the black paint and drew the curve of the canyon's base. To best utilize the scarce amount, she traced her line over again, collecting the excess paint for the walls.

But there were problems from the start. The green did little to fill her rigid canyon. The shade was too dark and lacked the flare Chiara had been able to mix. The look was too solid, her technique was off, and she struggled to duplicate the appearance of water.

The remainder of the paints were swirled together, to make brown for the earth around the canyon; what was achieved was more of a burgundy than she intended, but she still brushed it around the outside.

The painting was placed on the table, leaning against the wall. Ren rested on the couch with her head tilted by pillows so that she could see her picture through the arched divide of the two rooms. Even from a distance, the mistakes were blatant. The result was pitiful compared to the aesthetic original: the canyon walls were uneven, the bottom was too wide, and the iris was nowhere to be found.

Despite these shortcomings, Ren felt a rush of comfort and pride. If she had enough paint, she would have signed it or at least inscribed the work with the original title—*Dono della Varmundi*—which Ren felt she finally understood. Varmundi was Chiara's word for the energy of life—something she feared that Chiara's was running out of.

. . .

The narrow hull of the subway car was excruciatingly congested, with passengers squished together, pressing against the metal casing, and as the car moved, they swayed as one.

When the train arrived at the city center platform and the crowd took its collective exit, it did not disperse but instead grew larger. The passengers spilled from captivity and were added to an already pulsing current in the streets—Des and Mar were powerless against it.

Mar didn't grumble as they were swept away; in truth, he found the strange gathering remarkable. Even Des suspended his claustrophobic displeasure for the sake of growing interest.

There were no cars, only the people in the street. There were no lines in their progression, but a single direction.

Signs were unraveled and held over their heads. Many wore shirts with similar symbols. A tremor rose to accompany the march, a low rumble that eventually burgeoned to a soaring crescendo—so many voices collected in a unified chant.

Des and Mar were not quite sure why the people were there, but the passion was palpable—even infectious— and soon the boys were shouting along in a stupefied fervor. The sound of the legion was deafening.

Mar recited the chorale and phrases, or at least their inflections. Even though no one else heard it, he felt pride when his voice joined the united cry.

Looking up, he could see that people were watching the march from the windows and rooftops. They were murmuring to each other and taking pictures, distracted from their regular business and routine.

They progressed in front of a stone temple. A golden woman stood atop holding a sword in one hand, but Mar could not see what was in the other. A stage had been assembled before the rows of columns, equipped with large speakers and mounted with a podium. An emphatic woman was crying through the booming amplifiers over the march. A troupe of reporters directed cameras at her, but she ignored them and spoke more to the herd.

Being in the thick of it was blinding and Mar wondered how far these people could see, how far the march stretched. But there had to be a leader and there had to be a destination. "I'm going on ahead, to the front. Come on." Mar had already put his head down and was pushing through the drove before his explanation was out.

"Mar! Mar, wait!" Des called after him. But Mar did not hear; he was already several yards ahead, crashing through the throng, bouncing around and diving between the bodies. He did not wait for Des to catch up, too motivated to see the head of the movement.

There was a long banner strung across the lead row, with protesters holding a sign at their waists as they walked, shoulder to shoulder. Some even locked arms. Mar joined this front rank but there was barely any room for him to take a full step, and he had to shuffle his feet to keep from falling, pressed as he was on all sides. He considered breaking ahead of the crowd, not only for the chance to breathe but also to get a full perspective of the assembly's size but found something more interesting right next to him.

An elderly man marched to his right. He wore a black suit with a large black tie, all covered by a tan trench coat. His silver glasses had large, square frames. He wore a gold watch that slid freely over his thin wrist. But beyond his immaculate attire, Mar's eyes were drawn more to his hands. Perhaps it was because they were pressed so closely and he didn't have much of a choice, but Mar couldn't help but stare at them. There were scuffs and blemishes in the skin. The deepest and most striking wrinkles looked like they might crack. And yet, there was an underlying strength to the hands. Mar decided they looked like rusting iron, weathered but still strong.

The old man was not singing or chanting like the others. He marched forward in stolid silence, but a lot was going on behind his eyes—Mar could see that. And he felt that he may finally get the reasons for why the people were there and what they were trying to accomplish if he could only read the man's eyes. Unfortunately, his learning was interrupted by something flying overhead.

A rock had been thrown from somewhere in the mass behind Mar. It soared ahead of the banner and was deflected off a shield wielded by an officer in thick protective gear that included a helmet, a mask, and a stick in his other hand. The officer stood in the front row of identical troopers set behind a wall of shields. Mar had not seen them coming—the aesthetics of the man's hands and the mystery in his eyes had been too distracting.

The wave of people stopped marching when the rock bounced off the shield, but the polemic continued to sound, and it was noticeably more aggressive. Mar no longer joined in their song.

Standing in the open door of a jeep parked behind the rows of officers, there was a man with a megaphone. The man also waved his hand toward the crowd, sticking his fingers forward and tilting his hand to the side, like the stroke of a swimmer. The voice became harsher and the veins in his neck started to bulge. His words were drowned by the rising chant—though the unity of words had somewhat been lost. There was more disorder in the crowd behind Mar; waves of shouting and jostling rippled from the back and broke over the backs of the front line. The banner was like a barricade. The front row did not obey the orders from the officers or the push from their followers, standing their ground. A second rock was thrown, and then a third, like embers from an igniting fire, ready to spread.

Mar could feel the tension. The hairs on his arms and neck stood up, telling him that he needed to get out. But before he could manage to remove himself from the tight space and start pushing back through the crowd, there was the crack of a gunshot. It split through the air and scared all other sounds away. The chanting stopped, as did the barking orders from the jeep. Both sides were suspended in a moment of reservation.

Then the pressure on his right side started to give. Mar stumbled that way a step or two, pushed by the uneven force of bodies. His scrunched shoulders widened with the release, but then tensed back up when he saw the old man sink to the street. The banner remained in the grip of those iron hands, but his eyes were closed, hiding the answers forever. Mar continued to stare after them.

The patter of gunfire erupted again. Mar heard the rippling sound from his left as the banner was punctured by the spray of bullets and more people fell. He turned around to run, thinking that the crowd would retreat as one; but, like a kicked wasp nest, mayhem reigned. The marchers and officers both broke their formations and scattered into a melee. There was no clear retreat; everyone moved for themselves.

Mar was plowed to the ground and before he had time to cover or curl, he was kicked in the back, and then under his chin, causing him to bite his lip. The next foot connected with his stomach, knocking bloody coughs out.

Mar desperately thrashed his body around, opening just enough room to stand. He made it to his feet but got clobbered again before the next breath. This brutal, unmerciful beating continued until, finally, the swarm around him became less congested. There was chaos, but Mar was at least able to stay on his feet long enough to decide which way to run. He didn't recognize any of the buildings. He had no idea how far they had gone away from the underground. But he knew he needed to run, so he did.

Mar barreled through the frenzy, breaking at each intersection to turn down random streets without the faintest sense of where he was or where to go. The chaos seemed to spread farther and faster than he could run; it filled every street before he reached it.

Due to his impulsive route, Mar inevitably doubled back on the same buildings and intersections. He didn't pause to think of how to correct his inner compass, he simply took a different turn. He didn't know how far he would need to go to feel safe, but he was determined to keep going until he found Des. With each gasping huff, he worked through his entire arsenal of foul words to curse himself for letting his friend slip from sight.

Mar continued to run even after the fever began to fall. The swarm of crazed people disappeared from the streets, replaced by emergency vehicles. He ran until his fiery fuel was gone and his body depleted, slowing into a sluggish stagger.

Mar tried to call Des, wishing that he could hear the whisper, but he had no voice left. His throat was still raw from the chanting. He could muster only a doleful, "I'm sorry."

When exhaustion forced him to collapse and sleep overtook him, no rest was found. In his nightmare, he did not leave Des, but instead, they went together to march on the front line, holding the banner in unison. Then he saw the rock, followed by the crack of the single shot, which triggered the spray of bullets. But it was Des who fell in the elderly man's place. Only it was not Des as he knew him—his friend had changed. He was older, much older. He had gained the man's wrinkles and even wore his suit. It was troubling for Mar to imagine him aging to ancient, let alone dead.

. . .

In her sleep, Ren swam in the green water with boundless energy. She kicked off the sides of the canyon and dove deep but never found the bottom. The people on the bridge, high above, lowered their buckets on the pulley rig and heaved them back up.

Seeing them brought her back.

Ren awoke with a start, having realized that she had forgotten to paint the bridge and the buckets. The more frightening matter, however, was that the supplies had been left on the table to be discovered and disposed of like the rest of it. Her only hope was for Chiara to not notice them, as she seemed to have with the food and other things Ren had scavenged over the years.

Chiara was already awake and sitting at the table. The painting and supplies were present, so Res assumed they had been kept from her sight. This relief was instantly defeated by shock.

Ren almost jumped to the ceiling when Chiara put her finger on the canvas and traced the bottom of the canyon. The finger followed the curve perfectly. With her other hand, Chiara removed some lipstick from her pocket and spread dashes over the green water, connecting the two sides. But Ren didn't notice this addition. She was already on the floor, clutching her shirt to her chest. Reeling in disbelief, Ren didn't trust her eyes, yet there was a booming sensation inside her—Chiara could see the painting.

"Chiara!" Ren yelled before she could fully understand her purpose. The name hung in the air as Ren's mind slowly caught up with her hope that if Chiara could see what she had made on the canvas, then perhaps she could now see Ren. She didn't feel any different, but Ren ignored this, reminding herself how instantaneous and unnoticeable the separation had begun. The girl's eyes flashed between the woman and the painting, which she hoped had been the tool to break the eight-year-long removal.

Alas, Chiara didn't hear her. She stayed glued to her work, without the slightest flinch at the hollering of her name.

Ren wished to remain suspended in her short-lived hope; she would try yelling the name three more times before allowing the weight of reality to bring her back to her separation.

So brief a chance and yet unimaginably profound, Ren struggled to grapple with the fleeting possibility of being seen.

Ren slumped her shoulders and shuffled to the balcony, where she came across another perplexing sight, one that she couldn't truly appreciate in her melancholy heaviness—one green stem was standing renewed, healthy, and tall in the flowers' soil.

· · ·

We were taken by them; I just lost my mind for a second, and it was like I was one of them again. We didn't even know what we were chanting for, but we wanted more. And we split from each other.

Why? What was that?

I think it was anger. In the end, that's all it was. That's all it turned out to be—anger. We should've seen that, but I didn't. We got lost in it . . . and now I've lost Mar. Another mean trick they played on us. Distract and separate. I should have pushed harder. Worked to be at his side. Stay at his side. I should not have let them separate us.

XV

San's recovery was delayed by her stubbornness. She refused her body the respite it so badly needed and traveled farther each day. She wanted to prove that she was strong enough to be on her own, hoping that Pab would leave her alone once he saw that the wounded pup had healed. She didn't know why Pab had stayed but made it her mission to break him, to be as oppositional as possible.

This even meant bracing through an immense onset of snow that slowed steps and a drastic plummet in temperature that made their bones feel thin and frail.

San's weary body made her more susceptible to the chill and she found herself falling, often. After one of these clumsy tumbles into a large snowbank, she was struggling to resurface and Pab stepped in to help her, chuckling at the comical shape of her imprint and shoveling the sides away to widen the gap. San was hoisted to a kneeling position and patted down. His hand stayed near her elbow, rubbing warmth into her frigidity. This seemed to work because San swiped his arms away with newly found agility.

"Get-t aweg!" Her words scattered by chattering teeth. She pushed out of the waist-deep wave of snow, only to pounce back at a different angle and deliver a shattering left hook across Pab's jaw. He went ragged and collapsed into another misshapen hole next to hers.

San stood over his body, poised to pummel him again at the first sign of retaliation. Her fists were balled, stretching and tearing slits in her mittens. She breathed slowly through a high-pitched whistle. This stirred a nauseating thrill in her gut, one strong enough to take her back to the dogfight. Visions of the three hounds circled in her peripherals, and their howls echoed in each ear. San shook these hallucinations away and steadied herself for the fight she thought she had started.

Pab's scarf trailed out of the hole with one end still around his neck and the other attached to his top hat, which had not made it quite as deep into the snow. San watched as more snow sprinkled on his back and the walls of his tunnel started to cave in on him.

The cold, or something else, cooled San's temper, leaving room for shame. Her fingers unclenched and hands sank to her sides, timidly seeking the chance to reach for Pab. But a darker instinct flared up in time to resist, telling her not to trust the limp body in the snow—it may only be a trick.

Pab's escape was so startling that she was unable to attack as she had planned. He didn't come at her but burrowed forward through the drift, creating a new tunnel for his exit.

The straps of his backpack were readjusted with puffs of exasperated breaths. But he made no sign of intent to strike back.

San suddenly wanted to say something, but was unsure for a multitude of reasons. The darker instinct held her thoughts captive. She thought there would be ample time for her to collect herself and compose a sentiment, seeing that his coveted top hat remained to the side, in the pile of powder, but she was wrong; he left the hat behind and marched into the flurry, leaving her to sheepishly whisper his name in repetition.

The top hat was retrieved and emptied of snow. It was so worn that it folded like paper, barely keeping its shape. There were so many bends and blemishes. None of which were directly caused by Pab's fall, but she still felt responsible for each of them and inspected it for anything she could mend.

How long had she lingered before pursuing? How much distance could he have gained? San pondered these things as she tore after Pab. Her form lacked stability and her pace was not quick enough to be considered a run, but it was all she could do, and Pab was still out of sight. The darkness and shower of snow made it difficult for her to see a few feet ahead, but something told her that he was much farther—he was no longer waiting for her.

San came to a cluster of trees at the foot of a sharp hill with a clearing to her right and drop to her left. This stalled her progress and she tried to guess which way Pab had chosen. His prints had been swept away, there was no way of knowing, and yet she banked to the right and picked up her speed; her discernment was driven by nothing more than the need to keep moving.

"Pab!" It hurt to yell. Sucking in the icy air was sharp on her lungs. But San kept calling if only to drown out the mocking howl of the wolves that carried in the wind.

San caught a glimpse of something out in the distance—a smudge of glowing light—and she corrected her course for it. She kept her head tilted up, refusing to blink through watery eyes, fearing that she would lose track of the light. The closer she came, the brighter the light grew. While it still lacked any definite shape, she hoped it was

Pab, who may have made a fire, hopefully in some dry cave or overhang.

San was concentrating so much on the light ahead that she did not notice that the ground beneath her was about to end; she ran straight off a rocky ledge. Her feet finished two quick steps in midair before the drop, which was quite severe. Her body rolled through a steep gradient of gravel and then over the edge of a boulder buried in the earth, finally landing on the narrow cleft of another large rock, farther down.

Unbeknownst to San, her ridge was the last precarious perch before a sheer drop to a wooded ford below. Had the pain not dominated her senses, she would have been able to see the tops of the trees below.

The cold was numbing, but she felt shots of slicing pains in any part of her body that dared to move. The slightest flinch would spark a series of escalating stabs, in turn causing a spasm elsewhere, and the vicious cycle would continue. San's bout with this agony culminated in a miserable spew of vomit. She managed to turn on her side and let most of the puke fall the rest of the way down.

The snow continued to layer her immobile body as she lay on her back staring up at the sky, dazed and forlorn. The light could have gone out or away; it was difficult to know. Her vision was too blurry to up look to the cliff from which she fell, she had lost her bearings during the slide, and it would hurt too much to sit up and look around.

Miraculously, the hat remained in her grasp, tattered and bent, but with her. San crunched it against her chest as she peered into the sky full of stars. Against the railing pain inside, the tranquility above her was almost soporific.

"*Oma!*" San's cry was muddled in a gargle from the bloody, vile spit. Swallowing this mouthful, she cried again and again. "*Oma. Oma. Oma.*"

San was taken away from the pain and dread for a moment, astonished at how much her voice had matured. Would her grandmother recognize her voice when she called?

"San?" The voice came with a particularly strong rush of wind. She bore the pain, sat straight up, and listened for her grandmother, but when she heard her name again, she realized that it was someone else. "San!" Before she could detect whether Pab was above or below her, a knotted end of a rope flopped down against the rock wall at her side. San immediately took hold, fearing that it would disappear—possibly a trick of her imagination—and tugged twice, telling Pab that she was there.

San required quite a bit more time before her pain subsided enough to rise. And even then, the trip up was extremely rough; she could do little to climb and aid the effort, relying heavily on Pab to reel her up.

Back on level ground, San expected to rest, but Pab wouldn't let her, hoisting her up and supporting most of her weight on his hip. Her feet barely touched the ground as they started for the light. San allowed herself to be carried, conserving her strength, but trying to help by getting in a few steps of her own every once in a while. Pab did not falter or complain, which only made her guilt insurmountable, worse than the pain that pounded her body.

The two stumbled in silence toward the light, which soon stretched and grew brighter, revealing itself to be a cluster of homes—an exurb neighborhood. When they realized this, the houses were still a good distance away and would take some time to reach, but the sight gave direction and hope.

. . .

Chiara's belongings had been taken from the closets and shelves. The cabinets were emptied. Some were packed away, but most had been donated—she was not taking much with her.

The small holes in the walls left from the numerous nails and tacks were filled. A fresh coat of paint was layered on the walls, concealing the murals. Chiara even had the carpet in her bedroom replaced. The apartment looked quite presentable, almost like it had just been constructed and was ready for its first tenant.

The drastic change was daunting to Ren, who couldn't stop staring and fidgeting around the vacant apartment. She hadn't enjoyed living in the frowzy mess that Chiara had allowed the home to fall into, but now it was too clean—the pristine sheen made her uncomfortable. The feeling of home and familiarity had been taken away, along with the grime and dirt. Wandering around the sterile rooms now, it was difficult for Ren to believe that it was the same apartment she had called home for so many years. She could not place her memories there—the good and the bad—they would not fit.

Having the slate wiped clean also challenged Ren to define what the apartment had meant to her. It was strange for the rooms to hold and invoke such stark, conflicting tempers inside her. She was unsure if she loved the apartment, or if the recent gloom had ruined it entirely. The happy memories were numerous, yet the unpleasantness was more immediate; the good days were distant, like a story from her dreams—pleasing, but too remote to feel real.

Chiara skipped through the door behind Ren, interrupting her inner crisis, the woes of which were completely lost on the women. Chiara adjusted her sandals and wiped the sweat from her brow without a second glance at the place that had been her home, refuge, and prison. Ren searched for a glimmer of the same turmoil in the woman but saw nothing of it. She bent for the last jumbled stack of boxes that proved too heavy for one trip. Chiara made an exaggerated grunt and snarl, playing a bit for her own enjoyment. She was brimming with joy and Ren watched her with the same curious uncertainty with which she inspected the room.

The woman's return to normalcy over the past months came about in stages. Before she prepared a feast for herself, she baked treats in the morning. Before she started singing again, Chiara hummed and whistled. Before she painted another landscape, she sketched on napkins. It was almost as if she was learning these things again, rediscovering her delights.

Despite these hopes, Chiara's hurt was lasting, and her foul habits were not disappearing without a fight. While she seemed happier, the grimness was detectable in her eyes from time to time, and it would continue to win out on occasion. Crying fits were still common, even abruptly intruding upon a lovely song. She could ruin paintings she had happily created hours prior. Some nights she would bring home a record—perhaps one that she had previously loved—and play it through, only to wake, crying, and toss it out again.

Chiara had cut her hair short, above her ears. Ren thought it was adorable, and cut hers as well, in solidarity.

But on the evening following the salon, Ren found her crying in the bathroom, staring in horror at the mirror and pulling on her short strands with regret.

This oscillation between delight and desolation made Ren nervous about the move. She feared that Chiara was acting irrationally and that the new home would be too big a change and bring about too much regret. She didn't want to think of how Chiara may respond then, perhaps sinking back into the misery from which she was just escaping.

Chiara had made improvements. She had brought music, art, and light back into their lives. But it felt so foreign that Ren was slow to trust. Like the room, it seemed strange that such complex and contrary forces could be at play within the same body.

. . .

It was a tight fit, the neighbors had not left much space, but the man impressed Mar by effortlessly swooping in and claiming the parallel-parking spot in front of his family's flat. It was his finely tuned memory that took the wheel, and the process did not even disrupt his telephone call.

Getting out of the backseat, Mar spotted three children lining the apartment's front window, eyes brimming with eagerness at their dad's return. There also seemed to be some relief. Mar guessed the father may have been running late, enough to spark a little concern. He imagined the dinner would be set, untouched and waiting. By the tired gruff in his voice, Mar read that it had been a trying workday. He could empathize; the sky was darkening on another lengthy, tiresome day of searching with no result.

Mar spent his nights and days in a state of torturous vacillation. There were countless places to look, but he rarely fully reached a destination. The moment his feet set a course for the subway or a museum, his divided mind would place Des at a different location—a park or restaurant—in the opposite direction. And Mar would then hurry toward that new destination only to freeze and retreat, back and forth and out again.

While his body carried him onward in constant motion, in truth he was paralyzed by indecisiveness, and the insurmountable odds of finding his friend. There were so many trains and stops and connections; Des could have taken any of them and wound up anywhere in the city or outside of it—on purpose or by blindly searching like he was.

Mar followed the man up the stoop and peeked inside. The family home felt welcoming; he would enjoy joining them. There would be a warm bed for him and certainly a hearty meal to pick from. But Mar chose not to stay—to stay would be to stop. That felt like admitting defeat, giving in to the people, and that was something he could not do. His meals were always taken on the move, swiped from street-side markets, never from a house or restaurant or anywhere he may be tempted to sit, stay, and rest. Mar would sleep, at least his body would, and that was only at the peak of exhaustion, tucked in the alleyways, park bushes, and other forgotten places—again, never in the homes, hotels, or anywhere that would tempt him to linger.

In his dream state, his mind would continue searching, scouring the city for places he could go. The only other visions were of the past, forcing him to relive the mistake he had made.

The separation had never felt so severe. It was as if there was a side of his reality that he had been ignoring.

Having Des at his side had allowed him to ignore it—the grimness of true solitude.

Guilt was his only companion; it was the only voice in his ear, telling him where he should go and why. His grasp of hope was gone. Logical choice and reasoning were slipping.

Mar walked the street, peering in windows and even stepping through a few doors. Every household seemed to be on the same schedule: dinner, television, and then bed. Slowly the lights started going out. Still wandering the sidewalk, Mar's restless mind took hold and scolded, recognizing that it may have been foolish to choose a residential area. Why would Des go to such a place? Mar could not say why, nor could he reason where his friend would be instead.

A boy drove through and delivered food to a neighbor's house, three doors down; he was fast in his business and his car sped away before Mar could hop in. The next sign of life was the sound of a front door opening. Since most of the people were asleep, Mar rushed down the street in hopes that, miraculously, Des had emerged, but it was just a woman stepping out for a late-night smoke; she was not going anywhere. A second car pulled up and honked its horn. Mar watched the door across the street fling open and a young man scamper down to the street. His friend scooted in the backseat and tossed some junk to the floorboard to make room and luckily there was enough for Mar as well.

. . .

The people fooled us. We fooled ourselves. I felt the need to be seen. In that need, I took part in their world. Tried to be a part of what they were doing, what was real to them, what is seen. And I was blinded. So briefly. But so seriously.

It happened again. The same distance. The same silence. And it came just as sudden. And I have been removed again.

I blinked. I was blinded, for a moment, and my family is gone again.

XVI

For such a metropolis, it had an abundance of gardens—quaint plots of tranquility that stood in stark contrast to the blaring traffic and towering skyscrapers.

The small landscapes were immaculate. Stone paths rolled through lush flower beds, dotted with tiny pavilions. Quiet ponds were richly populated with orange and white fish. The manmade paths, bridges, and shelters seemed not to disturb, but to complement the natural surroundings.

The collage of flowers could not be duplicated with any paint or skill, although many artists were present to try. They sat with their sketchpads, easels, and journals to capture what they could.

San settled in a squat and observed over the shoulder of an artist as he brushed the foundational outline of the scene, but she was drawn to something the artist was not including in his rendition—a family of three gathered in a pavilion nestled across the pond.

A husband and wife had their backs to San with a grandmother taking their picture from the opposite bench. The elder mother snapped a few photos and then showed them to the couple, who seemed eager for more.

The three adults soon left the small shelter, venturing on to find another backdrop, and as they stepped out of the pavilion, San saw what they had blocked from sight in the close quarters—a young girl, slowly trailing, but not in a rush to keep up. They did not acknowledge her lagging behind, nor did they call to her when she stopped, turned, and retreated to the pavilion.

San brought the six-year-old girl to Pab's attention, and they approached, passing behind the grandmother as she took more pictures of the husband and wife under a willow. The man stood behind his wife, placing his hands gently on the bump in her stomach.

It was not the notion of finding another removed child that bothered her; it was something in the tone of her appearance. She did not seem removed *enough*. When San was first separated, she had slept outside, ate scraps, lost track of herself, and her appearance had shown it. But this girl was different. It was like she could still fit in with the people. Her appearance, from her clothes to her posture, was well-kept like someone was still attentive to her.

When they entered, her eyes flashed up at San but did not show surprise, joy, nor fear. Of the three, Pab was the only one to give any indication that something special had occurred, rejoicing with an awkward spell of laughter that ended in a hiccup. San stayed focus, paused, and turned to check on the parents, now perched on the railing of the bridge she had just crossed, for the smallest sign of acknowledgment, but nothing came.

Like a second layer, San's imagination filtered and added to the scene. In the stranger's place, she saw her family—at least her father and what she could imagine of her mother who had left when San was young. They were posing on the bridge. Her grandmother returned as well, taking their picture. She captured a series of poses and loving embraces, as her father caressed her mother's belly.

Had her father found another woman? Had there been more children after her? How had her family moved on without her?

"The replacement." San glared at the expecting mother's stomach and then at the glee in her eyes—completely ignorant of the pain in her daughter's. "They are replacing her."

One foot stamping with agitation, San claimed a seat on the side opposite the girl and offered her name as a greeting: "San." She didn't know how she would proceed from that but did not need to.

The girl came to her, without another word or thought, in a hurried scuttle. Desperation and liberation accompanied the embrace, and the façade vanished; the girl no longer worked to keep her composure, while her clothes were still pristine, she wilted within them. The girl wept and buried her face in San's shirt.

San's body had been rigid. She had not noticed this state, and she wondered how long it had been cast in such sharp iron—hours, days, or longer. How long had she been keeping her body so tense? She only realized her hardened state when the child broke it with her embrace. San was liquified; she adjusted to better receive and hold the girl, frame bending to fit like a cradle.

San was suddenly conscious of her own foul smell and how rough her bruised hands might feel on the child's unblemished skin.

She didn't know if Pab would protest; she doubted he would, but she stated her resolve that they would not leave without her—they belonged to her.

. . .

Ren listened for the sound of Chiara's return, her attention jumping between her pencil and the sounds from the corridor outside the door. She sat on the kitchen counter with the paper pressed to her leg as she drew. This version of

Gift of Varmundi was a bland and rudimentary skeleton of its predecessors and the original. It was one she could draw with simple strokes as it had grown too tiring for her to paint the full canyon, with great detail and color, only to have Chiara look through it.

The woman had changed so much.

Ren had never seen Chiara so gregarious; the shy, aloof hermit was gone. She was no longer intimidated by crowds. Instead, she was constantly out at the busiest times, striking up conversations with anyone who crossed her path. She loved the job she had found, and her coworkers. The new classes were treating her well. And friendships were blossoming in every part of Chiara's life. These developments were terrific, except for the fact that they took Chiara away in more ways than one.

At first, Ren had been excited for Chiara when she found a consistent group of friends. They would go out to dinner, walk in the park, or simply chat at one's home. Chiara loved them, and Ren had tried to as well, but it was strange to listen to them converse and attempt to squeeze herself into the happenings. She quickly felt excluded and out of place, more than ever before.

Ren couldn't help but miss the more reserved and silent side of Chiara. Even though the woman had never spoken back, she had always felt there was a strong exchange taking place. But that space was now being filled, and Ren was not proud of her unnerving jealousy.

Despite the turbulence in their relationship, Ren stayed with Chiara, hoping for another miracle, another glimpse across the distance. Chiara had seen her drawing—Ren didn't know how—but it had happened. Somehow, she had sent a message across the separation. It had awoken something in Chiara. Varmundi was

Chiara's word for the gift of life and Ren believed there had been a renewal in that gift for her. It had been a slow and difficult recovery, but Ren knew that she had sparked the fire. She knew that she had caused it and she had named this kind of awakening—destarsi.

Chiara didn't see that Ren was there, but she had seen her drawing and that gave her hope. And this hope was expressed in the numerous attempts Ren continued to make to reach across the removal again. The cord between them was there—Ren could still imagine the tether that had first held her to Chiara. But she feared that it would disappear if she didn't make another contact and Chiara drifted too far.

Ren sat with the drawing in hand, contemplating where she would put it for Chiara to see. Honestly, there were very few places she had not yet tried. The only option that came to mind was Chiara's books. Ren could stick her drawing in the pages of the new book sets that had just arrived—a recent purchase that continued a spending spree.

From her perch, a hundred eyes stared back at her from every surface in the apartment. They were carved into the wood, drawn with marker on the walls, or painted on paper tacked to the ceiling. Chiara had seen none of them. Ren's efforts to breach the separation stared back at her, telling her what she already knew, but wished to postpone.

The jingle of keys and click of the lock made her heart leap.

The frustration she felt toward Chiara instantly dissolved; she would not allow herself to spoil their time together by holding unfair grudges.

The door swung open, and Ren's anticipation was spoiled when she discovered that Chiara was not alone; she walked into the apartment with two strangers but they did not go far beyond the doorway. Their jackets and suits were dark and overpowering, but they each had warm and friendly smiles—it was a strange combination for Ren to read. One was hauling luggage and the other had a stack of papers in her hand. They gave everything to Chiara, setting things at her feet or on the nearby counter. The three had a lengthy exchange, speaking rapidly and excitedly, but that was not why Ren was having trouble understanding them. She could barely hear a word. She was too distracted by what Chiara was holding—a small child.

The boy, who was perhaps two-years old, played with Chiara's necklace for a while before he got distracted and snagged a pen from the clipboard in the stranger's hand. The quiet steal was soon noticed. The man at the door playfully tugged at the pen and the boy pulled it away with a chubby grin and a prolonged blabbing that made the three adults gawk and giggle. The boy mimicked their smiles and laughed as well. His rounded, rosy cheeks only added to their delight. The only one who wasn't laughing was Ren. She stared, suspended in her eddy of emotions.

Ren closed her eyes from the scene and wondered how she could have been so foolish, so blind to the obvious; Chiara had been making accommodations for another. The larger apartment, the shopping spree—she was adopting a child, a course that Ren had never imagined for Chiara. No matter how many friends Chiara had made, Ren had not thought that she would bring a third member into their home, especially not another child. But when Ren's eyes opened, the child was real.

The only thing that had changed was the disappearance of the two strangers. Chiara was closing the door behind them.

There was a sense of embarrassment like she was not supposed to be there—she was not supposed to be seeing such a private moment. Ren felt like an outsider, intruding on the happiness.

Chiara carried the boy around the rooms, giving him a tour of his new home. The woman was so happy; clearly, she had what she wanted. And she wanted a child because she didn't know Ren was there—she didn't know that she already was a mother.

The toddler waddled in cumbersome steps around the room. He dug through the bags the strangers had brought. He touched and tossed everything within his reach, testing his new world. Chiara knelt on the rug in the middle of the room and watched him explore. Ren slipped down beside her, closer than usual, rested against Chiara's back, and propped her head on her shoulder. She may have been sixteen, but she chose to forgo the maturity that she had gained over the years and sought, one last time, to simply be a child seeking the touch of her mama, wrapping her arms around her and nuzzling into her hair.

Ren's final plea for Chiara to feel her, to hear her, to ask her to stay was not received.

The preparation didn't take long. With tears welling, Ren gathered a few keepsakes: a brush, a record, and a lipstick of Chiara's most common shade. One trip around was all she needed.

Chiara came to the middle of the cluttered floor, brimming with excitement. It appeared as though she had the urge to run but had nowhere to go. Her head then began to sway from side to side, with her palms pressed together and fingers barely touching her lips. The sinuous motion traveled down, from the flick of her hair to the roll of her hips. In the next instant, her entire body was taken. The woman danced, without any regard, twirling freely in the small space, waving her hands and bouncing her shoulders. She spun around and around and yet her eyes always seemed to be fixed on the boy. Her shoes were kicked off as she stepped and spun to the music in her heart—Ren thought she could hear it, too.

One last look was savored, standing in the outside hall with the door ajar, capturing the lovely sight for her memories: Chiara dancing with her son. She held his arms, helping him balance. Ren was tempted to change the picture in her mind, to imagine that it was her in the boy's place. But she didn't. It felt somehow cruel to steal the moment from Chiara and make it hers.

Overwhelmed with sadness at the utter finality of her departure, Ren stopped before reaching the stairs and returned to Chiara's door, but didn't reenter, only reached and carved one more canyon into the wood of the frame—a message of love, meant not only for Chiara but for anyone who may see it—to know she had been there.

. . .

Des mounted one of the four bronze lions guarding the column. He rested his chin on the mane, letting his eyes wander and scan the faces. They were mostly adults, but Des remained focused on the random youths scattered in the mix, picking out those who matched Mar in height, build, or ever so slightly in look.

"You're stalling, Des. Keep moving." Ada's voice rang in his ear. Her tone was firm but not harsh.

He was relieved to have the vision and not just the sound of her voice. It was a gift that had been more frequent since Mar had been gone, a gift that had accompanied his fourteenth birthday—the first spent without his brother in almost a decade.

As he walked, he thought about those early days—meeting Mar at the gas station—the park that he had been left at.

"I saw you, and I knew you were on my side," Des recited Mar's words aloud, unashamed to call them out to Ada.

The family RV came clear to his imagination. With it came a wave of anger, anger that rose to an insurmountable height. He needed a release.

He parked the rickety, bulky vehicle in the forefront of his mind. Every detail was fresh and renewed. There was rust on the bumper, a chip in the taillight, and the family's bicycles strapped to the back. Everything was as it had been. Then Des lit it on fire. The bus was engulfed in flames so forceful that he could feel the warmth on his face and the skin of his arms.

"Does this help?" Ada asked.

"Yes."

"Relieve it."

Ada stood beside Des in the oasis of his imagination. He saw her face in the light of the inferno. She placed a hand on his arm, which made him feel warmer than the fire. Avoiding her eyes, he looked to his arm where she touched him. On his sleeve, there was something stitched, something that hadn't been there previously—an emblem of some kind, like she had worn at the dance. But before he could lift her hand to fully reveal it, Des noticed that Ada's hand was missing fingers.

The fire suddenly gave out and the bus disappeared. This was startling because Des was enjoying the fire, he wanted it to keep burning, so the abrupt darkness made him feel less in control of his daydream.

But they were not left in complete darkness. A cool blue light shone before them, and inside this spotlight cast by a high moon was an animal, too faint and too far to recognize.

It was large—he heard its paws scathe the ground—and the wingspan was immense. When the wings spread and flapped, he could feel it like a gust of wind. There was a foreboding presence from the animal, felt even at their great distance, and Des was put on guard, guiding Ada behind him.

The animal took flight or at least tried to, ascending slowly. The wings working vehemently to lift its weight, the rear claws holding onto the ground. The line of the horizon upon which the animal had been resting was then raised. Higher and higher the animal flew and brought the earth with it until a mountain was formed. The animal released the peak and let it settle. The lone mountain was massive and blocked most of the moonlight.

In an arc, the animal flew and then dove straight down but didn't bank to avoid nor land on the mountain it had just formed; instead, the ground gave to it. The mountain started to fold inward, like sand in an hourglass, pulled by the dive of the animal at its center.

The horizon didn't resettle at the even line it had held before; the creature pushed farther down, and the earth beneath his feet moved, toward the hole that was forming, and he was a helpless passenger.

A strange certainty arose that, even though he couldn't see inside, it was not just a hole but a cave, with a wide mouth and deep tunnels. When the pull beneath his feet stopped, Des continued to move forward of his own will. He crawled through the caverns, lured in by not sights but sounds; Des could hear voices coming from deeper in the cave. The further in he went, the louder the voices grew, and the better he was able to distinguish them. The beckoning calls of Mar, Ada, and his family quickly brought him to a back room with stone wells formed in the ground. There was boiling water inside these deep cauldrons. In the dim light, Des watched the surface ripple and send up bubbles. They didn't fly high in the air before popping and releasing the voices. Des listened for and found the well from which Mar called. The water deep within was hotter than others, and as he leaned in, he saw a fire. There was fire beneath the water. It was not moving. The flames were frozen, and they sparkled like gold.

Des was knocked hard to the sidewalk. A man exiting a cab hit him with the door. He hadn't seen the car, but he truly had not been paying attention to anything. His mind had taken him elsewhere, through the mountain and the cave. What he had seen and heard had felt so real. The sound of the bubbling water lingered as did the heat on his cheek. He also noticed that he was still clutching his arm where Ada had placed her hand.

But only one thing truly remained—the fire.

Something was towering over nearby buildings, a monument in the shape of a column with gilded fire on top. The golden fire—he recognized it and not just from his daydream. He and Mar had visited the monument during their first days in the city. The dragons sculpted into the side first had caught their attention and the boys had even taken in the sights of the city from the high platform.

It took longer than expected to reach the monument. The stone structure was farther away than it had originally appeared and there were a maddening number of buildings and blocked roads. It was dusk by the time Des made it to the tower, but the journey was worth it—Mar was already there, sitting at its base.

They recognized each other from afar, both reeling in the sensation of being seen again, but neither hurried the reunion. Des's approach was slow, and Mar did not rise.

"Found you," sighed Des.

"Can't get rid of you, can I?" Mar asked, light in tone, but with a solemn expression.

"Guess not, huh?" Des stared at Mar with the same astonishment that he received. There was enduring doubt; neither boy believed that the other was real.

Mar squinted out into the street and courtyard. "This city, blah. Terrible idea coming here."

"Uh-huh. Well, I don't know. I've had fun. But nothing good to eat, that's for sure."

"How'd you find me?" Mar asked, still without looking at Des.

"What makes you think I was looking for you?" Des gave a tired grin. "Came here by accident; I was enjoying my break from you."

"Were you?" Mar gave a sarcastic smirk.

"Oh, yes. I kept busy. Loads for me to do without you slowing me down. First, I met some locals. They showed me the city. We went everywhere. Good people! I was on my way to see them when I bumped into you."

"Sounds like you've had a nice vacation." Mar gave an exaggerated bow and clapped his hands. "Finally getting over your shy nature."

Des leaned against the towering monument, putting his back to the stone and sliding down to sit next to Mar.

"Oh, I've always liked to talk. Just never had anyone worth talking to. And yourself? What have you done since you ran off? Have you been here this whole time? Just been sitting here, waiting to be rescued?"

"I don't need rescuing," Mar shot back. "I was enjoying being away from you. Making new friends. Finally, people who like my ideas and want to hear my stories. Then . . . I met a girl. Oh yes, I did. I met a girl. She's terribly pretty. You see, I don't have to imagine them like Ada. She's real. Really real. We danced . . . and kissed."

"And where is she now?" Des stretched his neck and peeked around the sides of the base.

"She ran off." Mar slapped his hands together and shot one out to his right. "You scared her off. Thanks a lot, you ugly bugger."

Des shared in the laugh at the teasing but immediately regretted interrupting the flow of the banter, as it was replaced with silence. He didn't know how to break it. What could they talk about? There was so much to ask and say, and yet Des was at a loss for words. Why was it difficult? He had imagined finding Mar, every day since they had been separated from each other, but the reunion had always been joyous, never forced or uncomfortable.

Ada's presence returned, sitting on the opposite side of Des, who didn't turn from Mar at first, like looking away for a second would make him disappear again. She gave him a moment to fight this worry, before taking Des's hand and drawing his attention away, to something he was astonished to see.

A great company of people was seated in a line beside her. All seated as he was, holding hands and facing forward in stoic unity. None were recognizable to Des, their faces began to blur only a few from Ada, and yet Des felt comfort from their presence.

Mar reached for Des's hand, matching Ada's strength. It was a quick slap of a grab as though he was not sure if his palm would hit the concrete, uncertain if Des was there.

The line of people remained; Des wondered if Mar could see them. Gaze down and head turned away, it didn't seem like he could.

"H-how?" Mar whispered in a stammering attempt to hold back tears. "I had g-given up."

"Me too. I . . . did . . . too." Des did a poorer job of fighting the emotion, he had to take a breath between almost every word. "Ada. It was Ada. She showed me . . . a vision. A warning. A way."

"I dunno what I would've done," Mar spoke quickly, trying to get as many words as he could in an already rushed breath.

"I . . . walked in this place. Where she took me. Through it. And came here."

"It brought us back." Mar kept his grip on Des's hand, but slid away and rested on the ground, wilting into a state that quickly neared sleep, as he finally allowed his body to rest.

Des was thankful for the peace on his friend's face but did not share in it. His need for sleep was just as formidable, but a greater urgency kept him awake, alertness that lingered from the dark place Ada had taken him. "There's more."

Mar did not come back up to be seated; he stayed on his side but opened his eyes and peered up, telling Des that he was listening.

"Something's coming."

Des looked back to his right, toward Ada, and down the line of faceless followers; their line seemed to have grown longer. More and more were joining. The progression was too great for Des to count, so he stopped trying to see its end and turned forward as they all were, to see what they were facing.

"Something's coming. And we will need to be ready. Together. We can't let them separate us again. Together. Never again separate."

. . .

I don't know what I would've done if I had lost track of him. I mean for good. Forever. If I lost him. Where would I go? Nowhere, that's where. We would just be lost again. Like we were before.

We are together again. My brother and I. And soon we will find Ada. And others like her. Others like us. Others for the Rahirrem.

Those things I saw. The walking vision. Those creatures and places. I believe they were a warning—a framtive—that's what I'll call it. A framtive. A warning for what is to come. Or . . . what may come if we keep making these mistakes. Keep taking part in what is seen. If we do that, it will divide us forever. They will divide us. The people. The people—they are our ruin.

XVII

The sky was pierced with an arrow of birds, soaring in unison until home was in sight; then each deviated. The mother, beckoned home to feed and protect, descended with ease. Senses keen, she fluttered from one tree to the next, wary of danger. The meal in its beak would sustain the younglings, pining and helpless, their wings not yet fledged. But she did not make it all the way.

Danger was sensed.

The tree she had landed in shook slightly as the train passed.

Milky waters flowed down a gentle hill encircled by the tracks; its spray reached the windows of the passing car. The train rumbled onto a straight length of the track, through a series of galleries and then a tunnel.

When the light returned, there was a grand valley with a stretch of thick forest and a sparkling tarn running down the mountain from the range's highest peak. A small village radiated from the banks of the water.

"Odd," Des pondered to himself. "What people see every day. It is odd. Where and why they stay. This mountain . . . not a bad choice."

He was soon consumed with the relativity of traveling; he could enjoy the view as a visitor, but there was a depth of familiarity or perhaps ownership that was reserved for those who were there permanently.

How long would he have to stay to *truly* know and appreciate the place? He couldn't venture a guess because there had never been a place he knew that well.

While he wasn't sure as to the exact day he was dropped from their world—he had been so young—he often chose the twenty-fourth of May as the mark for when his new life had begun. If his mental calendar was correct, then he was just days away from the twelfth anniversary.

As the train reached the boundary of the village and began its deceleration, the townspeople came into view. Des studied them with great attention, and yet he and the train were treated with disregard. It was nothing more than a temporary, albeit expected, disruption in traffic and schedule. At each intersection, commuters, joggers, and delivery people lined up at the crossing, stopped by the blinking light and bar. A few could be seen checking their watches with expressions of defeat, but most seemed to have accepted the inevitable delay. Des could imagine it may even be a part of their morning routine, sitting there and watching random travelers pass by. Soon, the train would be gone, the roads would reopen, and the day would continue without great consequence.

Envy spiked at how fortunate they were to be able to live their lives out in the beautiful valley. The sunrises, Des assumed, would be breathtaking and the breaking light would vivaciously play on the water. And the cycle of seasons, the people knew how the landscape might change, in small increments and all together; Des could only imagine.

"Look at the view!" exclaimed Des.

Mar didn't respond immediately; he was not as transfixed nor feeling as contemplative.

People outside of the train seemed to have grown complacent, going about their days without a second thought or hint of appreciation. Familiarity could breed numbness, Des diagnosed and wondered if his senses would dull to the splendor of the mountains, too.

Over the intercom there came an announcement of the arrival, a friendly farewell to those departing, and an expected time for departure. A handful of the passengers stirred, gathering their bags and starting toward the exits.

"Does that mean you want to get off, here?" Mar finally said.

Eager travelers began to pour out onto the tiny platform through the narrow station doors before the train lurched to a halt. The weary conductor yawned as the doors opened with a hiss and clap but put on a brighter face to thank those exiting and greet those entering as the two lines collided. Patience was pled, times and orders were repeated, but the final solution required train attendees to herd the ticket carriers to the side, to make room for those who had to get off.

Opposing phases of the journey were played out—the beginnings and the ends. The platform was a temporary stage for acts of human drama and Des had a balcony seat from the car's upper deck. Embraces were offered, tears were shed, and lasting kisses were held. It was difficult to distinguish which scenes were farewells and which were reunions. A curtain call eventually came, much to the displeasure of those waving goodbye and at last, Des answered. "No, let's keep moving. Somewhere better. Down the line."

. . .

The girl lay stretched out on the twin bed, a blanket wrapped around her, toes pointed at the headboard as she worked on her puzzle.

Organizing the pieces by shape and color, small nests of alike pieces were spaced along the edge of the bed. Her favorite doll was propped up next to the box in front of her for encouragement.

Her focus was such that she didn't notice that the rest of the house had gone silent. Though her bedroom was at the rear of the house, she could usually hear the murmur of the front-room television—it had been off for almost ten minutes. A problem piece refused to fit where she thought it ought to, distracting her until there was something she could not ignore: the crack of the recliner's leg rest snapping back into place. That was the readying call.

Her shoulders locked, but her eyes remained fixed on the puzzle. This was stubbornness fighting her reflexes. He was leaving his chair, earlier than usual, but that was not a guarantee that there would be trouble.

There were sounds of running water and stacking dishes from the kitchen. Why was he taking so long? Did he know she was listening? Did he want her to expect something?

When he cleared his throat and coughed, he was already in the hallway. That was it. She rolled off the bed. The blanket came along in her hurry.

The window's top pane was loose and had to be propped up with the puzzle box to stay open. She considered hopping out but doubted she could outrun him. It was also cold outside; she had a long-sleeved shirt, but short pajama bottoms, and she didn't know how long she would have to stay out if she were to elude him. There was no time to add layers, he was already at the bathroom, knocking on its door and coughing her name.

Leaving the open window, her closet was a desperate alternative; she dove in, pulled the clothes from the hangers, and burrowed into the pile. The tiny cupboard was not a perfect solution—it had not always been a successful hiding place—but where else was there to go?

Her left knee was jutting out and uncovered when he came to her bedroom door. But she could not risk moving. When he said her name, she couldn't tell if it was a question or a demand. Did he see her?

His tone sharpened and he repeated himself once—a pause—then her name again.

Then he entered. She braced for him to plunge his hand into her den. His anger rose, but he directed it out the window, taking the bait of her ploy.

He turned and stormed out of the room, but her fear didn't dissipate. He was headed upstairs, his progress easily followed in stomps that seemed to rattle the house. If her brother was up there, her father would return—he knew she would not go alone—not without her brother. With luck, her brother had snuck out, without telling her, and her father would give up and go to bed alone.

Waiting, there was nowhere to go but further within herself. She had to substitute what she heard, what she saw, and what she felt—until everything and anything was new, of her creation. Then she had to make herself feel small, small enough to be safe. She folded in half and half again, shrinking until she was too tiny to mind, and the outside surrendered. But she could not vanish, not completely. *If only,* she wished, too deep within for the words to find their way out. *If only.*

. . .

Three years as a wanderer, a freelance seeker of illumina-
tion, a Vandar as she would call it, but she had never seen
anything quite like this funeral.

There was vibrancy, music, and color. The crowd
trickled into the square from all corners as if drawn to
the hypnotizing rhythm of the chanting. A circle of dancing and marching was formed. Ren kept her distance,
climbing a wall that quartered the square to see more of
the crowd.

The space filled but it was not chaotic. Everyone
moved in unison. A steady beat was played on a shekere;
the beads that dressed the hollow gourd rattled. Pictures
of the deceased were held overhead in praise of the life
lived.

Ren had lived among many groups and found that
each had a unique approach to death. Most were solemn
in the face of the inevitable, bowing to it. Others tried to
deny it or master it. But this ceremony was one of the few
that seemed, if her interpretation was correct, to taunt
it with a celebration—her clear preference. It was a reminder that the people did possess a deeper sense of life,
that they did possess varmundi—as Chiara had called it.
Removed, Ren believed that she was naturally gifted a
greater wealth of it, but they had it too. It was faint, she
had to look for it, but it was there.

The scene was deserving of an attempt, and Ren
sketched what she felt from it.

The coffin was represented by a large square with thick
lines. The left-side line was broken up by several horizontal dashes; moving inward, these roots sprung into wild
curves, but as they progressed across the box's center,

their waves began to match frequencies. Then they wove together, tighter and tighter, becoming less distinct and chaotic, forming a single cord. Once it breached the confines of the box, the lone stream then curved up, around, and back on itself in an infinite loop.

Her pen remained at the ready, hovering over the board, in case further inspiration struck, but there was absolution to the product. Ren was delighted with it, but would the people be able to see it?

Ren joined the procession, holding the tribute over her head. Within a single lap, she realized there was no change in the distant haze of their eyes.

. . .

While nothing is foreign, nothing will ever belong. We never belong, because we're forever foreign. Removed from the people and by the people. The people may not appreciate their world enough, but they are at least a part of that world. They have that.

My color had been removed from the palette.

XVIII

Tall prairie grass waved in the wind on its north and south shores of the remote pond, while a sandy beach grew from its western side and a patch of trees loomed on its east. A lone house rested atop a hill, many yards away, isolated in the prairie as though it had dropped from the sky. Siding in shambles and roof caved, it was difficult to guess how long it had been since the three-story structure was last occupied.

Des's heels were the only part of him in the water. He fanned his toes to shake the murky gunk from between them. His sodden denim pants clung tightly to his legs, and he fought the urge to peel them off. The sun dried his bare chest. The sand beneath moistened, collecting the water from his back. His hair felt gummy when he combed his fingers through it, working out the knots and spreading the strands out around his head.

A chittering in the water rang in his ears, making Des wonder if Mar had returned after hunting the opposite shore for a rabbit he had spotted.

"Catch 'em?" he asked. Mar didn't answer, but the splashing drew nearer to Des's shore and it was soon accompanied by a scintillating laugh that set lively embers loose in his chest.

Ada, the red-haired girl, was glowing as she knelt and slid to her elbows in the sand beside him. Her wet hair curled off her shoulder and along the straps of her swimsuit. The glistening drew his eyes to the water droplets on her smooth skin. The gems in her eyes were impossible to ignore.

Des's flimsy smile felt more like a snarl, but it seemed to tickle Ada, whose laugh now came through her nose, detoured by lips bit between her teeth.

"Leaving your mark? You're squirming like you got an itch."

"Just bored. Nothing to do."

"Don't act helpless." Ada wagged a finger. "You only have yourself to blame. Why not play with Mar? He's finding fun because he's looking for it." She nodded toward where Mar's had gone into the wood, but Des didn't turn, scared she would disappear if he looked away.

"I'd rather stay. Stay and talk with you."

Ada blushed, tried to hide it behind her arm, then came back up with a speckle of sand stuck to the end of her nose. "Good choice . . . Hmm, what should we talk about?" She tilted her head and the bundle of wet hair slid from her shoulder. "Oh! The anniversary. Of the day you met Mar."

Des smiled, but the feeling inside was bitter. "He wouldn't know. He doesn't care."

"Were you expecting a party?"

"H-he's forgotten," stammered Des.

"Oh, don't be raw at him." Ada smirked with sympathy. "He doesn't know what year it is or how old he is. That's part of the bargain he made when he gave up keeping time. Tossed those things out of his head. So he can stay young and away, forever." Ada put her fingers to her temple and flicked them away.

Des grunted, "Maybe I should do the same. Maybe I wouldn't envy them then. Comparing my years. I would—"

Ada jumped in, "Remember." She leaned closer until he had no choice but to stare into her eyes. "You've already seen more than they will in a hundred years."

Des finally turned away. He didn't want to hear this. It was the same thing Mar would have told him. *They should be envious of us.*

There was a brief window of silence and Des feared that his vision had already slipped away until he felt Ada's warm hand touch his cheek. "Peace. Be still with this. Please." She lightly scratched at the scruff on his chin. "What's going on here?"

Des reluctantly followed her in the change of subject. "I need a shave."

"Why? I like it. Makes you look . . . mature and why—"

"Makes me look like him. Like my dad." Des cut in and immediately scorned himself for doing so. Why was he being so adversarial? Why couldn't he just be happy with her? "I've been avoiding my reflection. It's like seeing him again. Can't have that. Hate that." Des and his father—their features were aligning. His hair color and eyes had always been replicas, but recently, his face was maturing and filling out. "We couldn't be more different. Opposed. And yet, I'm doomed to be him, to have his likeness."

Ada brought her hand to his chest, resting on his fish hook necklace. She scooted closer to him and nudged his shoulder with her nose. Des couldn't help but smirk; he could feel it pull on his burnt cheeks.

"You still looking at me?" Her soft, slender fingers cupped over his eyes and then parted to allow him to peek. "You are!" The hand then moved down and molded his skin, readjusting the smile from his face. "*Stop!*"

"I can't." Des shook his head and spoke firmly, interrupting her nervous laugh. With a simple shrug, he said, "I don't know when I'll be this close to you again."

Ada's hand left his lips and hovered in the air. A bird flitted above them, almost as if she had summoned it. Des watched it fly out of the corner of his eye, with rising anticipation that it might circle down and land on her upstretched hand. But the bird was not a part of his dream and thus could not be so manipulated.

As though its weight had grown too great, Ada let her hand drift back down, slowly, until it came to rest gently on his cheek. "You'll find me."

Des breathed those words, in and out, sounding their echo through his entire being he felt a sense of peace sweep through him—but it wouldn't last.

Mar interrupted, "Is he waving at us?"

He nodded to the field between the house and the pond, but Des didn't look; instead spinning back to find that she had vanished.

"Can he see us?" Mar asked more earnestly.

Des murmured a couple of curses and then looked across the pond grudgingly.

It was a boy, bouncing down the hill through the tall grass. Every few steps, the boy would leap into the air and wave his arms over his head before sinking back into the grass.

Des stood and began to dust the sand off his chest, stealing a concealed, hopeful glance at the sand, studying the bumps and shadows for the slightest indentation left in Ada's departure.

When the boy reached the opposite shore, he lifted one arm in a wave, then bowed.

Mar returned the gesture and the newcomer accepted this welcome. The beach suddenly felt uncomfortably crowded with the stranger standing with a beaming posture and energetic presence. He put a threadbare top hat on his head and held it there as he bowed. The hat was stained and had a poorly mended tear on one of its sides.

"Pab!" the stranger announced, then flashed a smile and arched a hand through the air between them.

"Mar."

Des knew it was his turn, but he was unexplainably distracted by the stranger's hat and lost in considering how, without it, Pab would be only a few inches taller than him.

"That's Des," Mar answered for him. "Don't be offended; he doesn't like to talk to me either."

Embarrassed, Des looked down. But the smile on Pab's face had not faltered.

"And here we are," Pab sang.

. . .

The next field they trekked had recently been scorched. Their steps kicked up clouds of ash that stained their legs as they walked along a line of rotting telephone poles.

The dreary scenery did nothing to hamper Pab's enthusiasm as he spewed forth one tall tale after another about his time with San and Bri.

"Bri is . . . nine. We found her." Pab stopped walking, and turned to look at them so suddenly that Mar nearly bumped into him. "At the start, I was afraid to pluck her from her nest. Thought it might be too soon, but San wouldn't leave without her. She saw how strong the little mutt is."

Pab was not subtle on this anecdote, driving it with an overzealous tone of admiration for San's kindness and compassion; he was setting a foundation to offset the un-settling first impression he predicted.

Demolished by a storm, as Pab presumed, and then picked clean before the people departed, there was not much left of the main house. Only the frame of the first story remained, the rest having fallen inward into the basement. Sparse debris had to be maneuvered in the yard as they passed on to the adjoining farm.

The barn looked as though it would soon face a simi-lar fate. Its walls were thin and warped. One side had already given way, causing the structure to lean to such a degree that it appeared to bow in defeat.

Once inside, Pab whispered to wait while he climbed to the loft. Mar and Des could barely hear him over the creak and howl of the waning structure around them; they looked ready to retreat at a moment's notice.

Pab climbed a ladder to what was left of the hayloft, stepped cautiously onto the landing, then shuffled to-wards San and Bri by the far wall. Bri began bouncing up and down excitedly, sending vibrations through the planks. He waved to them but didn't take his eyes from his steps. There was a tiny layer of hay left on the slanted floor, which at times concealed pitfalls in the wood.

"You found more." Tied into a single braid, Bri's jet black hair flipped and spun behind her.

San remained sitting with her legs folded, then slowly turned to the open side of the barn and stared at the field outside. Pab and Bri went silent and waited for her to join the conversation. When she finally spoke, it was in a high, haughty tone. "And you left them downstairs. With our bags. *Our food.*"

Bri gasped at this accusation and Pab had to calm her down by saying, "They aren't like that. They're like us."

Bri knelt and looked past Pab to the ladder. "I asked them to wait because I wanted to talk." A pause was given to allow San time to start her rejection, but she didn't take it. "This could be good. They are separated—I think they have been for as long as us. It'd be good to be together."

San didn't answer. Her face relaxed, her eyes gave nothing in their unfocused daze, trailing downward to stare at her feet.

. . .

The group moved back to Mar and Des's pond to combat the heat.

They stayed in the water for hours, aside from San, who sat stewing on the shore.

"Fish! Fish!" Bri hollered then plunged beneath the surface. "How did they get here?"

"The people who lived there must have brought them. To fish. For sport," explained Pab.

"Can we catch them?"

"How about it? Shall we show them how to catch a day's meal?" Pab called to San; Bri joined the effort, splashing back to the beach and burrowing into her lap.

"We can do it." Des untied his necklace and held it up, watching the metal hook catch the light. Mar scoffed at his showmanship. Des went still, as he waited for the school to grow comfortable and curious with his presence, hyper-aware of every quake he caused. One hand rested on the surface, brushed the water's surface—as though he could smooth away the wrinkles he was causing instead of creating more—and the other held the hook, slightly submerged, deep enough for the fish but close enough to still reflect the light.

204 · JESSE BANNER

"Blimey!" Mar exclaimed, perturbed by the lack of progress and jealous of the awe it received. Des didn't respond. He ignored Mar's taunt—a skill well-practiced in their time together.

One came close enough. There was a short struggle; the catch was very clean. Des brought his arms up in a smooth motion and flung the fish over his shoulder where it landed on the beach with a plop, followed by several flops, splattering San's legs.

Pab and Bri roared with applause. Mar, who had seen the trick on numerous occasions, was less impressed. "Yes. Well done. Yes. But we'll need more. Any chance you could speed things along?"

Des sneered back. "You're welcome to try."

Mar grinned back. "What do you say, Bri?"

San tried to reign Bri in, caging the giddy fluttering in a tight embrace in her lap. This was quite a fear. The effort of San to hold the child and simultaneously maintain the stoic, indifferent expression proved too taxing, and she relented.

"San could help. She's the best catcher. Hunter," Bri explained as she waded to Des's side, mirroring his stance but having trouble matching his patient, motionless composure. "Catch and kill anything she wants. The best hunter!"

Mar looked to San hoping for what would be the first sign of commonality. When she noticed Mar looking at her, she smiled, but he didn't like it. The spirit of her smirk was ominous and eerily intentional. Mar read it: *Let me show you what the child means.*

. . .

One or two. That's it. That's all. In all our time, Mar and I have only found a few who were like us. Forgotten. Unseen. Separated. The kids were the same. Scared. Trapped. They would refuse to go with us. Basically, dead. They were waiting for what'll never come. But this is different. Never has there been a group. No, I'll call them a pack—that's already together. Pab, San, and Bri. Now there are five of us.

XIX

To the west of their campsite, an impressive peak was alluring, but they needed their rest for such a climb.

A spread of trees separated the mountain from the grassy ridge on which the group had stopped for the night. Within it, a river could be heard, but the trees were so thick that it could not be seen. The echoing sound of the river's flow was quite soothing, a sweet treat, lulling them to sleep.

San was the first to drift, despite great determination to be the last awake; the long hours spent vigilantly watching over her companions were taking a toll. She didn't like how comfortable Pab and Bri were with the newcomers—especially Bri. San read harmful, ulterior motives in every interaction between the child and the boys. They were not to be trusted; Mar and Des would turn on them soon; she was sure of it.

As she bobbed in and out of consciousness, she could hear the others' voices and she fought to stay awake; she wanted silence before she slept, wanted to know that Mar and Des were down before her. Pab yawned and laid back onto the ground, head turned up to the stars and eyes closed; she hated how easily he lowered his guard.

In each nod of her head, as she momentarily resurfaced from a restless sleep, the fire withdrew more and more, and it was in one of these fleeting breaths that San saw Mar and Bri, sitting and facing each other. In the faint firelight, San saw his fingers fumbling with one of her buttons.

What was he doing with her coat?

"This one is giving us troubles, isn't it?" Mar's whisper thundered in San's ear. It shook the ground beneath her and pushed her to her feet.

She spotted the long knife with which they had cut the evening's meal sitting on a flat rock, its blade jutting out over the fire's glowing coals. The metal sang as she snatched it from the rock.

She soared over the campfire and hiked her knee into the side of Mar's head. She was on top of him before he even stopped rolling. She slammed his head to the ground and put the flat of the blade to his neck producing a sickening sizzle as Mar's skin seared. His body convulsed through an intensifying scream.

Bri's scream pierced the air. "SAN!"

Pounding her weight on his head through her elbow, San reached a hand toward Bri, but her words of comfort were lost on the child, who recoiled from her. San was confused by this response, which blinded her to the galloping feet coming behind her in an imminent attack.

Des brought the charred log down with a vengeance barely missing her head and connecting with her shoulder with a crisp crack, a toss of embers, and a puff of smoke. Her hair was then wrenched back and San was peeled off of Mar. He spun her onto her back and dropped his knees onto her ribs. She grunted and wheezed under his weight as he straddled her midsection, fixing each of her arms under his knees and making her defenseless to the pummel that proceeded until blood spurted from her nose.

Pab screamed, "Get off her!" Des responded by lobbing the chunk of wood at his head—a warning not to interfere.

Just then, Bri's petite hand rested on Des's shoulder and his balled fist fell to his side as if the tiny pebble of ice was enough to cool his scolding rage. He turned to look at the girl. Amidst the distraction and cease-fire, San wriggled her hand free and slapped it against the exposed side of Des's head, clenching his ear and using it as leverage to yank him over.

"Tell your br-*awer tah* keep his *ands* off *er*." San's threat was slurred through blood pooling around her gums and seeping from swollen lips.

"Mar! Stop! Stop! Stop!" Pab begged between hysterical sobs. San delivered the last pop across Des's slacked jaw, then focused on Mar stomping toward her, wielding her hatchet.

San hurled herself forward, walloped his side with her fist, and then launched her knee toward his groin. Mar leaped back, avoiding San's more devastating blow, then hunched forward as he tried to draw breath.

Grasping between his grip and the head of the blade, San nearly pulled the handle from his fist, but another set of hands emerged from the darkness and squandered her efforts. She expected Des, coming to the aid of his friend, but it was Pab.

The three danced awkwardly around the camp. Their huddle churned, bodies bumping and feet shuffling. Linked through the hatchet, it pushed and pulled and swayed them as though it had a will of its own.

Pab was the first to lose his footing and fell backward, pulling the others off-balance as well. The momentum of their bodies followed Pab, who was the first to release, midfall, to brace himself. He was knocked to the side slightly and the other wrestling bodies landed on top of his outstretched, left arm. There was a series of grunts and thuds—followed by a *snap* and *crack* like a twig underfoot, soft yet powerful enough to stop all other sounds and action.

Blood spurted over them, and they all looked in horror to see that the hatchet had fallen onto Par's hand, mangling his middle finger and cutting his ring and pinky fingers clean off at the first knuckle.

Mar and San rolled off of Pab, who drew a breath, then let forth a howling cry of agony. He lay on his side beating his right fist into the ground.

San stepped forward and hoisted Pab by the shoulders to a seated position. "*Pawv,* lemme see—" Her plea stopped as Pab yanked his bleeding hand away from her. It took two stumbles and falls before his legs were ready to carry him away from the fire.

Watching him disappear into the night, San hawked a stream of blood to clear her mouth and powered through the pain and puffy lips to deliver her first clear word, "Asshole!" She spun around and aimed an accusatory finger at Mar, who was standing in a line with Des and Bri.

"Us? H-how the hell?" Mar stammered, baffled. "You started it. You attacked me."

San's finger moved to Bri. "*Er* . . . h-her. You're *meshed* . . . messing . . . you were touching her!" She was struggling for power in her words as pronunciation through a sore and bloody face. "*Tawking* her . . . clothes . . . off. Undressing. I saw you."

"I was helping her button her coat you freak," Mat roared. "Putting it *on*. If you had just waited, for one second—" Mar stopped, seemingly cut short by a surge of pain, his fingers gingerly dabbing the weeping burn on his neck.

San looked to Bri for support, but she remained at Mar's side, shaking as she looked at San, her eyes wide with terror.

It was enough to send her running blindly into the darkness, but San didn't make it far. The icy daggers inside had numbed her legs. She collapsed to the ground only a couple of yards away. Her vision was blurred by the swelling. The guilt inside was worse than her excruciating bruises. Unable to escape, she lay there in defeat, helplessly watching the huddle of shadows of the three moving frantically as they tended to Pab's stoic figure.

. . .

When Mar woke at daybreak he looked around the camp and saw that Pab was already up, nestled against a lone crooked tree, looking out at the rising sun. Mar walked over to him and put a blanket on Pab's shoulders. He didn't acknowledge the gesture.

Mar leaned against the opposite side of the tree, trying to rest his head but the branding on his neck was tender.

"Not like her. I was always the troubled son." Pab started mid-sentence, mid-story, but spoke as though Mar had been privy to the entire thought. "Mother would scold me and say, *mind your sister. Be like your sister. Follow her, you wicked boy.*" Pab heightened his tone to a squeak and playfully impersonated his mother, with a finger-wagging in the air.

Mar looked down at the thick bandage encasing Pab's hand, then forced himself to look away.

"They may not see me. But I see them. I see them hurt each other. That's all they seem capable of doing . . . " Pab's words quieted into a mumble.

Although he had only known Pab for a short time, it was disturbing for Mar to see him in such despair. From their first meeting, he had struck Mar as a spring of continuous energy and hope.

"And I thought *we* could do better. I thought we could be decent and kind. Thought . . . maybe that's why we were separated. To become *wema*." Pab spoke the last word in a hush, filled with sorrow and longing.

Pab dropped his hand back to his lap and stretched his three remaining fingers wide, then tensed his arms until they shook, and his veins popped as though he was trying to force his fingers to grow back. He tipped his head back and looked skyward then moaned like a wolf howling at the moon. "I thought that. I believed in wema. That we could be different. That we could be decent. But we hurt each other. All the same. We are not above, just hidden within."

. . .

San placed her head back on her pillow and closed her eyes when Mar passed back through the camp, gathering their packs and departing for the river hidden in the tree line.

She had been listening to the murmurs carried in the morning breeze from the warped tree. She could only understand fragments, but what she did hear only added to mounting guilt and shame that had been weighing on her heart, telling her it was time to go.

Eyeing Pab's back at the tree, San felt the urge to go to him and beg for forgiveness before she left. But something held her back and she told herself that if she wanted him to heal, then the only thing she could do would be to re-move herself from his life entirely.

There were two stray strands of hair dangling over Bri's rosy cheek. San wished to reach down and brush them behind her ear but didn't want to wake her. She couldn't bear to hear Bri cry and plead for her to stay, much less the alternative of silence or even commands to go—that was her greatest fear.

"*Rafiki yangu.*"

San spun, startled as though Pab had screamed at her.

Pab bowed his head and continued his descent by dropping to his knees.

"If you want to go . . . I won't stop you, San, but you have to say goodbye first."

When he looked up, San searched Pab's eyes for anger, but they held nothing but pity.

She also noticed, perhaps for the first time, how fluid and creamy the brown in his eyes was. It was hard for her to miss, now that they were held on her with steady and unmerciful focus. Not far from that, she saw his small round nose and sensed how this somehow added to the innocence of his grin. She had noticed this before, the same way she had observed the small gap in his teeth. These things stirred feelings in San that she despised more than guilt, and all she could do was run from them. San rounded into a sprint.

Moments into her retreat, San was crying, softly. Her tears came as easily as breaths.

A short open field stretched between the camp and the wood. The wind started whipping through the trees. With it, came the sound of her name in her father's voice. It hissed and stretched through the air.

"Vati!" she cried back and ran harder to get to him.

He was calling to her as he once did, back home, when she would be out in the field with the horses and the day was spent or the family's dinner was ready. He called to her, and San ran harder to get to him. More tears came, and her chest tightened because she knew she would never get home—no matter how fast or far she ran.

In the cover of the forest, her father's call stopped. But San escaped one torment only to be treated with another—visions of the three hounds. Flashes of gray and black fur blazed in the tight gaps of the trees. In the mud, San could see their tracks. The incline of the mountain started in the middle of the forest, making it harder for her to outrun them. Their snarls and howls bellowed from behind each tree, near and far.

When the trees ended, the grade grew steeper, and the ground was harder. The hounds stayed in the shadow of the woods, but another animal caught San's eye. Her horse galloped ahead, up the hill and around a craggily bend. It was a considerable distance away, but San recognized Anelie's brown hair and white socks. The magnificent beast was impressive in its speed and agility and San could do little to keep up.

"Anelie," San called, whistled, and smacked her lips, but her horse didn't come back to her. It galloped forward, out of sight.

San collapsed on the ground, rolled to her side, and cried openly. The pain wasn't physical; her body had not yet been spent; she could have climbed several more miles. Her spirit had finally given out.

San lamented the separation. She missed her family and finally let herself truly feel the distance. The longing to return that she had long neglected poured forth in abundance. Her defenses were finally down, and she was laid bare, utterly vulnerable to the whips of neglect that she had been evading for so long.

Her life was played out, though still images in her mind's eyes, and San was forced to reckon with the misfortune. She relived the storm that had toppled the barn; her anger had prayed for the destruction. There was the morning she had left home; this was the last time she would see her father and grandmother as they were. The years of solitude were even more painful to relive through her mind's eye.

Pab came to mind and San beat herself on the inside for what she had done. He had tried to help her. Despite her abrasive manner, he had persisted in providing her with the connection she wanted so desperately—he was her friend. And she had punished him for it. She had hurt the first person to see and care for her since she had been separated, crippled his body and spirit.

Racked with guilt, San lay on the uneven earth. She cried until her eyes couldn't give another tear. She then went to her back and stared, wistfully, at the sky that looked as though it could crash down at any moment. Feeling as though she were under attack, she tried to think of a place to go and something to do where she could find rest. But there was nowhere she could go. Every option seemed worthless if she were on her own. She no longer wished to be cast-off as a pariah. She wanted to belong. Being with the others was the only true shelter she could ever have, and she had evaded it.

"San!"

San feared that her father's voice had found her again. But instead, she soon heard beating steps and the breaking of brush, and Des came into sight. San was surprised to see him and astonished to find that he had come on his own.

His face was pale and beaded with sweat, and he was breathing hard. "There you are!" he gasped with relief, then bent forward, rested his hands on his knees, and gulped for air.

"You're fast." Des grinned. "Nice of you to wait for me." He huffed out a few laughs.

Des looked up at the mountain that loomed over them. "I've been eyeing this climb." There was a comfort in his voice that San did not expect. "Should be a spectacular view." He passed her and took a few steps up the steep grade, then looked back and nodded at San. "Come on. We're not even halfway up."

Des let out a long breath and straightened his back. Marching in place for a moment, he rotated his body at the hip to stretch his back. San realized that he was giving her a chance to get off the ground, but she didn't take advantage of it. She sheepishly turned and looked back towards where they had made camp.

"They can wait." Des's placid voice rivaled the storm brewing in San. "Come on. We should make it up before midday. Before the storms." San nodded and stood, then began to follow after him.

· · ·

She was forgiven and she had to forgive herself. That was the only way to stay together. To forgive and trust. We'll stay together. And it's a start to becoming whole.

X X

*T*he shabby pavilion provided little shelter from the monstrous downpour, and the group had to press tightly together on a picnic table to keep dry. Pab, Des, and San were seated on the table's top with Bri and Mar plopped on its bench, their backs to the three sets of knees.

Pab busied himself by carving with a pocketknife. It was difficult to see, but it appeared to Des to be the same collection of shapes, over and over.

San dried Bri's hair by ruffling it with a spare shirt and then began to braid. Her fingers passed the strands with ease, forming beautiful designs, yet she was never satisfied. She only scrutinized her creations a moment before opening her fingers, allowing the hair to fall, and combing it out to start again.

Des looked on, captivated, leaning over to watch San's fingers until his chin brushed against her shoulder. She froze, then raised an eyebrow at him. He was steeped in embarrassment, then started to scoot away but was surprised to see her raise her hands, with the hair spun mid-braid, toward him. He nodded ardently, slid closer, and took the soft strands in his hands. She took his hands in hers and guided his fingers while patiently instructing him through every turn.

Des tried to be gentle, despite San's insistence, worried that he would hurt Bri, but the girl didn't fuss in the slightest. She remained motionless throughout the pulls and tangled mistakes—she didn't seem to notice at all and stoically stared out at the rain.

The water cascaded off the roof in sheets, distorting the playground that stood only a few paces away. The wind blew the swings back and forth, taunting Bri's spirit to play. A deep scowl evolved on her face. Mar playfully mirrored this grimace. He reached over, traced the slant in her brow, brought his hand back, and drew the same arch on his face, his features forming to his touch like clay. Piece by piece, his malleable expression flexed as he traced and duplicated Bri's hardened frown. The transposed frown remained as he turned towards the veil of water running off of the roof but as he leaned into it, drenching his head, it was washed away. A smile appeared on the other side of the flood.

He pushed further until his shirt soaked through and stuck to his torso, then hunched his shoulders and rolled forward into a somersault.

Rising in the rainfall, he performed for his friends' amusement. A palm was raised to feel the rain, then pretended to adjust an invisible faucet with the other, until he was seemingly pleased with the temperature, and scrubbed himself with an invisible bar of soap as the others laughed encouragingly. He lifted his hands, stacked one atop the other then pretended to extend an umbrella and huddle beneath it. The wind picked up, and Mar incorporated it in his act, staggering around in mock shock as the wind tried to wrest the imaginary umbrella from his hands. They howled with laughter.

Bri charged through the sheet of water, her hair slipping easily from Des's grip. She pirouetted in the rain, spinning until she reached the plastic slide, then climbed the jungle gym.

San ventured out after her, kicked off her shoes, and sprinted forward. Mud and clumps of grass coated her shins. *"Owww!"* Her howl rang skyward as she bowed and then tossed her head back, hair flipping in a high arc.

Pab answered the call but Des held back, curious for a closer look at the carvings.

They were copies of the same basic shapes. In the middle, there was a waterdrop. Hugging its sides, two lines sprouted up. One was thick with several smaller curves shooting off. The other was thin, bare, and straight. Both split near the top into distinct branches. One branch from each met at the top of the carving, where the waterdrop started.

Des studied the carvings intently, trying to understand the meaning, but couldn't make any sense of it.

"Stand there and stare. You, there.

"Stand and stare. Look through?"

San started to sing, so Des gave up and joined them in the rain.

She shook two fingers in the air then brought them to her chest.

"We don't need your eyes. We'll steal an ear!"

The choir erupted in yips, cheers, and screams.

"Stand and hear if you cannot see."

The floodgates had opened, and the rain fell harder than ever, but none of them cowered. Mar drummed his palms on the slide, and a beat from the fat, hollow tube. Pab watched him, then took up two sticks and began to tap along the metal legs of the swing set. San took Des and Bri by the hands and they formed a circle as she continued her rhythmic chant. San had the most ballon in her dance, but the others did their best to keep up. Bri stared glowingly up at San, mouthing the words as she heard them.

"In the shadows, in the shadows of your empty towers,

"Of your empty towers, we will revel!"

The others emptied their souls in a resounding holler. *"Oh, we see how they tremble!"*

San feigned shock, let go of Des's hand and pointed at the sky. *"Stand there and hear, if you cannot see!"*

When San closed the loop again, Des felt a course of energy and passion tremble through the three of them, and his heart raced in the ebullient flow.

"Close your doors. Shut us out.

"But we won't knock or fight.

"All you have done is left us to the light."

Des and Bri stuck out their tongues and wagged their heads at the sky, joining San as she taunted the people for their mistake. *"Danke. Danke. Danke!"*

Des thought Mar was going to break the slide from its bolts, he was smashing his fists against it with such power. The booms of his drum matched the rolls of thunder.

"Stand there and hear, if you cannot see.

"And we'll tell you how great are we!"

Des felt like his feet would be lifted when his arms were raised for the final call.

"Rahirrem. Rahirrem. Rahirrem!"

. . .

The shopping cart was waiting for them on the curving sidewalk—their rendezvous spot after individual scavenging tasks. To keep it from rolling away, the front wheels were set against a mailbox at the tip of the cul-de-sac.

Pab and Des were the first to return. Night had fallen and only streetlights illuminated the neighborhood. The cart shifted as they filled it with the shoes, socks, and blankets.

Mar and Bri were the next to appear. Their haul consisted of mostly food, which they tucked into the folds of the blankets and stacked in the bottom rack of the cart. Mar had brought an empty duffel bag slung over his shoulder.

Other than that, the only pull that Pab noticed was a purple bracelet on Bri's wrist and a matching hairpin. The bracelet looked handmade—it could be important to someone. Pab feared that it could be missed. His instinct cried that this was reckless—even something so small could be personal and precious.

"Where did you get that?"

"A little kid's room," answered Mar.

"Do you think . . . that was good?"

"Why not?" Mar asked back.

"Maybe the child will . . . miss it."

"They never notice," Des joined in.

"Yes. Yet . . . the child could have loved it. It could have been precious to her."

"She had so many. A box full of them. A closet full. A room full!" Bri tried to justify herself.

"Yes? Yes. Then that is good for you to have."

The others were confused by his behavior but let it pass.

Don't take what is seen, Pab told himself.

They could take from the excess, but they should not exceed their reach. Taking something *seen* could breach the separation, as he had with Wallace, a story he hadn't told the others—not even San.

Only now was Pab beginning to understand what had occurred after taking Wallace's locket. The necklace was still *seen* by Wallace. Not in his excess, it was precious to the man and therefore Pab was not meant to interfere with it. He had come to this conclusion based on the great sense of fear and shame he had felt when Wallace had raged at him.

Pab wanted to tell the others this story, but a crippling caution overwhelmed this plan; he was unsure of how they would react.

Would they agree that it was wrong? That they were meant to remain separated.

Or would it only be a greater incentive for one of them to take something that could break the removal? Then what would be their punishment? Surely, not obeying the warning of experience would lead to more severe punishment than the anger of a feeble old man—Pab was certain that it would be much worse than that.

Another hour passed without San, which was surprising since she was usually the first to finish during their scavenging trips. There was some talk about going to look for her, but no one was certain how far she could have gone or which house she would be in.

They were huddled around the cart trying to come up with a plan to find her when Pab heard a soft cough coming from the middle of the street. She cleared her throat twice more until the rest of them turned and saw the single find San had returned with after her long absence—a girl. She appeared to be Bri's match in size and age, though her features were obscured by a curtain of long brown hair that was hung about her face and a scarf covering her neck and mouth. San introduced the girl as Wes.

"She's an adorable turtle!" Bri shouted in a giggle. Pab knew she meant this as a welcoming compliment, but the girl seemed to take offense, shrinking further into her layers.

Des took the top blanket from the cart, poured the food from its folds, then wound the tattered cover around his neck. "Well, if you are a turtle, then I want to be one too."

He dropped to his hands and knees and crawled up to the girl at a glacial pace. Pab shook his head at the bizarre sight. The girl seemed more curious than scared as Des came to squat at her side then began to nudge her elbow with his bowed head. His sunglasses slipped from his head and rattled on the pavement, and he picked them up sluggishly and placed them on the girl's face.

Wes remained pressed against San, the scarf slowly fell away, and she smiled brightly beneath the glasses. She was just reaching for Des when her hand recoiled at the sound of a bark.

"You should have talked with us before you brought her here."

The others stared at him with bewildered eyes.

"How many of you think—" Mar cut himself off, threw up his arms, and stomped off.

Wes shook with every angry step Mar made as he made his exit, disappearing around the side of the house. San muffled the girl's whimpers in an embrace, rubbed her shivering shoulders, then leaned down and whispered directly into the girl's ear. "Don't worry about Mar, Wes. He didn't mean it."

. . .

Des trailed after Mar at a deliberate distance, fuming at having been given the task of retrieving his irate friend. He found Mar sitting on a curb three blocks away. His head bowed, Mar sensed Des's approach and spoke as soon as he was in earshot.

"Of course I want to bring the girl with us." Mar already sounded defensive. "There have always been more. More like us." Mar's lips didn't appear to move. His grave features seemed etched in stone, all but his eyes, which blazed into the darkness. "We just haven't been looking for them."

Des didn't know where the words came from—he had not planned to respond but spoke with surprising confidence all the same, "Maybe we should have."

"Yes. But," Mar began again, "then *this* will end." There was a lot packed into Mar's few words. Their time together had Des well-versed in unpacking a novel from the selective and short phrases Mar would give when he was upset. "We need a place—our place."

Des heard what he was trying to say; if they were going to bring more in, it would be better to have a home. If their numbers would grow, they couldn't keep living off rations and fit in the spare spaces. And so their days of free wandering may need to end.

. . .

How many are there? How long has this been happening? How far has it reached?

Have I ignored them? Neglected them, as the people have. Been blind.

It's true that we may not have the same freedom. We are giving up the wandering, and there was something special in that. It hurts Mar to give that up. But he will soon know that this is best. And it's simply the price we will pay if we choose to belong.

XXI

At first, Pab thought the building was empty and possibly a potential site for their home. But then he heard music coming from the upper level and discovered that it was not abandoned, only closed, with some floors waiting for new tenants.

The door to the small studio gave the only light in the dark passage, giving the faint echo of music drawing Pab a more ominous tone.

The grand piano was in the far corner. The floor space was filled with an assortment of instruments and sound equipment. The walls were filled with speakers, shelves of records, and very strange squares of fabric with grooves. Pab held his breath like he was being pressed into a crowd, even though there were only three other occupants.

The teacher sat on the right end of the bench, her student at her side, perched atop two thin pillows. She poked at the keys, softly and slowly following her teacher's instructions. The woman played with her right hand as she bounced her left index finger from note to note on the stand's page. In a quiet hum, she counted in beats of four, patient with the child's learning and only breaking to assist when the girl's hands struggled to extend far enough for the chord.

The lid to the piano was propped, and Des was bent over the opening, watching the vibrating strings. He then moved to stand next to the teacher, reached over her shoulder, placed his hand on hers, and allowed his fingers to move with hers. This is how he found the rhythm. When he took his hand away, his fingers kept the energy, dancing in the air until he brought them down to play the keys, farther down the board. His accompaniment sullied the duets' harmony, but they did not notice and neither did Des. When the song ended and the instructor clapped gleefully for her student, who smiled bashfully, Des gave a quick bow himself.

The woman flipped through the booklet on the stand to find their next song, but Des noticed a guitar on a stand near the door and moved for it, hand reaching. Before he could cross the room, Pab snatched him by the wrist.

The lesson continued. The teacher and pupil kept their backs to the boys. Pab's knuckles went white, his grip more constricting than he intended, and Des had to yelp in pain to get him to let go.

"Oww! What are you doing?" hissed Des.

"Don't take what is seen." Pab blurted out.

"Seen? Don't take what is seen?" Des repeated it back to Pab with a skeptical squint. "This again? You mean they'll miss it?"

"Yes! Don't take it, if they'll notice it's gone."

"You know they never do." Des scoffed, shaking his head and glancing back toward the piano.

"They do . . . sometimes," Pab spoke softly, uncertain of how he was going to proceed.

"What the hell are you talking about?"

"There are rules to this, Des. We can take from the fringes of their world. But not something so near."

Des's face softened to a stunned expression and then to one of understanding. Pab thought this was strange.

He expected Des to be agitated, not sympathetic, but it seemed as though Des knew what he was talking about.

"How do you know?"

Pab didn't know where or how to start in his story, so he made a desperate move and started from Des's.

"A framtive! Like you did. I received a *framtive*."

Des had told them about becoming separated from Mar in the city and the vision that had brought them together—and the warning he believed had come with it. He called that vision, a framtive. Pab hoped he was using Des's word correctly.

"Pab," gasped Des, astonished that Pab used the term he and Mar had introduced. "Pab, what happened? What did you see?"

"In the *framtive*? The dream?" Pab sputtered.

"Yes!" Des exclaimed. "What did you see?"

"A hospital. Or maybe it wasn't a hospital. There was a bed. There was a man asleep in bed. And he looked sick." As Pab began to walk Des through his interaction with Wallace, he fudged the facts with fantastic elements and blurred the scene with prose.

Pab claimed he hadn't known Wallace, much less his name, and in his telling, it wasn't a locket he had taken but a locked box—contents unknown—because Pab could not think of a lie quick enough to fill it.

"I don't know why I had to take it. I just had to. I wanted it. And that's when the attack came."

"The man attacked you?"

"No. It was a beast. A horrid beast attacked me. It was asleep, but when I took the box, it woke."

Des's fixed and certain gaze gave Pab the impression that he was following the story to its farthest implications.

Pab continued, "The beast is what awaits us if we take what is seen."

Des didn't stop pacing, but his mind returned for a question. "What made the box different? What was inside?"

"It doesn't matter!" Pab waved his hands frantically. "It doesn't matter what was in the box. Wanting to know, being tempted to know was enough. Whatever was inside was precious to the man. To meddle in such things would be to step back on their side. We are meant to remain outside of the box."

Des stopped pacing. "You're right. My framtive came after Mar and I were tempted. There was this march. A movement. And we joined . . . just wanted to be a part of it. And that's when . . . it separated us . . . from each other."

"But you're back. Together."

"Yes. But now we know."

"We do. Yes, we do."

Des glared back at the teacher and student with disdain as though they had purposefully baited him with the guitar. "Don't take what is seen."

"Don't take what is seen," repeated Pab.

. . .

San was trying to be more amenable. That was the only reason she had agreed to search the towns for a home—a task that was already taking months—and had not been more outspoken about her preference to leave the people and their cities completely. If San had her way, they would not be inspecting abandoned buildings to convert into a home, they would be striking out into the country and starting from scratch. It was an absolute solution the others had unanimously denied, believing it too difficult to sustain themselves without the opportunity to salvage supplies from the people. She first tried to tell them how she, herself, had done just that for quite some time.

"There are more of us, now," Mar said in response, adamant that they needed to be well-supplied for the hundreds and hundreds that he was convinced would come.

"I could show you," San replied, restraining her tone and temper. "I could teach you how to hunt . . . and you'd see how I did it."

"Didn't you almost die?" Des asked, cynically.

The scoff shared between Mar and Des had ended the discussion, at least in their eyes, and San was left with Pab's soft compromise. "Maybe you can still teach us after we get settled—then, one day, we would be more prepared to follow you out there."

Mar was presently testing her patience again, kicking up dust as he paced across the garage and sighing louder than a siren. "Not as much space as the store."

Feeling as though they had found the best option the area could offer—the abandoned storefront in the old downtown square—Mar wanted to head back and gather the others. So he was throwing a tantrum when she, unconvinced that the store would be best, searched too long in the deserted automobile shop.

Mar threw his arms up and screamed, "There's nothing for us here. The store is our best option, and you know it!"

"There's potential," San nodded her head around the dismal place.

In truth, there was little to see, but prolonging Mar's wait was very satisfying. It took four laps of looking at nothing for him to catch on.

"You're stalling. Come off it! There's nothing here."

"Potential," hummed San.

Then she whipped the can of red spray paint from the pack at her waist.

The bead inside rattled, the can was nearly empty. She pressed down the trigger, held the can close to the wall, and sprayed. In one continuous motion, she drew the curves of the river, rising to its crest on the horizon. The can sputtered to an empty hiss. She shook it back to life, then made the finishing touches—two trees—one with curved branches and the other straight.

"What's that?" asked Mar, his aggravation seemingly dissipating.

"It's our sigil. We leave it when we find a place we like." With her finger off the nozzle, San mimed the action of drawing the symbol over again. "Our way of showing we were here."

"Pab drew it before . . . what are those shapes?" He tossed his hand toward the wall.

San answered slowly, "When Pab found me, I was dead . . . or something near it. I imagined a river. I was in a river that flowed uphill." San slowly swam her finger up the bend, closing her eyes, briefly swept up in the water's rush in her ears and current's tug in her stomach. "And at its crest were two massive trees. I mean truly massive— the size of mountains." She traced the lines that sprouted from the river's edge and split near the oval's top. "I call it the *axonis*. Pab says those trees, that river, this place were mine, or ours. A gift."

. . .

The old school building was the only one on the block without holiday decorations, disappearing into the darkness, and yet this brick edifice loomed over its neighbors and beckoned to Des.

One of the two dormers on the east side of the roof had buckled and caved inward. There was a hexagonal cupola tumbling at the center of the roof, topped with a bent weathervane that teetered. Cracks in the masonry were evident enough to be seen in the dull moonlight. The great, double-hung windows lined the front of the building—twelve on each floor. He could not find one that was not cracked, broken, or missing.

Still, he couldn't help but feel an affinity for the bulky beast that towered over its diminutive neighbors, stubborn against the changing trends in surrounding décor and persistent against the decay of time. He felt a commonality with the place as if the building could speak and sympathize. Like them, it was unwanted, disregarded, and overlooked.

"Have you been waiting for us?" whispered Des.

Busting in through a window, he flipped on a flashlight and crept forward despite a sudden foreboding shiver. A damp smell permeated. The sound of water dripping water echoed from different corners of the darkness. It felt like he was exploring a tomb or a cave.

A central corridor ran the full length of the school. Turning from side to side, his light faded down the hall, barely reflected in the windows of the side doors. The wide hall was barren, except for a few lockers and empty display cases.

The front half of the building was made up of classrooms, most of which were empty. Some had tables and chairs stacked along the wall. A few were full of boxes and crates, for storage. Boards were fixed to the walls with chalk and erasers left in the trays. There was a utility closet at either end of the hall.

He was surprised by the number of books remaining on the shelves in the classrooms and the library. The collection was primarily dictionaries, textbooks, and multiple copies of the same few novels. Their pages were tattered, and some slipped from their bindings.

Exploring elsewhere, a black cat with green eyes was discovered, painted on the walls above the backboard in the gymnasium. Long dark curtains were drawn across a stage that ran along one side of the court, opposite a four-tiered set of stands. The court appeared smaller than most that Des had seen. The two rims seemed too close, and both were missing the nets.

Through the windows behind the stage, he could see the shell of a bus sunk in the untamed grass of the recess lot, alongside a rusty metal slide, tilted merry-go-round, and cracked asphalt courts.

All he saw thrilled Des, but it was not until he reached the cafeteria that sat at one end of the first floor's corridor and found the long lunch tables, with a hundred seats ready to be filled, that he felt peaceful and resolute. "We're home."

. . .

Our castle. Our home. There's plenty of room for more to come. Like Ada. I now have a place for her. To find me. To find each other. All of us. We will find them. And they will find us. Our haven—a home for the Rahirrem.

XXII

*P*ab was awoken by Bri and Wes, both looking quite
pathetic as they rubbed their bellies and asked about
breakfast. With Des away on a reconnaissance expedition, the cooking rotation was thrown from routine;
Pab stepped in and prepared the morning meal in a flash,
and the family enjoyed it despite the persistence of yawns,
stretches, and nodding heads.

Afterward, Mar shirked his chores, and lumbered back
to his room, mumbling some small assurances that he
was just letting the dishes soak and they would be done
by midday.

The days' task then focused on recovering the school,
making it more comfortable, if only inhabitable. This list
consisted of the grimy hallway floors, the caving ceiling
in the classroom, the basement flooding, the unstable
stairs at the side entrance, and the leaks everywhere.

Pab decided to start with the stairs outside and work
his way in. Lumber was salvaged from a few busted tables
and rummaged from the attic. Mar wouldn't let Pab rip
anything from the stage or the scaffolding around the
gym, earnestly vowing to put the space to good use. Wes
assisted by holding boards in place as he drilled and testing the work with light bouncing.

At lunch, San prepared a smorgasbord of deli wraps
with toppings to each person's preference. An assortment of canned soups was heated in a backyard fire. Mar
spoiled the younger ones with bags of candy and cereals

added to the table, but San monitored the portions and scolded anyone who avoided the healthier option.

Early afternoon, the school was hushed to a whisper when everyone found a quiet place to read. The books they had discovered in the library had sparked a marvelous interest in literature and books had been added to the list of required supplies on scavenges.

The large leather chair tucked behind the desk in the principal's office was Pab's favorite spot, but on his way there he was distracted by a pair of voices coming from the library. San and Bri were cuddled on the floor, the younger girl wrapped in her lap with a book propped against her feet. He joined them but tried not to intrude on the lesson. San's finger inched across the page as a guide. Bri rarely faulted, demonstrating a growing comprehension of the written language so vastly different from her native tongue.

Bri's book detailed the turmoil of a meager family driving across the country with their entire belongings stored in a beaten car—a predicament Pab felt they could relate to. The story was interesting, but he was feeling drawn away by his own literary expedition. As such, he pushed himself up to his knees, only to feel a tug on his back. San clung to him with two fingers hooked on his shirttail. Bri was so involved in her efforts with the book that she didn't seem to mind whether he stayed or not. Still, Pab quickly slouched back onto his bottom, feeling quite embarrassed and guilty. He thought San may be sore at him for trying to leave, but then she leaned back against him, giving Pab some relief that she was not upset—but his racing heart didn't get much of a break.

Never taking her full attention away from Bri's progress, San propped her head on Pab's arm, occasionally flicking her eyes up at him. The way her brilliant eyes glistened beneath her long eyelashes made Pab's chest flutter, skin tingle, and legs go numb—he couldn't walk away if he wanted to.

After about two hours, everyone began to fidget in the stillness. It was quiet enough to hear the walls creak, almost as if the school was talking to them, begging for activity. Then a howl thundered through the halls; Wes was calling for a game. Everyone else gathered by the front door, counted with their eyes closed, and then howled back to tell Wes they were ready to hunt.

Mar and Pab bowed out after three rounds to work in the gymnasium on a separate project—Mar had written a story he hoped to perform and Pab had offered to assist with the preparations. Although Mar refused to reveal anything of the story, he had drawn several shapes to be cut—silhouette puppets. Pab listened to the instructions, doing his best to make the characters and sets the right size until the product matched Mar's imagination. There were also tests to be done on the lighting on different walls and at various distances.

San later joined them on the dark stage, sat between them, and watched as they worked by candle.

"Pick a song, Mar."

Mar grinned without taking his eyes from the light cast on the wall. "That one that repeats and repeats, *whispers from the waters* or something of that sort. I liked that one. The one Des made up. During that storm. So cold and wet, our teeth chattering, we could hardly sing."

"Somber choice, lad," San laughed.

Pab felt a twinge of jealousy, seeing San ask Mar first. "That one doesn't even rhyme." He felt foolish as soon as the words had left his mouth, but this and the jealousy

were gone before he could dwell on them as San leaned to
her left, putting more and more weight on Pab's side until
he toppled over. Then, laughing, she started to sing.

I was only a child,
When I first heard the whispers
    Watery whispers from the deep
They called from a cavern
Too dark for youth to enter
    Watery whispers from the deep
But now to find my truth
I answer their siren song
    Watery whispers from the deep
I sever my tether
Leap from the world I've known
    Watery whispers from the deep
They bid me further in
The cold tunnels down in stone
    Watery whispers from the deep
I climb without my sight
Follow the sounds to their source
    Watery whispers from the deep
Earth's cauldron awaits
Voices rise from boiling ripples
    Watery whispers from the deep
To hear how I knew them
I drink from the ancient well
    Watery whispers from the deep
There are many whispers
I only listen for one
    Watery whispers from the deep
I do not hear her voice
And my soul is satisfied

To know her sound is still with her

. . .

It was almost an hour after the library had closed and the place was completely deserted. The boy climbed the central spiral staircase, holding the brown paper bags in tired arms, then hustled by the rows of the general collection, and darted across a large room full of desks with computers. The screens were blank, but he could hear a soft hum of one left on. The boy then wove through a labyrinth of book nooks—twelve numbered cubicles with doors and walls that didn't quite reach the ceiling—until he came at last to the Special Collections room.

Wide windows made up two walls of the corner room, the others were lined with massive shelves, nearly touching the ceiling, and made of thick wood. Two additional shelves jutted from the wall into the middle of the room, leading to two high back chairs facing the windows. People came to the room so infrequently that at times it seemed as though the room had been forgotten. The books were carefully maintained by the staff but rarely visited.

As he came to the farthest row, he noticed many books had been knocked and jostled, disrupting the spaces and footholds that he used to access his nest atop the double-sided shelf.

He crouched down to place a bag on the floor and that's when he heard the sound of rustling pages from above. He froze and listened closer but heard nothing. He looked up; the bookshelf appeared taller than ever—it stretched away into the darkness.

The climb, which he had made many times, now required all his concentration, not due only to the extra weight of the bag stuffed inside his sweatshirt and the frequent stops he had to make to reposition the books, but also to the unexpected sweat on his palms that was quite profuse by the time he slapped the top of the towering shelf. He pulled himself up to see that his bed of blankets was in a bunch, papers scattered, and flashlight teetered on the edge.

By his size and the stubble growing on his chin, the intruder appeared to be in his later teens. He didn't look up from the drawing in his hand. "These're good," he whispered, tapping the edge of the shelf with one of the boy's pencils. "I'm afraid I dropped one, earlier." He chuckled, as if they already knew each other, then set the paper and pencil down gently onto the boy's pillow.

The boy removed the paper bag, placed it gently next to his stack of books—the only part of this nest that had not been disturbed—and scooted to the opposite end of the shelf.

"How do you sleep up here?" the stranger asked as he peered over the side. "I'd be afraid of rolling off." He then made a high-pitch whistle that sank and ended with a soft pop of his lips. "*Phew*, you and San can climb anything. You're like a couple of little monkeys," the stranger said, trying to project a sense of calm as his eyes tensely shifted from side to side and his shoulders were pressed firmly to the stone wall.

Without leaving his seat, the intruder kicked a long leg out, brought his foot down on the boy's bag, and began to drag it towards him. "Name's Des." He stated with cheer as if Tic had asked "What's yours?"

"Tic," answered the boy, before he could consider whether or not he wanted him to know.

Des nodded, then nabbed Tic's flashlights from the edge and reached inside the bag.

"You know you could take anything you wanted from that store, but all you want are finger paints." Des laughed more to himself. "But Tic, your drawings are very good."

"You like them?"

"Oh, I do, Tic. I do . . . and I know some people who would love to see them," Des began. "Would you come—come with me and bring your drawings?"

"There are more of ya?"

"Many more," Des answered casually, as though this was obvious.

Tic leaned away and had to brace his balance; his mind shattered by the prospect of more people like him. Ignoring Tic's bewilderment, Des held up a drawing. "Is this where you're from? That place. Is that supposed to be a castle?"

"Caisleán. Yeah . . . yeah. That's it." Tic's tone fell as he came back down from the soaring heights of resounding joy he had felt at the mention of more unseen people, suddenly stung with the lonesome weariness that came with thoughts of home. "They don't have castles, here."

Des's eyes widened. "Aye, they don't—but we do."

. . .

"There once was a grand land. Rich in beauty and magic." Mar had the entire story written down in front of him, but he hardly needed it—the words came fluently as he worked the puppets in front of the lights.

"In this land, there was a magnificent mountain range." Mar placed a long, jagged strip of paper in front of his lights, and the mountains grew on the wall. *"In its midst, there was the palmy village of Patrin."*

The applause of the four on the gymnasium floor echoed in the open space, making it sound like a great company had come to see the performance.

"Patrin. The name was given long ago. So long that its true meaning had been forgotten. But many who lived there believed it came from the name of the eldest and most ancient ganfolk—the magical and powerful people. You see, this village was special because it was home to a long bloodline of ganfolk, who protected the people, the village, and the blessed garden within it. The garden was the source of their power.

"Our story takes place in the days of the twelfth generation of those protectors. This descendent was a girl. Her name was Kya. She used her magic to protect the gift plant of the garden that provided fortune and protection to the village."

Mar placed the figure in front of the light, and the thinly-cut wisps of her hair waved as her image appeared on the wall. Wes gasped in awe, as if a real woman, with spell-binding beauty, had suddenly appeared in front of her.

"But first we must meet another who lived in the valley. His name was Ash. To all in the valley, he was the tailor's assistant, but more so, he was seen as an outsider." The scrawny boy Mar had created appeared on the wall beside Kya. *"You see, Ash wasn't born in Patrin. His mother was found by the gates, her baby in her arms, nearly dead, and though she was allowed entry, the villagers never accepted them as their equal. They were seen as carriers of misfortune."*

"Where's his mom?" inquired Bri with a hand in the air. Mar didn't have the time to make a puppet for that character but didn't want to pause long enough to explain this.

"One morning, Ash worked diligently on a patch and cloak for Patrin's favorite son, a young warrior, Ebb, who was to be honored at a festival that very night. A festival with food,

music, and dancing. Ebb was to be named as the village's chief protector. Furthermore, it was said that he was going to use the occasion to choose his bride. Everybody knew that he would choose Kya; he had fancied the ganfolk girl since they were young. And the entire village approved—that is, except for Ash."

Mar paused for dramatic effect; a series of whispers wondered what would happen next.

"Yes, our boy loved Kya. He had since he could remember. You can imagine, then how he must have felt as he stitched the cloak for the man who would marry the girl he loved."

Wes and Bri shared a groan of sympathy for the character.

"Ash finished the cloak and slowly trekked across the village to deliver it to the soldier when he spotted an unfamiliar horse tied in front of his mother's hut—she had a visitor— and she never had visitors. The village shunned her even as she lived in their midst. She was reclusive, usually unresponsive, and mostly considered a mute, only speaking to Ash and even that was on rare occasion.

Inside, he found his mother sitting in front of the hearth, wrapped in blankets. She did not acknowledge his arrival, staring blankly at the fire—Ash had grown accustomed to this. The visitor's back was to Ash as they tended to the cups on a tray and then to the pot and kettle, steaming over the low fire. When the guest finally did take down her hood, Ash saw that it was Kya. A heat burned in Ash's chest at the sight of her."

Mar moved Kya's puppet into the glow, facing the tall boy with straggly hair.

"Kiss her, Ash!" bellowed Wes, and everyone laughed.

"She offered a greeting, with a smile that couldn't be matched, told him that she had come for tea with his mother. Because it pained her to see. To see how his mother was ignored by the

others in the village. They sat together. And she asked Ash if he was coming to the dance at the festival that night.

"Now, Ash had never attended any of the village's festivals or celebrations. He always watched from afar, knowing that his presence made people uncomfortable. But when Kya pled with him to come that night, to dance with her, he decided that he could muster the will to go, at least for one dance."

The shadow puppet Mar had made to represent Ebb's band of horses was rough; it looked like a black, loaf of bread. He cringed at the sight of it, but the others didn't seem to mind. Mar tried to repay their attentive imaginations with a more robust voice.

"When Kya and Ash took walked outside the hut, Ebb was there. The young soldier, Ebb, with his riding partners. He had been waiting for his cloak, and when the tailor and delivery were late, he had come looking for the assistant. Ash could tell by the look on his face that Ebb was disturbed to see the woman he preferred walking with the town outcast."

A round of boos and jeers rumbled from the group and Mar knew they were about to get louder.

"Later, an hour before the festival, Ebb's frustration had consequences for Ash. The tailor was shutting the doors when Ebb pranced up on his prized pony. He demanded that Ash be punished, claiming that he had found a torn trim in his cloak. He produced the cloth for the tailor to identify and, indeed, there was a hole. Ash knew that Ebb had torn the fabric himself and he was truly being punished for being seen with Kya but the tailor wouldn't hear any of his words.

"To this end, Ash found himself sitting alone in the shop with needle and thread, carefully examining and redoing his previous work. He could see the glow of the lanterns and hear the music falling down the hill."

"Liar!" As Mar had predicted, the small audience erupted in a monstrous fit of rage at the injustice and misfortune that he had described. "Cheat!" They pounded on the floor and tossed everything they could grab at Ebb's image on the wall.

" *'You gave me your word on a dance,' stated Kya, who had come alone to fetch Ash."*

As loudly as they had heckled, the four audience members now cheered with even greater energy and enthusiasm.

"Ash tried to apologize and explain the cloak and his master's orders. All the while, he tried harder still to cover his watering eyes. She asked him to come to the dance with her, but he refused, not wishing to disobey his master's orders. Kya simply reminded him again that he had promised her a dance. 'Can you hear the music?' asked Kya softly, and Ash nodded. So the two danced in the shop, and as they did, Ash gathered the courage to ask if Ebb had made Kya his bride. Kya smiled and shook her head. 'No, and he wouldn't be able to . . . if someone else marries me first."

Their joy reached a fever pitch, and Mar decided that he would leave them wanting more. "Now, is that not a beautiful place to leave our friends? Huh? Let's leave the rest for another night."

· · ·

Soon we will fill every room in the school. Our family will be so vast. San, Pab, Mar, and me—we four are the leaders, and the kids will look to us. And we will not fail them. We won't break. We won't lose each other.

XXIII

The theme park's paths were chaotic and congested. Parents herded their children in pods or pushed them in strollers. The little ones mixed and mingled, making it difficult to tell who belonged with whom. Adding to the gridlock were salesmen loudly hawking souvenirs from their carts and brightly-vested teenagers beckoning them to try their hands at ring tossing and balloon popping. Flashing lights and buzzing noises competed for Mar's attention, but he did his best to focus on the boy, whom he had seen slip through the gate without any alarm or hassle from guards and other adults—the first indication that he was unseen.

Taking advantage of the separation, the boy never had to stand in the queue but just hop out after a ride and wait for an odd-sized party and empty seat. The delay was never long, the boy would often ride several rounds in a row, which eventually started taking its toll on his stomach that had been filling with cotton candy and soft drinks. Mar laughed under his breath as the boy staggered from the coaster's platform and hurled two prolonged streams over the ledge.

A water ride was chosen as a suitable intermission, allowing his stomach to settle, and Mar decided that it was time to start his introduction—but first, he would have some fun.

A huge conveyor belt carried large, circular rafts through the loading dock where riders were helped in by a woman in waterproof overalls and rubber boots. Each raft had six inward-facing seats centered around a metal wheel for the riders to turn.

The cycle was plentiful with many rafts being sent into the simulated rapids with only three or four seats filled.

The teenagers ahead of the boy looked to be about Mar's age so he jumped in with them, pretending the duo was a trio. The woman in squeaky boots didn't offer the boy her hand, passing over him to help a grandmother and her granddaughter—the last in the queue.

The other two parties started conversing, and Mar did his best to sound interested and involved, laughing with them and joining in their anticipation as the raft was lowered into the water. The boy looked at Mar and then away again, assuming the forced distance in his eyes was as natural as the rest.

Mar focused on the smallest things around the raft— the grandmother's watch, the girl's water-soaked shoes, the wheel in the middle—anything to keep from looking at the boy. He didn't want to end the joke, too soon.

He raised his hands with the strangers when the raft was taken down a small drop and even reached in the water that was pooling at their feet to playfully slap water at the girls, who were already laughing and splashing each other.

When the raft entered a tunnel, water poured over them. Their joyful screams echoed in the darkness. Just as the light appeared at the far end of the tunnel, Mar put his face next to the boy's, grabbed him by the arm, and bellowed, "GOT YOU!"

The boy yelped and fell out of his seat. Fortunately, he tumbled toward the center instead of falling out of the raft.

Breaking into daylight, the raft was rocked by another wave, and the boy was thrown hard against the metal wheel and then fell back into his seat. Mar wailed with laughter while the boy stared at him as if he had bloody fangs and pointed horns.

"I—am sorry." Mar gasped for air and his voice cracked. "Couldn't resist." The overwhelming smile on his face made his sympathy less convincing.

"You can see me?"

"Obviously."

The boy looked as though he might be sick again, and Mar inched away, but all the boy came out with was a question—or half a question. "All this time?"

The ride reached its end, the raft reached the conveyer belt again and was lifted from the water.

"You're like me? They can't see you either," the boy asked, gesturing to the other four as they got up and stepped off the ride. The boy and Mar kept their seats as two new passengers came aboard, though Mar had to switch to another before getting sat on.

"My name is Mar. I was sent for you."

"Who sent you? How do they know about me?"

"Well, not you *specifically*," responded Mar, raising his voice over the excited screams of their fellow riders. He flashed his eyes at them for rudely interrupting the conversation. "There is a larger group growing. A home for people like us. And we are taking turns, going out to look for more. I found you and thought you might want to come back with me."

"To stay with you? Eh, no."

"Really? What else you got to do?"

"Go anyplace else. What kind of place is it?"

"It's an abandoned school, but we think of it more as our castle."

"A school! Boring. I'm separated so I don't have to be stuck in there."

"The others would like to meet you. They'll be glad I found you."

"I didn't want to be found. I can do it all by myself."

"Do what?" Mar asked but then had to pause and appreciate the similarity. It was like meeting a younger version of himself—angry, combative, and out to win. "At least come for a day or two. So you know who we are and where to find us."

"Wasted your time, Bar," sniveled the boy, sneering as he intentionally mispronounced Mar's name.

The boy turned his back for the remainder of the ride.

When the ride pulled into the station the boy scrambled out of the raft.

It had been eight months since they discovered the school—which they had dubbed Caisleán. In that time, this boy was the second removed child they had found. Considering that gathering a family was the purpose of the home, he knew the others would want him to give more effort, to run after the scared child, to convince him to come. But Mar had been put off by the snobbish response. He took a third ride by himself, suddenly feeling sorry for Des for having to deal with this kind of pointless combativeness.

However, when Mar finally left the ride's dock and walked down the exit ramp, he found the boy waiting there for him, arms crossed, looking more pathetic than stern. "Hig." Mar did not respond, still surprised that he had inadvertently called the boy's bluff by not chasing after him. "I'm guessing you want to hurry back home."

Mar smirked, gestured at the rest of the park, waiting to be explored, and said, "No hurry."

. . .

Their closets were bare, the trunks emptied, and the beds stripped; every stitch of cloth taken and repurposed in the library—a grand fort that consumed the room.

The bookshelves provided a suitable framework for the halls and rooms of the miniature castle, with blankets pulled between their tops like canopies. Only one of the library's double doors could be opened; the other was jammed shut, holding up a blue sheet, parallel to the stone wall, and another draped overhead. Following this entrance hall, Pab had to crawl to fit through the next tunnel, leading to a central hub. The overlapping slips were tied to the ceiling at its middle. Here, he could stand and observe several other passages and smaller tents. A sign was pinned to the cloth overhead: *No Boys Allowed.* He recognized that it was San's handwriting and chuckled to himself.

"San!" Pab called. "Where are you?"

Her response was faint, indistinct, but clearly not within the fort. It came from the hall.

They were supposed to be with the rest of the family, in the old bus outside, ready to go on their routine scavenging trip. He had come back for her when he discovered the fort.

"Where?" Pab asked again, exiting the library.

"102."

Pab followed the muffled voice to the classroom.

"I saw your fortress. No boys, huh?" Pab called as he skipped down the hall and found the classroom. The numbers were faded on the closed door.

San laughed from inside, "Oh, that is the start. We will get more sheets, and we're going to expand. Soon, it will spread to cover the entire first floor, maybe even both."

Pab smiled as he reached for the door handle. The lever had been locked and didn't budge, but the door had not been fully closed so it still opened to his push.

"Don't worry. We'll leave you boys the basement," San's voice continued as Pab walked into the room, which was awash in the sunlight streaming through the large open windows. He froze. There in the shadow of a diaphanous curtain hung to divide the room was San, shirtless and removing the bra straps from her shoulder.

The door hinge squeaked, and San looked up and yelped, then yanked her arms up to cover her bare breasts.

Pab stumbled backward into the door that had swung back and closed behind him. He covered his eyes, bowed his head, and slapped the wall behind him, feeling for the knob. His heart raced, pounding in his ears, but that was not the only sensation that was making his head dizzy. Although a rapid exchange of apologies flashed through his mind, not a single word made it out; his tongue was tied in knots. Sweat dribbled down his temple and the air suddenly felt scorching.

Pab's clammy three-fingered hand finally found the handle, but he did not make his exit. The heightened stirring within him commanded him to remain in the room, in the sensation, for a second longer.

His request to stay was unintentional, subliminal, almost instinctual—Pab would not have had the courage to speak it.

She spoke first, just his name. And the longer he remained, the more he came to feel like she was drawing him in—an invitation he was very hesitant to obey.

"Pab." His name sounded like a lyric from one of her sad songs.

There was a steadfast plea in her voice, as though she had taken a step out and was asking him to follow.

Aroused and petrified, Pab answered by sheepishly lifting his head to face her, but his eyes were averted.

"Pab."

San's arm fell away from her chest. She lowered her hands to her sides, where they swayed weightlessly, as a breeze wafted through the window and rippled her hair. Her fingers lifted and touched a birthmark near her navel—its shape reminded Pab of an arrowhead.

Pab was filled with fright, evident in his awkward and anxious demeanor.

San, on the other hand, was calm and assured.

The space between them somehow, inexplicably, felt a hundred miles long and simultaneously nonexistent.

Her eyes were steadily piercing into his, unwavering despite her vulnerability. Within them, Pab found her hurt and anger and drive for survival, which he knew all too well. Yet there was also her warmth and tenderness and lonesomeness. It was the culminating sensation of truly taking in her exposed presence that completely overwhelmed Pab.

"Pab! San!" Bri's call sounded miles away. "San! Where are you? Let's go!"

San's eyes went wide as she rushed to gather up the clothes. Pulling her bra and shirt on, San's eyes finally released and left Pab. They did not return to him as she hurried from the room, brushing by his arm and out the door.

. . .

Des steered the half-full cart around and started back toward Caisleán. His haul barely met the essentials of his assignment and only one of the special requests. He didn't care. He was regretting having come to the far neighborhood. The issue was not the available supply, but the condition of the things he had to choose from. The neglect the people had toward their things made him feel more than pathetic, foraging through their leftovers.

The cart's wheel was caught in a crack in the sidewalk cement when he heard the shattering of glass behind him. He spun around but saw nothing out of the ordinary—the houses and street remained still.

A second smash narrowed his focus to a particular house, but the neighboring windows remained empty. And no one came out to see about the noises. Des quickly connected this kind of disregard to that which was typically reserved for those unseen. He felt a twinge of excitement, thinking that he may have stumbled upon another who was separated.

The front door of the two-story house seemed to be slightly off-centered with the rest of the house, but it could have been an illusion due to the wayward tilt of the roof extended over the cement porch. There was one window on each side of the front door. Des could spot shadows through drawn shades. One shadow grew larger as the noise grew louder, and the front door burst open with a force that seemed surprisingly strong for such a little girl. She slammed the door shut behind her. Both hands pressed on the storm door, she planted her pink striped socks in a wide stance, bracing for some unimaginable impact. But nothing came.

Panting, she hung her head. Messy blonde hair fell around her face. Des stepped forward, brushed her hair aside, and studied the young girl.

She could not have been older than eight or nine, with spindly limbs, a gaunt face, and a shirt so long that it reached her knees. The baggy sweatpants made her look even frailer.

"Shut it!" This demand came from across the lane, a man in the window was shouting at the girl and whoever was making the noise inside. Des looked around at the surrounding houses and watched as more appeared to peek out doors and windows, shout some fowl words, and then close their homes to the noise. He sighed. The girl wasn't like him—she was seen.

The window to the left of the front door flew open. Its frame would not stay up on its own and the burly man had to hold it with his shoulders when he poked his head out. The lack of screen allowed him to lean farther out and berate his neighbors to mind their own business. While his fury was concentrated on the other houses, the girl released the door and ran toward the driveway alongside the house and hid on the opposite side of a car.

"Come back 'ere, g-girl!" His shout was disrupted by a burp that stopped in his throat.

Des left him shouting at the front step and walked toward the car but the girl had already moved on to the next hiding spot. It was a good choice because she seemed to disappear; even Des could not see her at first and neither could the man who came to the edge of the porch, peeked over the car, cursed under his breath, and went back inside.

Des noticed rough tracks in the garden in front of her neighbor's house, leading to the lattice beneath the front deck. A section of it was loose, Des could see where it had been pulled away, displacing the soil in a broad sweep. He squatted in the garden and peered through the gaps in the pattern. It was difficult to see the girl, only one eye blinked from the dirt; she had burrowed far and deep, but he could hear her sobbing.

. . .

She wants to be like us—but she is not. To be seen, for her, means to be hurt. She would love to be invisible. She wants our separation—but it has not been given to her.

XXIV

Foot traffic filled the teeming plaza, particularly congested in the open-air atrium surrounded by three of the tallest buildings in the metropolis. Strips of hedges and flower beds lined its perimeter as well as cut toward the center, where a massive black stone fountain caught Mar's attention amid the lunch rush.

The female statue with a flowing robe stood with her hand raised over her head. From her palm came the spring. The shower came upon smaller statues, children at the tails of her robe. Some held cups to be filled; others held small animals to let them drink from the sitting water that circled the woman. Mar stepped over the knee-high stone ring that enclosed the fountain and waded up to the statue of the woman, knelt next to the children, and let the water wash down his face.

Mar observed the courtyard from within the fountain, using it as an overdue shower. The dirty clumps in his soaked hair dissolved. Each time he puffed, spewed and scrubbed his face, there was less of a crowd to see. The courtyard was emptying quickly as the midday rush was finishing. The people were returning to their workstations inside. The benches were mostly vacant. The trash bins were filled. The nearby café staff was clearing its outdoor tables. Slowly, the rumbling noise died to a mellow babble.

Refreshed, he clambered out of the fountain, clothes heavy with water, then stood dripping on the courtyard pavement, still marveling at the mother.

A hand patted the toes of his shoes; Mar waddled back, startled, flinging water from his clothes as though he were a mutt drying itself, the spray soiling a spectacle of colorful. The chalk mixed and its colors faded in his wake.

These colors were a part of a larger picture being formed. The farther he moved away, the more clearly he was able to see it. The picture encircled the entire fountain, and Mar had to stand atop one of the cement benches to keep from soiling more of it. Although it was lacking any recognizable image, the drawing was mesmerizing. The boring gray of the cement was being transformed into an unyielding array that seemed to move and flow on its own.

The young woman was kneeling with her head bowed low, near to the pavement; her clothes, skin, and hair were powdered with a rainbow. She gave her entire body to the creation. She swayed and flung her body with a rhythm. There was no hesitation or contemplation. Always in motion, she never stopped to consider what to do next. It was as if the shapes and designs were forming themselves and she was trying to keep up with their music.

He wondered if she would ever acknowledge her sole audience. He knew he had gotten her attention when he was dripping on her work, so she must have been able to see him. And yet, she never paused to peek over to his bench.

As the girl reached out, a passerby stepped on her hand causing her to wince in pain. Mar scooted forward to offer comfort.

"Hurt?" She heard him. Mar could tell by the way her head turned. But she ignored the pain and his question and was already back to work.

"I wish they could see this." Mar immediately felt foolish. He hated the way his voice rose and quaked.

When she was done, the young lady hurriedly gathered up what was left of her chalk piece, stretched her neck from side to side allowing Mar to catch a glimpse of her face for the first time—she was stunning.

Her dark eyes radiated strength and allure. A minuscule mole perched on her cheek, to the right of her nose, caught Mar's stare. She flashed a radiant dimpled smile, but it quickly faded into stoicism.

The girl was about Mar's age, probably a bit older, but he found her intimidating—he felt painfully plain in her exotic presence.

The girl clapped her hands, brushed them on her pants, and made to leave. Mar's mind raced as he searched for something—anything—to say. His name was all he could manage to blurt. "Mar."

She finally looked at him, Mar was petrified as her gaze fell to the branding on his neck and bashfully clapped a hand over it. Closing his eyes for a settling breath gave her a chance to disappear.

. . .

San was sitting next to Tic and Bri in the otherwise empty cafeteria, eating a late-night snack of rather stale biscuits and jam by candlelight, when a tremendous crashing noise came from overhead, followed by a long groan that resounded throughout the building like they were in the hull of a stressed ship.

The cupola had become dislodged—that was San's guess—it had always had an alarming tilt.

Briskly jogging from the table, San called over her shoulder at the youngsters to get back to their room before pushing through the double doors and into the main corridor. As she passed the first room she heard a small voice, Wes asking what the matter was. San smiled reassuringly, told her everything was fine, waved her back to bed, and continued down the hall.

Des and Pab were huddled outside the central office, San joined them in their debate of whether it was safe to stay inside with the roof sounding like it could fall in.

Then came the theories about what was making the sound.

"Someone's in the attic!" shouted Hig startling San from behind; he sounded scared but more excited by the prospect of danger. "Could be intruders. What are we going to do about them?"

"No. I think the cupola collapsed. Or maybe one of the chimneys," San proposed, dismissively.

"The what?" Hig's head tilted to the side and then up to stare at the ceiling.

"The small domed thing with the weathervane."

"But the sounds are moving." Des pointed down the hall, farther into the darkness, and then brought his hand back to the ceiling over their heads. San was not sure if her mind was playing tricks but there was a sense that the creaks were moving.

"How would someone get up there?" asked Pab.

"*Why* would they even want to?" added San. "No. Those are not footsteps."

Hig and Des ignored their questions and logic and began to formulate a plan, that quickly became quite elaborate. Des listed reasons why the intruders were there. Hig strategized their defense, how they would fight back.

The noises overhead stopped suddenly, everyone froze, and looked at the ceiling in unison, listening, but the roof finally seemed to be at rest.

"There. Can we stop this nonsense?" San asked sternly, flipping her hands toward the three boys.

"The roof was in poor condition. It may have given." Pab gently patted the wall next to him, reminding San of the way her father would pet his weary horses after a day in the pasture. "We'll stay on the first floor tonight and check out the damage in the morning."

Des nodded, satisfied, and agreed that everyone should try to sleep. They decided upon the library and began splitting off to gather bedding from the first classrooms.

San started in the opposite direction, toward the side exit, until Pab stopped her. "Where're you going?"

"Going for a walk. Doubt any of us will get back to sleep tonight."

"Don't go up there. We'll see about it early, at the break of day."

San was slightly perturbed, given the fact that she had been seriously considering climbing to the attic and didn't like to be told what to do, but she also found Pab's tired voice and pleading to be adorable, and this squashed her stubborn spirit.

"Think the intruders will get me?" San teased. "Maybe I'll join them." Pab squinted and frowned. San winked then slowly raised her arms and a knee into an exaggerated runner's pose, he took her arm, and she playfully pretended to get away, gradually allowing his gentle tug to pull her in closer. "Trust me. I'm just going outside. A quick check. I'll stay on the ground."

But Pab was persistent. "I can't stop you from leaving. But—first, you've got to say goodbye."

Pab leaned forward to kiss her, but San was afraid that the others would come back out, so she pulled away and gave him a small smile, then hurried down the hallway and out the door.

San walked out onto the front sidewalk and looked at the roof. She was surprised to see that the cupola was still attached. The angle of the chimney's tilt may have sharpened and, even in the poor moonlight, there were clear gaps and bends in the roof, but she wasn't sure if those had already been there.

Tall grass and weeds consumed the backlot, she couldn't see much of the play equipment as she rounded the building, except for the basketball hoop and old bus, which she decided to climb for a better view.

She was nearly there when something rushed through the grass behind her. It was gone or hidden when she turned around; nothing could be seen between her and the school. She watched the grass for the slightest split where the thing could be crouching.

Her body tensed at the pounding of approaching feet or paws, again behind her; their tempo quickened and then released. She scrunched her shoulders and braced for the leaping attack, but none came.

After some breathless, silent moments, there was a loud metal pop as something landed on the bus's shell. San dove into the grass, her hands instinctively grasping for her knife and hatchet, though she had not carried them on her person in quite some time.

It had been a long time since she had been on the hunt or felt hunted and San's instincts were rusty and torpid. She had to continuously remind herself to stop moving and to focus on the essentials. Realizing that she had little to defend herself with, San concentrated on mapping the best route of escape. The abandoned school bus was in the far corner of the lawn; she was closer to the building than she was to its rusting shell. If the predator was heavy enough to bend the hood and chassis in such a way, then she hoped that it would be slow—at least slow enough for her to make it to the gymnasium window. But this was a desperate assumption.

She rolled onto her back and began to sit up to see what she was up against, initially cautious to stay low and concealed, but once she got a glimpse of what was on the bus, all regard for safety vanished—she couldn't believe her eyes. Out of spiking fear and sheer bewilderment, she pushed herself forward to her knees.

The roof creaked under its massive weight. Its rear legs resembled a lion's and long claws jutted out of its paws like bony fingers. A tail ending in a narrow spike whipped through the air. There were wings. And within the tempest of feathers, San could barely make out the head. The mouth opened, the animal bayed an ear-splitting cry, and San pressed her hands over her ears to muffle the sound, curled into a ball, as small as she could become.

This was the end for her; San was sure of it. A memory sprang up and San embraced it—hoping for some refuge from reality. Her father, grandmother, and another woman—whom San assumed to be her mother—were standing at her side. San tried to cling to the woman, but she pulled away, repulsed by something about San. The memory was too real, too painful, and San retreated from the place her fear had taken her—there would be no sanctuary.

But she was not attacked. And when the noise of the animal's call and her crying faded, San stood again. The animal was gone.

. . .

Des watched the girl as she sat at the edge of the bed wearing her backpack, earnestly waiting for the school bus. Her small fingers brushed her hair and then the few strands left on her favorite doll, mouthing the number of strokes, as she worked through the tangles.

Des had lost count of the times he had visited her but it was enough for him to know her home, family, and daily life well.

Zoe—he had given her the name. She had her own, one that her real family had given her, but Des didn't feel it fit her, because she didn't seem to fit with her family. Her brother and father were rough and wretched, but Zoe was gentle and sweet. Des thought of himself as a more appropriate brother.

And though she was a quiet, timid girl, he couldn't help but marvel at her incredible strength and resilience.

Her father was brute of a man, hard and cruel, who meted out insults and beatings as if they were candy at a parade, and while her brother didn't directly contribute to Zoe's misfortune, his apathetic behavior was just as horrid, in its own way. He did little to nothing to defend her from her father's outbursts, or even to draw the man's eye from Zoe.

And yet despite this, she adored her brother.

Zoe's brother stayed away from the house whenever possible, and most days, Zoe was left alone with her father, whose name Des had also replaced with something to match his inhuman, formidable spirit: Runach.

Zoe avoided her father when she could. When he couldn't be cleared, she tried to appease him by removing other inconveniences. She cleaned up after him and cooked meals with an efficiency that was surprising for her age—doing everything in her power to keep the smallest annoyance at bay.

Runach was also a study in extremes. He could be cruel one day, warm and attentive the next.

On the good days, he would wake her up with the smell of pancakes and bacon for breakfast, drive her to school, and let her choose the radio station. Instead of splitting off to their rooms, her dad would insist upon eating at the table or in the front room, like a "proper family." He may even let her sit in his chair in front of the television.

The stains in his teeth were concealed in his sideways smirk. The same rasp in his voice that accented the curses also found its way into his infectious laugh. The calloused, rough hands would reach to stroke her arm or tickle her sides, and Zoe would flinch away from the unfamiliar intent, signs that the malicious Runach was brimming under the surface.

Sure enough, she was right to be wary. On nights following these shifts, the man seemed to have a proclivity for Zoe to share his bed. He would earnestly plead and persist that she did not sleep in her bed. Des could never bring himself to enter the man's bedroom or stay in the house at all on those occasions. Though he wanted to watch over her, the touches and abuse he imagined transpiring in the man's bed were too horrific for him to witness. But Des would be quick to return the day after—as soon as he could.

And on that morning, the house was empty. The two men had already gone.

"It is clear, Zoe," Des told her with a smile, even though he knew she could neither see nor hear him. He wished that she could. He wanted her to know that he was there, hoping that he would somehow ease her fear. He sat with her until the bus arrived, at which point she stowed her favorite doll in her backpack and hurried out the door.

. . .

We are the Rahirrem. *And we're wema—or whatever you want to call it. But . . . Zoe could be, too . . . so, why us? And not her? What is it that's in us, that led us to be unseen? She deserves to be, she wants to be, but she's not, and never will be. Zoe's already beyond the age of separation.*

XXV

"Not quite. The wings were larger. So were the legs. Larger." Impatient, San grabbed the chunk of graphite from Tic's smudged fingers, drew over his work, and blocked the outline of the beast's features. Tic winced as her haphazard scratches marred his meticulous attempt to create a visual to accompany her story. The rest of the group had abandoned their lunches, half-eaten, and were crowded around them at the end of the table, listening to San's words and watching the animal appear on the page.

Des, who was the only one who hadn't left his seat, stared forward and pensively picked the last crumbs from his plate, his mind wandering across town—to Zoe.

"A bird?" Bri asked with her nose inches from the paper on the table.

"Birds don't have legs like that," Pab responded.

"Maybe if there was more than one animal," suggested Wes.

San shook her head. "It was one creature. Like nothing I have ever seen before."

A storm of curiosity—*"Think it'll come back?"*—simmered in whispers that were passed within the circle—*"We could catch it!"*—and then, building energy until it spilled over into shouts that interrupted Des's daydream—*"Too big. If it scared San, then we should leave it alone."*

Des eyed the lively deliberation with disgust.

"What do we name it?" Mar proposed with a smile.

Des bristled. San's monster story felt trifling to him—a figment of her imagination. His problem was real. Zoe was real. And even though Des had not spoken to anyone about it, he somehow felt slighted when their concern was placed elsewhere.

"I did. I call it the abaphim." San squared her shoulders and her body rippled with delight.

"*Aba*-what? You should leave the stories to Mar." Des did not intend for this to come out so loud, loud enough for the chatter to hush in response.

San barked back, "Don't believe me?"

He tried to keep his mouth shut, but couldn't help himself and scoffed, "I'll check under the beds and in the scary attic."

"Why can't this be real?"

"Stop filling their heads with fantasies." Des waved his spoon around the group, who avoided his eye-contact with him and San, wishing to stay out of their spat.

"Just because you didn't see it."

"I didn't see it because it doesn't exist!" The heat in his chest gave way. The aggravation, brewed by how helpless he was to Zoe, finally had an outlet.

"So you say."

"Mar and I went all over. And we never saw—"

"You went from city to city. I was the one in the wilderness."

"Telling yourself fantasies and imaginary friends to keep yourself company."

"Fantasies? We are invisible to the people. Can you explain that?" San slapped her hand on the table and swiped the paper to her chest, protecting it from Des. "No, you can't! So who are you to say there are no other things. Other things they can't see but we can."

Suddenly, a howl from the hall echoed from the hall. Heads spun toward the entrance.

"Greetings, my faithful and flea-ridden wolfpack," laughed Pab, opening the double doors just enough to poke his head between. He scratched the hair behind his ear and licked the back of his wrist like it was a paw. When Tic started to giggle, Pab looked up in mock surprise, smiled, and said, "We have a new pup."

Pab pushed open the door to his left as though there were someone else waiting but the space beside him was empty. Pab looked back down the hall and started whispering to whoever was there.

Des could see the child's shadow and for a moment, he let himself believe it was Zoe. He imagined she stepped into the light, doll in hand, then joyfully raced into the cafeteria. The others welcomed her with celebration. Her presence seemed to brighten the entire room and stirred smiles all around.

Des rose from his seat, ready to be the first to welcome his little sister home, but her image faded, disrupted by the boy who shuffled into the room. He took her place and stole the light from the room.

"Loc," Pab placed a hand on the top of the boy. "This is your family."

His words brought the others to cheer, but they burned Des. He hated hearing the welcome and applause that should have been for Zoe.

. . .

"It was not long after they had announced their engagement—to the shock of the village and dismay of Ebb—that Kya came to the shop and told Ash that there was a beggar at the gate with rags for clothes and a wooden leg. And she asked if he had the extra fabric for a blanket and if he would mend the man's rags.

"*Many such migrants had made their way to Patrin's gate, but very few were allowed in. Citizens were able to pass food and resources through special portals in the wall. But they were not allowed to open the gate. Kya took pity on the old man, giving him bread and water, each day.*

"*One day, when the sun just began to rise, its light was muted by a menacing storm. It brewed in an instant, out of the cloudless sky, and swept against Patrin's magical walls but did not breach them.*"

Mar turned on the fan, raised his voice, and sprinkled confetti-sized bits of paper over his puppets to simulate the snow as he read.

"*As the storm roared outside of Patrin's walls Kya could think of nothing but the old man and with pure love in her heart, she used her magic to open the gate. She and Ash welcomed the beggar in, but as soon as the ragged man took Ash's hand and stepped foot inside the wall, he . . . transformed.*"

Mar rolled his voice into a growl. He lit a match and set the feeble character ablaze.

"*Where the old man had once stood there was suddenly a column of fog—a black mist that enveloped Kya. Ash couldn't hear her, but she appeared to be screaming, her voice trapped in the fog with her. Ash rushed forward to enter it, only to have the mist transform again.*"

As the small fire died down, Mar produced the largest and most detailed figure he had ever made—a long, slender monster with a cloak, hood, and hooked fingers.

"*Many of Patrin would later say that this villain was a dark creature. Some would say he was hideous with fur and claws—Ash would say different. He saw this evil. He looked in its face, and he would say that it was nothing more than a man. All that was different were the eyes—filled with a white haze, no color.*"

"*The sword flashed out of the robes and sliced Ash's chest. The other hand gently flicked the air and a great force sent Ash flying through the air.*"

"*In her pain and fright, Kya burst from the mist and ran to Ash's side. She touched his wound—her gleaming hand was stained in his blood. Then she leaned to him and whispered in a magical tongue—words only Ash could understand. And he was saved, for the moment.*

"*Kya had not been able to heal him, not fully, for her strength had been depleted. Only a taste of life was returned to him. Ash could neither move nor speak. She needed to replenish her strength to bring him back. But the monster took her from the garden.*

"*The evil was gone and the gate was once again closed. But the monster had taken the garden's gift, and without it, she would not be able to save Ash or the others who had been attacked.*

"*Within days, the village changed. All hope and joy were gone. Fields dried up. Devastating storms no longer stopped at the wall. Many considered it to be the end of days. But Kya refused to accept the defeat.*

"*While Ebb and the other soldiers were too frightened to pursue, Kya gathered a few weapons and a small band of followers, including two loyal friends, the siblings—Fin and Kin.*" Mar sheepishly held up the two characters he had honestly forgotten to introduce earlier. "*And they left Patrin to purse the evil one known as Dol, retrieve what he had stolen, and save Ash's life. The next chapter is coming soon.*"

. . .

"You missed my show. My welcoming gift for Loc. That's not a good start. You always say how important it is for all to feel welcome."

Des heard but did not turn to address Mar's intrusion into his room or his reprimand, keeping his face away and trying to clean the tears from his eyes—he had expected Mar's performance would last longer, he thought he would be alone for the night.

"Oh." Mar's scolding was shut off when he came around and saw the mess of tears and pain on Des's face.

Des's instinct told him to shove Mar and send him away, but he was spent; all that was left was a melancholy detachment. The next option was the opposite, to tell everything. But Des knew that any effort to explain would lead Mar to the same conclusion—the same that Pab, San, and any of the Rahirrem would face—Zoe was seen, and they were not meant to mettle with what was seen.

Mar put a hand on the back of Des's neck, pulled him in, and embraced him

"What's in your head, huh?" Mar rapped on Des's head with his knuckle, asking to be let in.

"Why are we spared?" Des lifted his head but didn't move far enough away to lose Mar's sturdy hand on his shoulder. "The people can be so evil. And we are spared. And why not . . . others?"

Mar didn't hesitate. "We are supposed to find others, and yet we do not know what makes us who we are—why are we separated, what do we have in common—and we don't have any say in who is next." There was no confusion in Mar's eyes. As always, he understood Des. "I've thought a lot about that too. And all I have found is that we have been chosen for something. You and I." Mar released Des to stand on his own again. "We . . . were chosen." He nodded his head toward the window and the peoples' homes outside, "I don't know why, exactly. But I am certain, this hasn't been by chance. It's not random."

Des mumbled, "It's not fair."

"Don't get lost in these questions. You must find peace. Don't be tempted. Remember the city. The march. Remember the last time we concerned ourselves in their matters . . . we almost lost one another."

. . .

The Rahirrem is at its best, but I count it as a loss. I don't share in the joy and freedom—not while Zoe is not able to. The removal is worse than ever. I feel it. More than with Mother and Pappa. More than my family, or Mar's, and Ada. Even worse than missing Ada! Because it's different. I lost my family, but they will be fine; don't even seem to notice I am gone. They have each other; they don't need me. But she does. Zoe needs me. Needs me terribly.

XXVI

Zoe's hair was shorter, lopped off in uneven layers. Des assumed it was her father's haphazard handiwork. It had once draped to her shoulders, but her blonde hair now barely came below her ears. Matted at places, random strands stuck straight up on top. And yet she was bouncing with joy.

Zoe's cheerfulness told Des that she had the house to herself—that her father was away for one of his frequent, weeklong excursions. Though it was a school day, Zoe stayed home, and Des fantasized that she had done it to be with him. To be with him to celebrate his birthday.

"It's not really today—it was last week. I'm nineteen years and one week old!" Des explained to the oblivious girl. "The others made me something special. Mar even helped me celebrate. We made a game of knocking these—" Zoe left the room in the middle of his story, but he spoke after her. "But it was incomplete without you, little sister."

She poured herself a bowl of her favorite sugary cereal. Her doll was given a spoon of its own. Milk slipped down her chin from an ornery smirk when the school bus arrived and then departed.

Zoe turned on the television with the remote she seldom got to use and tuned to the cartoons she rarely saw and sat down in his chair thatwas forbidden.

The volume was turned high.

Two hours later, while Zoe was watching the second movie of the morning, the phone in the kitchen rang, but Zoe ignored it. Des guessed it was Zoe's school, inquiring about her absence. The calls kept coming—there were three before the second movie's end, but she was not threatened or deterred.

Des told himself that he wouldn't stay much longer. In truth, he had not intended to spend the entire morning at Zoe's, but time seemed to pass so well in her company. The ease contrasted with the dread that had captured the house. He did not have to watch or worry. He could just be there. And his defenses were lowered so much that he fell asleep.

Zoe and Des both woke with a start, to the sound of someone pounding on the front door. They simultaneously jumped from their seats in the front room.

Zoe was still alone in the house; her father and brother had not returned, but there were cars in the driveway. Des presumed that it was the authorities, come to see about Zoe's unexcused truancy. The school may have gotten worried.

Zoe walked with high steps and soft feet on the wooden kitchen floor and then dashed on the hall carpet. Des stayed in the front room, head swiveling between her retreat to her room and the officers outside. He heard a thump in the hall. Zoe had dropped something or knocked a picture frame from the wall.

An officer started making his way around the house, peeking and showing a light at every window.

Des moved ahead of him, toward Zoe's bedroom. In the hall, just as he reached the doorway, his foot came down on her doll.

Zoe was digging herself deeper into a pile of blankets in her closet.

A flashlight beamed in through her window, and Zoe went still or at least tried to; Des could see the rise and fall of her breathing as the flashlight moved on.

Des then looked down at the doll. He knew that Zoe would want to have it with her. She may even break her cover when she realized the doll was missing. "Shh, stay there, Zoe," Des whispered as he bent down and scooped it up, "I got her."

Des heard Zoe yelp in alarm and something stirred within him. He dropped the doll and bounded into Zoe's room to see what was the matter, bumping to a stop against the bed.

Nothing appeared different or alarming. Zoe was hiding under the clothes in the closet. The officer was outside. Having moved on to the neighbor's house, he was striding through their yard to knock on the back door.

"How'd you do that?" The question quaked came from the closet, escaping through a gap in the stacked layers of clothes and covers.

The pile on the floor began to rise. She slowly sat up. The layers of clothes fell away until only a stubborn pair of jeans and a jacket sleeve clung to her shoulder. Her eyes were wide with wonder, locked on Des.

They stared at each other for the longest time. Des's mind was mayhem, working in overdrive to figure out what had happened, how it was possible, and what it meant. Each possibility was like a spreading vine, branching off into infinitely more alternative explanations and consequences, and Des was soon lost in the tangle. But every time he looked back at Zoe, sitting and staring back at him with amazement, the confusion was overcome by overwhelming joy.

Somehow, he had made the connection he had been hoping for, and even in his rush of confusion, some part of him was able to appreciate that.

The amazement in Zoe's stare turned to fear, and she opened her mouth as if to scream. Des held out his hand and asked with a surprised tone of glee, "You can see me?"

Mouth still agape, Zoe tilted her head and the last few articles of cover fell. She didn't take his hand but tried—with a few false starts—to answer his odd question. "Mhmm . . . you were there . . . but no. What do you mean?"

"Well, there are few who can."

The astonishment returned and widened Zoe's gaze.

Des proceeded to explain the separation, as best he could. "Most people don't see us. To most, I am unseen and unheard. I—and those like me—live apart from your lot. On our own. Invisible."

"You're invisible? But I can . . . no. No." The astonishment was wearing off again, quickly. Zoe started to get defensive, as though Des had not only broken into her room but tried to trick her as well. "I'm not stupid. I don't believe you. You need to . . . get out."

"It's true," laughed Des, not at Zoe's growing concern but at the bounding zeal and delight he was feeling.

"Prove it, then," Zoe demanded. "Disappear again."

"What?"

"Do like you did before." Zoe pointed to the hallway outside her door and snapped her fingers. "Go away. Disappear. Vanish. Then come back. The same way."

"That's not how it works." Despite the bubbling joy inside, Des was just as puzzled by the whole situation. He had not quite regained his bearings on his state—the notion that he was dreaming was still within the realm of possibility. His voice therefore severely lacked confidence, which led Zoe to insist on proof again.

"Do it again."

"Well, you see . . . " Des then drifted off, unsure how to answer.

He didn't know if he would vanish again—if this was just a pause in the removal. He couldn't say what had happened, or what would come next. He didn't know if the separation remained or—considering Zoe could see him—everyone could. Was he one of the people again?

The last suggestion was the worst. If he was seen by one of the people, would he be blinded like them? He feared that he may have lost the ability to see or be with the Rahirrem—Mar and any of the others. If he ran back to Caisleán at that moment, what would he find? Would he be able to see his family, or would the school be empty to him, like it was to the people?

The crackle of a radio fizzed from the backyard, and Des saw the officer through the window again. The man had come back for a second look.

More desperate than Zoe, Des wanted to know. He walked to the window and pushed the curtains aside. "If this is it?" Des took a deep breath through his nose, hiding the trembling in his body. "Let's see then."

Des jumped from the window. It was a short fall from the first story room, but he landed awkwardly on his ankle and stood with a sting, but that was not the cause of the tears coming down his face. It was the faces in his mind—Mar, San, Pab, and all the Rahirrem—faces he may never see again.

Away from Zoe's interrogation, Des had his first moment of clarity—the doll, it was the catalyst for the shift;

it was precious to Zoe, and Des had taken it. He had broken Pab's rule. Was this the punishment? To be seen by Zoe but separated from his real family?

Des didn't wait to reach the officer who was standing at the backdoor. As the man knocked, Des wailed at the top of his lungs, pouring out his desperation.

The officer didn't hear him.

He yelled again, but the man didn't see or hear anything.

Des's chest began to shake in a strange mix of laughter and crying to express his relief. He rejoiced in his renewed freedom and played the scene for Zoe who was watching from the window. He slapped the man on the shoulder, tickled his neck, and rambled nonsense into his radio, but the man didn't notice a thing. Pacing backward, he stayed in front of the man as he returned to the driveway, facing him, long enough for Zoe to see how he looked through Des, who had never been happier to see the dull haze in the man's eyes.

"Are you a ghost?" asked Zoe after Des returned to her room, utilizing the door this time.

"No, not a ghost." Des chuckled at the question as if it was ridiculous, despite having wondered the same thing on multiple occasions. "I can't walk through walls." He smacked the solid wall to his right with the palm of his hand. "Here, take my hand. See for yourself."

Zoe shook when Des reached out his hand.

Des sighed, "Don't be afraid, Zoe."

"Zoe?" She snorted at the sound of the name. "M'name's not Zoe."

Des pulled his hand back with a wince and paused to collect himself. "I am unseen. And only others who are chosen, like me, can see me." Des could tell Zoe wasn't following. "Zoe is your name, now." Des was talking slowly and pausing frequently. "We get new names . . . when we become separated."

The room was silent for quite some time. Zoe wrestled with what Des had said. Her eyes grew wide and then dulled. She looked at him and held up a hand to look at herself. For the longest time, she closed her eyes and, with the silence, Des thought she may have passed out. The sun set and the headlights outside disappeared.

"I'm like you?" asked Zoe, without looking up to direct the question to Des, who simply nodded in response.

Another substantial delay followed.

"The police. The man outside. Would he see me?" The officer was long gone but Zoe did not seem to notice how long she was taking.

Des shook his head for several beats before answering. "Not anymore."

. . .

Despite Des's pleading, Zoe refused to leave her room for the rest of the night and nearly the entire next day.

Des brought her water that she gulped down and food that she barely nibbled. He offered her books, blankets, and movies, but she refused them all. But he kept trying because it was all he could do. He felt so helpless, watching her come to grasp with what he had lived in for so many years.

They sat in palpable silence, interrupted only by her intermittent inquiries. Des was quick to answer, often rambling and giving more than she asked for, striving to present their lives with the utmost appeal and grandeur.

"Chosen?" Zoe was caught by that phrasing. "Did you choose me?"

"No, it isn't for us to decide." Des knew this was a lie, that he had caused it, but until he better understood what he had done, he didn't know what else to say. Zoe never mentioned the doll; it seemed as though she had not noticed him taking it. She thought that he had suddenly appeared and that she had already become unseen.

"Was it surprise like . . . *poof*? Was it a surprise for you like that? I was surprised."

"Yes. I can't even tell you when exactly I became invisible. It took time for me to notice." This was not a lie. The smallest truth he could give in the mounting uncertainty was a relief.

The silence returned, for what seemed like hours, but was mere minutes. Either way, it was long enough for Des to realize he needed to leave, but he wanted Zoe to come with him, afraid that she would go on her own as soon as he left.

"Would you like to come to our home?"

Zoe shook her head.

"You're one of us. And Mar says that we can sense it in each other. That we're drawn together. I was meant to find you." Des felt foolish relaying this idea, as it was one that he had often disagreed with before. "We can wait. I'll get you dinner."

On his way to the kitchen, Des stopped to pick up the doll, which he had been avoiding for hours. He had also been dodging the questions that still needed answering. He had opened the box from Pab's framtive. That which was precious, valued, and seen was tarnished. If the warning was correct and he had done something wrong, what would be the punishment? When would the beast come?

Des returned to Zoe with a bowl of soup and gave the doll back to her, which brought Zoe more joy than the food.

"I'm going home, Zoe." Des didn't stand up, not yet. "If you're going to stay here and wait for them, then I'll come back. But I must warn you, the way they look through us—" Zoe pushed the spoon around the bowl, mixing the broth as it got cold. "It always hurts when it's someone you care for."

. . .

Des's mind was clouded with questions as he walked Zoe back to Caisleán. Their journey happened in the middle of the night; it had taken a couple more hours for Zoe to agree to go with him. He had promised that she could come back to see her brother and dad after she had adjusted to being separated. But he hoped that she wouldn't want to do so after experiencing the better life he knew she was joining.

All they had to do was make it home, then she would see.

Being so late in the night, the yellow cab that came over the hill ahead was only the second car that had driven by on their walk back to the school, but Des was not keeping count. He only really noticed it when the driver kicked on the brakes as he passed the pair walking on the opposite side of the road. The screech of the tires and red glare of the rear taillights were signs that something was wrong. Des heeded the feeling inside, took Zoe's hand, and quickened his pace.

"What's wrong?" Zoe asked, but Des didn't respond.

The cab was stopped, idling a little farther down the road. The red brake lights continued to glow.

Des saw the cupola of the school's roof rising above the houses and trees, and his heart lifted.

"Cross here," Des ordered and pulled Zoe into the street.

The lights dimmed, but Des was able to see that its door was now open. The driver had gotten out to follow them.

"Run!"

Des had been mistaken. Taking the doll broke the separation with Zoe but she was still seen. He realized that that the driver must have seen her, a little girl walking alone in the middle of the night, and that was why he had stopped.

They sprinted off of the street and through a series of yards, sticking to the shadows as they tried to keep the cupola in sight without compromising their cover.

"Why are we hiding?" asked Zoe in a forced whisper.

"I t-thought I saw . . . something." Des was out of breath.

Zoe scooted closer to Des and started to tremble. "You saw what?"

"I'm not sure," Des said, stalling as he tried to concoct a lie.

"What?" mumbled Zoe. Des shook his head. "Was it a dog? There are a lot of dogs. Was it? Was it an animal?"

"Yes." Des bit his lip, trying to keep the lies in, but there was another part of him that was desperate for Zoe to believe him. "But not a dog. A monster. San's creature."

"Who?"

"San." Des pointed in the general direction of the school. "She thought she saw something in the night. I think I did. Back there."

"Is it mean?" Zoe's body shook and her voice quaked.

"Don't worry, Zoe. I just got a little spooked. That's all. We just need to get back to Caisleán," Des took her by the shoulder and lifted Zoe to her feet. "Come on, let's get home."

No one was awake when they arrived. This struck Des as peculiar—the notion of rest seemed so foreign to him after such a night—and he had to remind himself of the time.

He showed Zoe to her bed and was relieved beyond belief when she passed the others in their rooms and beds and asked for names—she could see them.

"This is Zoe." In the morning, Des introduced her to the Rahirrem as her new family. He didn't tell them about taking the doll at first, and though no one questioned where he had found her, nagging guilt made him want to confess everything.

It wasn't until they sat down for a meal, together. And Des watched Zoe become more and more comfortable that he cleared that from his conscious. He considered that perhaps he had done the right thing. And he could wait until he knew more before telling the full story.

. . .

There is no sense to it. The only thing I know is that Zoe is home, just like I wanted. And she is away from those who would hurt her.

I am worried though. About the others. Staying at her house for so long, they think I went farther. Not just to the edge of town but far out and found her. She may tell them she is from this town, but I hope she doesn't. It would be better if they don't know. Fewer questions; there are too many already. They ask only a few, but I can see the rest in their eyes. And I have several, myself: Will they accept her? Will Pab be suspicious? What would he or the others do if they knew she's seen? If they knew I had broken the rule?

XXVII

Casleán's attic was an open loft that ran the length of the central building. Pab had blocked certain areas off due to the instability, mostly at the east end; the floorboards and supports were either missing or ready to crumble. What remained as safe was a narrow alley starting at the western stairwell, lined with wooden rails and rope, and leading to a bulb-shaped deck.

Here, the group settled and listened to the rumble and watched the rain fall through a huge breach in the roof, just beyond their easternmost boundary. The attic's wood flooring beneath it, exposed to the open sky and weather damage, had given way as well; they could see down to the second-floor hallway.

Hig constantly ducked beneath the makeshift fences, immediately scolded by Pab and Des, but this only spurred his reckless behavior further, treading on the insecure boards and jabbing at the roof with a broomstick.

Seeing the attention Hig received, Loc tried to heighten the daring feats. At the eastern edge, he braced his legs against the rail and tested Pab's work by leaning out to fill a tin can in the rain. Pab ordered him back and held on to his wrist.

"Can I try?" Zoe asked, appearing at Pab's side and eyeing the cup.

Loc brought the cup back, took a drink, and shook his head.

"I'm taller. I could reach farther," Zoe offered.

Hig scoffed, "Prove it."

But she was not the only one. The others began to gather, and each wanted a turn to fill the cup.

Hig matched Loc's reach while Tic was unwilling to lean out far enough to fill the cup. Wes beat them all, stretching out far enough that her shoulder and head got wet. Hig instinctively grabbed the hand that held the rail, but Wes was able to pull herself back under the shelter. Her soaked hair whipped around and slapped him in the face.

Pab was steaming with anxiety; San enabled them. She found a stack of dry, unused boards and slid one beneath the rail. With the counterweight of a couple of bodies, each in the group was given a turn to walk the plank and stand in the shower. Most would inch out and hurry back, standing only for a moment under in the rain, not even reaching the edge of the board. Hig, however, taunted them to push the boards out farther on his turn. With his toes at the plank's edge, he felt the bend of the uneven leverage. Staring down into the second-floor hall that was starting to flood, he boasted that he would not be outdone. But as soon as he was back on the safe side of the rail, San ran the length of the narrow board with nimble agility, bounced like a spring, flew through the column of rain, and landed on the other side. The ruined wood there was not ready for any weight and gave quickly, but she managed to make it to the brick wall and cling to it.

"Monkey!" called Des with cheerful laughter.

Everyone cheered, except for Hig, who spurned with jealousy.

"How are you going to get back?" Pab with a smile and a shake of his head.

. . .

San wove the needle through the shirt's fabric as fast as she could. As soon as one hole was mended, her tired eyes would spot another, and she had to wonder if the fabric was so frail that it was torn more by her handling.

Pab playfully bumped San's side after entering the library with yet another box of scavenged goods, adding to her pile of work.

San let a breath out, sounding like a bull snorting before the charge, and flashed a glare at him.

"What'd I do?"

San closed her eyes, sealing herself in and shielding herself from the ignorance of his question. Unfortunately, within her mind, she found more frustration. It had been there for days, wearing her body down from the inside. "I know you want to stick to the rules—don't take the best and only pull from their excess—but do you have to take their trash?"

Pab slowly squirmed at the shoulders, shaking off San's antagonizing tone. More of his attention was paid to unpacking the box and categorizing the content.

"Did you at least find medicine for Wes?" Her voice rose as if she had not heard her.

"I did. From what I recall, this will be best." Pab nodded and looked around, "I can't tell you which box it ended up in. But it's here somewhere."

San was too exhausted to search for the medicine, the piles were growing and Pab probably had more stuff outside.

Pab continued, "I don't think she needs it anymore. Seems fine to me. She was playing with Loc and Hig when I got back. Looks to be back to her regular self. They were whispering about something." He smiled and put his palms on the table as he bent forward, lowering his tone to a whisper. "I think they're scheming. Better be alert."

San's tone and expression remained stern. "They're probably talking about Zoe." She bit her lip and aggressively crumpled the shirt she had been stitching into a rough ball and tossed it, in no particular direction. "I caught those three mocking her."

Pab sighed. "Give them time. She is a new child in the family. Siblings fight. Has it even been a week?"

"It shouldn't take them any time to welcome her! Why the hell are they treating her like some unwanted guest?!"

It had been infuriating to see Hig turn away when Zoe spoke, Loc exclude her from games, and Wes refuse to share her room.

"It is peculiar—how old—that she was separated so late," Pab mumbled. "She's almost ten."

"Old! What are you talking about? She's one of the youngest!" San shouted.

"Yes, but she was only separated now. They are the same age but have been this way for many years. Everything's new to her . . . not just the Rahirrem and our home. Every part of being unseen."

"That's awful. You children are dreadful."

"I'm not mistreating her!" Pab made a poor attempt to deflect. "I'm not excusing their behavior, simply explaining what I have gathered and guessed."

San hated hearing this—the judgment, the adversarial way he spoke about one of their own.

San decided that she would deal with the other kids another day. Right now she had Pab as her target. "Excusing? No, it's worse—you're encouraging it. I don't think you like Zoe, either."

"Whoa, peace." Pab waved his arms in front of his chest as he stepped forward. San thought it was a strange time for him to brave coming closer. "I like Zoe. I do."

San was not convinced. She was not shy about her doubt, wearing it with a purse of her lips and a shake of her head.

Pab sighed, "Be that way, don't believe me, but I'm not lying. I do like Zoe. She reminds me of . . . someone."

"Who?"

Pab's strong advance slowed, yielding to what appeared to be embarassment.

"Umm," Pab laughed in his discomfort. He fidgeted with his hands turning over on one another. San was caught by his awkward composure. His high-pitched and scratchy chuckle made her momentarily forget herself, and she started to smile as well. "Another girl from a long time ago."

"Oh?" San threw her head back as if he had just said something astonishing. "Another girl?"

"Not a girl, I suppose," Pab said bashfully. "A woman."

"A woman?" San teased again, but with an unintentional flare of temper—it could have been jealousy.

"When I was younger, younger than Zoe, and I was alone, far from home . . . I would tell myself that, someday, I would find a new mama. And she would take care of me. If I was scared, I would dream her."

San could tell Pab was gone. He could see this woman again in his imagination.

"I think my real mother loved me, but she was not nurturing. Not in the way my new mama would be. She would see me . . . and this was back when I thought no one else could . . . pick me up in a great hug. And nothing could ever be bad again. I would live with her, as her son. And I wouldn't have to be alone anymore." Pab's smile was persistent, but it had changed in some way, less comical and more tranquil. "Zoe reminds me of her. A tenderness.

But that dream was different. She didn't look like Zoe. And she was older."

"You thought you would find a mother?"

"Yes," Pab looked up at San, afraid to find her mocking him. "Is that so ridiculous?"

"No," San said softly, trying to put him at ease. "It's sweet." But she only exacerbated his mortification.

San was honestly touched by his story; she found it endearing. And even though she had been furious with him only moments ago, San was drawn to Pab's gentleness, attracted to his strong and vulnerable spirit.

San tried then to remember her mother, but the person who came to her mind more readily was her father; there were just so many more memories of him in comparison. Thinking of her mother only brought up her absence, which in turn drew looming questions about why she had left.

"Can I tell you what I imagined? What I hoped?" San paused, Pab didn't respond, but she continued. "I told myself, for a time, that we didn't deserve this. We were too young; we couldn't have done anything to deserve being taken away. But what if they did? What if they did something wrong? The people we came from—our parents and our people—what if they were the problem, and their punishment was losing us?"

San didn't truly expect Pab to answer, but he surprised her.

"I've never thought of that. Makes as much as sense as anything else."

"There does seem to be something rotten in them, the people we come from. Your mother. Even my father was a hard man."

"How so?" Pab asked, pushing the clothes aside and sitting on the table in front of her.

"The only memories I have of my mother are of her leaving. I always thought it was my fault somehow, but he may have some blame. He could be a brute. I know people feared him. Maybe I was the punishment for his manner. And if he—" San's memories rushed forth and clouded her mind, blocking her words. Pab's arm slid around her, a comfort that allowed her to continue. "If there was something rotten in him, in them—then it is in us too. We came from them."

"Don't say that."

"And how they are treating Zoe. That proves it." San was directing this at the children, but she recognized that Pab would be hurt by her words as well. "And it reminds me of myself."

Pab put both hands on San's face. "You?"

"The way I was . . . maybe I still am." Contrite, San was tempted to pull away from Pab's grasp, but instead, she took hold of his hand, the one from which she had removed two fingers. "The anger . . . is there. He gave that to me."

Pab put his other hand over his injury. His grip tightened on hers with a reassuring shake. "It's up to us. Even if we came from a rotten patch, we could choose something different. A path that leads to *wema*."

"If there is any good in me, it's because of you." San caught the way Pab was looking at her. She placed a hand over his eyes. "You are my good, my better path. You are my *wema*."

As her lips touched his, Pab's mouth twitched slightly at first and he almost backed away, not certain whether to trust it, given her temper and the heated way she had been speaking to him earlier in their conversation.

To reassure him, San made her kisses softer and gentler, present but also coaxing his return. Her thumb rubbed his cheek, and her nose would nudge his. It didn't take long for Pab to press back, sliding his hand to her back and pulling her in.

· · ·

Des had been eavesdropping at the door long before the kiss. The sight knocked him back, out of his hunched-over posture, and he shuffled his feet backward, creeping away as quietly as possible.

When he was a safe distance away, Des allowed himself a smile. "Took you long enough." He laughed under his breath and stepped down the hall, away from the library door, finally giving Pab and San their privacy. He had not meant to linger so long, but their conversation about Zoe had caught his attention because it had also confirmed his worst fears—the others were wary of Zoe.

Des had taken note of this, but he had tried to pass it off as paranoia. There had been many indications. Des would catch Zoe's name being passed in whispers. The other kids didn't ask her to be a part of performing Mar's stories. He had seen their disinterest in sitting with her at meals. There was often a subtlety to their actions, easy to explain away with a half-hearted excuse. But having heard Pab and San speak with such conviction on the matter was the final straw. No one had guessed that Zoe remained seen nor had they discovered that Des had broken the separation, but they were getting closer, and he was getting worried.

Zoe may have been kept at bay by the others, but to him, she was still home. It was better for her there than with her foul father. And it was better for Des.

He had a little sister again. Zoe had taken to him, their friendship was just as he had imagined, and there was no way he would give it up.

Time was all he needed. Des believed, once they saw Zoe as he did, they would be more welcoming. They would be more willing to accept her and forgive him. Then it would be safe for Zoe to explore the new coexistence he had brought her into.

"We're trapped!" Wes's voice echoed down the hall, as she raced from the eastern end of the main corridor, Wes called into every doorway. She barely noticed Des walking the other direction, skidding to a stop a few steps short of him. "Des! Come help!"

He followed to the side entrance, where Loc was throttling the door. A chain had been crossed over the exterior handles. The school's front had always been locked in this manner, but never the side doors or rear entrance to the basement. Red tape had also been added, along with a laminated notice on the window—the building was being condemned. It was going to be torn down.

. . .

I have lost our home. We will have to wander again. And Zoe is still one of the people. She is still seen. And the second she steps out the door, Mar and the others will know—she will know.

Something must be done. We are sending Pab and San out. Far out. Mar went to search as well. We have to find a home that can't be taken away. And I have to find a way to get Zoe there.

XXVIII

Zoe was eager to learn, but she had fewer teachers; with so much going on, those willing to answer her questions had dwindled to Bri and Tic.

The squeak from her chair, caused by her bouncing, apparently annoyed Tic, who paused his autobiographic narrative to look under the table at her seat; she wrapped her feet around the legs of her chair to contain them.

The globe shared the tabletop with Bri, who sat with legs crossed and elbows resting on a stack of books—mostly encyclopedias and atlases for reference.

"The letters are faded, but I recognize the shape—that's home," Tic pointed at the globe.

"You came from there? All the way here?"

"Yes," Tic affirmed in a dismissive, underwhelmed tone.

Zoe was glad Tic spent time with her. She didn't know exactly why he helped her, while the others would not, but she guessed it was his distinctively mature nature. While the other kids competed and challenged one another, Tic went this own way—never hurried, always patient and pensive.

Tic transitioned to the books, finding pictures he recognized to talk about cities and various places he had been.

"And here, in this city, there are rivers like roads. Flat, narrow boats—"

"Gondolas," Bri blurted. Tic gave a doubtful squint, and Bri had to prove it by flipping through another book for the word with picture and definition. This was her typical contribution, random tacks on Tic's stories.

Zoe loved Tic's description of his home country and the other places he had gone. His words were rich in detail, even though he would have been quite young when he was there. Deeper than this, something was alluring in the way he spoke of the places. There was a form of familiarity. Tic spoke of these faraway places—not just his home, but all corners of the world—with such awareness. She could best relate it to how she might speak of her house or her school. Tic talked as though he knew them well and he could visit them again in a day's journey. She was jealous of this. To her, they felt like other planets—places she had heard of but had never dreamed she could see.

Zoe wanted to go everywhere Tic and Bri had been and more. And she was overjoyed that she was about to get the chance. She had never felt that Caisleán was home, and she was thrilled at the prospect of traveling with the Rahirrem.

"And you?" Zoe asked, trying to keep Bri engaged. "Where'd you start?"

Bri pointed farther east on the globe, but she was giving more of her attention to a stampede of steps overhead.

"How long—" Zoe's next question was interrupted.

Wes was calling for Tic, from the hall. Her voice was then joined by the ecstatic laughter of Loc and Hig.

They squeezed through the door and into the library. They spoke rapidly amongst themselves, gesturing excitedly with their hands. Hig broke away first, asking if Tic knew where the tennis net was stored.

"I'll show you!" Bri chirped, obviously excited to have an excuse to leave.

"Don't know," Tic mumbled under his breath, as he flipped through the pages of a dictionary.

Hig, Loc, and Wes finally looked over to their table and stopped in their tracks, eyes wide at the sight of Zoe.

"What do you need the net for? You hated those games," Bri laughed, spinning away from Zoe and Tic, knocking over the stack of books.

"We're going to catch the abaphim!" Hig clapped Wes and Loc on the back.

Wes looked at Zoe and loudly explained, "That's a creature that San found, flying around the roof."

It took Zoe a moment to realize that Wes was teasing.

"I know! I saw him. I saw the abaphim," Zoe lied.

This was a lie. Zoe had not seen the creature that had spooked Des, on the night he had brought her to Caisleán, but she liked to tell the others that she had. She thought it could make her a part of the stories, but this rarely worked. The others did not seem to believe a word, constantly demanding a description to prove it. All she could say was that the animal was larger than anything she had ever seen, with giant wings and a tail and the feet of a great beast—details relayed from San's account.

"Never mind. We'll find it," Hig said, making for the door while pulling Loc by the sleeve.

Tic tried to continue with the lesson but quickly realized that he had lost their interest, both girls were staring at the empty door.

"Zoe, don't worry," said Tic softly, closing the book. "They'll get—"

"I did see it, and, and if I . . . " Zoe interrupted Tic, only to trail off herself.

Bri sighed heavily, "Zoe, just give them a breath." Zoe was caught off guard by how genuine she sounded. "No matter what they say, you're here. You are one of us. And they'll see that."

"Why not today," Zoe announced, pushing her chair out and bounding for the door. She made it to the hall when she realized that she was being rude to Tic, and she considered going back to thank him, but then she spotted the other three and started after them without another thought.

"I could help!" Zoe offered, running after them. They stopped near the entrance to the central office and let Zoe catch up. "My dad took me hunting, so I could . . . umm . . . do things." They waited in silence as if she needed to say more to make her case. She knew they were only humoring her for sheer enjoyment, but she was desperate for the chance to prove herself and fit in. "Me and my brother. My dad would take us hunting. I could show you. I mean. I could help."

To debate her proposal, Hig, Loc, and Wes began conversing in a different language. They spoke loudly and quickly, knowing Zoe couldn't understand anything they were saying. This was a mean trick they had enjoyed playing ever since they had learned Zoe could only speak one. Zoe tried to follow their meaning through their body language and tone, but it was all nonsense to her. The more she listened, the more a swirling tide of shame grew inside her. They kept conversing for an extended amount of time—Zoe thought she noticed them switching freely between tongues. All the while, they took turns peeking over to Zoe, holding her in great anticipation. She hoped they were debating whether or not to let her come but knew better.

"Sorry, we don't want you to get in trouble with Des," Wes finally said, breaking eye contact with the others.

"Des? Why'd he care?"

"He forbade you from going out," Hig answered, playing along.

"Doesn't think you can handle it," Loc chuckled.

"I can go out. He didn't say—Des just said that I won't be a scavenger—I can go out and play with you." Zoe swung her arms in a whirl of nerves and frustration as she rambled.

"This is not playing!" Hig barked, putting up a hand in Zoe's face to stop her from offending him again. "*Mierda!*" He then spiraled into a string of profane words, none of which Zoe understood, but she could feel their intention.

"Why risk it?" Loc shook his head and walked casually past Zoe. His insult was the shortest, but it burned the most. The other two followed his lead and bumped Zoe's side.

. . .

Ren had rehearsed what she would say. If he was there—and something inside told her he would be—then she promised herself that she would manage to speak, or at least look him in the eye, not like last time.

It was not fair, Ren thought. She had been by herself for so long, with no one to talk to. Her social skills were non-existent. She was distracted. The first person to see her came out of nowhere—and he was cute. She had failed to say a single word.

But this time she would do better or at least more.

Sitting on the circular rim of the fountain's basin, she slowly took out her supplies, one at a time, and placed them in her lap. Unconsciously, Ren was playing with her hair, brushing it away from her face, only to flick a few strands down again to bite. She kicked off her shoes as well, a nervous tick she had inherited from Chiara.

The people hurried along. They passed quickly, and Ren did her best to compare each face against the one in her memory.

Ren started with chalk, drawing on the cement rim. A portrait of Chiara slowly formed, recognizable only to Ren. She often drew Chiara when she was feeling down.

At the edge of Chiara's figure, Ren drew a line, curing out toward where she sat—the tether, the daydream connection she had originally felt to Chiara. If she closed her eyes and reached out, Ren was convinced she could still sense it, stretching all the way back to Chiara.

"She's pretty. Is it you?"

"*Vorrei*," Ren answered before she fully escaped her reverie of Chiara. "I wanted to be her, and I—"

The line she was drawing suddenly swerved when she realized who she was talking to. The piece of chalk almost snapped when she clenched her fist. She looked up timidly and locked eyes with Mar. He shifted his hands from his hips and brought his arms across his chest nervously.

"That's ugh . . . what's her name?" Mar asked, clearing his throat again.

"Chiara."

They both studied the drawing, mutually thankful for something else to look at.

"Chiara? That's a good—I've never heard—could be—" Mar tripped over every word, "And . . . and what's yours?"

"Ren." Smiling, she pointed to the other side of her drawing, offering him a seat and a piece of chalk.

. . .

There were no other early risers in the family, so Des would usually have a good portion of the morning to himself.

On that morning, he gathered a plate of blueberry muffins left from the previous night's dinner, along with a glass of milk, a piece of fruit, and a narrow slice of lemon pie that he could simply not resist. His meal was taken on the move, finishing the pie before he made it out of the cafeteria. With a quick step into the library, he nabbed the book he had been reading, his father's fish hook tucked inside to hold his place. The best reading spot, in his opinion, was a large, cushioned armchair in front of the second floor, bow window overlooking the street; but he found it was already taken.

Zoe was slumped in the chair with her legs out-stretched and her feet perched on the windowsill. Her strung-out hair clung to the fabric of the chair above her head. The collar of the large, turquoise sweater she had worn to bed was pulled up to her ears, her chin retreat-ing into the hole like a turtle. She stared out at the sparse traffic, expressionless, seemingly unaware that Des had arrived.

Standing behind the chair, Des tried to amuse her by balancing the small plate of fruit and muffins on her head; she remained stoic, apathetic to the gimmick. Even when she spoke, she seemed to be talking more to herself.

"She lost us our home." Zoe's voice was whiny and child-ish. Des couldn't tell who she was trying to imperson-ate. "They made a mistake, spoke my language when they didn't think I was there—behind them."

"Who said that?"

"It's her fault. Went wrong. When she came—" Zoe stuck her tongue out and wagged her head, but then took a

breath and answered, "Everyone." She slapped her leg a few times, then clutched the armrest, and threw her head back against the chair. "I just want to be one of them! But they won't let me—neither will you."

Des waited for her to finish before asking, "What do you mean?"

"Why won't you let me scavenge? I want to go out with the others." Zoe asked, her voice measured.

"We all have our roles here." Des had placed the same restrictions on Tic, hoping this would mask his intentions, and claimed that they needed to start dividing up the work.

Zoe let Des's answer hang in the air, unaccepted.

One of the open windows was closed by the breeze, but the toes of Zoe's slippers nudged it back out.

"I miss my school, my friends." There was a real pain in her voice, replacing the childish grumbling. She kept her eyes forward. If she had turned, she would have seen how pale Des had become.

They heard the chatter of a group of children passing on the far side of the road. Toting their backpacks and lunches, they jogged along the sidewalk. Des watched them with rising suspicion, as it finally occurred to him that, even though they were far from her home and neighborhood, she may still recognize someone by just looking out the window.

But Zoe stayed in her seat until the road fell silent again.

"Do you miss the people you had to leave behind? I know—"

"Every day." Des interrupted her with an earnest answer. It was a truth—one that he wouldn't admit to many, but he felt Zoe deserved his honesty.

. . .

San and Pab must hurry. The Rahirrem is splitting; they want to blame Zoe. They've linked the timing—Zoe arrives and Caisleán is condemned. What would they do? The chaos. If they knew what I have done.

She speaks of friends, but no one was there, I don't care what she says. I saw how she was being treated. The abuse and perversion. Others may have seen it, but they did nothing. They turned away. I didn't. I saw Runach's malice and disturbed delights . . . and I saved her from them.

XXIX

fter a long afternoon of riding, they leaned their bicycles against two large trees on the shoreline. They then knelt on the stream's bank and splashed water on their faces.

"When we move on, would you come with us? Would you join—the Rahirrem?"

"No, I don't belong there."

Her response startled Mar, but this in of itself was something he was growing accustomed to—she always surprised him. She never acted nor spoke as he would predict. Her rationale, the way she saw and approached the separation and herself, was the first thing he had found foreign in a long time.

"Yes, you do—you would. Come and meet everyone. You'll see," begged Mar.

"I'd love to meet them, but I wouldn't stay and be one of them. I have a different calling." Ren spoke so confidently, Mar wondered if she had predicted his offer and had prepared her denial. "You call yourselves Rahirrem? Well, I am a Vandar—a wanderer, a seeker of varmundi."

"Is that a place?" Mar tried to follow. "Our sigil is based on one—San's place."

"No, not a place. It's . . . ."

"What?"

"I've never had to explain it before."

"Try. Please."

Ren opened her palms to Mar and wiggled her fingers. "Think of it like . . . this."

Mar flapped his hand to mirror her.

"No." Ren smiled and bit her lip. "All that is here and now."

"Today?"

"It's not just today. It is not just a number of days. It is all moments. Varmundi is the happening—everything in a moment—the life-breath potential."

Mar was genuinely curious and put aside his efforts to convince her to come. "So, you're looking for varmundi?"

"Well, I don't need to. Not really. We. You and I. The Vandar come by it naturally." Ren began to excitedly sway and wave her arms in the air as though she were painting something for Mar to see. "We have been taken outside of their lives . . . and brought into this freedom. Out here we have a wealth of it."

"Then what do Vandar do?"

Ren pulled her wet hair back, gliding her fingertips along her scalp, and scratched to help her think of how to proceed.

"We are separated from the people, but we are not that different. They share the capacity for varmundi as we do. And that, Mar, is the meaning for *all* of this." Ren paused and let her words sink in. "We are meant to wake them to this gift . . . and I have found a way."

Mar was transfixed by the flare in her eyes.

"You speak of a deeper connection. Within your family, yes?" Ren clapped her hand on Mar's shoulder where San's emblem—the two trees and river—was stitched, but he could focus only on the warmth he felt from her touch. He had to lean back against the tree to stabilize himself. Ren wasn't aware of her effect and kept talking at an impressive rate. "You believe that you had a sense for the others, even before you knew them. You were drawn together."

"True. It did seem like we knew there were others. One of us was sad—very sad—truly grieving—others could feel it. Without knowing where or whom it came from."

"It is at that same depth that we must reach the people. Speak in a way that reaches beyond sight. Before I left, Chiara saw my painting. Not me. My message. And with it came freedom. She was revived. Replenished with varmundi. I will do that again. An awakening. A destarsi—as I call it."

Ren glissaded down the slick bank and into the water, then turned and held up a hand to Mar. His descent was not so smooth. Mar slipped several times and was soaked, head to toe, by the time he reached Ren in the waist-deep stream.

"If you go. You cannot help them. Breathe it in. Be a part of it. If we learn to stay immersed, then our varmundi will last, and so shall we."

Scrunching her nose and holding a deep breath, Ren leaned backward and kicked her feet up. She floated a short distance away, suspended for a moment before sinking. Her long ponytail was last to be pulled under; beads braided into the strands were resistant, floating atop like a fishing lure. From above, Mar watched her figure shimmer and waver, smiling to himself for a moment at how beautiful she was to him. Then he dove in after her.

. . .

Pab had asked for a campfire, anticipating a quaint crackling flicker, but San would not settle for such a mundane burning. Some pyro spirit had awoken in her and was eager to create.

The flames tested the boundary of the pile of timber. He couldn't help but lurch forward at times, as the flames appeared to engulf her. But she never faltered, immune to the sting. The fire was seemingly within her control; it whipped and rose, responding to her touch, like a colt being broken under her reins.

After much coaxing, San was finally content with the blaze and backed away on her hands and knees, marveling at her work like it was a piece of art. Pab was a little disappointed when she didn't join him, stretched on the blankets and with their packs under his head. Instead, she nestled into the trunk of the tree closest to the fire, its lowest branches and leaves being tossed by the smoke and energy of the fire below. He watched as her being seemed to expand and trickle into the ground. The moss and bark around her spread to enclose her, welcoming her to be a part of it all.

Pab had heard San's stories and knew she favored forests to towns, but he saw now that it was so much more than a preference for solitude or bitterness toward the people—it was a union, a belonging.

Ever since they had left Caisleán and trekked into the countryside, San's spirit had come alive. Blossoming, her presence shed its rigid and edgy coating, becoming something more fluid and natural. While Pab marched and broke through the brush and sticks, San would float. Not passing through or visiting, it was a homeward return.

There seemed to be so much that only San saw and heard; Pab could only follow her lead. Her link would intermittently spark what Pab called excursions, in which she would stop abruptly, spin in a completely different direction, and run with incredible haste. There was rarely a sound or sign on Pab's radar. Hurrying to keep up, he would follow San through the thickest of trees and over stretches of hills until they arrived at what was calling to her. He was confused, but always enjoyed what they found, whether it was a herd of grazing animals, a waterfall, a tree bearing deliciously juicy fruit, or a quiet pond.

When it came to the goal of their journey, Pab was searching in a desultory fashion. He knew they needed plenty of space and expected to build their home from the ground up. Otherwise, his standards were slim. Countering this, San seemed to have a more established criterion of their needs and resources, but she neglected to share much with him.

No matter how perfect the glen or river that San led them to, she never seemed quite satisfied, and Pab began to wonder if they would ever find a place that she thought was right for their family, or if she was content in an everlasting search.

When Pab inquired of what exactly she was searching for, San would always reply with the same vague answer, "We'll know when we get there."

. . .

Shoppers sped in and out of the storefronts and cafés. Des had long grown accustomed to being bumped and shoved in crowds, but this unrelenting punishment around their holidays was especially brutal.

He caught a glimpse of a woman with red hair pouring out from under a purple hat. It was very conspicuous in the army of dark hoods and scarves. Her color shined through the gray exhaust coming from the jam-packed traffic.

Des raced after it. He was unmerciful in his pursuit, no longer idly taking the bumps but shoving them back ferociously. He wrestled his way through the crowd, keeping his eyes locked on the swaying waves of scarlet hair and the bouncing ball of purple fuzz on top of her hat. The closer he got, the easier his pursuit became, and he soon discovered why—she was not alone—she was a part of a couple that seemed to have a strange effect on the crowd. Like a rock in a stream, the flow of hurried foot traffic broke and parted for their gentle glide.

"It's not you."

The man's heavy coat made his proud shoulders all the more imposing. The woman walked in tight steps as she kept both arms wrapped around him. Together, they seemed to move in some sort of stupor, looking into each other's eyes, blissfully ignorant of the path ahead, their feet swaying in step like they were on an empty dance floor, and Des followed in the safety of their wake.

He imagined himself in the man's shoes and when he looked to his side, there was Ada. Her freckled cheeks were rosy in the chilly night air. Her hazel eyes enchanted him with every twinkle. She unwrapped her scarf and whipped it around Des's neck, pulling him and kissing him.

"Hey, you," Des whispered, his lips pressed to her forehead, tasting the wool and smelling her scent.

"Hey, you," Ada answered back in her euphonic voice. "Missed you."

Des was about to steal another kiss when a passerby bumped into Ada's back hard, pushing her deeper into his arms.

"Sorry about them," Des nodded to the crowd, then shook his head.

"Don't be cross," Ada said firmly.

"I'm raw. I'm raw all the time. At them . . . and myself."

Ada laughed then lifted one of her hands and began to caress his neck. "And what have you done to bring this anger? What are the charges?"

"I lost our home," Des said, pulling away and reaching to tuck a few of her loose strands back under the hat and behind her ear.

"And now you are flying with the others?" there was a harsh rasp in her voice.

"You don't want me to? We have to."

"You have to?" Ada crossed her arms over her chest and began to cry.

"We will build a home that is safe. Untouchable."

"If you go that far . . . " Her words were tampered by the tears.

"Ada?" pleaded Des, reaching for her hand. "I thought you'd understand. I'm—"

"How will you find me? You're giving up on me."

"Never." Des stepped in and kissed her tear-stained cheeks. He found her lips again—any responsive affection was attenuated—and then moved down her neck. "I'll never stop looking for you."

Ada dropped her head, and she seemed to shrink five inches. Her pitiful whimper puttered through pursed lips. "But will he let you go? Will he follow you?"

"Who?"

Ada buried her face in his shoulder, which muffled her cries. "See all that has been lost." She struggled to keep control of her voice, amidst sniffles and hiccups.

"But see what I have gained. Zoe. And . . . soon . . . you will join us . . . this will be for all of us." Des tried to put as much vigor in his voice as he could, but it was not enough to revive her lowly spirit. Her watery eyes were mesmerizing as their color changed, but Des held her stare. "Hear this now. We'll be together. I promise." Des held her closer. "We're building a home. A place that will be ours." His words were his plea for her to stay. "*Ours.*"

"It won't be enough." Ada shook her head. "You know what we have to do—to be free."

. . .

Mar is gone, more and more. And I don't think he is a bit concerned with finding a home. I don't know where he goes. He just goes. Comes and goes. Abandoning us . . . me at my greatest time of need.

XXX

"**K**ya, Fin, and Kin journeyed through many lands, in *search of the country of Dol. To find the evil one's fortress and recover the gift he had stolen from Patrin*," Mar bellowed from the gymnasium stage.

The performance was transitioning into a second act, there was little intermission or delay in the action, and yet his voice continued to project prominently. In the audience, Wes was impressed with his dedication and stamina to keep the story going, despite its author's absence.

"*They had journeyed far but had yet to catch up with him. But signs of his evil were left in his path. Ruin, fire, death, and destruction. Towns set ablaze. Strange illnesses. Starvation.*"

Bri played the protagonist—Kya—and led Tic and Mar around the stage. Their roles were more fluid, stepping into whatever part was needed, scene by scene. Currently, they were her two trusted companions—Kin and Fin—who had followed from Patrin. Wes was unsure who was who at the moment.

"*Their pursuit brought them to the city of Murron, where they came upon a mob beating a man unconscious. Kya used her ability to clear the way to the man's side. But the mob grew and they were overwhelmed, beaten, and taken as prisoners.*

"*As they were dragged through the city, people came out from their homes to hurl insults and spit on them. They were brought to a building at the center of the village and down a* staircase that spiraled into the rock and dirt for what seemed like an eternity. After a maze of tunnels, they found themselves at the bottom of a massive pit."

The actors sat, huddled in the center of the stage, and stared up. The distance in their eyes made the depth of their despair more believable, and Wes experienced a sinking feeling in her gut.

"The man they had tried to save woke. But instead of thanking them, he cursed Kya and her companions for saving him. Saying he would rather die than go to their true prison, for the place they sat was only the court.

"Once a natural spring and plentiful well. Now it had dried. Into just a pit. It was reformed to a court. Judges sat atop. They carved a council into the rock."

Clank. Clink. Clink. Clank.

Mar rustled a chain leash across the floor while Tic tapped a pot with a spoon.

"The rattling of metal came from above. Four pairs of chains were lowered. The man instructed them to lock themselves by the wrists. Or they would be left to starve."

Clank. Clank. Clank.

Tic beat the pot harder, and the sound rang louder.

"The chains pulled the stranger up by his wrists and out of sight, silently, helplessly drifting away.

"The sound stopped. They worried the man would be dropped and die. There was a scream but he did not reappear. He had been taken. Judged."

Clank. Clink. Clink. Clank.

The three characters rose to their feet. The banging around them was thunderous, and yet Mar's narration was clear.

"*Then, all at once, Kya, Kin, and Fin were lifted. As they rose, the chains attached to either hand began to separate, pulling their arms up and out at the same time.*"

Bri stood at the end of the stage, hands straining, then began to spread her arms.

"*Enormous metal wheels were incased on both sides of the well, driven in the wall, and were holding the winding chains.*

"*Just as they reached the top of the pit, and felt as though the chains would pull them in two, the wheels stopped.*"

"*What crime do you confess to?*" Tic hollered, adding gruff to his voice to distinguish the simultaneous characters.

"*Men and women clad in armor and feathered hats were sitting on carved stone benches that encircled the pit. The three claimed to have committed no crime, but the court charged them with aiding a thief, and deemed them 'unfavorable.'*"

"*We shall mark them with the lot,*" screamed Tic, forgetting to alter his voice. "*Scar them, until their bodies can hold no more.*"

Mar continued with the narrative. "*The council conferred and agreed, but a voice in their midst declared, Not satisfied! He demanded one be made a sacrifice.*"

"What!" Wes shouted.

"*Choose! One of you must die! Choose and atone.*"

Wes searched the actors' faces for a sign of who would live and who would die.

"*Kya pleaded that it should be her, but her friends cried out and volunteered their own lives.*"

Bri, Mar, and Tic shouted over each other, as the audience watched, breathless.

"*They pleaded. And as they did, the wheels began to turn and the chains pulled again, until—*"

Clank.

Mar cried in agony, then hid one arm behind his back as though it had been ripped off at the shoulder.

Clank.

Mar dropped to the floor.

"*Kin!*" Bri screamed.

The flashlights on stage went out, and the gym fell into darkness.

. . .

Pab and San ventured deep into the mountains until they were beyond the people's reach. It had been two days since they had passed through a sizeable town. The homes and streets were thinning.

After hours of passing through thick wild woodland, they came to an open field. Pab noticed the remnants of a roadside park and went to investigate while San gave a wide berth.

The foundation and lower plumbing remained from what could have been a rest stop or shelter. Rotting benches, rusty trash bins, and toppled light posts littered the tall grass. There were three abandoned vehicles: a shabby two-door with its tires missing, a busted RV, and a four-wheeled rover. Pab wished they could get one of them to run; his legs needed rest.

On the far end of the field at the base of a mountain, he could see buildings that were in a similar state as the park. A tall sign with a notice for prices and vacancy stood in front of a deserted building. Pab couldn't tell if it was once a store, hotel, filling station, or all three. But it was made to look like a two-story log cabin with a rustic exterior likened to the timber that climbed the mountain behind it. Connected to this were the ruins of an extensive patio and a smaller building that had been mostly demolished by the tumble of massive trees. Farther along, there was a motel that appeared to be in the best condition.

Overgrown, the park's entrance lane was barely visible, but Pab managed to track with it and found where it met the paved road. Too thin for Pab to believe vehicles could safely pass in opposite directions, this road was in much better condition, winding away to the store and then around the bend.

Upon closer inspection, white lettering hung on the boarded-up storefront, but it was difficult to guess the name with so many letters missing. The pumps were gone but Pab could see where they would be placed beneath their canopy, now tilting and crumbling.

The motel's walls were nothing but a thin veil on a decaying frame. Vines had spread and weeds were growing inside some of the motel rooms. All the windows were busted. The siding was peeling away.

And yet, Pab could not help but wonder if the place could be salvaged.

San whistled for his attention then gestured at the patio with a nod of her head.

Pab did not know she had followed him to the road, but now she did not wait for him before crawling into the pile of downed trees.

A few minutes later, she gave another whistle and called his name, having made it through the mess, and climbed a good distance up the slope behind the complex. She was jumping and pointing farther ahead, toward a dirt road that dashed up the mountain in a series of switchbacks.

Pab was excited but chose to circle the motel for a cleaner route.

"We're close now." San craned her neck to look up the mountain path as she offered Pab her hand, and they started the climb together.

The ascension was a slow process; the trail cut back several times while maintaining a challenging angle.

Resting at one of the turns, Pab sank to his bottom and cut the legs of his pants short with a knife to let his aching calves breathe.

He asked San to help him to his feet with exaggerated weariness and slumped against her shoulder as they walked. More and more, his weight relied on her until he barely lifted his feet to move forward. She then removed his arm from her shoulder and let him fall. After a playfully apathetic brush of her hand and a shrug, San kicked leaves over him for what she deemed, "A fitting burial."

Pab rose with a growl, and she yelped, speeding ahead.

The fun chase ended when San slowed and allowed herself to be caught. He put his last spurt of energy in a leap and tackle. He wrapped his arms around her midsection, and brought her to the ground.

Laying on their sides, panting for breath, Pab pulled San in closer. He let his heart pound into her back. San gnawed at his arm, but he only held her tighter. She still managed to wiggle in his constricting embrace until they were facing each other.

"Look." San nodded her head up.

The dirt trail flattened out into a small gravel lot at the center of an abandoned campground, on a level shelf in the mountain's slope. Closest to the hub stood a giant three-story hall built into the incline of the hill. A wrap-around porch ran was meant to run the full length of the cabin, but half of this walkway had collapsed. A collection of smaller buildings—cabins, outhouses, shelters, and sheds—were scattered throughout the surrounding woods, connected by walking trails.

"It's perfect. Too perfect."

"Why do you say that?" asked San.

"They may take back the motel, down there," Pab pointed to the road that had brought them to the treasure. "And what if that leads them back here? They'll take this place back."

"Don't worry, they can't have it." She smiled as though she found his concern endearing and took his hand "We won't let them."

. . .

Des heard the commotion coming from Zoe's room, a spare space behind the gymnasium. Since none of the others had volunteered to bunk with her, it was rare to hear a gathering there. The closer he got the more hostile the voices became. Imagining that the other kids may be trying to scare or tease Zoe—which hadn't been uncommon as of late—Des charged into the room and found his worst fear realized: Zoe was gone.

In her stead, there were the usual suspects: Loc, Wes, and Hig, pitted in a struggle over Zoe's bedding. Looking over their wrestling match, Des noticed the open window and instinctively thought they had scared or threatened Zoe into leaving and were then fighting over her stuff.

Demanding answers, Des joined the altercation, only to be struck hard by a stray swing. Hig had done so without intention, but the anger in Des and the fear of having lost Zoe took it as a challenge.

A swift and devastating response was delivered to Hig's ribs, and he crumbled to the floor.

"Where is she?!"

Des was struck on the back by a large book, wielded in the hands of Wes. His vision was distorted and everything outside his reach was obscured. Des turned to where the open window should be, but that side of the room was now blurred. He took a particularly long breath and slowly released it against the throbbing pain, hoping this could somehow increase his field of vision. For a moment, it was working. Like blowing air into a balloon, Des's concentrated breaths seemed to expand his focus and the pain ebbed.

When Wes tried for a second strike, he was ready and knocked the book from her hands, cuffed her shirt, and throttled her against the wall.

"Where?!"

Loc put his shoulder into the attempted tackle at the waist, but Des didn't budge.

"Des!" Zoe cried. The doorway slowly came into focus. "Let them go!"

Senses gradually returning, Des felt the frantic slaps on his arm and Wes's nails digging into this skin. Zoe's begging sounded again in Des's ear. He released Wes and she dropped to the floor.

Des felt a bit outside of the scene and—in an unsettling way—was frightened of himself. He was both the primary source of the fear and was sharing in it. Torn by the strange sensation of wishing to run from himself and realizing that there was no comfort he could offer, Des made for the door. Zoe shuddered as he passed.

. . .

I was not wrong about the others—they were planning to do what I feared. They wanted to ransack Zoe's room. They want her gone. Loc thought that was too far. Too mean. He claims he was trying to stop them. And that's where I found them—in a small scuffle about how to best get rid of Zoe.

But I lost myself in anger.

I have exiled myself. From the group. For a day and a night. Or as long as I must. Our castle has become our cage. Beasts in a cage, clawing and growling at one another. Pab and San must hurry—or we'll eat each other.

XXXI

"This was only the beginning. The beginning of all things."

Caisleán and all of its wonderful unrealized potential plagued his imagination. He saw a bright sun sparkle through the windows on a hall full of energy, laughter, and smiles. Some faces Des recognized, some he didn't yet know. The air teemed with anticipation. They were celebrating something; Des was unsure what.

Pab and San and the others mingled with the crowd. And Zoe was there as well, happy and accepted. To the new arrivals, she was no different than any other member of Rahirrem.

But this fantastic daydream only added to the dread of reality; the school would soon be taken. It was no longer Caisleán, no longer home. It was just another place they didn't belong.

The beat of Des's footsteps echoed back to him, gradually accompanied by another's steps—Ada's.

Des was happy to see her, but her physical appearance was different this time. Her cheekbones were more prominent with a more gaunt and elongated face. Tiny dashes of paint encircled her alluring eyes and drew a swirl on her cheeks. Her long red hair was straightened and was also longer, flowing down her chest and reaching her navel. While she often appeared in casual clothes, Ada now wore jewelry and a black dress that suggested an occasion of mourning.

"Are you like us? Or going to be like Zoe?" Des didn't want to waste the fleeting time he had with Ada on trivial matters. He wanted to discuss what had been encumbering his soul. "Will I have to break it for you too?"

Ada glided forward for a passionate kiss. Des put his arms around her. She was real again, for him, and he wanted it to last.

"I wish you could meet her. You'd love Zoe. And you would see what I do." He kept his hand on the small of her back as though at any moment she could slip away. "Did I do what was best? She was being mistreated. I cannot describe . . . and I saved her from that. I did, yes? But I ruined our future, here. The Rahirrem is breaking. Our family—our fellowship, ending. It won't last even if we find another home."

Ada then leaned in again. Des closed his eyes, expecting a kiss, but her cheek grazed his, and she whispered in his ear. "It's good. She's good. Des, you have done right."

Des came to the school's side entrance and pushed against the doors, opening them as far as they would go against the chains looped between the handles. He squeezed through the gap and held it open for Ada, but she had vanished—he didn't get to say goodbye.

. . .

The frigid wind howled through the stripped shell of the bus as Mar and Des huddled together on the skeletal seat frames.

Mar had returned empty-handed, again. Des remained suspicious of how much effort Mar would giving to the search, but he was also glad to have his friend, home. And he decided that they should spend their time, reminiscing about better times.

"Remember, huh? Remember when—you wrote your new language? Because we were going—a team—we were a *tribe*. You said that—and you—our own lingo," Des was laughing so hard that he could barely get the words out. "You walked around, snorting and—and adding sounds . . . *ollo, err,* and *eena* to random words. Tell me . . . how do you say, '*Morning, brother*?' Come now, let's hear it."

Mar felt his face flush and shook his head in embarrassment but eventually obliged by clicking his tongue on the top of his mouth, making a low chuff like a tiger, and finishing with a whisper of "*Nay-nay.*"

Des laughed so hard that he almost fell out of his seat.

Mar smiled "Don't forget, you ate that stuff up. It wasn't hard to get you jabbering that nonsense. You followed, easily. As always. As in everything!"

"I—didn't follow—in *everything*. You were just a bossy bugger."

"No. You tried to look like me. Wore my shirts and tried to be . . . me! Even cut your hair like mine."

"Now, you're jawing!"

"Guess how I know?" Mar stuck his chin in the air and raised his eyebrows. Des had his lips pressed tight in an embarrassed smile, red in the face. "Because you shaved your head. All your hair—gone."

"What's that prove? I did that more than once." Des's eyes went up like he was checking if his hair was still long enough to touch his shoulders.

"And both times, you were following my lead. I did it just to see if you'd follow."

Des slapped his hands over his face in embarrassment and groaned, "I got a sunburn on the top of my head—weirdest feeling."

Working off one another's memories they cobbled to-gether the story of how they had met, of their days at the theatre, and making holidays

The longer they talked, the more uncomfortable Mar got in his cold metal chair, but he didn't want to cut their reunion short.

"Oye! I've missed seeing you laugh, friend." Mar reached out and took Des's hand.

"I've missed you, too. It's hard not having anyone to laugh at."

"I'm sorry that I have been spending so much time away," Mar said with difficulty, knowing that it was largely a lie.

"You're looking for a home."

"Yes. But there is . . . something else. I have been look-ing. But I have found something else. Someone else."

"I should have . . . I think I did know. In some way."

"Her name is Ren."

"Bring her along. She can help us find the next stop."

Mar knew he should tread lightly but didn't know any other way of saying it. "She won't come."

Abandonment was the phrase Ren had used; she felt that the Rahirrem were abandoning the people. She strongly disagreed with the prospect of leaving for a separate and secluded existence and neglecting what she believed to be the purpose of being unseen. Mar wanted Des to like her and thought it best to filter those harsh critiques and extreme motivations, so it had truly been his choice to delay their meeting. He wanted to prepare both Des and Ren—equally stubborn and certain—before their polarizing views collided.

"She wants . . . to stay with the people," Mar answered in a calm and purposefully paced voice. "She believes . . . that we can still communicate . . . with them."

Mar had spoken softly but Des reacted as though he had just shouted, cowering and putting his hands up in defense. "How! That's nonsense. Wishful thinking. We would waste so much more time. More than we already have."

Mar gravely considered how their relationship would be tested if Des knew how far he had strayed, if he knew the fondness for the people that had been cultivated by Ren.

. . .

"Our home rests on the slope of a mountain. Surrounded by pure, natural beauty—untouched. The people have left this part of the world for us." Pab and San had hoped for a nap before speaking to the group, but everyone demanded an immediate report. Hig, Loc, and Mar were huddled over the map he had kept. "We were wandering and searching for quite some time, and I know we were gone for so long. But there is a much faster and more direct path."

"Patrin. It's our Patrin—the village from Mar's wonderful stories." Tic was almost in tears. He was smiling and squealed over the buzz of the room. "Removed. Blessed. Protected."

Claps and hollers rang out. The consensus was instantaneous and unanimous.

San was in the corner of the cafeteria, propped against the wall, wearing sunglasses to conceal her sleep. Wes and Bri jabbered next to her, oblivious to her slumped posture, as they packed bags full of snacks as though they were leaving in the next hour.

Mar poured over the map with a sour expression then asked, "Should we wait?"

The air was snatched from the room; no one spoke nor breathed.

Hig dropped the map and stared. Loc and Tic stopped, half-way out the door. Wes and Bri stopped packing and their sudden silence shook San awake.

"There may be another way. My friend, Ren, has many interesting . . . abilities. She's found a way to help the people without them seeing us. She could teach us to do the same."

There were so many questions and Pab's mind had to wake up and work quickly to deal with the overwhelming load.

"Would you let her come and show us?" Mar begged. "It would mean staying in Caisleán for a few more days—but not long."

Before Pab had time to answer, a swift fit of rage escaped Des, tossing whatever he could get his hands on. "Stay! In their world!"

"No. Please understand." Mar searched each face for sympathy and support, but no one looked him in the eye, they were avoiding Des as well. "The camp sounds perfect. All I'm asking for is—"

Des was out the door with Zoe in tow before Mar could finish. Everyone looked at each other, but no one seemed to know what to say.

"She's close. She could be here. And it would only be a little while," he begged those who remained. "If what she has told me is true, it could change . . . everything."

"Right then," Pab started just to end the silence, uncertain of what he wanted to say. "Everyone is tired. Mar. Everyone. We'll pack and plan the trip for the next three days. Within that time, Ren can come and speak. We'll hear her."

. . .

We have found a way out. And just as we are breaking free, on our own for the first time, Mar . . . how is it Mar . . . gets scared and cries that we need to stay. Like a timid child who needs to nurse, he wants us to stay and suckle at the elusive teat of an unloving mother.

The people want us to leave. Every day that they have ignored us, every time they look through us, they are telling us to go and find another way—another life outside of theirs.

XXXII

"**W**es, you are . . . lovely." Ren pulled Wes in for an embrace that felt rigid—it also lasted a little too long, as if Ren didn't know what to do or say next, so she chose to keep Wes in her hold.

The rest of the children were treated with a similar awkward greeting as introductions were made. "Bri, lovely . . . Loc, handsome . . . Hig, happily." The smile on her face appeared genuine but the words sounded forced, scripted.

Wes perceived her entire presence as strange, aloof. Mannerisms couldn't be ignored, such as her response to any question being just a pinch delayed, her greeting smile thinning too small, and her eye contact seeming too constant.

They took their meal in the gymnasium and gave Ren the stage. Wes felt they were gathering as a favor to Mar, not out of interest. She couldn't believe that this young woman could teach them anything about how to communicate.

Instead of standing on the stage, Ren knelt in front of it with her back to the audience. An uncomfortable silence fell on the space, everyone waiting for Ren to turn and begin. The first sound was Mar, lightly tapping a beat on the bottom of a plastic bucket. It woke something in Ren. Her back was kept on the audience as she emptied the contents of her bag. Paint and tools were spread around her.

Wes scooted forward, instinctively curious, but then returned when she saw that no one else had moved.

Ren began to paint on the front of the stage, starting at the far-left end.

First, there was an eye with a swirling green iris.

Then there was a faceless woman who appeared to be in the middle of a dance.

"Chiarra—not the mother I sought, but the mother I needed to find."

Slowly, the wooden front was filled with minimalist dark figures, set against an array of colors that progressed like a tide overtaking a beach.

Pages from a book were painted, floating away and gradually taking flight as birds. A parade of four-legged creatures. A woman curled in a circle surrounded by dark, intimidating spikes. Directly before Wes, there was a deep and empty canyon with a thin bridge strung between the ledges.

Her voice was captivating. The curt tone was gone; her voice was so elegant and graceful, it almost sounded musical. This combined with the visual to form an enticing message, but one that was not concise nor immediately comprehensible.

Though she largely worked from left to right, the events and images did not follow a clear order. The truths of her life were presented with abstract imagery and poetic prose, not a linear story like Mar's tales. She would even at times shuffle back and paint something over or around her previous work, to fill in the literal and imaginative spaces.

How she was separated, what she had learned, and what she wanted of them were woven together.

Wes didn't realize how far she had moved forward until she had to wobble back to get out of Ren's way. She did not feel ashamed this time; everyone had crawled closer.

There was a challenge to listen on multiple levels. Meanings came without strict definition or clarification. Silence was offered as a player in the story, a hushed assistant to keen ears. It was as though Ren's proposal was a piece of poetry that was meant to be felt, not simply heard.

Ren returned to the canyon and filled it with a watery green. "She saw what I had made. She heard me through this medium. And was changed, renewed. With new eyes, a new life began."

Ren dropped the brushes and set the paints aside, finally turning to face her audience.

Wes's initial disregard had turned to voluminous admiration.

There was something new at work in her, born of awe and curiosity.

. . .

Zoe could see that Des was upset by Ren's suggestion, and so she felt torn on how she should feel about it. The prospect of traveling more was appealing. As opposed to moving to a remote camp, following Ren would provide a greater opportunity to see more places and prove herself. But it would also mean giving up a home and disappointing Des.

Ren wanted them to stay with the people instead of moving to a permanent and removed settlement like Patrin. She believed that they could help the people, Zoe understood that much. But as to how they would do so—that was a little unclear to her. The others seemed to understand it. Even if they didn't believe Ren's testaments were true, they understood them, which made Zoe feel like an outcast again.

"So . . . what is varmundi?"

"Dunno. We've never heard of that. Varmundi is Ren's belief. Honestly, I couldn't quite follow what she was rambling on about." Des turned away from the window and whispered, "There's something dodgy about her."

Zoe nodded her head with a grin. But there was a flicker of shame for agreeing with him. "It'll be tough to get everyone to go now."

Des's body lifted like a huge weight had been lifted from him. "Is that what you want? To go to the camp with me?"

Zoe smiled and nodded again. "But why not go along with her for a little bit? Just for a few days."

Des groaned dramatically as he lowered himself to her eye level. "I wanted to go back once. I hated being invisible. I—"

Des had such shame in his eyes that Zoe couldn't fathom what he was about to confess.

"But what's wrong with going with her. For a day or two at most."

Des only continued with his story. "I needed to belong again. I thought that if I could find my family, my home, I would be one of the people again. That would . . . fix it."

"Did you ever find them?"

"No. Never. But I searched for them for years. *Years.*"

"Years?"

"I was stuck between lives and couldn't accept that I had to move on. The worst part is that I held Mar back with me. Maybe even gave him ideas that he would, once again, be one of them. He'd never admit it, but I feel that he started to hope for it too."

Zoe was having trouble concentrating on what Des was telling her. She could hear the slow progression of the others spilling into the hall from random rooms and the yard. There was no talking, not even in a whisper—only the patter and squeak of shoes on the floor, sounding at a lethargic pace. No one was eager to arrive at the meal, where a decision would be made.

"Now it is happening to him again. Someone is leading him down an empty path. And it's the same lie that I told myself. That I told Mar."

Zoe narrowed her focus forward, knowing that Des wanted her to hear what he was saying. She asked, "It's a lie?"

The clanking of pans rang from outside; Hig was calling everyone in for the meal.

"It is. And Ren has new words and seemingly new ideas, so they start to believe that . . . *maybe this time will be different*. This time, *we will belong again*. But that will never be the case. We'll never belong here again."

"We should go then . . . right?" Zoe asked.

His voice sounded much older. "Would you stay with them, with Ren and Mar? Or will you let go of the people? Would you come home?"

Zoe looked at the brother whom she adored and hugged him tightly. Des returned her embrace with a kiss on the top of her head. "That's all that matters. Come."

In the hall, Des marched vigorously, with little regard for Zoe keeping up.

"*Oooowoooo!*" Des howled, startling the rest of the family, who were seated at the same long table. Everyone turned their heads and stared at him. "What is wrong with you lot? We have a guest. And you are so cold and dead. What sort of family are you?"

"I'm sorry. I didn't mean to cause division!" Ren cried out from the far end of the table. She sounded defensive like Des was starting her trial.

Des laughed brashly. "Oh, don't think so highly of yourself. You could never split them up. No, they are doing this to themselves!"

A few glares fired up at Des from around the table. Zoe backed away, pressing herself against the wall near the double doors.

"Forgetting that they're Rahirrem. That we're all Rahirrem. That there's a reason we found each other." The smile that lit up his face was genuine, sparked from somewhere deep within. "Tic was with his grandad. Along the Bann. Bri is from *J-Jiangsu*, correct?" Des didn't wait for her to confirm before high stepping over to Zoe. "And Zoe was here." Des snapped his fingers in Zoe's direction. "The distance between us didn't matter, and it never will." Des planted a foot on the bench beside Wes then stepped up onto the table. "We found each other in the dark. We're Rahirrem. Family. For me, the choice is Patrin. I want to try and live in a world that's away from the people. Say your choice."

Pab and San stood. On the other side of the table, Bri did as well. Zoe came between San and Pab, hugging them both. The rest of the table kept their seats, but Des didn't let this rob any of his enthusiasm.

"Come now, the abaphim calls us!"

Loc stood up so quickly that the bench lurched away from the table. Des clapped his hands together, then leaned down and shook Loc's hand.

"To you who are going with Ren, I give you blessings. Wema, my brothers and sisters. And know, we will always be your family."

Tears brimmed in Mar's eye. His face was so red, that it looked as if he had not taken a breath since Des started to speak.

Des sang, "And Patrin will always be open to you."

. . .

The police cars cast their strobing lights over the homes and storefronts as they canvased the streets. They moved slowly, meticulously searching for something or someone. Officers were on foot, surrounding the cars in rows. The tight squad gradually dispersed, filling each side street and lane.

"Now even the adults have a curfew." Des quipped as he and Mar walked in front of the procession.

He quickened his pace every time Mar matched his stride until they were pitted in some kind of jogging race.

"It's getting more dangerous out here. This town is falling apart," Mar admitted.

"That's what the people do. They break things"

"Which is all the more reason to stay with them, show them another way," Mar pleaded earnestly. Des scowled, but Mar didn't seem to get the message and continued, "We've fought them long enough. They're not the enemy. They're our profound purpose."

Des slowed into a sluggish stumble as if Mar's preaching was draining his body of strength. "Look, agreeing with Ren is one thing . . . but you sound ridiculous when you try to talk like her."

"*You'll be a home for us*, huh?" snarled Mar. "Rubbish!"

Des fired back quickly, "Come now, really, I said what I had to. If I move against her, she'll just play the victim, and more will rally to her side . . . out of pity."

The wail of a siren rang through the air, and the thinning swarm in the street moved aside to allow an armored vehicle to pass. Des watched it go, waiting for the scream to fade enough for him to continue.

"I'm not going to debate her. That's what she wants. No, I'm just going to let her plan fail."

A bullhorn crackled from the line of houses to their right and a commander started barking orders through it.

Mar spoke over it. "I thought you'd be with me on this. You more than anyone should understand why it's so important that we find a way to breach the separation."

Des had to yell to be heard but kept his high volume after the horn stopped. "The separation is absolute! We had to face that long ago!"

"That's not true—you know it's not true." Mar's voice was suddenly quiet, muffled by the boots charging down another road in unison. "I don't know how, but I know you've found a way."

Everything went quiet. Des didn't know if the officers went still or if the nauseous feeling that rose in his chest had clogged his ears and silenced the world for him.

"Zoe." Mar kept talking, but Des barely listened. His mind was scrambling, trying to formulate a plan, minimize the damage of the situation, convince Mar not to tell the others—if they didn't already know. "She was the one you were talking about. The one who was still seen and left behind. The one you wanted to choose. You call her sister, but I can see it in your eyes when you look at her—you're afraid. Afraid of the rift, even though you found a way to cross it."

Des couldn't look at Mar.

"I know you Des—you can't give in. Can't quit, even if you want to." Mar's voice quaked like boiling water, not with anger but sympathy, and Des was tempted to get a better look to see if he was crying. "Maybe that's just it. Even though you've broken the separation, you can't leave the fight. We have been in it for so long that it's all you know."

"Enough." That was all Des could muster.

Mar took a sharp breath in through the nose and held it like he was about to dive into deep water. "Or . . . do you regret bringing Zoe over?"

"Enough!" Des stamped his feet, halting what had progressed into a considerable pace, and put a hand to Mar's chest. "You won! Sure, you didn't get the lot, but some have fallen for it. Some are going with you." He grabbed Mar's shirt. "Profound purpose? This whole thing has nothing to do with the separation, the people, what we can do—any of that. It's all about Ren—that's where it begins and ends."

Mar sheepishly bowed, his posture curling inward, and started rubbing his hands together.

The patrol had moved on and houses were dark and quiet. Des raised his voice as if he still had to compete with the commotion.

"I know you, Mar! I know you as well as you know me. I see the way you look at her. You may have tricked her into thinking you were after something of her mind and mission. You've managed to conceal the way you drool and yearn like a mutt in heat. But I see it!"

Mar looked at him with searching eyes like he was trying to find his place in a book, lost. He mumbled, "This isn't about her. It's about what you've done."

"I'm sure she will be pleased that you have nabbed some followers to her pointless cause." Des took a step back, thinking that Mar may retaliate with a swing. "And when the bitch finally does give in—and for your sake, I hope it's soon—and you've had your *feel* and your *full*, you will realize that chasing that tail has led you astray." Des snapped his fingers and patted his leg like he was calling a pet. He stared down at the imaginary dog, pretending to be lost in the fantasy. "Sadly, only then will you realize how you've allowed others to be misled as well, and all thanks to your—what was it again—*profound purpose*?"

Des grinned malevolently and kicked into a swaggering exit.

Mar stood his ground. He wouldn't chase after Des, but he also refused to let him get far. "What's stopping me from telling Zoe! What she is! And what you did!"

Des feigned laughter, then tossed his hands in the air, and shrugged.

"I don't know what sort of magic you think I possess, but Zoe is one of us—always has been—go ahead and tell her whatever nonsense you want." Des's smirk vanished as soon as his back was turned and he hurried away before Mar could see the sweat that was slipping down his temples.

. . .

We have lost our home; now, we've lost ourselves. I've lost him.

Did I cause this split? Is this my penance for Zoe?

I called his bluff; he didn't tell Zoe. Perhaps he was only guessing, and he wasn't confident enough to push her. I would like to think that, but I have another awful suspicion— Mar is certain of what I did, and he is only keeping my secret as a kindness for me . . . because he is my brother.

XXXIII

There was a plan. The Vandar—Mar, Ren, Hig, Wes, and Tic—were supposed to leave after the first meal while the rest of the Rahirrem prepared for their journey to Patrin, scheduled for the following morning. As it happened, the farewells were delayed and prolonged and it was late afternoon by the time they walked away.

San, standing at the sidewalk corner, was the last to watch them go, or so she thought; Des was watching as well, not waving but hiding in the garden farther along the outside wall.

His eyes began to burn as he stared, unblinking, after his friend.

Mar and Des hadn't said a word to one another since their argument the night prior. They addressed each other cordially in the group's talk, masking the fight and passively agreeing not to allow it to ruin the camaraderie and unity that had returned to the family.

"Do you trust her?" San had moved to the garden's edge, making him wonder how long or who else had known he had been hiding.

"Yes." The frankness of his response surprised San and himself. "I don't believe her, but I trust her."

"There's something about her. Like an innocence . . . goodness, a purity that I have only seen in one other."

Des knew she meant Pab.

He crawled out and stood at her side.

"Promise me. Promise me we'll see them again," San pled.

And it had been in that moment, standing in the shadow of Caisleán and watching the travelers disappear, that Des truly came to comprehend that he was finally without Mar—his brother and oldest friend.

Fourteen years together had come to an end.

. . .

The top comforter had been taken from the bed, leaving the sheets and pillows tossed. Other than this, Zoe's bedroom was untouched. The mess she had made in the closet remained. Her clothes, books, and toys were preserved on shelves or in drawers, just as she had left them.

It had not even been five months but felt like more than five years since he and Zoe had met and left together, and yet, Des was able to step back into the place with surprising ease and familiarity, giving him the feeling that Zoe could as well if she were there.

Runach walked through the door after work, going about his routine just as Des had seen him do countless times before, as though nothing had changed. The man moved to the television where he would remain the stretch of the evening.

Des removed the crinkled map from his back pocket, and carefully unfolded it.

Options were dwindling.

Des had considered altering the course Pab had planned, staying in the rural areas and countryside as much as possible. The schedule could be altered to travel more under the cover of night. The parties could be divided further, so he could go with Zoe alone, taking the route and time as he pleased. Some combinations of these could keep Zoe out of sight until they made it to the camp.

But why—how could he explain them. He could not conjure any reason or deceit for these changes that would not produce more skepticism.

Des stayed with Runach through several programs but watched the man more than the television.

When Des leaned against the mantle, he nearly knocked the clock off with his shoulder. He swung around and stabilized it, then examined the piece with a strange sense of recognition—it had an astounding resemblance to one his family had owned. There was the same pendulum, gears, and face with fancy lettering. A gold strip curved along the border of the wooden frame, which was fixed to a granite base.

It had been many years since he had allowed himself a return to his family home, to that part of his memory, and yet it was a quick and seamless journey. He stood in his front room. There was the fireplace, a lively crackle welcoming him. There was the same furniture, with warm, soft cushions inviting guests to have a seat. And there he saw his mother, winding the gears with care and smiling down at him when she let the pendulum swing.

A messy laugh from a mouth full of food brought Des back to the room. When he looked at the clock again, he did not see the past, only a reminder of the late hour and what soon needed to be done.

There was much to do at Caisleán—they would be leaving in the morning—and yet Des lingered in Zoe's home, telling himself that he would leave when Runach had given him what he wanted, the slightest indication of remorse, guilt, or brokenness—anything resembling change.

So much strife had been created, he needed to know that it had had some collateral effect on the other side, on the people, on Runach. Des had taken Zoe to protect her and to punish Runach, but it was he who felt defeated.

Des crossed his arms, walked forward, and stood between Runach and the television. The same distant blur in the man's eyes met his, which were tearing.

"Why couldn't you care for her?" Des asked. "If you had loved her, then I wouldn't have done it!" He brought his hands to his face and rubbed his stinging eyes. "Why couldn't you see her? Why couldn't you be what we needed you to be?" The question was out before Des realized that it wasn't directed solely at Runach.

"She should never have been yours. She is good and kind and everything you people are not. She is wema. And you'll never know! You'll—"

The clock was seized and the hefty base was swung with ease as Des brought the clock down on Runach's head. The top of the timepiece fractured, the frame split, but the granite slab remained. Runach spilled forward. Des went to his knees next to him, then lifted the clock's solid base over his head and brought it down hard on the man's temple. There was a sickening noise, and Des instinctively yelled over it. A tremendous reverberation shot through his arms, but he managed at least three more powerful blows—he lost count.

The weapon was finally tossed aside.

Des's body lurched with each colossal gasp for air. He kept his arms outstretched to the side. This did little to help him regain a sense of balance. Even on his knees, Des felt as though he could tumble and would fall forever.

Des couldn't look at his hands or any part of his own body—the spray of blood was tremendous.

"*Nahg* . . . sorry. Why — 'm sorry — whyn't ya —"

Des was unsure of the question that was coming from his mouth, but a particularly sharp *wheeze* from Runach stopped it. It raised his back and put an arc in his spine. His shoulder lifted, and he pushed on his wrists for support. His head stayed on the floor. Blood gushed from his wound and soaked the carpet.

Runach's green eyes flashed at Des, who immediately put a hand over them. He wasn't sure if the distant haze was gone—but he didn't want to know.

"*Puh.* S-s-sorry. Naw. No. No —'m sorry. *Cgn* ... can't let."

Des brought his other hand to his chest and slid it inside his jacket and removed his dad's fish hook.

"Ru—Ru ... I'm sorry, Runach." Des's voice was steadier.

Scooting around on his knees made a gross sloshing sound from the carpet. There was another gargle of pain, and Des feared that Runach could now feel the hand over his eyes.

Weeping, Des clasped the hook in his fist and plunged the point into Runach's throat, ripping it under his jaw and yanking upward, until it caught bone.

When it was over, Des removed the hook and returned it to its pocket, then got to his feet—all the while avoiding Runach's eyes. He looked around for something to cover the body with, settling on the thick blanket that had fallen from the back of Runach's recliner. Des wiped his hands with it before moving back to the body.

For a moment, it felt like he was tucking the man into bed. There was a strange peace to this thought. But that momentary bliss was disturbed when he stepped back and recognized the comforter he had used to bury his sin—it was Zoe's.

. . .

"When Kya awoke, her entire body felt pain. Blood and a strange ink were seeping from wounds all over his body."

Loc had woken with shortness of breath that made his chest feel as though his blanket weighed a thousand pounds. He had been screaming in his dream and wondered if it had made its way out; that would explain his raw throat and painful chest. The same fright that had caused the dream scream followed him out. He sat upright, shaking. If his roommates—Hig and Tic—had been there, he would have woken them up. But having the room to himself for the last night, Loc was left to calm himself.

He wandered the school that felt so much emptier, arriving in the gymnasium where they had shared so much celebration and imagination. The jumbled scraps and notes Mar had left on the stage—stories not yet told nor performed—were waiting for him, meant to distract him.

"Kya and Kin had stood trial, found guilty, and scarred with tattoos—labeling them as criminals. As they had not confessed to a single crime, they were given the lot. Marched back through town, they were brought to the border wall. Towering and thick, the wall was made of cells. Drawers for people. Tombs for criminals."

Loc could relate to the claustrophobic feeling.

"Tight spaces. Just enough for them to slide—"

A series of crashes and knocks in the hall interrupted his reading and brought him to investigate.

Three shadows were looming at the far end of the hall: San, Bri, and Pab were standing in the dark hall, outside Zoe's door. They did not acknowledge his arrival; he was welcomed by a painful wail coming from inside the room. Spooked, Loc thought of the scene he had just read, prisoners crying within walls.

"What's going on?"

"Don't know. Des tore up the kitchen and then barricaded himself in Zoe's room." Pab grunted, putting his shoulder to the door. "Something was wrong with him."

Another furious racket and Des's muffled holler sounded from within.

Internally, Loc made a connection to his dream.

The elder four had spoken before of warning, receiving dreams and visions. Perhaps, the ailment that had caused him to wake in such fright was now troubling Des.

There was some exchange taking place. Voices were raised and lowered. The deeper mumble was Des, but Loc was listening for Zoe's voice.

The handle turned and Zoe emerged. She walked a few steps into the hall. When the door shut behind her, she whispered, "He isn't good. I've never seen him like this." Concerned looks were exchanged in a cycle around the group. "He yells and cries, but none of it makes sense."

"Is he hurt? Sick?" San asked.

"In a way. He is in pain. And believes it is another framtive."

Loc had only heard this word from Pab, who he asked, "You had one too, before, right? What's going on?"

Pab's eyes darted and his words stammered. "Umm . . . I did once . . . long, long . . . he said what?"

"When we do something wrong, right?" San asked, trying to steer him around.

"Yes. When we do something wrong. Or when we are about to. It is a command. A warning of what could happen."

Bri closed her eyes and covered her ears. "That makes no sense!"

"What did Des do? Or did someone else do it?" asked San.

"Umm. It's not him; it's us—all us. Des says—I think—that it's not what we *did*. Uh, it's what we *haven't done*—what we have put off—and that's leaving. We have lingered too long, and he says, this is our warning. He wants you to go. To go to Patrin. Now! Get ready now. I'm going to stay behind."

San looked over Zoe's head at the closed door behind her. "No. We won't go without you."

"Yes, you will! I only need to stay here for a little while, just a little while. Once he's better, we will follow. We'll meet you at the camp. At Patrin."

Pab argued something about unity, but Zoe would not hear it. She suddenly sounded and appeared so much older to Loc.

"I'm not going." Zoe's words were firm but she did not look Pab in the eye. "Me. He wants me. I should be the one who takes care of him."

. . .

I see it—again and again—I relive it. And I'm never able to stop myself.

Every time I close my eyes, I see his green eyes staring at me. There is such fear, but there is also recognition. He can see me. And he knows me.

XXXIV

They should have reached Patrin; the journey was taking more time than necessary. Des kept the map close to his chest, rarely taking it from his pocket when Zoe was looking, but she was not so naïve as to believe that they were taking the most efficient way.

On the rare occasion that her apprehension grew too great to contain, Des would respond with something resembling fear and give nothing more than, "Zoe, we must."

It was clear he knew something she didn't, but while she found this concerning, Zoe trusted that Des was doing what he felt was right, that he was protecting her—like he always did.

In addition to the prolonged route, their travel was slowed by Des's strange heavy sleep, consuming most of the day and forcing them to travel at night.

The changes in Des's features were more troubling still. He seemed to have aged years. His face was weathered, his gaunt frame was stooped, and he favored one foot as he walked.

As the sun began to set Zoe started to pack up the camp quietly, so Des could get a few more minutes of sleep. A scuttle through the surrounding forest caught her ear. She squinted into the darkness but could not make out what animal made the sound.

Des stirred, opening his eyes and following her gaze into the woods.

"Who's Runach?" Zoe asked, without expecting an answer, as Des rarely responded to anything anymore. "You say his name when you are sleeping."

Des sighed and leaned forward. His hands slid through the dirt and his backside reared up as he stretched. "He is the man I'm not, but one that I am afraid of becoming."

Zoe was too surprised by getting an answer at all to ask for clarification.

He squinted into the dark sky as though he were blinking at the brightest sun.

"We come from them, so a part of us will always be . . . *them*."

Zoe had heard something similar from others in the Rahirrem. "San told me that any evil in us comes from them."

"Aye, that's true. And we must work to correct it. It may be harder for some of us. For me, it is almost *tangible*. Runach is that piece, their likeness in me."

"I don't feel any different about them," Zoe admitted in a whine, wishing she could better grasp what Des was talking about.

"You're lucky, Zoe. He is my ghost of the life that could have been if I was not separated."

"Is he scaring you?" Zoe asked through a gasp. She finally felt like she was getting closer to Des again. She was shaking when he nodded, and Zoe whimpered, "Why?"

"He is the past, but Runach is also the framtíve. The one that pushed us to go. He has shown me that something is coming for them—but not for us. And that we are right to leave. We must break away and escape it."

"What about Mar, Tic, and the others—will it get them?"

Des's eyes unfocused for a second, and Zoe was worried that she may lose him again. "They will be safe with us soon. We will be together again."

"What if Runach comes for me? Will I see him?"

"Don't worry." Des pushed to his feet and offered a hand to Zoe. "He can't hurt us where we're going."

. . .

Paint bucket and brush in hand, San walked on the porch, as far as she could, to the point of its collapse. She knew that it would be safer to wait until it was fully repaired and better supported, but was too excited for caution, determined to mark the axonis in a proper place—the center of the hall's outer wall. It was the most visible spot for those coming up the trail, and she was envisioning hundreds of arrivals.

The axonis formed. The river's curve mimicked the motion of the uphill current. Replenishing her brush from the bucket, the two trees hugged the riverbanks. One was thick with curly, looping branches. The largest of these sat atop the tree, a deep curve. The other tree was dried thin. Its branches were few and straight.

For once, the drawing was deserving of her satisfaction, encapsulating her rich memory. San felt the majesty and grandeur of what she had seen all those years before was finally reflected perfectly in the simple shapes.

"San!" Pab yelled from the field as he sprinted toward the porch like it was about to tumble. When San walked out to the rail to tease him, she saw that he was also hurrying to stop Bri from climbing up the last of the support posts to join her.

"Stay off!" San ordered.

"Why?" Bri smiled up at her, pushing and shaking and testing the give of the wooden beams. "You didn't."

"I didn't go that way, you little runt!" San yelled. The porch started to sway as Bri began clambering up the supports. "Quit!"

Bri ignored her and tried to get the best grip on the unsteady boards. To discourage her, San dumped the paint on the girl's head. Then a little was saved in the pail to splash on Pab when he got close enough. But before he came in range, there was a howling echo from the trailhead. Everyone spun in time to see Des and Zoe walk into the clearing.

The bucket tumbled off the breach of splintered wood, the small pool in the bottom of the bucket splattering on the ground. San sprinted to join the radiant embrace that had already formed. Hollers of laughter grew as the world outside their huddle disappeared, along with the delicate dread that had formed in their brief estrangement. The days they had spent in waiting were over, and tomorrow was spotless and bright; they were finally whole and home.

But amidst the family's celebration, San sensed a foreign presence, like a new smell had been imprinted on a familiar flower. None of the others seemed to notice, but San found it slightly unnerving and wondered at its source and if it was permanent.

. . .

Des's body was plagued with an erratic sleep schedule. This forced him to retreat to bed for long but restless slumbers and wake at inopportune times.

So when he opened his door to a burst of sunlight beaming through the trees, he thought it was daybreak until he reoriented himself with East vs West, and determined it was closer to dusk.

Walking backward, San came into view around the corner of the adjacent cabin, carrying one end of a stack of boards. The planks stretched on until, at the other end, Loc and Zoe appeared, hobbling shoulder to shoulder.

San was singing a lovely melody—one that Des didn't recognize, but it made him smile. It had been so long since he had heard her sing so freely. The younger two were mumbling along at a slower pace. Zoe did her best to parrot the words, while Loc tried to translate them for her.

He said, "*Ever over the waters, ever to create, and ever to renew.*"

Des and the others spent the next few hours trying to salvage lumber from the wreckage of the porch.

It was the first hard day's work, and while everyone understood that there would be many more to come, there was an undeniable sense of accomplishment and excitement.

A quick night snack was shared, and Des hoped it would spark some further energy. He was not tired in the slightest.

Loc took his leave for bed while Pab and Zoe explored the trails that snaked up the mountain. San and Des clambered down the mountain to scavenge one last trip. They broke into the main filling station and hauled a load of supplies back up to the camp on a sled of wooden planks. They returned to the fire to find Bri huddled there, writing by firelight.

"Last time Mar read to me, they were in prison." She tugged a page loose from the book trapper and thrust it in San's hand, too busy to explain further.

"They were saved," San whispered to Des, either from memory or Bri's note. "The well. That deep and natural well Kya, her friends, and the thief had been taken to.

After they were judged and locked in that wall of prisons, the well suddenly sprung new life. The waters returned and poured from the well, flooding the surrounding world. A great wave. Destroying the town. But! Those in the prison with the strong and sturdy cells were saved, spared. The wall was broken. The coffin-like cells floated like rafts. The waters set them free . . . free to start over."

The tone she used changed from a distant whisper to a vibrant, song-like laugh. But Des wasn't truly listening. He was thinking of Mar, who he missed terribly.

"Now it's my turn. Mar said that. Now it's my turn to continue the story. Mar gave it to us. It's ours now."

San wished Bri well but urged her to go to bed. The two argued back and forth. Des smiled as he watched San take the motherly role and preach the importance of a proper night's sleep. Bri cursed and pouted but eventually followed orders, which San tried to pass onto Des as well with a kiss goodnight.

Des took labored steps back to his cabin. He wished that he could somehow force himself to sleep, to realign with the others. But even if he were tired, he didn't want to sleep. Because that would mean dreams. He knew that if he did sleep it would not be restful, it would be hellish.

And it was.

As he often did, Des started in Zoe's room, but he couldn't linger—he wanted to make it farther.

The hallway felt endless. Not only that, it seemed to slope downward before him. Des caught himself leaning back and shuffling his feet.

The walls and floor of the front room were bare—all furniture had been removed. The room was closed off. The kitchen and other doors had vanished. The only way in or out was the warped hall leading from Zoe's room, which Des doubted he could return to.

The other strange alteration was a window—a wide window that consumed most of the wall, before it stood Runach with his back to Des.

There was a flash of light outside. As it faded, smudges could be seen on the window—handprints. Hundreds of them were smeared on the outside of the window. Des read the collage and imagined a frenzy—he felt the panic.

A low rumble was heard. Then knee-high water rolled toward them, outside the window, and cleansed it of the prints, before receding.

The walls and window were sturdy, yet the ceiling had somehow been stripped away with the tide. A vast expanse was now overhead. Des peered into it and saw strange forms in the low light. They came to a point, directed at him. Tic had taught him the difference between stalactites and stalagmites, but he could not remember which these were.

A second wave—the water level was higher and hit harder, crumbing the wall, carrying its debris with ease. But the window remained. The water broke around it. Des and Runach were safe in its wake.

The soft carpet was gone, replaced by charred earth. The ash was spread and pushed into the air with the smallest movement. It wafted up and clogged Des's throat. He tilted his chin to get a clear breath, but it was stolen by the horrific sight of bones scattered around him. They were massive; most were taller than him. There was some pattern to the bones, and by the curve of those closest to him, he figured he was kneeling in the empty ribs of a whale-sized creature.

"I am glad you've come back for our end." Runach was facing him. The man was naked, his clothes lost in the last wave. His skin was stretched over a spindly skeleton.

"This is not my end."

Runach sagged in posture and his head hung to the side. He offered a hand to Des. "You can see me?"

The wave returned once more, demolishing the window and rushing over Runach.

The water overtook them. Runach's question sounded in his ears, muffled by the water. He saw Pab, who was in the water as well, reaching for him. He didn't know if Pab was trying to save him or push him farther away.

The waves crashed through the window and consumed Des. Memories and dreams swirled in his suspended state until he was given a final push, tossed from the sea of sleep and back onto the shores of reality. This was not a graceful return; in his agitation, he rolled off his bed and onto the dirty cement floor. It was a short but startling drop from the makeshift cot; he was thankful that he had not chosen one of the higher bunks that were pressed into the corner.

He had the cabin to himself; there were enough for them to have their own space—for the time being. If they had still been sleeping in the school, he would have surely woken Mar and Pab, who he had shared a room with, and perhaps the entire family—noise had an eerie way of traveling to and from all corners of that run-down place. Des had once despised the building's age and instability, but as he stepped into the open air of the camp and saw how distant each cabin was from the next, he missed it dreadfully. There had been a sense of unity, if not claustrophobia, in their first home.

But he was also glad that his restlessness would not be noticed. He did not want his nightmares to dampen the jovial spirit that had thrived since their arrival.

Dawn was approaching and bringing a new day. Based on how late the others had stayed up, working and celebrating, he knew it would be several hours before anyone else joined him.

When they did wake, it would be another long day of manual labor, but Des denied himself another moment of sleep, not even the attempt, knowing that he would only be returning to the nightmares.

As if his internal strife could spread like sickness and seep into his friends' slumber, Des decided to temporarily remove himself from their midst. He started down the trail that led to the old, scenic highway and the abandoned roadside station that had first caught their attention.

It was an arduous trip down; his legs were tired, stiff, and in no shape to handle the steep grade.

Des walked in the gravel lot and observed the remains of what could have been a vacation destination or at least a familiar pitstop. The station had doubled as a store and restaurant, and there were plenty of rooms in the motel so he presumed that it must have been popular—given its remote location—and then wondered what had killed it. The station and motel had fallen into disrepair; he didn't know long it had been since the people had last resided there.

Des and the others had already begun scavenging from the remains to revive the cabins and houses higher up the mountain. Soon, he imagined the plot would be bare and the forest would be free to recapture it, and then the trail would be completely concealed.

"We will be hidden." He grinned at the thought as though anyone was actually looking for them.

He hoped the people would never return but almost as an act of immediate spite, a car appeared, cruising the long stretch of road. Des watched it on approach with a wary scowl. He knew it was not going to stop, there was no reason for it to, and they were probably lost.

But he could not deny that this car or any other may, at any time, come to reclaim the camp and send them wandering again.

He knew, in his separation, there was little he could do to stop them.

But there was a part of him that at least wanted to try because when he looked down, his hand suddenly held a rock. Des had not been conscious of picking it up, but it required tremendous effort to let it drop—he would not hurt anyone else.

Des walked toward the road to watch the car pass. And as it disappeared, he reached into his jacket pocket and removed the long thin blade of the fish hook—the heirloom he had stolen from his father.

Thinking back on the last time he had seen his father, he still didn't know when exactly it had happened. When exactly had he been removed from their mind and sight?

No matter—his father had chosen, taken, and cradled Des's brother, leaving him behind.

But what if it had gone differently? What if it had been Des who had gone into his arms, accepted, and claimed?

Des considered his life on that alternative path, the one previously set for him before he was removed.

It would have been a singular life, he imagined.

While separated, he had been able to observe and he had seen so many different lives, in so many places; it was difficult to imagine himself in just one.

That family wouldn't know him as Des but the name he had left behind. The name that was given, instead of chosen; he no longer recognized it.

His planning would be based on what others had done and said before him—step by step—to a sure and stable expectation. By his age, he would be looking to start his work and soon after, maybe a family. Was Ada waiting for him on that side?

Des would stay in his home—the one house. They may travel for leisure once or twice a year, but his life would be in that one place instead of spread around the globe.

Des could guess what he would do, but he didn't know who he would be.

There was good in his life, but all Des could presently see was the trouble he had caused. He had done such terrible things. And he feared that he had ruined his life and those around him.

Lost in the memory of his family that he had not seen for almost fifteen-years, Des did not pay attention to where he was walking and found himself standing in the road, facing a second car as it neared, gaining speed on the straightaway.

The headlights were hardly necessary given the breaking daylight but they removed any doubt that the driver should be able to see Des, standing in the middle of the road.

He did not move, grounded with the belief that things could be set right if he was completely taken away.

"How long have you been coming for me?" Des asked and then recited the words that had haunted his dreams. "Can you see me now?"

He screamed this again as the car drew closer.

"Only stop if you can see me."

There was no sign of alarm or change.

"Right then. Enough now."

He thought of his friends sleeping in the mountain-side camp—his friends who he considered his found family.

"Goodbye."

He peeked back to the trail that had brought him down the mountain. The forest was clear. No one had followed. The others were asleep in the cabins.

When they did come after him, what would they think had happened? He knew each would have their explanation and way of grief.

He thought of his longest and closest friend, Mar.

"I'm sorry, Brother."

What would last? How would they remember him? Would his presence linger with them as they built their new home?

He thought of Zoe.

"I thought I could help. I thought that's what this was for."

The blast from the headlights engulfed him, and he was ready to be taken.

But in the last moment, he thought of her—Ada. And his longing for her was strong enough to make her appear at his side.

Ada grabbed him at his hip. With a force greater than that of the tidal wave in his sleep, Des was knocked to the side, turning as he did in the water, but staying upright to stagger just far enough to be clear. He felt the rush of the vehicle passing.

No horn sounded. No last-minute turn or avoidance. The driver never saw him and so kept the car on its course, unaware of the part it had played in his existential ultimatum.

"You missed? How could you miss?" Des asked rhetorically of the driver as the car disappeared around the mountain bend.

Des knew that he would die in the removal. He knew the cost of even a crack in the wall between them would be more costly than simply his life. "They are our ruin, and we are theirs."

Consumed with his delayed but inevitable end, it was fitting that when he looked into the open field on the other side of the road, he discovered a remnant of his old life, his beginning—the family RV.

The junked hulk of metal was difficult to distinguish from the muddy ground from which it grew; Des briefly feared that it had merely been a mirage caused by his warped and troubled mind. Only when he was close enough to touch did he trust what he had found.

Two of the wheels had been removed and the others were flat. A latch to the rear exterior luggage carrier had been broken open. Every window was either cracked or broken out completely. Bird droppings dashed what was left of the front windshield.

There was not much left, not much to see, but that seemed all the more fitting for Des, who felt beaten and bare, himself.

He knew that it was a different model than the one his family had driven, but it was similar enough to spur his memory. "Found it, Mar. Finally caught up with them."

Des rammed and pried at the door until a hinge broke and it titled forward. Nothing came scurrying out, so Des crept in.

When last he was with his family, the bus had felt massive from his five-year-old perspective, and it had remained that way in his memory, with the ceiling high and the rooms spacious. Therefore, it was strange to duck under the ceiling and shuffle and squeeze through the tight space between the shelves, seats, and counter. He felt like an odd giant.

Shouldn't he be able to fit in his memories?

A spiderweb spread on his face while his hands were busy at his side, retrieving the hook. If he had known he may have prepared something, a speech or words of farewell, but as it was, returning the stolen hook was quite unceremonious. He tucked it into the sun visor over the driver's seat and folded it back up. "Sorry, Dad."

He had tried to toss it away countless times in the last few days, but the bus seemed the only fitting tomb for the token he had made into a weapon.

He had carried it long enough.

It didn't feel right to sit in the driver's seat, so he lowered himself to the floor. A padded bench with storage space beneath the cushions was packed behind his father's chair—there was no room for the blankets and pillows that he and his brother had slept on.

"I'm back," Des whispered into the bus. "I'm back." He reached into the recesses of his life, to places he had closed off. "Please. Come back."

Des heard the pandemonium of their arrival. The voices echoed across the years but sounded so close. He heard his father announcing their arrival, his twin brothers bouncing around the hull, his mother berating his dad's driving.

Des's father knelt and gently pulled the blanket from atop his two sons, but only saw one.

"You can see me."

Des closed his eyes when he heard the words. And for a second, he was back in his dream—captured again. But Runach's voice was gone. It had changed. Two voices replaced one. In front of the window, Des saw his parents. They stood with their arms out to him. They could see him. But Des didn't want to be seen—to know the man he had become.

"I'll be better for you."

Des was alone in the rusted bus again, but the faces hovered in his mind. They kept him company as he sat in silence for a long while, waiting for the absolution, the resolution that he had always hoped would come upon his return. He had made it back—everything should be put right.

But it was not to be, at least not yet.

"But I have to let you go."

Des sparked three fires in distinct sections of the bus—two under and one within. The wood of the interior furnishings was quickly lapped by the scarlet tongues.

The heat of the inferno baked his skin through his shirt, pushing him back one step at a time. Embers hurtled into the sky like enemy arrows, but fell as gentle as a winter's first snow, masking the punishment they'd deliver if he would allow them to rest on his skin.

Des watched from the road, hoping that Mar—wherever he was—somehow knew and could see it as well. He needed someone who would know.

And so, Ada soon took his hand. He knew she had not yet arrived. When he turned, he saw only one shadow behind him, in the light of the fire.

It was right to see the relic perish, but in its place, there was an opening. There was now a vacancy in the oldest parts of himself. True, he breathed easier in his lighter state. His shoulders squared. Aches were relieved. But he suddenly felt vulnerable to the elements and wished to be grounded again, the sooner the better, by something new. He didn't know what it would be, but he was excited for it to find him soon.

Des had expected a time of reminiscence but could only think of tomorrow. He decided to see this as a promising sign and share it. "To what end?"

ABOUT THE AUTHOR

Jesse Banner is from Missouri and a graduate of Truman State University. He has worked for a variety of educational and trauma-centered youth organizations. When he is not writing or reading, he is hiking, camping, or really anything outdoors.

www.jessebannerbooks.com
Instagram: @jesse_banner_writer